Midwife
of the
Blue Ridge

Midwife of the Blue Ridge

Christine Blevins

BERKLEY BOOKS, NEW YORK

THE BERKLEY PUBLISHING GROUP
Published by the Penguin Group
Penguin Group (USA) Inc.
375 Hudson Street, New York, New York 10014, USA
Penguin Group (Canada), 90 Eglinton Avenue East, Suite 700, Toronto, Ontario M4P 2Y3, Canada
(a division of Pearson Penguin Canada Inc.)
Penguin Books Ltd., 80 Strand, London WC2R 0RL, England
Penguin Group Ireland, 25 St. Stephen's Green, Dublin 2, Ireland (a division of Penguin Books Ltd.)
Penguin Group (Australia), 250 Camberwell Road, Camberwell, Victoria 3124, Australia
(a division of Pearson Australia Group Pty. Ltd.)
Penguin Books India Pvt. Ltd., 11 Community Centre, Panchsheel Park, New Delhi—110 017, India
Penguin Group (NZ), 67 Apollo Drive, Rosedale, North Shore 0632, New Zealand
(a division of Pearson New Zealand Ltd.)
Penguin Books (South Africa) (Pty.) Ltd., 24 Sturdee Avenue, Rosebank, Johannesburg 2196,
South Africa

Penguin Books Ltd., Registered Offices: 80 Strand, London WC2R 0RL, England

This book is an original publication of The Berkley Publishing Group.

This is a work of fiction. Names, characters, places, and incidents either are the product of the author's imagination or are used fictitiously, and any resemblance to actual persons, living or dead, business establishments, events, or locales is entirely coincidental. The publisher does not have any control over and does not assume any responsibility for author or third-party websites or their content.

First edition: August 2008

Library of Congress Cataloging-in-Publication Data

Blevins, Christine.
  Midwife of the Blue Ridge / Christine Blevins.—1st ed.
    p.   cm.
  ISBN 978-0-425-22168-6
  1. Midwives—Fiction.   2. Women pioneers—Fiction.   3. Scots—United States—
Fiction.   4. Blue Ridge Mountains Region—Fiction.   I. Title.

  PS3602.L478M53   2008
  813'.6—dc22

                                                    2008004475

PRINTED IN THE UNITED STATES OF AMERICA

10 9 8 7 6 5 4 3 2 1

For Brian
my life, my love, my heart

ACKNOWLEDGMENTS

It is best to begin at the beginning. I would have never begun or completed this novel without the loving support and excited encouragement of my wonderful family.

I will be forever grateful to my sister, Natalie Frank, for a lifetime of sharing stories and books, and for bringing about the dinner at the Three Chimneys Restaurant on the inspirational Isle of Skye that sparked a storytelling session and my first desire to write. A special thanks to my brother-in-law, Peter Morris, for the simple but all-important suggestion of "just get a notebook and write it down . . ."

For giving me guilt-free time to research and write, and for taking their mom's ambition to finish and publish a novel seriously, I thank my four fantastic kids: Jason, Natalie, Bob, and Grace.

For sharing insight, critique, and expertise, I would like to give thanks to all of the writers who attended the evening Writers Group at the College of DuPage with me, especially my core brothers and sisters of the pen: Tom McElligott, Jo-El Grossman, Farheen Dogar, Holly Stoj, Gerry Ryan, Chris King, and instructor Kristine Miller.

I want to extend heartfelt appreciation to my fantastic literary agent, Nancy Coffey, for loving this story, and to my wonderful editor, Jackie Cantor, for championing this book to publication. I also offer thanks and admiration to talented artist James Griffin for capturing the spirit of Maggie Duncan so beautifully for the cover illustration.

Most of all, I want to thank my best friend and the source of all things good in my life—Brian Blevins—for always being right there to squash my self-doubt and push me forward in everything I do.

Midwife
of the
Blue Ridge

PART ONE

Lochiel, Lochiel! Beware of the day
When the Lowlands shall meet thee in battle array!
For the field of the dead rushes red on my sight,
And the clans of Culloden are scattered in fight.

They rally, they bleed, for their country and crown;
Woe, woe, to the rider that tramples them down!
Proud Cumberland prances, insulting the slain,
And their hoof-beaten bosoms are trod to the plain.

CAMPBELL

In 1746, the last battle ever fought on British soil was fought on the Culloden Moor in Scotland.

"It's a rare thing for a child to be delivered at my convenience . . ." Hannah launched herself from the warm cocoon of her bed-covers. A midwife is never surprised by a knock on the door in the middle of the night, but Hannah Cameron was indeed surprised when she opened the door and found a strange, bedraggled mite of a girl on her stair step.

"Hurry, mistress . . . he needs yer help." The agitated girl bounded from the step and disappeared around the corner of the cottage. Hannah tossed her plaide about her shoulders, snatched up her basket of supplies always kept at the ready, and rushed out the door.

Rounding the corner, the midwife could make out two figures huddled near her stable. The little girl crouched next to a scruffy man, gripping him by the hand as he sat propped against the stone byre—his familiar eyes glimmering with the light of a waxing moon.

Hannah stopped cold and blinked hard, certain her own eyes were playing mean tricks in the dark. The basket slipped from her fingers and tumbled down the slope as she ran to his side.

She didn't need to see the wound festering on her husband's body. In the cool damp of the moonlit night, the reek of poisoned flesh was overpowering. In that spare moment, Hannah knew her Alan was a dead man.

"Darlin' lad! Ye shouldna be lyin' here—c'mon, up—up on yer feet—"

Hannah struggled to hoist her husband to a stand. With effort, Alan Cameron placed his left arm around his wife's sturdy shoulders. They stumble-stepped into the cottage, Alan's right arm dangling erratic, like a tool on the tinker's cart as it banged along a rutted road.

"Och, aye . . ." Alan Cameron sighed and nestled into the comfort of his own bed. "Home at last."

Hannah tossed peat clods on the embers and touched a flame to the oily wicks in the cruisie lamps. For a moment the midwife became lost in a frantic search for her elusive scissors, at last finding them in the tangle of her mending basket. Clutching tight the shears in one fist, Hannah pinched the bridge of her nose between thumb and forefinger to silence the clamor in her head. She drew a deep breath, forced a smile, and stepped back to the bedside.

"Well, love, let's see the sort of mischief yiv been up to." She snipped away the remnants of what had been Alan's best shirt, exposing a filthy, bloodstained bandage bound above the elbow of his right arm.

Alan said, "It's but a wee saber slash . . . hardly more than a scratch . . ."

"Scratch or cut, ye should've cleaned it proper, like I taught ye."

"At the time, I was a bit concerned with savin' the rest of my hide."

Hannah kept her eyes on task. "Ye were there, then? Culloden?"

"Aye, Culloden . . ."

"Right in the thick of it, too, I'll wager . . ."

"In the thick of it, aye, that I was, lass."

Hannah gulped back the angry retort sprung to her lips, just as she had nine months before when Alan'd answered the call to arms. The time for scolding had long since past.

Mouth pursed, she snipped at the bandage—the sweet-rot odor more distinct as each layer of crusty linen peeled away. Hannah pressed a warm, wet compress over the last fragment of cloth that had bonded to his skin with a stubborn glue of dry pus and blood. She kept her eyes averted from the blue poison trails racing across his chest toward his heart.

Hannah peeled away the last of the bandage and her hand flew to cover her mouth. She fought to choke back bitter bile rushing up her throat.

It was by far the worst case she'd ever seen—dead, black skin surrounded by rust-brown, oozing blisters. The surgeon's saw would not save her man. The gangrene was far too advanced.

Alan grasped Hannah's hand with his left. "We never stood a chance—Cumberland's artillery cut us to ribbons before we could even begin our charge." His grip tightened. "All for naught, Hannah. The courage . . . those brave, brave lads . . . all for naught . . ."

Hannah wrenched her hand away. "I—I need to clean and bind yer wound." She ripped a discarded petticoat into long strips, the words *all for naught* tolling like a church bell in her head. Tiny hands appeared and draped a cool wet cloth across Alan's fevered brow.

"That's verra helpful, lass." Hannah had forgotten about the little girl. Glad for the distraction, she asked, "And what are ye called?"

"Maggie," the girl offered with a smile and a bob of the knee. "Maggie Duncan."

Hannah picked at a twig stuck in the snarl of the girl's black hair. It struck her odd—the strange lass had not turned or retched from the horror and smell of the gangrenous wound.

"Alan, where'd ye find this wee slip?"

"In truth, she found me."

"And where would that have been?"

"Och!" Alan winced as Hannah began swabbing his wound with a wash of marigold petals steeped in warm water. "The English are steadfast in hunting those who escaped the field of battle." With a soldier's discipline he concentrated, refocusing from pain to the past. "I've been hiding by day and moving only under cover of dark. Made my way to Bailebeg—knew the people there held strong for our cause—hoped they'd give me aid." Alan paused, glancing at the little girl who stood at his side. "But the English—they'd got there afore me." He tensed and shivered as if to shake the memory away. "They'd massacred them all. Every blessed soul. Old folk, women . . . children . . ."

"Women and children! But why . . . ?"

"Cumberland." Alan spat out the name and settled back in the bedding. "Th' butcher ordered no quarter given to supporters of the rightful king. I was daft with fever, and so tired, I lay down there—just to bide a wee and rest a moment. When I woke, I found Maggie beside me." He reached out and stroked the girl's head. "She brought water and shared what bits of food she'd scavenged."

Maggie left them to freshen her cloth with water from the pail.

"The lass escaped the massacre?" Hannah whispered.

"She willna speak on it, but I figure her folk are counted among the murdered. There was no leavin' her behind, Hannah—not there. Ye ken I could never . . . never have left her there . . ."

"Ah, now, darlin' . . . dinna fash. O' course ye couldna leave the wee lass behind."

"No—and in the end, 'twere Maggie who brought me home."

"Aye, she did . . ." With loving fingers Hannah smoothed and erased the worry from his brow. "Maggie brought you home to me."

Alan smiled and closed his eyes, never seeing the tears tracking quiet trails down Hannah's cheeks.

1

The Village of Black Corries
Spring 1760

An obedient girl, Maggie Duncan usually heeded Hannah's admonitions to keep her eyes downcast so as to not ruffle anybody's feathers. But today, Andy Scougle could see the girl was being carnaptious.

Andy stood at the window of his shop and watched Maggie trounce down the muddy thoroughfare, greeting every person she met with a defiant, direct gaze. Grinning from ear to ear, she clearly derived pleasure from their anxious hand gestures of protection and fervent clutching of talismans. The people of Black Corries believed Maggie Duncan possessed the evil eye.

The talk began years before, when Andy's brother-in-law, Alan Cameron, returned from Culloden mortally wounded and in the company of a strange child.

"Her own folk are all dead—the whole of Bailebeg is wiped out," the villagers said. "Send the lass away, Hannah. She must be bad luck."

But Hannah paid them no heed. Mercifully, Alan had not lingered long. At his passing, grief-stricken Hannah's attachment to the little girl intensified, as did the villagers' fear.

"First her own folk and now your Alan—mind, Hannah,"

they said. "She's bad luck, that one. She's no place here in Black Corries."

As village midwife, Andy's sister was accustomed to easing dreads and fears. Gentle words and reason were the remedies she used to soothe and placate her neighbors.

"What blether. If not for wee Maggie, my Alan would have died a cold and lonely death." Hannah insisted God's hand was at work the day Alan brought Maggie home.

Andy agreed. His childless sister needed the company of a kindred spirit. Little Maggie possessed high intelligence and a natural aptitude. Most important, she exhibited true empathy for those in need of care. So, as their mother had taught Hannah, Hannah taught Maggie, and Maggie learned. The lass became Hannah's shadow, attending the births, nursing the sick, tending the injured, and laying out the dead. Just as Andy'd seen his sister grind the ingredients of a remedy together in her big stone mortar, Hannah gradually mixed Maggie Duncan into village life.

Under Hannah's tender nurture, Maggie's apprenticeship progressed smoothly. She learned to find, grow, and prepare the agents required for Hannah's vast store of medicines. She studied their healing properties, learning the best ways to prepare tinctures, decoctions, teas, and poultices. Years passed, the girl's skills improved, memories faded, the villagers mellowed and allowed Maggie to treat their ailments. But then, no one expected Hannah to be struck down by illness.

At first, Hannah insisted her cough was but a pesky remnant from a bout with the croup. Andy wished it were so, but he'd seen the disease too often—the continuous, paroxysmal cough, the thick, blood-streaked sputum, random fevers, weight loss— the symptoms of consumption were, unfortunately, very familiar to him.

Consumption, Andy thought, *such an apt name*. The same disease that consumed his mother had been slowly consuming his sister Hannah for two years, and he knew nothing could stop it.

Fear and ignorance triggered virulent whispers as it became evident their beloved midwife was afflicted with the tubercular disease. "Alan Cameron died of rot . . ." Heads wagged. "And now Hannah's cursed with the Graveyard Cough. That Duncan lass brings bad luck to everything she casts her evil eye upon."

Hannah's condition worsened and so did the rumors. Maggie was at fault when Widow MacKay's hens stopped laying. When Liam Menzie's milch cow went dry, he laid blame on "Dark Maggie." Maggie's nickname, benignly referring to her thick black hair, had taken on a more sinister connotation.

The doorbell jangled and Maggie stepped into Andy's shop.

"Och, bloody hell!" she swore. Striding right past Andy without seeing him, Maggie marched straight to the counter, where his wife, Emma, worked. Maggie proffered a cloth sack to be filled. "Two pounds of meal and none of yer guff, Emma Scougle."

"I've done tolt ye afore, Dark Maggie—we dinna want yer custom here. G'won . . . away with yer bad eye." Emma spat on the floor as a measure of protection against any sort of retaliatory curse and turned her back.

Maggie grabbed Emma by the shoulder and spun her around. "Shut yer wicked gob, Emma Scougle. Ye didna have a care about my evil eye Monday last when yer lad Colm needed his head stitched, did ye now? Fill the sack, Emma. Hannah's waiting on her breakfast and I'm owed."

"Emma! For shame!" Andy inserted himself between the squabbling women.

"But Dark Maggie's cursed poor Hannah with her evil eye!"

"I'll not suffer such blasphemous talk in my shop, wife. It's not for the likes of you to question God's will." He pushed his wife toward the door. "To kirk with ye . . . pray . . . seek forgiveness for yer less than Christian behavior."

Though Emma shot him a look that illustrated Andy's personal definition of the evil eye, she obeyed his order and left the shop.

"Emma's easily swayed by the opinion of others," Andy said as he prized the sack from Maggie's clenched fist. "I'm sure she's contrite and means you no harm."

"That may be"—Maggie shrugged—"but there is little ill-said that is not ill-taken."

"Ah, Maggie, still, ye ought know better than to tangle with folk that way."

Andy scooped far more than two pounds of oatmeal into the sack. He always held a soft spot in his heart for Hannah's foundling, watching her grow to become the most attractive young woman in the glen. A solid, buxom lass, Maggie stood taller than most women. She was blessed with a clear olive complexion, free of the blemishes and pockmarks that so often marred a pretty face. Maggie bore a foreign cast to her features that set her apart, and Andy was of a mind there might be a bit of the gypsy traveler in Maggie's lineage—her liquid, dark eyes held the wisdom of a thousand years.

Under normal circumstances the local lads would be coming to blows vying for Maggie's favor, but folk believed a woman with the evil eye held the power to curse a man with impotence. The threat of being so eye-bitten was too much for simple highland lads to overcome. At twenty-one years of age, Maggie Duncan was doomed to lead a spinster's life.

Andy handed over the sack of meal. "I stopped by yestreen to sit with Hannah for a spell."

"Is that so? I must've been out gatherin'. She said naught to me."

"Hannah's not faring well, is she, Maggie?" Andy's eyes squinched as if he were wincing with pain, casting a pall over his eyes. "I've never seen her lookin' so peellie-wallie. She's naught but skin and bone, a mere shadow of the woman she once was . . . and she's worried about ye, lass, aye . . . rightly so."

"Och, the two of ye . . ." Maggie scowled and draped her woolen shawl over her head. "No need to waste yer worry on me. I can fend for myself all right."

"Ye can pretend otherwise, Maggie, but ye ken as well as I there's danger in this evil-eye blether. Hannah's right to be worried. What's to become of you once she's gone?"

"Hannah's no goin' anywhere, Andy. She's had bad spells afore and she's always pulled through."

"Ye think she'll pull through?" Andy brightened. "Fine weather's a-comin'. Hannah's always been a great one for spring."

"Aye, mark my words, Andy, she'll soon be on the mend."

⚜

Maggie eased the door open and slipped inside the cottage. It was dead quiet. She removed her wooden clogs, tiptoed over to the bedstead, and heaved a sigh of relief. Although sleeping Hannah labored for every breath, she was still breathing.

On the decline for months, Hannah had reached the final and most agonizing stage of the disease, and Maggie could only dread the inevitable—her world without Hannah Cameron in it.

She stoked the fire, prepared a pot of parrich for their breakfast, and then settled down on a small stool near the hearth. Rather than worry over Hannah struggling for every breath, Maggie leaned elbows on knees and rested chin on fists to contemplate the oatmeal breathing in the pot. She watched the thickening meal rise and bellow upward, anticipating the puff of steam exploding from the center of each bubble.

Hannah's weak, wheezy voice broke the silence of the room. "Yer mind is always chasing mice, lass. When are ye goin' to the village?"

"A good long sleep ye had, eh?" Maggie smiled over her shoulder, gave the parrich one last stir, and pulled the pot from the flame. "I've been to the village and back again." Spoonfuls of cooked oatmeal plopped into a wooden bowl. Maggie added a splash of thick cream and a dollop of heather honey.

Hannah's fever-glazed eyes glittered like bright buttons from within their sunken hollows. "How d' ye fare today?"

"Och! I wish ye could have been there to see it. Emma Scougle and I near came to blows over the meal she owed." Maggie settled Hannah into a sitting position. She took up the bowl and spoon and sidled onto the bed. "Andy got between the two of us and sent the auld besom to kirk with a flea in her ear. She's right now begging Our Lord for His forgiveness."

"Mmmph! Our Lord best think twice. Emma gains much pleasure holding a stick over others."

Maggie popped a spoonful of oatmeal into Hannah's mouth. "Aye! Ye must eat—a few spoonfuls at least. It's no wonder they say I've the evil eye. Look at ye—skin and bones!"

"Listen to me, lass," Hannah managed between spoonfuls. "I've been thinking . . . after I'm dead, ye need to leave Black Corries. Leave this place and find yerself a good man."

"Stop yer claverin' and eat!"

"Aye . . . a big braw man is what ye need, Maggie. A man t' protect ye and keep ye warm at night."

Maggie laughed. "I'll tell ye, if it's a good man I'm after, I'll surely need t' leave Black Corries. If only ye could see them scurry, Hannah—so frightened I might cast a wicked spell upon their pitiful parts." She sighed, wistful. "Och, if only I could . . ."

"*Fiech!* There's not a pair of bollocks worth cursin' in this village. America . . ." Hannah closed her eyes and nodded. "Aye . . . yid be bound t' find a real man in America . . ."

"*America!* Are ye daft?" Maggie took the dirty dish to rinse in the washbasin.

"Did I ever tell ye, Maggie, how Alan and I once thought to emigrate as bond servants to Virginia?"

"Virginia! Ah, g'won . . ." Maggie shook her head in disbelief.

"We were young and full of our own dreams then." Hannah's words gasped out in staccato bursts. "Alan said we can slave our whole lives for the laird, with naught to show for it . . . or slave four years in Virginia and have a wee patch of land to call our own in the end. I was game. We had no weans—only our own selves to look after . . ."

"So what happened? Why did yiz not go?"

"Och . . . the call to arms . . . Culloden . . ." Hannah gave a feeble wave of dismissal and fell into a violent fit of coughing and retching.

"Enough palaver." Maggie rushed to fill a kettle with water. "I'm fixing ye a cup of comfrey tea. 'Twill help to heal the lesions in yer lungs."

"Pah! Keep yer comfrey tea," Hannah rasped between coughs. "The only thing t' help me is a generous sprinkle of monkshood on my parrich."

Maggie turned about-face. She marched back and plunked down onto the bed. Monkshood was the deadliest poison in Hannah's medicine cupboard.

"Ye ken well I canna bear it when ye blether on so . . ."

"But I'm weary . . . so weary of the pain. It's a merciful thing, helpin' a body onward in peace." Hannah struggled to catch a breath. "I've done so for others, and there's no one but you to do so fer me."

"Ye will get better! Ye have in the past . . ."

"Na, Maggie-love, there's no gettin' better—ye ken tha' as well as I." Hannah reached out and touched a wizened finger to Maggie's temple. "Dig deep—find th' strength to help me onward—for I canna get the thing done on my own."

Maggie could not speak for the anguish clogging her throat. She trembled and took Hannah's hand in hers.

Hannah smiled. "I'm not afeart—my Alan's there—waiting for me."

2

Spirited Away

A smirr of rain and fog clung to the city, muffling the bong of the evening church bell. With the raveled selvage of her plaide in a clutch beneath her chin, Maggie gripped tight her basket and wove through the crowded streets of Glasgow's Gallowgate.

The pittance Maggie earned helping the washwomen on the Green paid the quitrent on a damp room she shared with eight others—nothing more than a place to lay her pallet. She earned a few extra pennies selling simple remedies on the street, enough to buy a bannock and bowl of pease porridge on most days. Two years of living a hand-to-mouth existence had brought Maggie to the end of her tether, taking two steps backward for every step forward, never quite able to get ahead.

At fifty paces, a slab of wood painted with a crude portrait of a bearded man in a turban creaked on its hinge. She hurried toward the Saracen Head, the coaching inn where her friend Jenny worked as a scullery maid. She'd agreed to aid Jenny's husband, Angus, one of the barmen in the public room. Angus had injured his hand, and in exchange for treatment, he promised to mend Maggie's sorely worn clogs.

She shouldered the heavy door open. Inside, the pub was snug with the spice of boiled beef, cabbage, and fresh-baked bread. Maggie waved to Angus, who was busy serving the lone customer at the bar—and she made straight for the fire to warm her chapped hands.

"Ho, Maggie!" Angus bellowed. "Jenny said ye might come." He was a broad, muscular fellow, with a head of thick ginger hair. His cheerful smile missed several teeth—lost breaking up one of the frequent barroom brawls. "Have a seat over by the hearth, that's the best light. Cider?"

"Aye, cider'd be a wonder, Angus, but I'll also be needin' a dram of whiskey, if it's no bother to ye." She sat down on a bench at the table he'd indicated. Angus set down a tray bearing a pint of hard cider, one small glass, and a bottle of whiskey. He settled into the chair opposite.

Maggie tipped her pint, taking a moment to savor her first sip, for cider was a special treat she could ill afford on her own. She then put the drink aside, ready to tend to business.

"Let's have a look-see."

Angus propped his arm, palm up, on the tabletop. Maggie untied the filthy rag wrapped around his hand, discarding it with some disdain onto the straw-covered floor.

"Aye . . . yiv a nasty wound here." She poked gently at the angry welt slashing across the palm of his left hand. Angus winced.

"I scratched it off-loading casks from the brewer's cart days ago. Ye can see how it's festered—throbs somethin' fierce. Jenny said yid fix it for me."

Maggie examined Angus's huge paw cradled in her small, capable hands. "Aye . . . I'll wager yiv a sliver lodged deep. Help yerself to a dram, lad . . . this is bound t' hurt." She dug through her basket and laid a few items on the table—a darning needle, a stubby candle, strips of clean linen, and a small clay pot sealed with a cap of beeswax.

Angus cast a dubious eye on the needle she held in the flame of the candle and poured a generous amount of whiskey into the glass. "Have a dram with me, Maggie . . ."

"Och, no! The hard stuff was always meant fer you. Now hold still, ken?"

He nodded, sucked in his breath, and averted his eyes as Maggie began probing with her needle. She glanced up. Other than a slight twitching in the muscle of his jaw, Angus bore up.

"Aahhh now, there 'tis!" Triumphant, Maggie showed him the pus-and-blood-coated shard of wood impaled on her needle. Angus jerked his hand away. Maggie pulled it back. "That was the worst of it, lad, but this wound needs dressin'." She drizzled whiskey onto his palm, slathered on a glob of soothing ointment, and bound the whole thing in a clean bandage. "Take the salve home. Have Jenny bind yer fist with a clean dressing every day— it'll heal quick that way."

"Feels better already." Angus smiled and flexed his fingers. "Tell ye what—the farrier's in the stable right now and he owes me a favor. Give us yer clogs—I'll have him tap on a bit o' leather straightaway."

Maggie felt a bit silly, sitting alone and shoeless in the pub. She focused on finishing her cider—aware she was being observed with some intent. The young man Angus had been serving when Maggie first entered the pub stared rather boldly in her direction. She decided to intimidate him with her best evil-eye glare. To her surprise and dismay, he broke into a smile and sauntered over to her table.

He stood very tall with wavy brown hair caught at the nape of his neck in a sky blue ribbon. His linen shirt and cravat sparkled white in the dim light. The worsted gray wool of his jacket spoke of quality; the buttons cast silver and the cut well tailored. She noticed the silver buckles on his leather shoes, and tucked her dirty bare feet beneath her chair.

"May I join you, miss?"

"To be certain, I dinna have a care where ye sit, sir." Maggie shrugged. "I'll be leavin' just soon as Angus brings my shoes."

"Are you married?" he asked, sitting down across from her.

"Married?" Surprised by his boldness, Maggie answered in kind. "That's no concern of yers."

"I'll get right to the point." The rude young man peered inside her basket. "I can see you have a valuable skill and I've a proposition for you . . ."

Maggie flipped the lid closed. "*Feich!* Proposition indeed!" She grabbed her basket and moved to sit at the next table.

Undaunted, the man simply slid his chair over. "My name is Ethan Hampton . . ." He held out a hand. "Just arrived from the Colonies—Virginia to be exact. Hear me out. Let me stand you a drink. I assure you, it's not at all what you think."

Maggie ignored his hand and leaned back in her chair, dropping her guard but slightly now that his odd way had been identified. She'd heard Americans tended toward brash. Her curiosity was piqued, and besides, the cider at the Saracen Head was awfully tasty.

"Barman! A pint of cider for my friend and a pint of stout for myself. Are you hungry?"

Maggie answered with a cautious nod. When the barman brought the drinks, Ethan Hampton ordered a full supper for two. She hadn't eaten meat in over a year, and the promise of supper earned this man Maggie's rapt attention.

"I'm ship's agent for the merchant vessel the *Good Intent*, charged with securing cargo for the return leg, and there lies the proposition I have for you." The American lad settled back in his chair, drink in hand. "Did you know, Maggie, most of the tobacco shipped from Virginia makes port right here in Glasgow Harbor?"

"Aye," she agreed. "Everyone kens tha'."

Ethan Hampton refreshed himself with a pull from his pint. "No shipmaster wants to sail home with an empty hold. There's no profit in that, is there?"

Bobbing her head in agreement, Maggie hurried to gulp down

the dregs of her pint. "'Tis all well and good, Mr. Hampton, but unless ye have an ache or malady of some sort, I dinna ken how I can be of any assistance t' ye . . ."

"It is *I* who will be of assistance to *you*." He flashed a brilliant smile. "What I'm offering is a new beginning—the means by which to start a wonderful life in the New World . . ."

"A *spirit*!" Maggie pounded a fist on the tabletop, drawing the attention of a group of customers stumbling in off the evening coach from Edinburgh. Men known as "spirits" haunted popular gathering places, beguiling young people into servitude with grandiose tales of the Colonies, and then "spiriting" them far away, never to be seen by their families again.

Unperturbed by her outburst, Ethan Hampton signaled the barman for another round of drinks. "Spirit!" He laughed. "Come now . . . do you really think I have the power to spirit you away, Maggie? Against your free will?"

"Na, I'm nobody's fool." Maggie punctuated her assertion with a gulp from her pint.

"Exactly so!" Ethan banged the tabletop. "I can see you've a native intelligence and you're doubly blessed with a pretty face and a marketable skill. Have you been trained in the healing arts, or is it you just possess a knack?"

Maggie blushed, flustered by his compliments and the effects of her bottomless pint of cider. "I was once apprenticed to a midwife of considerable skill. She passed away, and I've had no luck finding another willing to take me on."

"You certainly seemed skilled enough . . ."

"Aye, but I've no repute—considered by most too young, ye ken?"

"I see . . . even though you've a skill, you're not well off. Life for you is a daily struggle . . ."

"Och, aye . . ." Maggie sighed, and toasted her host with a tip of her tankard.

"But, I ask you, who can expect to get ahead here? Only

those of proper lineage, that's who! Those lucky enough to be born into the right class." Ethan Hampton hit his stride. A few of the other patrons edged close to listen in, and he raised his volume.

"Tell me if I've the right of it—no matter how hard you are willing to work, no matter how smart or how pretty you are, Maggie, you are only allowed to go so far in this life. And when you can't find steady work, what will you do to fill your empty belly? Sell your beautiful hair . . . your teeth—or resort to even more desperate means? Do I speak the truth?"

Maggie found herself nodding, and the others who'd gathered around also grunted in agreement. Ethan reached into his pocket and pulled out a document, which he unfolded with great care and set on the table.

"I offer you Opportunity."

Maggie shook her head. "I canna read."

"It says this—" Ethan smoothed the folds of stiff parchment. "You will receive transport and victuals aboard the *Good Intent* leaving two weeks from this day, heading for Richmond, Virginia. You'll be bound for four years' labor to whoever purchases your contract from the ship's captain . . ."

"And if no one purchases my contract?"

"Not much chance of that, Maggie. There's such a shortage of domestic servants, I'm certain you'll obtain a fine position . . ."

"Ah, no . . ." Maggie shook her head again. "I dinna possess a Character . . ." She'd been deemed unqualified for domestic service for lack of a "Character"—the referral document necessary to obtain such a position.

"You don't need a Character in Virginia. They're clamoring for girls—Scottish girls especially are in high demand. And, Maggie . . ." Ethan edged the contract toward her. "You will be well cared for—three hearty meals a day, a clean, warm bed at night, clothes and shoes whenever you need them."

"Aye? Clothes, ye say?" Maggie bunched a handful of her

threadbare skirt in her fist. She spent much of her spare time repairing the worn odds and ends of her meager wardrobe.

"After four short years, you'll receive your Freedom Dues. It's all listed right here, see?" Ethan pointed out a section on the paper. "At contract's end you're promised three pounds ten shillings, one suit of clothes, stockings and shoes, two hoes, one ax, and three barrels of corn."

"Ha! And why would I be needin' an ax?" Maggie pushed the parchment away. "To protect myself from the Red Indians what come to hack off my hair?"

"Wild tales!" Ethan laughed. "I'll admit there are one or two savage tribes deep, deep in the backcountry, but the few docile natives remaining in Virginia are very tame. No"—he slid the document back toward Maggie—"the tools and such are for starting out on your own. There is land for the taking in the New World."

"A wee bit of land to call my own . . . tha' would be fine." Maggie began to plan the herbs she would plant in her garden. "I could make a living from tha', na?"

"Three pounds ten shillings—an enticing dowry for some young man looking for a wife." Ethan winked. "You're a beautiful girl, and I would be remiss not to warn you—there is no shortage of marriageable young men in Virginia. Be prepared to have your pick . . ."

"Aye . . ." Maggie nodded. "Someone once told me good men are to be found in the Colonies . . ."

"Not only good men—the best men! Strong and handsome— rich . . . oh, Maggie, they're waiting for you . . . a better life is waiting for you! All you need do is sign here . . ."

ᕙ❀ᕗ

When Angus returned with Maggie's clogs, he found her huddled over the table with the American lad, struggling with a quill to make her mark on a sheet of paper.

"Maggie! What have ye done?"

Maggie looked up, her smile wide. "I'm off to America!"

3

A Region of Calm

As Captain William Carlyle mounted the stairs to the aft quarterdeck, the last curve of the sun slipped behind the horizon. The captain caught himself doing something he rarely did—questioning his ability. The *Good Intent* had left port six weeks before. Skimming along smartly, she eased past the Portuguese coast on a westerly course, but just beyond the Canaries she'd blundered onto the notorious region of calm known as the Horse Latitudes and now they had sat adrift without a whiff of a breeze for six days running.

The evening sky glowed with residual light from the setting sun, still a bit too bright to make out the stars. Carlyle turned his attention to the silent crowd assembled on the main deck. Most of the ship's inhabitants—seamen and passengers alike—gathered every evening to hear MacGregor read aloud from his cherished copy of *Robinson Crusoe.*

"*...we committed our Souls to God in the most earnest Manner, and the Wind driving us towards the Shore, we hasten'd our Destruction with our own Hands...*"

One hundred and twenty souls crammed together like so many hogsheads of tobacco—in daily peril on the high seas—all mesmerized by the adventure of a solitary, shipwrecked man. Although Carlyle found the irony amusing, he was grateful for the diversions that kept tensions from running high. Periods of calm could be just as life threatening as a hurricane, for the longer his ship went without touching the wind, the greater the chance of running low on rations and fresh water. *I would do well to recall what befell the Sea-Flower.*

Stocked with only eight weeks' worth of provisions, the *Sea-Flower* floundered lost at sea for sixteen weeks. Forty-six people starved to death as a result of their captain's poor planning. In the end, the *Sea-Flower* survivors resorted to cannibalism and ate six of the dead, the captain included among those consumed.

"Mr. Stark!" Carlyle shouted. His lanky ship's mate quickly disengaged from the crowd of listeners and scrambled up the quarterdeck stair.

"Aye, Cap'n?"

Carlyle lowered his voice. "If the wind's not shifted by tomorrow, move to half rations—victuals and water."

"Aye, Cap'n." Josh Stark nodded in agreement.

Mr. Stark kept the crew on their toes, making use of the idle time to maintain first-rate condition and keep the ship tight. The ship's mate saw the bilge pumps engaged and the corrupt water collected in the bottom of the ship purged. He had the caulker seal every leak with oakum and tar, and the sailmaker finish mending all three sets of sails. Tackle, blocks, and rigging were all examined and repaired. To minimize infestation, today all bedding was aired and the sleeping berths sweetened with a swabbing of vinegar.

A groan went up from the crowd when MacGregor snapped the book shut and slipped his precious spectacles into the breast pocket of his jacket. Daylight faded completely and it was a strain to read by lantern light.

Someone called for a song and the Duffy twins began to tune their instruments. The good-natured brothers had boarded with nothing more than the shirts and the fiddles on their backs, and never needed much encouragement to oblige their audience. Moira Bean, a robust Glaswegian washwoman, stepped up to join the fiddlers with a powerful voice. After two bawdy songs and one soulful ballad, Carlyle signaled Pebley, the boatswain, to begin dousing the ship's lights. Fire was the ever-present and most deadly danger aboard. It was Mr. Pebley's duty to see every lantern extinguished and collected, save one lamp to illuminate the compass and one for the watch.

The passengers hurried to settle their sleeping places below before Pebley called for all lights out. They collected their pallets from where they hung along the rail and took turns shuffling down the hatchway stairs to tween deck.

Located between main deck and the cargo hold, tween deck quartered all passengers traveling on indenture to the Colonies, providing both space for their berths and storage for any baggage they'd brought aboard.

The captain never ceased to wonder at the endurance of these desperate pilgrims. His own tiny cabin was a luxurious retreat compared to the cramped quarters of the tween. Carlyle knew he could not suffer even one night in that airless pitch black, sandwiched between strangers, privy to his fellows' every grunt, groan, snore, and fart.

Tween deck measured a scant five feet six inches from floor to ceiling. Most of the emigrants housed there could not stand fully upright. Baskets, wooden chests, and canvas sacks were stuffed into every available nook and crowded the narrow aisles. Ventilation was poor at best, and in the event of rough seas with hatches battened down, fresh air was nonexistent. On those days, the stench of vomit and latrine buckets could be particularly hard to bear.

Will Carlyle had weathered hurricanes with the force to split sails and snap a mainmast in two. His ship had been boarded and ransacked by pirates. He'd twice been washed overboard and lived to tell of it. Able to endure the worst of a seaman's life, the captain still avoided going down to tween deck at all costs—and so did Maggie Duncan.

Carlyle smiled. *There—she stands her post like clockwork . . .*

Maggie dawdled at the portside railing every night. Will Carlyle sympathized with her plight, but he could not have the beautiful young woman distracting the watch. As it was, half the men aboard were besotted with the well-rigged healer, and the other half stung by her rejection of their coarse overtures.

Though a pretty woman aboard usually spelled trouble, Captain Carlyle considered Maggie Duncan to be the most valuable passenger his agent had recruited. Unlike many of his peers, Carlyle understood that be it tobacco or laborers, the quality of the cargo determined the amount of profit he reaped at voyage end. Will Carlyle maintained a solid reputation up and down the Virginia coast as a merchant who always delivered top-quality goods. Maggie Duncan occupied her time maintaining the good health and humor of his cargo, forever delving into her basket to bring comfort and relief to passengers and crewmen alike.

The staunch champion of her fellow shipmates, Maggie earned praise early on by standing toe-to-toe with Cook, who was not an easy man. She asked Cook to prepare a clear broth for the unfortunates racked with seasickness, as they were unable to stomach the usual fare of salt pork, hard cheese, and biscuit. She did not relent until Cook obliged her request.

But Cook bellowed like a bull elephant when Maggie suggested the ship's drinking water be boiled and strained. Maggie insisted Carlyle inspect the most recently opened cask of water.

"Captain," she began, "though I dinna doubt this water was once fresh, 'tis no longer the case. Look here—every cask coated with this vile green scum—" Her nose crinkled in disgust as she stirred the contents with a stick. "Dead bugs and worms form the second layer. It's no great wonder so many are laid low with the flux. Boiling our water is but a small bother for Cook, and there are many willing to help."

The captain saw no harm in the suggestion and ordered surly Cook to follow Maggie's advice. The effect upon everyone's health was immediate and Cook ceased his grumbling.

As much as Carlyle liked and admired the young woman, she tried his patience every night with her continued dawdling on deck after hours.

"Mr. Stark, please escort Miss Duncan down to the tween . . ."

Joshua Stark skittered down the stair before the captain could even complete his order. Carlyle grinned. His stalwart mate was definitely counted among the severely lovestruck.

⊙

She leaned into the rail and stretched her underused muscles, determined to delay the trip down to tween deck for as long as possible. Maggie'd grown accustomed to the many discomforts of sea travel, but she would never grow accustomed to the tween's unholy combination of fetid air and total darkness. Most mornings found her curled in her plaide at the bottom of the stair, where a trickle of fresh air managed to filter down.

"Och, the evil hour is upon me," Maggie muttered when she saw Mr. Stark ambling toward her. She did not budge from her post by the rail. She smiled. In this game, she held all the cards.

"I'm sorry, Maggie, but Cap'n says it's time for you to get below . . ."

Maggie ignored him, and bent over the rail, searching for something alongside the ship.

"What're you lookin' for?" Joshua peered over her shoulder.

"Ol' Pete says there's a huge sea beast lurking beneath us—a *remora*. Pete claims he's seen one latch onto a ship's keel and pull it under the waves quicker than a blink of the eye. D'ye think it's true?"

Joshua relaxed and leaned onto the rail next to Maggie. "I'll tell you what I think, Maggie. I think Pete should spend less time spinning frightful yarns for gullible girls and more time mending the canvas."

"Ah no! Ol' Pete's a darlin'." Maggie gave the ship's mate a playful elbow to the ribs. "I ken it's but a tale—a tall tale at that. Don't be bothering Ol' Pete on my account . . ."

"I won't scold Pete. He's been at sea a long lifetime, and Lord knows, these ol'-timers have seen a thing or two to tell about. But really, Maggie, you need to get below . . ."

"Joshua, look!" Maggie flung her arms wide to the perfectly smooth sea stretched before them like a huge black mirror reflecting the spray of stars twinkling in the heavens. "I ken fair wind is the seaman's best friend, but I canna help but think this calm is verra bonnie indeed."

"I'll grant you," Joshua said. "On a still night like this it's easy to imagine creatures lurking beneath the surface. Sailors have the most—"

An unfamiliar noise interrupted his speech. Maggie and Joshua both glanced upward in time to see an eerie, liquid blue fire hiss and crackle at the top of the mizzenmast. For a few seconds the blue light danced along the uppermost spars and rigging before dissipating into the atmosphere.

"Megstie me!" Maggie inched close to Joshua. He slipped an arm around her shoulders.

"Just a bit of St. Elmo's fire. Why, I've seen where the blue flames shoot across the spars and climb up and down the shrouds for hours at a time."

"St. Elmo's fire!" Maggie sniffed the ozone in the air and stared in wonder at the topmast, hoping the strange event would repeat itself.

"Some say it's a good omen—a blessing from the patron saint of sailors. It's not really fire as such—more like lightning. They say St. Elmo's fire portends a strong wind on the way."

The helmsman turned the hourglass and struck the aft bell, signaling the beginning of the first watch. "Come along now,

Maggie." Joshua slipped his arm from Maggie's shoulder and glanced toward the quarterdeck, relieved to see Captain Carlyle engrossed in his celestial navigation. "I'll be whipped and pickled if Cap'n sees you're still on deck during the watch."

"Joshua, I was wondering." Maggie laid a warm hand on his forearm. "What harm is there in my finding a wee corner to curl up in, here, on main deck? Quiet as a mouse I'd be . . ."

The mate's gaze swept across the ordered chaos of the crowded deck. Spars and spare mast pieces rested amid coils of tarred rope. Yards of anchor cable caked with dried mud were piled near the iron-banded casks filled with water, salt meat, and other stores. Near the chicken coops and pigpens, the four mariners standing first watch were busy arranging sea chests around an upended cable reel for their nightly game of euchre. In all likelihood Maggie's presence would go unnoticed.

"All right . . . but mind, steer clear of the watch," he warned. "If anyone finds you out, Maggie Duncan, you're on your own."

They tugged her pallet far from the quarterdeck, back behind a stack of canvas near the foremast. Maggie bid Joshua good night, very happy to be granted one night's reprieve from the grim quarters below.

⋘❦⋙

"G' way . . . leave me be . . ." Maggie groaned, dismissing her tormentor with a wave of her hand. Her eyes blinked open. A cool breeze washed across the deck and the ship bobbed on waves slapping up to the rails. Bright lights flashed in the distant sky. Propped up on one elbow, she pushed the frizzle of hair from her face and squinted at the dark silhouette hovering over her.

Relentless, the prodder persisted in poking a stick between her ribs. "Get below, you filthy guttersnipe! Your kind is not allowed to pollute this deck after hours . . ."

"Sod off, y' drunken skulk . . ." Maggie pushed the stick aside, irritated at being so rudely wakened from the first deep sleep she'd had in days. The knob end of the stick caught up under her chin, and the man forced Maggie to rise unsteady to her feet. Though she had never before laid eyes upon him, she recognized her tormentor at once.

A queued, beribboned powdered wig sat askew on his head, exposing a patch of close-clipped dark hair. He moved close, his pallid face inches from hers. "Filthy Scots vermin! Infesting the deck by day—by God, I will not allow you to haunt it by night!"

"I beg pardon, yer grace," she croaked, stretching up on tiptoes to alleviate the discomfort of the cane lodged against her throat. "I misspoke . . . I mistook ye fer one of the watchmen . . ."

He lowered the silver-tipped cane. His misbuttoned shirt was trimmed with fine lace and stained with the luxuries of claret and beef gravy. His sour breath stank of wine and garlic. The man stood only a wee bit taller than herself, and his clever blue eyes observed her closely as well. "I am most definitely not the watch, but I shall call for it . . ."

"No! Dinna call the watch! I swear, it willna occur again, yer grace . . ."

"It most assuredly will not." His words were harsh, but the voice behind them mellowed.

"Aye, yer grace." Considering herself dismissed, Maggie bent to gather her bedding. The man continued to stand over her, his ominous proximity making her anxious for the squalid safety of the tween deck.

The nobleman suddenly tossed his cane aside. Maggie's eyes followed the polished black walking stick spinning and skittering across the deck planking. He grabbed her from behind and forced her forward several strides, trapping her hard against the rail. Certain the madman meant to toss her overboard like so much rubbish, Maggie squealed, squirmed, and struggled to break free. It almost came as a relief when he began grinding his hips against her rear end and groping for her breasts. Maggie stopped struggling immediately.

Mistaking complacency for acceptance, the nobleman relaxed

his grip. "Good girl—that's the way . . ." Panting heavy in her ear, he struggled to shove her skirts up with one hand and fumbled with the buttons on his breeches with the other.

In a swift, practiced movement Maggie whirled around with a clenched fist, striking her molester square in the face with all the force she could muster. He staggered back. She shouldered past, hitched her skirts, and ran to the nearest stairway.

The man turned in time to see Maggie escape down the hatch to join the denizens of the tween deck. Dazed and more than a little drunk, he plopped down onto a pile of canvas and rubbed his aching face.

❦

"Nimbly, boys, or we'll be meat for the fishes!" Stark shouted over the wind. He marched two crewmen onto the foredeck, barking out orders to remove the sails from the bowsprit and foremast. Cables squealed through pulleys as men battled time, preparing their vessel to face the oncoming storm.

Mr. Stark was surprised to find the ship's phantom passenger sprawled out on a stack of canvas, for Viscount Julian Cavendish never left the sanctuary of his cabin, choosing instead to weather his crossing in a semicomatose state of inebriation.

It was unusual for Captain Carlyle to transport members of the peerage, as the *Good Intent* was not fit out with much in the way of accommodations. But in a desperate effort to extricate his youngest son from some nefarious tangle, the Duke of Portland himself had discreetly arranged the young viscount's passage at the eleventh hour. Stark recalled the duke being much more concerned with the speed of their departure than with the suitability of accommodations. Canny Carlyle negotiated an extra-generous compensation for the inconvenience of having to give over his captain's cabin.

"Beg pard'n, sir." Joshua picked up the walking stick rolling around the deck and handed it to the nobleman. "We're coming into some foul weather."

Julian took the cane and used it to propel himself to his feet.

"Mr. Stark—are you aware a young woman has made her bed here among the sails?"

Stark's eyes darted over to Maggie's deserted pallet. "You're mistaken, sir. Passengers other than yourself are not allowed the freedom of the deck during the watch. You but stumbled across one of the ordinary seamen catchin' a bit of shut-eye."

"Oh no, Stark—I am quite certain *she* was no ordinary seaman." Cavendish winced and touched two fingers to the purple swelling beneath his right eye. "One of the indented creatures—a lovely, wild thing—black hair, dark eyes, luscious round arse— do you know of whom I speak?"

"No." Joshua's mouth formed a hard line in his face, his hands balled into fists, and he struggled to maintain a level tone. "There's no one aboard who answers your description."

"Indeed, Mr. Stark . . . no one?"

"There's a bad storm coming—I must insist, sir—your quarters . . ."

"When this foul weather clears, I think I will join the rabble on deck. Yes . . . good business to fully peruse Carlyle's merchandise in advance of the auction, don't you think, Stark?" Cavendish staggered with the pitch and roll toward his cabin. "After all, I'll soon be in the market for a serving girl."

༒

Maggie wended her way through the maelstrom of the tween deck. The ship's lurching after six days of calm disturbed everybody's sleep. Boots thumping across the upper deck and the muffled shouts of the crew added to the passengers' distress. Those prone to seasickness groaned. Those prone to fear mumbled prayers. The pragmatic struggled in the dark to secure their belongings.

Supported by wooden uprights, platforms measuring six foot by six foot lined both sides of the tween deck. The platforms were stacked one over the other, with little more than two feet separating bottom bunk from top bunk, and top bunk from the ceiling above. Four passengers shared each platform with feet pressed against the bulkhead and heads facing the aisle to catch what little air there was.

One after the other, the hatches slammed shut. Unidentifiable objects slid and rolled up and down the narrow aisle, banging into Maggie's shins and ankles. After tripping and feeling her way to the end of the row, she found her assigned space on the lower platform occupied. Moira Bean, a young woman of generous proportions, took advantage of Maggie's absence and lay comfortably curled on her side. The space allotted each passenger did not allow for anything as exotic as sleeping on your side. Maggie gave Moira a shove. "Roll over, dearie . . ."

"Ummghh," Moira moaned loud, and swatted at the air.

"C'mon, Moira! Make room!" Maggie tried to squirm into the little space left her. Moira's body twitched and contracted into a tight ball, forcing Maggie back into the aisle.

"Och, Moira! What's gotten into ye?"

"We've not had as much as a wink of sleep for all her moanin' and groanin'," one voice complained from across the aisle. Others grunted in agreement.

Maggie pressed hands to Moira's forehead and round cheeks. The woman felt clammy, but she was not feverish. Moira was not one to suffer with seasickness, but she might well have eaten spoiled food. "Moira, are ye ailin', lass?"

"Leave me be."

The sea grew more turbulent. One after another, booming waves slammed against the bulkhead, pounding the ship without letup. "God Almighty!" the occupant of the upper bunk cried out in a panic. "There's naught between us and certain death but the thickness of that planking!"

Moira lashed out at the platform above her and banged it hard with an angry fist. *"Stiek yer gab, ye bletherin' gobshite!"*

The outburst did not deter Maggie. "Dinna fash. Most likely something ye ate, Moira. Have ye pain in yer belly? The beef

Cook served up today was hard enough to take a good polish . . ."
She pushed and cajoled the hefty woman to lie flat on her back in
order to poke and prod her generous, soft abdomen properly.

Moira's big belly was not soft at all—it's hard roundness tightened and bunched beneath her palms. Maggie leaned forward
and whispered into her friend's ear.

"Why Moira Bean . . . yer birthing a baby!"

⁂

"Hold her steady into the wind!" Captain Carlyle shouted at the
helmsman. Sheets of rain whipped across the decks and veins of
lightning cracked the sky directly above as the *Good Intent*
churned through the roiling waves. Carlyle smelled sulfur in the
air, fully confident he'd once again bested the sea by having
weathered the worst of this storm.

A burst of wind howled through the rigging. The topmost spar
snapped and tore away from the mainmast, thudding into the
pigpen in a tangle of canvas, rope, blocks, and tackle. Squealing
pigs scrambled over the fallen spar and out of the pen. The disoriented pigs staggered drunkenly with the pitch and roll, silly in
their attempt to make good their escape.

Joshua and the boatswain cleared away the debris as the other
crewmen scurried to capture the pigs. Just as the last squealer
was deposited back into the pen, Mr. Stark noticed a rhythmic
pounding and shouting coming from a nearby hatch. He pulled
back tarred canvas, unbolted and opened the hatch a few inches.
The Duffy brothers' cherubic faces peered out.

"No worries, boys," Stark said. "Pass the word. Naught but a
busted spar . . ."

"Mr. Stark! We need a light!"

"Can't you see we've a storm here? None of your jaw
now . . . get below, both of you . . ."

Jim Duffy shot his scrawny arm through the opening as Joshua
began to lower the hatch. "Maggie sent us!" they both squawked.
"Maggie needs light . . . Moira Bean's birthing a baby!"

"*What?*" Stark pulled open the hatch and the two brothers scrambled out onto the deck, shouting in turn.

"Moira Bean's birthing a baby . . ."

"Maggie needs a light . . ."

"Aye, and yer no t' worry . . ."

". . . there'll be no fire . . ."

". . . we'll mind the light."

The fair-haired twins waited as Stark digested the message. "But Captain Carlyle does not allow pregnant women aboard his ship," he shouted back.

"Moira's birthin' a baby nonetheless," the twins replied in unison.

"Here . . ." Joshua grabbed a lantern and shoved it at Tim.

"One thing more . . ." Tim grinned. "Maggie sez yer t' '*stop the bloody ship from bloody rockin*'." The two boys returned to the tween and the mate went up to the quarterdeck to break the news to Captain Carlyle.

"Have a look, Joshua." Carlyle handed him a spyglass and pointed at the clear band of pale dawn on the western horizon. They would soon sail free of the squall.

Stark handed back the glass. "Maggie sent the Duffys up for a light. It seems one of the women is having a baby."

Carlyle snapped the glass shut. "Come with me, Mr. Stark."

Joshua followed the captain into his quarters, waiting patiently as Carlyle hung his dripping sea cape from a hook and then searched through a cupboard for his bottle of whiskey. The captain swallowed a mouthful and offered the bottle to his mate. "Tell me, Joshua, how did a pregnant woman manage to stow away all this time?"

"She's no stowaway, Cap'n. It's Moira Bean—the big girl who sings."

"Damnation! Hampton knows very well I do not contract with pregnant women!"

"She's a large woman, Cap'n, and in all fairness, I doubt

Ethan knew Moira was carryin' when he signed her on. After all, she's been aboard for weeks, and neither of us had a clue. There's naught to do 'bout it now; she's squeezin' the mite out as we speak."

"They never survive, you know." The strain of the storm had caught up with Will Carlyle and he sank down onto his berth. "I've seen it so many times before. The sailor's end for them . . . mother and child sewed into a piece of old canvas with a load of iron shot to weigh them down . . ."

"Buck up, Cap'n! Moira's a stout heart and Maggie knows a thing or two. She'll do what can be done to help Moira and the babe survive."

"If the baby survives, then I've a dilemma of another sort." The captain rolled to lie on his side. "The storm's abating . . . go find some sleep, Joshua."

Stark woke several hours later to find the ship in full sail, riding a strong, steady breeze on gentle swells. To his surprise, he found Moira Bean up on deck, perched upon a feather bed, nursing a very pink baby boy. He congratulated the proud mother and ran up the stairs to meet the captain on the quarterdeck.

"Everyone seems to be faring well, Captain."

"Aye, Moira's a strong woman and Maggie pulled them through." Captain Carlyle seemed pleased. "I've decided on the solution to my dilemma."

"Dilemma?"

"Aye—the baby." Carlyle waved his hand toward Moira. "If I auction Moira's contract, it's doubtful the buyer will accept the child as well. And though there are those who would not hesitate, I will not separate a mother from her child. If I do find a buyer accepting mother and child, the law binds the poor baby into servitude till the age of twenty-one. Dealing with men and women who enter into an agreement of their own free will is one thing, but condemning an innocent to decades of slavery weighs too heavy on my conscience. I've decided to have Moira repay her debt of passage as a domestic in my home. With our girls married off, Lord knows my Sarah can use the company."

Joshua spotted Maggie coming up the hatchway stair. She looked up to the quarterdeck, smiled, and waved before going to sit with Moira. Stark and Carlyle both waved back.

The door of the captain's cabin slammed open and Julian Cavendish emerged, attired in the same disheveled clothing he'd worn the night before.

"Good day to you, sir," Carlyle greeted him. "It cheers me to see you leave your cloister and join us on this glorious morning."

"Yes, yes . . . good morning." Cavendish yawned, bleary-eyed and hungover, the purple bruise vivid on his pale complexion. He stood for a moment, scanning the main deck, closely examining the crowd. "Aha!" He pointed to Maggie with his walking stick. "That one, Carlyle. The raven-haired girl. Name your price and have her sent to my quarters."

At first struck speechless by the audacious demand, Carlyle recovered quickly. "I—I'm sorry, sir, but my partners frown upon the practice of advance sales."

"Name your price, Captain, for I've no patience haggling with merchants. I'm quite certain your partners will have no complaint with our transaction."

"Again, I apologize, sir, but I must abide by the rules and decline your generous offer. I'm afraid you will have to attend the auction and enter the bidding with all buyers."

"It is most unfortunate, Captain, that we cannot come to terms." Clearly unaccustomed to having a request so rebuffed, he turned on his heel and descended the stairs to the main deck.

"What partners?" Joshua asked. Carlyle grinned.

Will and Josh chuckled, watching Julian Cavendish, so alien to the environment of the ship, pick his way through the crowd with much effete distaste. Maggie noticed the viscount heading her way. She muttered something to Moira, and slipped down the hatchway.

"Why, that pompous powdered Bob . . ." Carlyle shook his head in amazement. "He's cast his eye on Maggie, and means to have her."

"Well, I've got my eye on him. If he bothers Maggie, I'll trim his fancy jacket and give him a good rubdown with an oaken towel, I will!"

"Steady now, son." Carlyle calmed his mate. "Just warn the girl. Tell her to steer clear . . ."

"But, Cap'n, she'll not be able to steer clear if he purchases her contract at auction . . ."

"Don't worry, Joshua, I'll see to it. Duke's son or no, Maggie Duncan is too good for the likes of that drunken scoundrel."

4

Just Arrived

SCOTTISH SERVANTS
Just Arrived
in the ship the *Good Intent*
A Number of healthy Indented Men and Women Servants
among the former are a Variety of Tradesmen,
with some good Farmers and stout Labourers
Indentures will be disposed of
on reasonable Terms for Cash by
Captain William Carlyle of Richmond, Virginia
April 4, 1763

"Yer certain there'll be women for sale?"

The elderly gentleman tapped the stem end of his claybowl pipe to the broadside tacked onto the notice board. "Well, it says right here—'men and women' . . ."

"Aye . . . and would ye happen to ken today's date, sir?"

The pipe smoker took a moment to reevaluate this Scotsman, who had so politely introduced himself with a request to have the auction notice read aloud. The young man's patched and grimy frock shirt was tied at the waist with a rough-cut strap of leather.

He wore deerskin breeches and his feet were encased in soft moccasins. Slight and wiry, Seth Martin stood only a mite taller than
the long rifle he casually leaned upon.

"I don't suppose you've much call to mind the calendar backcountry, eh, son?"

"Na . . ." Seth shrugged. ". . . one day's much like the one afore."

The older man chuckled, having a certain regard for the life-
style led by the frontiersman. "If you aim to buy yourself a
woman at that auction, best make your way riverside, for today
is the fourth and most auctions tend to get under way about
midday."

Seth Martin glanced up at the sun shining directly above. He
thanked the man and hurried down to the waterfront.

⋘❤⋙

"*There's one!* Look there! A Red Indian man!"

The immigrants rushed the portside, where Jim Duffy stood
shouting and pointing like a madman. It'd been two weeks since
the *Good Intent* snaked its way up the James River to the fall line
at Richmond, and the newcomers had yet to sight a single savage.
Maggie wriggled through the crowd and leaned out over the
rail.

"Where? Where d'ye see a Red Indian man?"

"Look there, ye gowk." Jim Duffy pointed to a tall man coming down the pier leading two laden packhorses.

"He's no a verra red Red Indian, is he?" Maggie noted.

"Do Indian fellas often wear beards that-a-way?" someone
else asked.

"He's no a Red Indian at all . . ." twin brother Tim challenged.

"Christ! O' course he's a Red Indian," Jim insisted. "Have
look at the clothes he's wearin'."

The first mate bullied his way to the front of the crowd. "Why,
you silly pack of greenhorns! That's no Indian." Stark cupped his
hands to his mouth. "*Ahoy, Tom!* Ahoy, Tom Roberts!"

The man leading the horses stopped and squinted into the sunlight. He whisked off and waved his battered felt hat, exposing telltale fair hair. "Ahoy, Josh!"

"Fry me brown, Tom, I never thought to see you alive! They said you were crow's meat by now."

"Whosoever told you that is a point-blank tale-teller. I've been on a long hunt, Josh—overmountain—beyond the ridge in *Kentake*! I've a year's worth of stories to tell and peltry to sell—"

"Hold there, Tom. We're buying goods for the outbound voyage . . . I'm coming down." The first mate impatiently pushed people aside, making his way over to the gangway. "G'won now! Get on back to where the bidders can give you a good going-over." He shooed the crowd away from the rail before running down to greet his old friend.

Freshly bathed and laundered, with their contracts pinned to their backs, the immigrants shuffled back to stand about as buyers wandered the decks previewing Carlyle's human cargo in anticipation of the auction. Indentured men who arrived armed with a trade such as carpentry or smithing were in high demand and garnered premium prices. Strong young men suited for work in the fields would also fetch a high price. A lucky woman would have her contract purchased by a well-to-do colonial in need of a domestic servant, for during planting season, there were those who did not hesitate to purchase females for backbreaking labor in the fields.

The captain warned them all to be on their best behavior during the preview, for no one would bid on a surly servant. To encourage their cooperation, Carlyle made it plain any contracts unsold at auction's end would be handed over to a broker known as a soul driver. Not known for their kindness or for the quality of their clientele, soul drivers herded their human merchandise through the countryside in search of buyers. Many an unfortunate lass wound up working the terms of her contract flat on her back in a brothel—an all-too-typical sale for a soul driver.

As much as Maggie wanted to impress buyers, she had a hard

time behaving well under their rude scrutiny. A man came up and ordered her to open her mouth so he could "have a gander," and Maggie struggled to keep from spitting in his eye. The prospective buyer moved on in search of a "good-natured girl" and she wandered back to the rail.

The indented passengers had not been allowed to debark, and for two weeks, Maggie leaned out over the same rail, longing for the day when she could set foot on dry land. Now that auction day had arrived, the precarious uncertainty of fate lay heavy on her heart and she struggled to quell the anxiety cramping in the pit of her stomach.

"Och, bloody hell!"

Silver-tipped walking stick in hand, Julian Cavendish strolled down the pier. Maggie spent the better part of the voyage hiding belowdecks to avoid the viscount's dogged pursuit, and she began the day hanging on to the slim hope that perhaps he would not attend. Captain Carlyle promised Maggie her contract would not be sold to Cavendish, but she worried nonetheless. Men of rank have the means and the habit of acquiring whatever they want.

Joshua Stark was helping his friend off-load the heavy bales of hides and furs when Tom Roberts suddenly burst out laughing. Josh looked up to see the young viscount, coiffed in an elaborate powdered wig and attired in silk and lace finery, strut past on high-heeled shoes. Josh thought it a good idea to run up and warn Maggie, when a barge loaded with a dozen hogsheads of cured tobacco pulled up alongside the *Good Intent*.

"Blood and thunder!" he cursed. "I'll have to deal with this lot. Tom, go on up and settle accounts with the boatswain—do me a favor—tell him to find Maggie and warn her that Cavendish is aboard."

"Maggie, you say?" Tom gave Josh a friendly shove. "Who's Maggie?"

Josh grinned and shoved him back. "Pass the message. I'll explain later."

"All right, I'll meet up with you at lamp-liftin' time—the King's Arms. As I recollect, you owe me a pint."

꩜

It was easy for Maggie to spot the tall man in the ever-growing crowd of buyers, sellers, and servants. At six feet two inches solid and strong built, Tom Roberts stood a good head taller than most of the men aboard. A large, ginger-colored dog accompanied him as he moved through the tumult of the auction-day throng with a smooth hunter's grace. He and his canine companion wove their way to the table near the quarterdeck stair where Mr. Pebley kept an accounting of the day's business. Maggie inched through the crowd, avoiding the viscount and moving close to where she could get a good look at the exotic colonial.

His rough hands rested large on the barrel end of the longest gun Maggie'd ever seen. He waited patiently while Mr. Pebley finished dickering with another man over the price of milled timber. At his turn the hunter stepped forward.

"How do, Mr. Pebley. I've five hundred half-dressed deerskins and three hundred winter beaver pelts . . . all top-notch. Josh tells me you'll be wanting the lot." His rich voice made Maggie wish she could hear him tell one of the tales from his hunt "beyond the ridge in *Kenta-ke*." He leaned in on the long gun that seemed almost a part of him and proceeded to bargain for fair price with the boatswain. His unusual attire sparked Maggie's curiosity, and it seemed she was not alone when the Duffy twins and MacGregor, the schoolmaster, sidled next to her.

"He may not be a savage, but he certainly dresses like one," fastidious MacGregor sniffed.

Tim Duffy asked, "Ye think mebbe he's one of those who lives among the savages?"

"Aye, most likely captured as a lad," Jim agreed. "I heard tell of such . . . 'renegade,' Ol' Pete calls 'em."

The hunter's long shirt of faded blue linsey was cinched at his trim waist with a wide leather belt. Among the many oddments hanging from his belt and shoulder, Maggie recognized a sheathed knife and a powder horn. The horn was a beautiful thing in itself—skillfully etched with a scene of mountains and words Maggie could not read. She pointed and whispered to MacGregor, "What's that say?"

"It says 'Tom Roberts, His Horn, 1755.'"

"See that there—" Tim pointed to the small axlike weapon hanging from the man's belt. "That'd be his 'tommy-hawk.' Aye, that's what he uses when he goes t' lop off yer scalp."

Maggie noticed all of the man's possessions were decorated in some unique fashion. A pattern of leaves curled up the carved handles of his tomahawk and knife. His belt and the leather sheath protecting his knife were tooled with intricate geometric designs. A cluster of brilliant colored feathers dangled from the polished dark stock of his gun, which was incised with fancy scrollwork and inlaid with a silver heart. Even his dog wore a collar woven with a zigzag of bright, tiny beads.

The hunter and the boatswain must have reached an agreement, for Pebley opened the strongbox and began counting out a stack of notes. "There's ten . . . twenty . . ."

"Silver."

Harried Mr. Pebley glanced up at the hunter. "What's that?"

"Silver." Tom Roberts pushed the notes aside. "This paper is worthless where I'm headin'. Them Spanish dollars you have in the box will suit me fine."

Pebley sighed, returned the notes to the strongbox, and proceeded to count out the agreed-upon amount in Spanish pieces of eight. The immigrants were agog at the amount the hunter received for his goods. Back home, hunting was a sport reserved for the peerage and the notion of hunting for profit was unheard of.

"*My Lord!* It's indecent!" James MacGregor whispered. "The man's wearing naught but a breechclout!"

Instead of breeches, the hunter wore a red woolen breechclout. Soft leather leggings came up to midthigh, just where the fringed hem of his long shirt began. His leggings were secured below the knee with red wool garters and tucked into the cuffed tops of laced leather slippers.

"He's dressed more decent than the soldiers in Glasgow," Maggie countered. "Those lads wear naught beneath their regimental kilts but what God gave them upon their birth."

Tom Roberts leaned over the table to gather the proceeds, allowing Maggie a better vantage from which to ponder the mechanics of the breechclout. He deposited handfuls of coins into a rectangular leather pouch, hanging by a beaded strap across his chest. Roberts turned and caught Maggie in the act of admiring his muscular upper thighs. He slung his gun over his shoulder and headed straight for her, a wry smile peeking through his dark beard.

"You're staring, miss. Do we know one another?"

Tongue-tied, Maggie shook her head no, and without knowing what else to do, she knelt down to stroke his dog.

"No harm intended, sir." Mr. MacGregor stepped forward. "Excuse the lass . . . she was but curious. We've never seen a body dressed in such a fashion, ye ken?"

"You her husband?" Roberts asked.

The Duffy twins guffawed and MacGregor turned beet red. "Husband? Och, no!"

"We're newcomers—from Scotland," Tim offered.

Jim said, "Maggie fancies yer dog."

The hunter laughed loud. "So *you're* Maggie!"

She leaped to her feet and tried to push past, but Tom Roberts grabbed her by the arm before she could get away. His hat had slipped from his head and his eyes shone ever blue in the bright sunlight. His provocative smile was quite unnerving. Maggie— who rarely found herself at a loss for words—found herself struck dumb by this man.

"*Maggie Duncan! Duffys! MacGregor!* The lot of you—go

line up with the others," Pebley ordered. "The auction's about to begin."

The hunter's blue eyes clouded over. The playful smile up-ended into a frown. Still having hold of her arm, he spun Maggie around to see the contract pinned to her back.

"Hmmph! Servants!" He released her arm, picked up his hat, and strode away, his dog padding after him.

Maggie stood astounded by this swift shift in attitude. "That was quite odd."

"Odd indeed!" MacGregor agreed. "Colonials . . . verra brazen, if ye ask me."

"Some men just don't cotton to the notion of folk selling themselves into slavery," Pebley said. "Rubs 'em the wrong way."

"We're no slaves!" Maggie argued. "Slavery is a lifetime. We've but contracted four years."

"It's all the same to a man like Tom Roberts. Those backcountry men walk the earth beholden to no one and no thing. Why, most of them don't even consider themselves Englishmen." The boatswain waved them along. "Get a move on now and join the others. The bidding's about to begin."

◖✦◗

A richly attired and very fat woman proclaimed her delight at acquiring a perfect matched pair of footmen for a mere seventy pounds after winning the bid on the Duffy brothers. MacGregor did not fare as well. A man building a crew to labor in his tobacco fields purchased the scholar's contract for a lowly twenty pounds. Maggie's heart ached as bewildered MacGregor tripped past, following his new master down to the pier. She waited her turn on the block, wringing her hands, choking back tears, utterly regretting the day she signed her indenture.

"Stop fretting," Josh Stark said. "How many times do I have to tell you? It's all arranged. The captain has a plan. Cavendish will not win your contract."

"Aye, but soon we'll ken who my master will be." She motioned with a wave toward the quarterdeck and burst into tears.

"Stanch them tears! No one will bid on your contract if you blubber and then Cavendish will certainly win." Joshua pulled Maggie from the queue and gave the next man a shove up the steps in her stead.

"They're gone—the Duffy lads, MacGregor—an' I didna have a chance to wish any of them a proper farewell."

"Don't cry . . . you can't cry, not now." Josh untied the kerchief from his neck and used it to swab the tears from Maggie's cheeks. "Chances are you will see them again one day."

"You think so?" Maggie sniffed.

"Sure . . . why, just today I met up with an old friend I haven't seen in years."

Maggie flushed with renewed embarrassment, and gave an angry swipe to her nose with a handful of skirt. "And how is it yer friends with that brute?"

"Tom? Ah, don't let his gruff looks frighten you. Tom Roberts is all wool and a yard wide. We were boys together—grew up at Penn's Settlement."

"Quakers!" Maggie couldn't help but grin at the notion.

"Well . . ." Josh smiled. "We were raised Quakers, Tom and me, but the elders claimed we were more suited to raise hell. The plain life held no appeal for either of us. As soon as we could, we bolted—Tom for the high timber, and me for the high seas."

Maggie winced as the auctioneer's gavel banged out a final bid. "I wish I could bolt right now."

"Everything'll be fine, you'll see. You'll get a position with a nice family and I promise to call on you whenever I'm in port. Now get ready, Maggie. You're up next."

⸻

The auction had been under way for some time when Seth Martin pushed his way to the front of the crowd. He counted only five women left standing in the queue of twenty waiting their turn up the steps.

They all seemed strong, clean, and well fed. These immigrants had weathered their crossing well compared to the sad lot he'd sailed in with sixteen years before. His heart sank when the first two contracts he bid upon went for more than the sum he had to spend. These were quality laborers, and as such they fetched quality prices.

Seth had sold four kegs of his best dram whiskey and one stubborn mule to earn the twenty-three pound notes clenched in his fist. *Not enough . . . not near enough.*

"Margaret Duncan—twenty-two years of age," the rotund auctioneer announced as the next young woman mounted the steps to the quarterdeck. Seth's heart sank farther. He didn't stand a chance of winning the bid on this girl—she was too pretty by far.

Her hair was plaited in one glossy black braid coiled at the base of her neck. Her faded yellow blouse accentuated the tone of her olive skin, coated with a sheen of perspiration, and the tight-laced bodice she wore emphasized the dip and curve of a very womanly figure.

". . . unmarried and childless, this girl is suited for service . . ."

"Yep! She can service me anytime!"

A pimple-faced young man drew a loud guffaw from the mostly masculine crowd with his play on words. The girl on the stair colored red and looked near tears. Seth pitied the lass, recollecting the helplessness he felt the day he had stood on the block.

"As I was saying," the auctioneer continued, "this girl is well suited for *domestic* service and has been taught additional skills that would benefit any estate—"

"I bet I can teach her a few skills!"

The crowd howled. Seth observed the girl struggle to maintain her composure, but hands flew to hips and angry eyes flashed.

Much to the crowd's delight, she stepped forward and addressed the rude young man.

"Ho there! Laddie! Aye, you . . ." She pointed. "You wi' the face like a tinker's spotty arse. Here's a sound bit of advice—best make friends wi' yer fist"—the girl punctuated her verbal assault with an explicit hand gesture—"for it's bound to be yer one true love." The crowd roared its approval and the heckler slunk away.

Seth liked this girl.

"Please . . . your attention, please!" The auctioneer banged the gavel. "Captain Carlyle himself attests to this young woman's extensive knowledge of medicines and remedies. Though young, she's served many years as apprentice midwife . . ."

Seth could not believe his ears. Providence had to have sent this lass in answer to his desperate prayers.

". . . and so we seek an opening bid of eight pounds . . . do I hear eight pounds? Aha, yes—I have eight pounds from the viscount. And nine? Do I hear nine? Nine pounds? Yes, there's nine . . . do I hear . . . I have ten from the viscount. Thank you, sir. Do I hear eleven?"

"TWENTY-THREE POUNDS!" Seth shouted out.

The crowd stuttered into silence.

"SOLD!" The gavel slammed down. "Sold for-twenty-three-pounds-to-the-small-man-with-the-big-gun!" The red-faced auctioneer shoved Maggie aside and scurried down the stairs, loudly proclaiming a dire need to "answer nature's call." The stunned crowd began to stir.

"*What?*"

"She's sold?"

"That can't be . . ."

"Well, when nature calls . . ." Someone laughed.

"Go on and get her, son." A man slapped Seth on the back. "Looks like that pretty gal's yourn."

When Seth saw some of the other bidders grumbling about the

turn of events, he did not waste any more time pondering his good fortune. He marched over and tossed the fistful of notes on the boatswain's table. "Where do I sign?"

Seth scratched his mark several times, anxious to secure the girl's contract before any protest could be lodged. The boatswain blotted the ink, dusted the parchment with a sprinkling of sand, and handed him a copy of the document.

"Quite a bargain, young fella—I'd say today's your lucky day."

"That's so . . ." Seth grinned from ear to ear and tucked the paper into the front of his shirt.

"My, my . . . it cannot even write its own name!"

Seth turned to the voice. The fancy Englishman—the viscount who had placed the initial bid on the girl—was standing right behind.

"I'll have that girl. Name your price."

"Not interested." Seth slipped the rifle from his shoulder to rest in the crook of his arm.

"Don't be a fool." The smiling Englishman reached into his breast pocket. "I'll pay . . . forty pounds. I'd say that's more than enough to purchase one of these other trollops to tend your hovel and whelp your brats and leave you with a few pounds to shove in your pocket as well."

"Aye—an' I say, ye can shove that forty pound right up yer own arse—I'm not sellin'." Seth smirked. Many of the onlookers were laughing at the viscount's expense.

"*Lout!* I'll teach you how to address your betters," the Englishman sputtered, and raised his cane to strike, but was stopped by the barrel end of Seth's rifle pressed cool beneath his right ear.

"Ye might take notice yer in Virginia, sir . . ." The hammer on the flintlock clacked back. ". . . and a lout like me can sink a ball in yer brain from a hundred yards with one of these. Take heed and leave me be if ye mean to stay out of my sights."

The threat drew a smattering of applause and a few "hear, hears!" from those who witnessed the scene. Seth pushed past the stunned viscount and skirted around the crowd of bidders. He spotted his girl waiting near the gangway, a large covered basket at her feet and a tall sailor planted at her side.

"Och, but pretty lassies are such a bother," he muttered. After the encounter with the Englishman, Seth was in no mood for another confrontation or tearful good-byes.

". . . but that *was* the plan, Maggie," Seth overheard the sailor say. "The auctioneer was told to accept the first bid over twenty from anyone other than the viscount . . ."

"Aye, Joshua, dinna fash . . . it's done now, isn't it?"

"Believe me, Maggie, no one figured a backwoodsman would—"

"This yers?" Seth interrupted, pointing to the basket.

"Aye," the girl answered.

"We're off, then." Seth picked up the basket and turned to leave.

Joshua laid a restraining hand on Seth's shoulder. "Hold on there, fella . . ."

Seth dropped the basket and spun around, his rifle still cocked. "This lass goes with me. I've paid twenty-three pound and have paper t' prove it!" He motioned for the girl to pick up her basket and precede him down the gangway. He glanced over his shoulder several times as he hurried after the girl, happy to be on the road leading home.

5

In-Country

One foot afore the other . . .

Maggie focused on finding her land legs. Solid ground proved difficult after more than two months aboard ship.

Set one foot afore the other . . .

The hard-packed surface of Richmond's dusty main street led to a wheel-rutted trail, which disappeared into a rough foot-path.

One foot afore the other . . .

Maggie trudged alongside the pack mule, each step taking her deep into the strange wilderness, not knowing where she was heading or even the name of the man she headed there with. Grit and bits of gravel weaseled into her clogs, abrading the skin on her feet raw. The kerchief she'd tied about her head gave scant protection from the hot sun. She swiped the sweat tickling a trail down the back of her neck, silently willing the man to stop for a rest.

But the man continued to march forward with grim determination to put much country between himself and Richmond-town. He held his weapon in a nervous grip, checking the back trail over his shoulder often. On occasion, her new master slowed the pace to wordlessly offer her a swallow of warm water from the tin bottle he carried on a string around his neck. Maggie moved forward without complaint. She did not want to stir the volatile emotions of this "small man with the big gun."

The toe of her clog struck a gnarled root snaking across the path. She stumbled, lost one shoe and her footing, and pitched forward into the dirt. Maggie scrambled back onto her feet.

"Are ye all right, lass?" He seemed concerned.

"Aye, just the wind knocked from me is all." Maggie brushed debris from her skirt and searched for her shoe, finding her master held the errant clog in his hand. To her surprise, he fell to one knee and jerked the other clog from her still-shod foot. The mule brayed and escaped into the brush.

"*Bloody hell!*" The man stuffed the clogs into his pouch and ran after his animal.

"My shoes?" Maggie asked, when he returned tugging the mule up onto the trail.

He shook his head. "Yer better off barfoot. Clogs will do naught but cripple ye, especially down the line where the trail gets rough."

Maggie stared in dismay at her sore feet, not even able to imagine a trail rougher than the one they'd been following.

"Dinna fash so, lass. Tell ye what—tonight, I'll fashion ye a pair of moccasins."

"Moccasins?"

"Aye, see?" He held up his left foot in example, showing her his cuffed leather slippers, similar to those worn by the hunter on the ship. "Red Indian brogues!"

"Are ye a shoemaker by trade?"

"Aye." He chuckled. "That's me—shoemaker, farmer, carpenter, hunter, tanner, blacksmith. Jack of all trades—master of none." He slapped the mule forward. Maggie fell in beside the man, a bit more at ease having exchanged a few words.

"How long till we get there?" she asked.

"Well . . . we set off wi' a late start—lost most of the day, aye?

If we press hard we might get home in six—na . . ."—he squinted at the sun, low on the horizon—"more likely seven days' time."

Maggie blinked. "*Seven days?* Seven days away? A body could walk across the whole of Scotland in seven days."

"Aye, tha's the truth. But my homeplace is upland." He pointed. "Near those mountains there—the Blue Ridge."

Maggie eyed the faraway indigo smudge along the horizon Seth pointed to and swallowed hard to squelch the tears. *Get a grip, lass. What canna be cured must be endured.* She took a deep breath, squared her shoulders, and extended a hand.

"My name is Maggie—Maggie Duncan."

"I recall." He grinned, and they exchanged a handshake.

Maggie sighed loud and blurted, "'Twould ease my mind, sir, to ken the name of the man who owns four years of my labor . . ."

"Och, did I no give ye m' name?" Without breaking stride, he pumped Maggie's hand a second time. "Seth Martin." He smiled. "From where in the old country do ye hale from, lass?"

"A wee village in Glen Spean called Black Corries. D'ye know it?"

"Ah no, can't say as I do. I'm an islander myself—from Raasay in the Hebrides—the only time I ever ventured from our bonnie isle was when I boarded the leaky bucket that brought me to Virginia."

"And when did ye cross the water?"

"Soon after Culloden. English burned us out and shipped us off. 'Threat to the Crown,' they said." Seth snorted. "Can ye imagine? Me, a skinny-malinkie half-starved lad of fourteen a 'threat to the Crown'—as if I even cared which horse's arse sat upon their throne." Seth's crooked smile vanished. "'Twere a rough crossing. The flux killed my mam and my wee sister. The sailors just tossed their bodies over the rail . . ." He kicked a stone from the path.

"Culloden." Maggie shuddered. "Bloody English butchers killed my mam as well."

"An' yer da?"

"Joined the Jacobites at the call to arms and I havna seen him since. Dead, I s'pose."

"Yer da may have been captured and transported. There were a few Jacobite prisoners aboard our ship. My ol' da never seasoned to this climate—he fevered and died soon after landing. 'Virginia bug,' they called it." Seth sighed. "Aye, sixteen long years ago, Maggie, I stood the block just as ye did this day. Puts a twist in yer belly when they start the bidding, don't it?"

"Ye were indentured?"

"Four years," Seth answered. "I earned my Freedom Dues and vowed never to labor for another man. I bought traps and earned good silver workin' the peltry trade. Two years ago I claimed a piece of land by cabin right."

"What's that—cabin right?"

"Free white men can claim up to four hundred acres. Ye must build a cabin and plant at least one acre of corn to hold the claim."

Maggie hopped on one foot, trying to dislodge a stone wedged between her toes. "Could ye no claim a piece a bit closer by?"

Seth grinned. "There's little land open for claim along the coast. I had to range out to find a good piece. That's why we settled yonder, on the edge of the frontier." He waved his arm toward the mountains. "It's rough goin', but I've no quitrent to pay and no laird to answer to. I'm my own master."

And mine, thought Maggie.

The mule became agitated as they approached a shallow, swift-running stream. "This ol' mule gets skittish 'round water. I need to coax him across." Seth handed his rifle and hat to Maggie and grabbed hold of the halter with a double-fisted grip. "Step careful as ye cross and keep that weapon dry. We'll make camp on the other side."

Maggie shouldered the heavy rifle, hiked her skirts, and stepped into the ankle-deep water. Midway she stopped to massage the soles of her aching feet on the smooth stones of the creek bed. Icy water rushed between her toes and she watched Seth cajole the stubborn animal across. She sensed they'd passed some invisible boundary, for Seth's face missed the pinched worry it'd worn most of the way from Richmond. He pulled the ornery mule up onto the bank and waved her over. "Move along smartly! We need to hurry and make camp afore nightfall!"

He doesna seem a bad sort, Maggie thought as she maneuvered the rest of the way across the stream. *But he certainly doesna seem the sort to have two pennies to rub together, much less twenty-three pounds.* She took a good, hard look at Seth Martin.

His shirt was torn and stained. It seemed he never bothered to pull a comb through his ill-shorn hair and his stubbly chin could stand the attention of a sharp razor.

Aye, but he does seem the sort to trade twenty-three pound *for a woman to warm his bed.*

Seth scraped up a pile of tinder and started a fire with flint and steel. He unloaded his gear, hobbled the mule, and disappeared with his rifle.

Maggie gathered dry wood. Not much time passed before the mule's ears twitched at the report of rifle fire in the distance. She heartened to see dinner was on her master's mind when Seth appeared clutching his hat filled with strawberries and a brace of pigeons slung over one shoulder. "Clean the birds," he directed. "I'll fetch a good stone."

Maggie stripped feathers and watched Seth search along the shore. He levered up a smooth, flat stone, lugged it to the fire, and set it atop a pile of embers raked to the side. He covered the stone with more hot coals. "I'm hankering after a few corn dodgers," he said.

Maggie nodded, pretending she understood what he meant. After gutting and rinsing the plucked birds, she skewered them on greenwood sticks over the flame. Seth filled a battered brass kettle with water and set it to boil. He dug through the pack baskets and extracted two small sacks and a pale sausage. Into the simmering kettle, he added a pinch of salt from one sack and sifted in several handfuls of pale meal from the other. Maggie watched him nip the end off the odd sausage and squeeze its gooey contents into the pot.

"What is that?" she asked.

"This? Bear butter."

"Bear butter!" Maggie wrinkled her nose.

"Aye, rendered bear fat—very tasty." Seth smacked his lips and used a stick to stir the concoction into a thick yellow paste. "We'll let that set a bit while I see to yer moccasins."

He unrolled a half hide of tanned skin. Maggie stood on the hide and Seth used a piece of charcoal to trace the outline of her right foot. "I'll cut the leather while there's still light. You mind th' birds and cook the dodgers." He nodded toward the batter thickening in the kettle. "Dust the ashes away and bake the dough on the hot stone just as ye would a Hogmanay bannock."

Maggie flattened dollops of dough onto the makeshift griddle. The corn dodgers sizzled nicely. The bear fat sputtering on the hot stone reminded her of smoked bacon. Using Seth's broad blade knife, she turned the dodgers to crisp the other side. Maggie washed out the kettle, refilled it with water, and set it to boil. She delved into her own supplies, tossing a handful of chamomile flowers and rose hips in to steep for their tea.

After Seth cut two matching shapes from the hide, he inspected the birds and declared them fit to eat. Maggie slipped the dodgers onto a piece of birch bark peeled from a nearby trunk, and they sat together to enjoy the fireside feast. As soon as Seth gobbled his meal, he removed his damp moccasins and stockings and set them near the fire to dry. He stitched Maggie's moccasins while toasting his bare feet on the flames.

Maggie sucked every bit of tender pigeon meat from the bone before tossing it onto the fire and she licked the grease from her fingers. She relished each sweet berry, perfect and ripe, but the corn dodgers were her favorite. A familiar preparation of unfamiliar ingredients.

For the first time in a long, long time her appetite was satisfied. She sighed with content, sipped her tea, and paid close attention to what Seth was doing. The ability to manufacture footwear was an important skill, and she meant to acquire it.

The leather had been cut in a clever pattern requiring but two short seams sewn at toe and heel. "Oneida style," Seth informed her. When finished with the sewing, he pulled a tin from the depths of his pouch and rubbed the substance into the surface and seams of each moccasin. Maggie held the tin to her nose and sniffed.

"Beeswax mixed with bear fat"—Seth answered before she had a chance to ask—"softens the leather and waterproofs the seams—helps t' keep yer feet dry. Ye'll do well in Virginia, Maggie Duncan, if ye remember this one thing: *always care for yer feet*. Upon my word, there's nothing worse than rotten feet. There ye go, try those on fer size."

Maggie secured the "wangs," as Seth called them—and took a few trial steps around the fire. She stretched onto tiptoes and back down, extending each foot in turn to admire her new moccasins.

"They might be a bit stiff at first," Seth warned.

"They're lovely slippers! I've never owned a pair as fine." Genuinely pleased, Maggie showed her appreciation by dancing a quick two-step jig. "*Losh!* I'm ready to walk the whole of Virginia. I am verra grateful to ye, Seth."

"Och, naught but a pair of moccasins . . . not much more than a decent way of going barefoot at best." Seth dismissed her compliments. "It's been a trying day, lass. Ye must be done in. Take a blanket and fix yerself a bed near the fire."

Maggie's smile evaporated. "And where'll you sleep?"

"I'm not goin' t' sleep just yet." Seth slipped one of his moccasins onto his hand and wriggled a finger through a tear in the sole. "I've mending to do." He tossed wood to the fire and settled back to patch the hole.

Satisfied with his answer, Maggie cleared a flat area of twigs and stones and spread a wool blanket. She draped her plaide about her shoulders and lay on her side, facing the fire.

Even though she was very tired, the nocturnal babble—chirping crickets, croaking frogs, and an odd creature sounding much like teeth of a comb dragged across a hard edge—thwarted her attempts to find sleep. Maggie propped up on one elbow. "Och, but it's noisy, na?"

"No noisier than the streets of Glasgow, I expect." He glanced right, to his big knife stuck point end in the ground. His long rifle rested beside it, barrel end up on a forked branch. "Yiv naught t' fear, lass. I tend to sleep with one eye open, rifle primed and knife at the ready."

The sight of his loaded weapon set Maggie's mind at ease, and she was a little surprised to be more threatened by what lurked beyond the glow of their campfire than by what might be lurking in the mind of her master.

Other than his initial gruff aspect, she could only classify Seth's behavior as kind—almost brotherly. Still, Maggie decided that she, too, must sleep with one eye open. She cradled her head on bent elbow, and her eyes grew heavy as she watched the dance of the flames.

⸙

Maggie jerked awake. She must not have been sleeping long, for Seth was still awake, staring catatonic into the flames, sipping from a leather flask and smoking a funny, long-stemmed pipe. She heard the noise again—growling, coming from the pitch black beyond. Seth slowly set his pipe aside and picked up his knife.

Maggie stared into the darkness, the tiny hairs raised on the back of her neck. Something stared back. "What is it, Seth?"

The twin red lights flashed and flew toward her. Maggie squeezed her eyes tight and screamed at the top of her lungs.

Seth laughed and shouted, "Friday!" He dropped his weapon to greet the dog bounding into the light of their campfire. "Stop yer gallie-hooin', Maggie—it's but a dog!"

She opened her eyes. Here, barking and leaping, was the same ginger dog she had befriended on board the *Good Intent*.

"Ye scared th' bejesus out of Maggie, Friday!" Seth scrubbed the dog's floppy ears. "No t' worry, lass. He's not one of them biting dogs."

Friday circled the fire twice and flopped with a grunt at Maggie's side. "I know this dog," she said. "He was on the ship this morning. Where's yer master, pup?" She stroked one finger along the velvet space between Friday's eyes and a moon-cast shadow loomed over her.

"C'mon, lad . . ." Seth waved Tom Roberts into their circle. "Yer always welcome t' share my fire." Tom stepped around Maggie to pump Seth's outstretched hand and slap him several times on the back. He settled next to Seth, immediately removing wet moccasins and stockings and stretching his feet to the fire.

"Nothing worse than rotten feet, eh?" Maggie observed, amused at the attention these rough men lavished on their feet. The hunter ignored her.

Seth splashed whiskey from his flask into a tin cup and handed it to his friend. "Och, 'tis good t' see ye, Tommy! Naomi'll be pleased t' hear yer still walking among the living."

Naomi? Maggie scooted closer to the fire.

"Hmmph . . . tell me, friend, how pleased will Naomi be when she sees what twenty-three pounds buys in Richmondtown these days?" Tom jerked a thumb Maggie's way.

"Ahhh . . ." Seth smiled and relit his pipe with a brand from the fire. "A braw man such as yerself would never stoop t' work fer a horse's arse of an Englishman . . . my best guess is the smitten sailor. Aye, he's the one who set the likes of Tom Roberts on my trail."

Tom tossed back his whiskey, gasped, and hammered chest with fist. "*Whooo-wee!* Your whiskey sure drinks fine. Kisses like a woman yet kicks like a mule." He poured himself another. "Yup, Josh Stark's an old friend of mine. He fancies himself head over heels with this servant gal. He's sent twenty-five pounds for her paper and I'm to fetch her back."

"If I were selling—and mind, I'm not—I wager I could get fifty from the Englishman." Seth tugged on his pipe. "Truth is, Tommy, I canna believe my good fortune. This lass is a godsend—an answer to a prayer."

Tom shook his head. "This gal's trapped you in her wicked snare along with Josh Stark, and most of the men aboard that ship. Why sane men behave like such fools over a woman . . ."

"Och, Tommy—ye dinna ken . . ."

Tom looked at sleep-tousled Maggie, her dark eyes shining bright with curiosity, her face flush with warmth from the fire. "No, friend, I do ken. I'm the first to admit the gal's prettier than a new-laid egg . . ."

Seth snickered. "D'ye hear that, Maggie? Sounds to me like ye managed t' capture this crafty rascal in that evil snare of yers."

Maggie giggled.

"What's gotten into you, Seth Martin?" Tom's voice rose and Seth grinned with the satisfaction of seeing his barb hit its mark. "You've got a fine woman tending your hearth and offspring, and here you sit, mooning over a bondwoman like a lovesick calf."

Maggie bristled at the way he spat out the word *bondwoman*. This man discussed her as if she were no better than a dockside prostitute.

Tom went on. "I'd not be much of a friend to either you or Naomi if I did nothing to discourage this foolishness . . ." He reached inside his shirt and drew out a stack of pound notes. "I keep my ear pressed to the ground and I know for a fact you'll be needing this cash money sooner rather than later. Now sign over the gal's paper or I'll have to throttle you."

Seth leaned forward. "What've ye heard, Tom?"

"I heard the Irish surveyor y'all hired to file your claims didn't do such a good job." Tom reached for the flask. "Fact is, your claim sets in the middle of a land grant deeded by King George himself to the Duke of Portland back in '51."

"Aye." Seth's shoulders slumped. "That sums it up. Drunken Irish bastard! If he'd have filed proper I would have learned straight off I had no right to settle that land."

"What do you intend to do about it?" Tom handed the flask back.

"I've no chance winning a dispute in court. I'm going to wait it out—in time I can—"

"There is no 'time,' Seth. Portland's already sent an agent to see to his holdings."

"So it's come to that . . . I s'pose we'll just have to begin anew somewhere . . . we'll just have t' move on." He drained the flask, heaved it into the darkness, and buried his face in his hands.

"Damn it, Seth!" Tom waved the cash in front of his friend. "You need this money more than you need that gal. Take the money and go home to Naomi."

Seth lifted his head and shoved the notes aside. "Naomi's dying, Tom."

"No . . ." Tom shook his head. "That can't be,"

"Aye, she's withering away before my very eyes."

"She can't be dying," Tom said, hoping there was more whiskey than truth in Seth's assertion. "Last I saw, she was fit, happy, and getting ready to birth that new baby."

"Born dead. Born too soon. I helped her as best I could, but Naomi lost so much blood—I was grateful t' have but one wee grave to dig on that day. She grieved terribly, and now she's a-childing again. Weak in body, unwell in spirit—I fear this time I will lose her." Seth swiped a tear escaping the corner of his eye. "I'm at wit's end, Tom. I went to auction willing to spend all I had for a woman to take on the heavy chores to give Naomi a chance to regain her strength. Maggie's strong, and she's a midwife—the answer to my desperate prayer."

"Brother Seth, I'm truly sorry for your trouble. Believe me, I know how much you care for Naomi, and so I was flummoxed as to why . . . well, it don't matter none." Tom placed his hand on his friend's shoulder. "You know best what needs doin'—but mind—this bondwoman only claims to be a midwife. These people tend to bend the truth to suit their own end."

"We need help, Tom."

"Maybe Naomi'd be better off with the aid of an older woman. How 'bout I take this one back and fetch a—"

"Awright! Tha's th' bloody end! I can no longer hold my tongue." Maggie leaped to her feet. "Yer an eidgit, Tom Roberts! Whether ye choose to believe it or no, I *am* a midwife." Maggie planted fists to hips. "Seth says his wife is in dire straits. Even if I were th' worst excuse for a midwife, any help for the poor woman is better than naught. If ye truly are th' good friend ye claim to be, yid see th' truth in tha'."

Maggie turned to speak to Seth. "My foster mother was skilled—considered by many the best midwife in the glen. I was but a wean when I began training and she trained me well. I swear to ye, Seth Martin, I will work hard and do all I can to help Naomi get well and birth a healthy bairn."

"Aye, that's fine, lass. That's fine." Seth squared his shoulders and took a deep breath. "Ye can start by helpin' me find my flask in the morning. Can ye believe I've done chucked away my best flask?"

Tom did not relent. "Seth, do you s'pose I can tell Josh that maybe . . . after the new baby's born . . ."

Seth shrugged. "Maybe . . . we'll see how it goes—"

"Seth," Maggie interrupted. "Joshua Stark is a good man and a fine friend, but there's nothing more between us . . . not on my part, anyway."

"What do ye mean, lass? Ye dinna want the sailor-lad?"

"My contract is yers to sell—but truth is, such a marriage—a body bought and paid for like some sort of . . . well, it's . . . it's not right is all. If ever I marry, I'll give my heart to a man of my own choosing. For now, I'm happy for a place where my skills will be of use." She turned to cast an evil-eye glare at Tom, surprised to find him smiling at her.

"Well, I did my best, but I guess Josh is plumb out of luck." Tom returned the money to his pouch and drew out a bottle. "Peach brandy." He uncorked the bottle, took a swig, passed it over to Seth. "Not near as fine as your dram whiskey, but it does in a pinch."

Maggie rolled her eyes. She understood the two men were a bottle of brandy away from bedding down for the night, but she was exhausted. "I bid good night t' yiz both."

"Aye, get a good night's sleep, lass," Seth said. "We've a long road ahead."

Maggie nodded and settled down in a comfortable cuddle with the warm dog.

"Friday! Git over here." The hunter slapped his thigh.

With a canine I-can't-see-you-so-you-can't-see-me reasoning, Friday burrowed his head beneath Maggie's plaide. She wound an arm around the dog. "Leave him be—I dinna mind." With her place in the world now defined, she allowed the hum of masculine voices to lull her to sleep.

⁂

The two men passed the bottle of peach brandy back and forth. "How much time d'ye think," Seth asked, "afore Portland evicts us?"

Tom shrugged. "He might not evict—but he'll surely demand quitrent. Either way, he'll first have some work getting surveys platted and writs of dispossession passed through the court . . ."

"I just hope I can harvest my corn is all." Seth worried the stubble on his chin. "Otherwise, we'll be awful hard-pressed this winter. Ye ken, I had t' scrape every penny t' come up with the twenty-three pound for the lass's contract."

"If you're strapped, I could always lend you some . . ."

"Och, yer a good friend, Tommy, but borrowing is aye a measure of last resort." Seth took the bottle and drained it.

"After I finish this business with Josh in Richmond, I'm meeting up with Guy DeMontforte for a summer hunt. Why don't you come along?"

Seth smiled. "Na . . . those days are behind me, lad."

"You're growin' soft on me, farmer boy! The garrisons along the frontier are paying good silver for wild beef. You'd be bound t' earn."

"Soft . . ." Seth relit his pipe. "Men dinna come any tougher than Bert Hawkins. He went overmountain a year ago last winter and no one's heard tell of him since. Long hunt's too risky for a man with a family."

"Bert'll turn up. That bastard knows his way about the woods." Tom stirred the embers with a short stick. "I s'pose Bess's lucky to have ol' Henry 'round, though—t' give her a hand with the farm."

"Bess Hawkins." Seth snorted. "She's not one to waste away pining after Bert, tha's certain. I'm no gossip, but ye ken well what I'm talkin' about, don't ye, lad?"

"You're a huge gossip." Tom grinned. "But I'll grant, Bess is a friendly gal. No one but Bert will be surprised if he comes home to find he's fathered a child or two in his absence."

Seth laughed. He stood, stretched, and gathered his bedding.

Tom dropped to a whisper. "You're probably wise to stay close to home, Seth. I didn't want to frighten the girl, but I've evil tidings—an Ottawa chief stirring trouble among the tribes up north . . ."

"Which tribes?"

"Those in the old French territories 'round the Great Lakes. There's been no call for militia. The Regulars are handling it so far."

Seth unfurled his bedroll. "Well, if the French keep out of it, it'll probably go no further."

"I hope you're right." Tom tied the laces of his moccasins together and strung them around his neck. "But then again, there's nothing as unpredictable as an Indian with a grudge." Yawning, he lay back and stuffed his felt hat under his head. "Leastways, Seth, best keep your family close and an auger eye out for trouble."

Maggie woke to a steamy dawn. She sat up, moved her hand across the warm, empty space beside her, and looked around the camp. The dog Friday and the man Tom Roberts were gone.

6

The Homeplace

"C'mon, Maggie . . . we're nearly there!"

She'd been lagging behind all morning. Seth began this last day of their journey with an elongated gait. To add to Maggie's difficulty, the pace had quickened a few miles back, when he spotted a pig bearing the Martin earmark rooting for mast at the base of a giant oak. She caught up to where Seth waited at the edge of a rough clearing planted with a haphazard field of corn—young stalks growing between the rotting stumps of trees felled to build the cabin Seth pointed to.

"There it is—the homeplace—for the time being at least." His voice betrayed a sad blend of pride and pique. "Odd, though," he said with forehead crinked, "nary a wisp o' smoke from the chimney." He gave the mule's lead a twist around a sapling then cocked the hammer on his rifle. With a finger to his lips he said, "Follow along, softly."

Maggie restrained the urge to race across the clearing and savor the solid luxury of a roof and four walls about her. She knew better than to question Seth's instincts. During the seven days between tideland and mountains, she'd come to admire her master's considerable woodskill. Seth skimmed the perimeter of the clearing, moving toward the cabin, careful to keep cover in the shadow of the forest. Maggie followed, close and quiet, at his heels.

The cabin was built on a rise with an unobscured view of the cleared acreage. Logs notched and mortised at the corners formed the walls—split wood clapboards, the roof. The chimney was constructed of mud-chinked stones. More than a dozen brown-feathered chickens pecked in the dirt in front of the cabin's stout oak door, and half as many noisy geese meandered between the smaller outbuildings scattered down the hillside.

"A war party on the move would have snatched all those birds," Seth noted.

This self-comforting muttering quite alarmed Maggie, who had not fully realized the basis for his concern. She tugged on his shirttail. "Red Indians?"

"Na . . . no Injuns here. See there? Window lites are open . . . and the latchstring is out." Nothing more than narrow, shuttered openings cut into the log walls on either side of the doorway, the window lites did not boast a single pane of glass. Seth spoke with assurance, but he double-checked the readiness of his weapon before stepping out into the bright of the clearing.

As they crossed the field, two hound dogs—one brindled, the other solid blue black—rushed forward, barking mad but wagging tails. A young girl came around the corner of the cabin struggling to steady two splashing buckets of water suspended from a wooden yoke across her shoulders.

"*Patch! Little Black!* Hush that racket or I will skin yer hides . . ." She stopped, squinted, and screamed. "Da!" Shrugging the heavy yoke into the dirt, the girl ran full speed, straight into her father's arms. Seth shouldered his rifle and swooped his daughter into an embrace.

"Winnie-lass!"

Winnie clung like a bur to her father and buried her face in his neck. The oldest of Seth's three children, Winnie Martin was nearly twelve years old, but slight, and an easy burden to bear. Seth set his daughter on her feet, and the girl eyed Maggie, who stood quiet off to the side.

"Aye, Winnie, I've brung help and it's help we surely need. Look at the state yer in—midday an' yer about in naught but a shift. I'm almost shamed to introduce ye to our new girl."

"Sorry, Da." Winnie cast her eyes down to her grimy toes and plucked at her shift, struggling to suppress an onslaught of tears.

"Och, now dinna fash on my account." Maggie stepped forward and wrapped an arm around Winnie's narrow shoulders. The girl leaned in with a hiccup and swiped her tears with the back of her hand. Freckles sprinkled across her nose, soot smeared across her forehead, and blue-gray circles beneath her eyes were all that lent color to her thin, pale face. A thousand wisps of auburn hair escaped from two braids trailing down her back. The girl looked especially exhausted, her skinny arms protruding from a dingy shift she had yet to grow into.

"Where's yer mam?" Seth asked. "Where're the boys?"

"Battler's napping . . . Jack's gone to the Bledsoes' for live coals."

"Dinna tell me ye lost the fire! Och, if I told ye once, I've told yiz all a hundred times—bank the fire properly."

"I tried, Da," Winnie whimpered, "but this morn there was naught but cold ashes on the hearth and I couldn't catch a spark for the life of me. Battler's been ornery and Mam's ailing . . ."

"Ailing?"

"Aye, she's abed with fever two days now."

Seth tugged on the latchstring to lift the bolt and the girls followed him into the crowded, single-room cabin. Three sharp shafts of daylight streamed in through the narrow window lites and open door, providing the only source of illumination. As Maggie's eyes adjusted slowly to the dim light, she stumbled along, following Seth to the bedstead tucked into the corner of the room.

"Naomi . . . Naomi, darlin' . . ." Seth called softly to his wife. Naomi Martin was blanketed from toe to chin. Her tiny flushed face was the center in the blossom of sweat-wet auburn hair exploding across her pillow. Seth's younger son, Battler, slept, curled in a tight baby-ball at the foot of the bed. Maggie eased the sleeping toddler into his father's arms and whisked the covers back. Released from the heavy prison of quilts and woolen blankets, the unconscious woman sighed in relief.

Naomi's small frame lay trapped in a damp depression in the straw-stuffed ticking, the soggy linen shift she wore tangled and bunched at her hips. The bulge of her six-month pregnancy seemed an obscene and unnatural addition to her emaciated body. Maggie laid a hand on the woman's gaunt cheek. "She's burnin' up. Winnie, has yer mam been pukin' or coughin'?"

Winnie shook her head. "No . . . but she's been racked with chills and mumbling crazy like. She won't take a bite to eat . . . though I did get her to sip some water earlier."

"The poor thing . . . naught but skin, bones, and baby." Maggie placed two hands on Naomi's distended abdomen. "But there's a braw bairnie inside, kickin' strong, and that's always a good sign." She smiled and rolled up her sleeves. "Winnie, lend me a helpin' hand. Bring rags, a basin of water, and at least a dozen big onions—more, if they're small." Winnie nodded, her face a picture of relief as she ran off to fetch the things Maggie needed.

Cradling Battler, Seth stood inert with worry and guilt. Maggie gave him a gentle shove. "Find a place to put that knee-baby and get a fire going. I'll need my basket—and more water."

Little Battler was plopped onto the floor in a fat, dazed stupor, and he watched his da strike a spark to the tinder Winnie had assembled in her failed attempt. Seth hunkered on haunches, feeding strips of fat pine to the blaze when his older boy skittered into the cabin. Young Jack set a tin bucket of embers on the hearth and leaped onto his father's back.

"Da's home!" Jack laughed. The two tussled and Seth gave his son a sound tickling.

After the fire established, Maggie hooked two big pots of

water onto the lugpole over the flames. Jack was dispatched to bring Ol' Mule in from his tether. Seth shouldered the yoke and left to fetch water.

Maggie stripped the sweat-soaked shift from Naomi. She sat on the edge of the bedstead, dipped a rag in water, and swabbed the woman's fevered skin. The sponge bath had an immediate effect. Deep lines of agitation around Naomi's mouth and forehead disappeared. Her eyes fluttered open, beryl blue and soft in dazed confusion.

"Dinna fash, Naomi. Yer goin' to be fine . . . everything will be just fine . . ." Maggie's crooning soothed the woman back into unconsciousness.

Winnie returned, deposited a woven string of onion bulbs onto the table, and wandered over to the bedside. "Are you daft?" The girl gathered the tangle of blankets Maggie had cast aside. "Mam's a-fevered! She needs be kept warm."

"Leave those blankets be, lass. Come, sit here and learn some healin'." Maggie smiled and patted the bed. Winnie's eyes narrowed, thin arms clinching the bundle of blankets tight to her chest. She glanced from her mother to Maggie, to her mother again, dropped the blankets, and sat down beside Maggie.

"Most folk dinna ken this—fever can be a good thing, for it rids the body of ill humors and corruption." Maggie sponged Naomi's naked limbs and torso. "But fever also weakens a body, stops a body from doing the things that need doing. Mark this, lass—more folk die from thirst and hunger than ever die from fever. Aye, fevers are most dangerous if not managed properly." Maggie dipped the rag in water and handed it to Winnie. "As the fever heats from within, we'll cool her from without. I'll roll yer mam to her side, you swab her." Winnie waited, compress in hand, as Maggie levered Naomi to face the wall.

"*Megstie me!*" Maggie gasped. The freckled skin on Naomi's back was crisscrossed with layers of silvery scars, telling a story of repeated, brutal floggings.

Winnie traced a finger over the perfect pink letter *R* seared into the skin of her mother's left shoulder. "Mam would run away," she explained matter-of-factly. "This's what the master does when yer caught out."

Whipping and branding a human being like an animal— Maggie shivered, unable to wrap her mind around it. "She must have had a verra cruel master—a devil."

Winnie shrugged. "Mam says most masters are cruel."

Shaking her head in disbelief, Maggie was suddenly grateful her own contract had found its way into the hands of these simple folk who understood the ignominy of bondage, and determined she must succeed in helping her new American family in any way she could.

"Winnie, is there a fresh shift fer yer mam to wear?"

"One to wear and one to wash—" the girl singsonged as she fished a clean garment from the cedar chest at the foot of the bed. Together, they dressed Naomi and spread a lightweight coverlet over her.

Disturbed by the sight of Naomi's scarred back, Maggie asked, "How old was yer mam when she came to America?"

"Oh, my mam was born here. She's a true Virginian."

"A Virginian? Then why was she held in bondage?"

"Her mother was a bondwoman. Mam was but a little gal when her mother died. The master kept Mam t' work off the debt in his tobacco fields."

"But what of her da? Could he no work the fields?"

"Mam was a come-by-chance child. She's not lucky like me. She has no da."

Jack came through the door, lugging the basket he'd been sent to fetch. The stringy muscles on his arms strained, struggling to heft the big basket onto the tabletop crowded with dirty trenchers, bowls, and wooden mugs. Maggie rushed to help the boy and avoid having her things strewn across the floor.

Where Winnie was a miniature version of her mother, ten-year-old Jack was the spit and image of his da. Jack's sun-streaked brown hair looked as though it had been clipped with a pair of dull sheep shears. His grimy tanned arms and neck were festooned with an impressive array of scratches, welts, and insect bites. A tentative crooked smile crept onto his face, reminding Maggie of the first day on the trail with Seth.

"I need a knife," Maggie declared. Jack produced a sharp knife from his belt, and in no time the onions were peeled, quartered, and stewing in the pot.

Jack and Winnie crowded around as Maggie inventoried the contents of her basket. She sorted through mysterious paper-wrapped parcels, packets, and soft muslin bags. Bottle after bottle and many small clay pots—all corked and sealed with wax—were set down on the table in orderly rows. A brick of beeswax and a stone mortar were the last things pulled from the basket. The children could not help but toy with the intriguing items.

"Keep yer mitts t' yerselves, aye?" Maggie snatched a precious bottle of sweet oil from Jack. Winnie sneaked the packet of rose petals she'd been sniffing back onto the pile. When little Battler dragged a chair over to the table to begin some hands-on inspection of his own, Maggie swung the sturdy toddler up into her arms to avoid certain mayhem. She laughed at the surprised look on the three-year-old's face. "And this busy laddie must be Battler, na? That's quite an odd name, young sir."

"His given name is Brian," Jack volunteered. "But we've been callin' him Battler since the day he blackened Mammy's eye with his fist."

"He din't mean to," Winnie added.

"I must admit, the name suits." Maggie set the toddler on his feet. "Jack, I need ye t' mind yer wee brother. Take him out to play." Jack rolled his eyes, sighed big, but took Battler by the hand and did as he was told.

Seth came in, setting two full buckets inside the doorway. He crossed the room and sat down at his wife's side. "She seems t' be sleeping easier now."

"Aye," Maggie agreed. Using a pothook, she hoisted the steaming pot of onions from the lugpole and carried it over to the crowded table. She wrapped the cooked onions in a double thickness of flannel and set the poultice at Naomi's feet. "Onions draw out th' ill humors and force a good sweat—that'll help to keep her cool."

"What sort of remedy will you give her for the fever?"

Maggie sat down next to Seth and pressed a cool compress to Naomi's forehead. "Truth is, all the remedies I have to break a fever would be harmful to the unborn bairn. The best I can do here is keep yer woman cool, and fortify her with nourishment when she wakes."

Seth frowned. "What d'ye mean, the best ye can do 'here'?"

"Well, I ken healing plants back home—how they work, where to find 'em—but here it's altogether different." Maggie sighed. "In my seven days crossing America, I have yet to spy a single thistle or bunch of heather. There are so many plants I dinna recognize at all . . . I'm a stranger in a strange land, Seth."

"I ken what yer sayin', but believe me, much is the same. Tell me this, Maggie, if we were back home, what could ye do t' help my Naomi?"

"Well . . ." Maggie rested her hands in her lap and closed her eyes, recalling her faraway glen. "I'd run down to the burn and gather a great apronful of gowke-meat. Then I'd crush the fresh leaves with heather honey and make a cool drink that would break the fever and not harm the babe in her belly."

"Gowke-meat?" Seth grew excited. "I havna heard it called so in years—wood sorrel is what Naomi calls it. Aye, there are great patches of the stuff down by our stream. I'm certain it's the same. Winnie, take Maggie down to the branch near the step-stone bridge."

Maggie jumped to her feet. "I'll need honey . . ."

"Naw, we've no honey . . . but in Richmond, I traded for some muscovado sugar."

"Is it sweet?"

"Aye."

"Then it will do." Maggie took Winnie by the hand and they ran out the door.

⟨❦⟩

It was candlelight time when Seth trudged in from the fields. He stopped to hang rifle, pouch, and powder on pegs mounted next to the door and gazed about the room. In the time he'd been out seeing to his chores, Maggie Duncan had wrought a miracle.

The puncheon wood floor was swept clean. Bundles of freshly cut sedge grass propped in the corners of the room sweetened the air. The table, cleared of all clutter, was decorated with a bouquet of elder blossoms.

Winnie and Jack sat at the table—hands, faces, and clothes all clean. They barely greeted their father, so focused were they on their bowls brimming with chunks of stewed chicken and cornmeal dumplings. Battler lay sprawled at the foot of the bed sound asleep, a horn spoon gripped in his chubby fist. Maggie sat at Naomi's side, feeding her small spoonfuls of clear broth.

Cheered by the sight of his woman alert and upright in their bed, Seth crossed the room in three quick steps and planted a kiss on his wife's forehead. They smiled into each other's eyes as he cradled Naomi's alabaster cheek in his work-worn hand. "Fever's broke?"

"Aye, yer woman's on the mend." Maggie handed him the bowl and spoon. "She's eating fer two, so mind that she finishes the lot. I'll go and dish up yer dinner."

Seth settled onto the bedstead, soup and spoon in hand. A Scotsman bred true to the bone, he leaned forward and whispered into his wife's ear, "It's certain I got the best of that bargain, na? This one day alone is well worth twenty-three pound."

7

A Good Clipe on the Head

A rooster crowed. She gasped and jerked awake, desperate to blink away the dark specter floating over her bed. The brooding figure spoke. "Maggie . . . wake up . . ."

Another voice lurked in the shadows. "It's day bust, Maggie . . . time t' wake."

"Och, Jackie . . . Winnie." Maggie elbowed up with a grunt. "Must yiz always give me such a start?"

The tin lantern Jack hung from the roof beam did little to illuminate the loft they shared, and in the dim light, Maggie could only sense their indifference. She resisted the lure of her pillow and scrubbed the sandy bits from her eyes in mute stupor. Winnie and Jack struggled into their clothes, and one after the other, the children disappeared down the hole in the loft floor. Three weeks on the Martin homeplace, and Maggie still required a moment each morning to reconcile her new place in the world.

Contending with a forest of snarls in her face sent Maggie searching through the bedding for the piece of string that must have slipped from her braid during the night. Annoyed, she abandoned the futile search, flung her clothes over one shoulder, and crawled on all fours to the center of the loft—the only spot where the sloping roofline allowed her to stand upright to dress. Maggie hop-stepped into her skirt and pulled it over the shift that doubled as her nightdress. She poked her arms through the sleeves of her bodice, gave the laces a halfhearted tug, grabbed the lantern, and shimmied down the hole, careful negotiating the ladder of stout pegs embedded into the wall.

Firelight mixed with the soft daylight just beginning to creep into the cabin through the open shutters. On his haunches, Seth fed fuel to the flame he'd coaxed from the embers. Naomi sat on the bedstead plaiting her hair into a single copper braid. Wide-awake, bare-bottomed Battler was busy "sweepin'" with the big birch broom.

"G' day, all." Maggie tried hard to put some cheer in her voice.

"Good morning," Naomi answered with a smile.

"Good . . . OW!" Seth yelped. Battler had thonked him soundly upside the head with the broom handle. Seth snatched the broom away and laid it out of reach, across the mantel shelf. After a moment's silent astonishment, Battler let loose a shrieking howl in protest.

"Th' wee lad's a menace," Seth said, rubbing his noggin.

Naomi agreed with a nod. "Takes after his da."

Seth took his rifle, planted a quick kiss on his wife's brow, and left to tend to morning chores.

"The lad's a menace with a bibblie-nebbit." Maggie swooped in and swiped Battler's snotty nose with the hem of her skirt. She swung him onto the bed and plopped down alongside, tickling his chubby feet as he scrambled to his mother for comfort. The little boy was immediately distracted from his troubles by his mam's hog-bristle brush, which Battler snatched up with enthusiasm and put to use on Maggie's tangled mane. She endured several minutes of Battler's "brushin'" before escaping out the door to see to her chores.

The sun had only just cleared the horizon and the morning was already sweltering. Maggie trudged from the stable, a wooden pail three-quarters full of milk gripped in each hand. Sweat-drenched frizzles of hair stuck to her face while rogue strands tickled her nose and hung in her eyes. Her waist-length hair was a hot and heavy bother, and if she'd had a pair of shears handy at that moment, she would not have hesitated to lop it all off. The rope handles on the buckets bit ridges into her hands. She hurried ahead, anxious to get on the shaded path leading down to the springhouse.

Adjusting to life in the Blue Ridge Mountains had proved more difficult than she'd anticipated. Almost every morning Maggie longed for the perfumed smoke of a peat fire and the cool, misty glens of Scotland. Besides being unaccustomed to the hot, humid climate, Maggie found since she'd been raised in a household that bartered a learned skill for necessities, she lacked many practical skills required for frontier living.

Seth was surprised when he needed to teach her the mechanics of milking a cow. The children showed Maggie how to work the hominy block and pound dry kernels of maize into meal. Naomi taught her to mix the cornmeal with sour milk and salt and bake it in the iron kettle for bread.

Maggie was eager to contribute to her new household. She liked her life with the Martins and was happy helping Naomi regain her health. But treating the symptoms of fever and pregnancy were simple tasks compared to the daunting task of lifting Naomi's spirits. A wounded soul is a troublesome thing, and hard to heal.

Maggie kept Naomi occupied with small tasks—carding wool, mending, shelling beans—not allowing her to wallow in despair and dwell on the baby she'd lost, or fret over the new baby on the way. She fed Naomi raspberry-leaf tea to strengthen her birthing muscle and dosed her with syrup of valerian root to ease her nerves. After several weeks of close companionship and reassurance, combined with steady nourishment and ample rest from the heavy household chores, it seemed her patient was truly on the mend. Naomi's predilection to "slip down into the mulli-grubs," as she called it, waned with each passing day.

Careful so as not to spill any milk, Maggie took her time traveling down the steep incline to the springhouse. She lifted the latch on the springhouse door and crouched down to step inside, for upright, her head barely cleared the ceiling rafters. The little stone house Seth had constructed over the running stream maintained a cool environment on even the hottest of summer days, and she shivered with delight at the abrupt change in temperature.

Wooden shelves lined the stone walls and provided storage for perishables like butter, cheese, and eggs. She poured the new milk into an empty crock and set it in a shallow trough built into the floor along the length of the springhouse. The icy mountain spring ran through the trough, keeping the items placed there chilled and fresh.

She ladled the rich cream floating atop the previous evening's milking into the butter crock and then poured the skimmed milk into one of her emptied pails. A dozen eggs and a lump of butter wrapped in wet oak leaves went into the other pail. Before leaving the cool comfort of the springhouse, she tucked the hems of her skirt into her waistband.

A pail in each hand, she waded downstream toward the Berry Hell—an ancient thicket groaning with ripe blackberries, and as far as Maggie was concerned, one of the wonders of her new world. Barefoot, she traversed the shallows, concentrating on balancing the disparate weights she carried and maintaining careful footing on slippery stones—so focused on her path, if he hadn't called out, she would have walked right past him.

"Good morning, Miss Duncan!"

Maggie startled, shrieked, and dropped her bucket of milk. Three eggs flew from the other pail, splat open on the stones, and washed away with the current.

"Och! Look what yiv gone and done!" Maggie tossed the

empty pail to clatter onto the shore. "Sneakin' up on folk with yer thievin' Red Indian ways . . . do y' even ken how to greet a body in civilized fashion?" She struggled to climb up the steep bank, but her bare feet could not find purchase on the slippery mud. "C'mon, lad," she yelled, "give a lass a hand up, aye?"

"By my reckon," Tom Roberts noted as he moseyed over to creekside, "you were the one sneakin' up on me." He grasped her by the forearm and yanked her up to dry land.

"Hmmph!" Maggie set the bucket of eggs on the ground and stood with hands on hips, inspecting his camp. A dapple-gray gelding stood hobbled, browsing on cress near a pile of gear. A field-dressed deer lay trussed near a small fire burning within a ring of stones. His faded blue shirt hung flapping from a tree branch.

Her eyes lit back on Tom, wearing nothing but his red woolen breechclout. Tiny droplets glistened in his dark beard and on the curly hair sprayed cross his chest. His shoulder-length hair hung loose, dripping wet. Maggie swallowed.

That is much man.

He had a rugged beauty about him—tight, lean—solid as a chestnut tree. His body was allover tattooed with the marks of his trade, the most prominent being three parallel scars slashing from his left shoulder across his chest to his sternum. The purple-yellow of a fading bruise wrapped his rib cage on the right side. A shiny, circular scar, the size of a Spanish dollar, decorated the firm muscle of his left thigh. The collection of scars added to his particular aesthetic. *He belongs here.* Standing in the wild, Tom Roberts fit.

He drew on doeskin leggings and secured the thongs to a thin belt holding his breechclout in place, all the while grinning. Sheepish under her scrutiny, he noted, "If you'd come by a mite earlier, you could have watched me bathe as well . . ."

"An' yiv no a speck of shame, do ye? Struttin' about half nekkid, like a savage . . ."

"Look who's talkin'—bare legs . . . loose hair, laces undone . . . like . . . like one of them gypsy dancin' gals."

She blushed at the truth of his observations and her fingers flew to tighten the laces on her bodice. "Yer a most angersome man, Tom Roberts!" Twisting her hair into a knot at the base of her neck, she held it there with one hand while jerking her skirt down to cover her legs with the other. "What are ye doin' here anyway? If it's on Joshua's behalf, I'll tell ye right off I'll no go back t' Richmond with ye . . ."

"I figure this will come as a shock to you, miss, but the sun and the moon do not rise and set around Maggie Duncan." Tom plucked his shirt from the branch, pulled it over his head, and slipped his arms into the damp sleeves.

He cocked his head and looked at her for a brief moment, stepped forward, and pulled her hand away from her hair, releasing the dark coil to roll down her back. His eyes went soft and his voice low. "Leave it hang loose—'tis pretty thataway."

Maggie stared at him.

Tom cleared his throat. "Where're you off to anyway? Cabin's back yonder."

"I—I was going t' pick berries . . ." Maggie stumbled to gather her pails. "I've tarried here overlong—I better head back for more milk." She scooted down the bank and sloshed upstream back toward the springhouse.

Maggie stopped and turned. Smiling, she called out, "Hoy, Tom! I expect we'll be seein' ye up the brae."

"Up the *what*?" Tom shouted.

"The hill! Come on up fer breakfast."

☙❦❧

Seth came in from his morning chores and sensed an unusual nervous energy in the air. Battler was once again armed with the broom, sweeping with great gusto. Seth skirted around the toddler and settled his rifle on the pegs mounted next to the door.

Jack struggled down the ladder from the loft with a slab of bacon, which he tossed to Maggie. She slapped it down on the table and carved thick slices into the three-legged fry pan setting over the embers. Winnie skittered in, dumped a load of firewood on the hearth, and ran back out the door. Only Naomi sat serene at the head of the table, wiping out her collection of treenware. Seth gave his wife's shoulders a squeeze. "Smells good. Where's my breakfast?"

"Maggie's cookin' up a company breakfast," Naomi said. "Tom Roberts is a-comin' by."

"Tom's about?"

"Yep. Maggie met up with him near the springhouse."

Maggie hovered at the hearth, stirring a mess of onions sizzling over the fire. Seth watched as she peeked under the heavy lid on the bake kettle, and he realized she'd forced her more buxom figure into a clean white blouse belonging to his wife.

"Maggie!" Naomi cautioned. "That spoonbread will never bake proper if you keep fussin' with the lid. I'll keep an eye on things here . . . you go fresh up—fix your hair."

Maggie flashed a smile, grabbed a bucket and Naomi's hairbrush, and ran out the door.

Seth took his usual seat. "Why all the fuss? I never rate more than a bowl of mush and a boilt egg—an' why is Maggie wearin' yer best blouse?"

"You might've taken notice hers is almost tatters, poor thing. We really need do somethin' about her clothes."

Seth shrugged.

Naomi stood and wandered around the table, setting a wooden trencher, bowl, and mug at each place. "I think Maggie fancies Tom . . ."

"Mmmph." Seth frowned.

". . . and maybe Tom fancies her as well. Maggie tol' me he was havin' a washup when she found him at the stream."

To this Seth raised an eyebrow, but then shook his head. "Na . . . all Tom Roberts fancies is the long hunt."

"Maggie also mentioned Tom had warshed out his shirt as well . . ."

Winnie came in with a bucket of water. "An' Tom tol' Maggie her hair was pretty, Da."

"He said that, eh?" Seth worried. "He can be a charming rascal, aye—I'd best warn the lass to keep a distance."

Naomi said, "Seth! Is that any way to speak on a dear friend?"

"Och, ye ken as well as I, between the whores and squaws he beds, the scoundrel never spends more'n one night under the covers with the same woman—exceptin' for maybe Bess Hawkins—and that's only cause she's married . . . *OWW!*"

Naomi gave her husband a good clipe on the head with a wooden plate. "You best mind that gossiping tongue, Seth Martin."

Seth rubbed his sore head. "I dinna consider the truth t' be gossip."

"Wouldn't you like for your friend to find true love?"

"True love!" Seth laughed.

"Aye—true love! Maggie's a wonderful gal—strong and smart—just the right sort of woman to make a man like Tom settle down. I don't recollect you bein' too keen on marriage, but you warmed up to it in the end, didn't you?"

"Aye . . ." Seth nodded. "Now I recall . . . yer belly bein' round and full o' Winnie had naught to do with it." He dodged the cup his wife sent flying in his direction. Winnie giggled.

Jack poked his head through the door and shouted. "Tom's a-comin' up the hill!" He ran off and Winnie shot out behind him. Maggie rushed in, her hair braided into a demure crown around her head. She hurried to get the breakfast on the table.

"*Feich!*" Seth grumbled. "Yid think the bloody king of bloody England were on his way."

Naomi shook a finger at her husband. "You'd do well t' remember that a certain Mr. Seth Martin would not be counted among the living if not for a certain Mr. Tom Roberts. I, for one, am goin' out to greet the man proper."

Chastised, Seth accomplished a neat two-step maneuver in order to dodge Battler and his broom. He gallantly offered an elbow to his wife and escorted her out to the dooryard.

"Och, woman, maybe yiv got the right of it after all. Would ye take a look at tha'—th' poor bastard's done shaved his beard."

Sure enough, Winnie held a clean-shaven Tom Roberts by the hand, tugging him up the slope. Jack, proudly sporting Tom's broad-brimmed hat, trotted behind with Friday.

"It's good t' see you returned safe." Naomi welcomed Tom with a hug. She reached up on tiptoes and touched fingertips to his beardless cheek. "It's been overlong."

"I'm sure glad t' see you so fit." Tom turned to greet Seth. "Hullo, brother! On my way to th' station at Roundabout and thought I'd stop by and see how y'all are farin'."

"I didna expect t' see ye so soon . . ." Seth said, greeting Tom with a handshake. "And I certainly never expected t' see ye without yer pelt." He laughed and slapped his friend on the back. "I forgot what a baby-face lad ye are . . . it's a mite odd."

Tom stroked the lower half of his face. "Feels odd—but a beard is bothersome. Too hot and itchy for summer wear."

Seth led the way toward the open door. "Let's eat."

"Hope you brung yer appetite, Tom," young Jackie chimed in.

"Why, I'm so hungry, Jack, I could eat the scraps off'n a buzzard's beak! I'll be right along after I tend to this horse."

Jack and Winnie bolted to the table and began to tussle over who would be sitting where. Naomi put a quick end to the argument, grabbing each child by an ear and plunking them down side by side onto the same bench. Seth settled onto his stool at the head of the table and Naomi at the foot. Maggie circled around plopping a steaming scoop of spoonbread onto each trencher.

Tom came through the open door, ducking his head so as not to bang it on the lintel piece. "Hello again, Miss Duncan."

It was plain Maggie needed a moment to form the link between the voice and the clean-shaven face. She tossed the spoon into the bake kettle and settled her hands at her hips.

"Losh! Yiv scraped away yer whiskers! Why, I would never have recognized ye! Who'd a thought such a well-favored lad lay beneath all that fur?"

Everyone laughed, and if Seth had not seen it with his own eyes, he would never have believed it—Tom Roberts blushed crimson. The tall hunter shuffled from side to side, reaching to tug at his nonexistent beard. Feeling sorry for his friend, Seth rose up from the table to take Tom's rifle. "I'll set yer weapon out of Battler's reach."

"Come and sit next to me, Tom." Winnie patted the empty spot beside her.

"Tom don't want to sit near a puddin' head like you." Jack stuck his tongue out at his sister. "Tom wants to sit beside Maggie. She's got pretty hair."

Flustered, Tom stumbled forward, tripped over Battler, got tangled up with the broom handle, and flailing for balance, fell with a crash to the floor.

The Martins and Maggie rushed around the table. Battler sat up, wailing like a banshee, but Tom lay perfectly still, knocked out cold. Maggie fell to her knees. Seth helped her to flip the man onto his back.

"Would ye look at the knot on his forehead?" Maggie said. "He banged his noggin but good on that table edge. Jackie! Fetch my basket."

8

A Wee Thump to the Head

Onions sizzling in pork fat wafted up through the floorboards. He nestled his head into the sack of barley that served as his headrest and turned the page . . .

In a little time I began to speak to him; and teach him to speak to me: and first, I let him know his name should be Friday, which was the day I saved his life: I called him so for the memory of the time . . .

His stomach growled—it must be close to supper time. Reading up in the loft always made him so hungry. The smoked hams and sausages dangling from the rafters were hard to resist, so he arranged his secret reading place far from temptation, among the sacks of grain and sweet-smelling bouquets of lavender.

"Tom!"

Mother called. He marked his place with a piece of straw, and scrambled to hide the forbidden novel behind the barrel of pickled beef . . .

"Tom . . ."

Tom blinked and looked up into Maggie's quiet, dark eyes, his head nestled on her lap as she massaged lavender oil on the space between his lip and nose. He tried to elbow up, but she pressed a hand firm to his chest. "Stay put, lad. Yiv taken quite a blow to the head . . ."

"What blether. Take my word, Maggie, th' lad's survived far worse." Seth bent over. Tom grabbed hold of Seth's forearm and rose up to his feet.

"A bite t' eat is what ye need," Seth suggested. "I could hear yer empty belly roilin' from across the room."

Disoriented and a bit wobbly, Tom plunked down on a bench facing away from the table, his backbone rubbing uncomfortable against the thickness of the table edge. The ringing hum in his head dimmed the bickering of the Martin children helping themselves to the breakfast laid out on the table. He fingered the large knot swelled near his left temple.

Maggie stood before him and took his face between her hands to study the bump. "I've arnica for that." She dipped into her basket, pulled out a slender blue glass bottle, and saturated a pad of raw wool with the tincture. She moved in to stand between his knees, one warm palm cradling his cheek as she dabbed the pad to the swelling, standing so close, the wool of her skirt tickled the bare skin of his inner thighs.

Maggie's fingers on his cheek triggered an unexpected and not unpleasant tug to his groin. Tom drew a breath—woman-musk mingled with the alcohol in the tincture she administered. He found his eyes level with golden flesh mounding up beyond the gathered neckline of her blouse, his hand reaching up. He quick collected his wits, restrained the impetuous urge to caress her breast, and settled his roving hand on the curve of her hip.

Maggie glanced down at his hand resting on her hip. "Are ye dizzy?"

"Dizzy? No—" Tom squirmed like a red worm tossed on hot ashes. His hand slipped down and plopped into his lap. Jack giggled.

"Leave the man be, Maggie." Seth seemed annoyed. "It's naught but a wee thump to the head."

"You just save your breath to cool your spoonbread, Seth Martin," Naomi scolded. "Maggie knows what she's about."

"I only meant the poor man's no doubt dizzy fer want of his breakfast." Seth glared into the mountain of food on his plate.

"Seth's got the right of it, Tom. Breakfast in yer belly will do ye some good. If yer head still aches after, I'll fix ye a cup of willow bark tea." Maggie tucked her things back into her basket and sidled onto the bench next to him. Tom turned around and focused on the food ladled onto his trencher.

After a moment Seth said, "Here's a thought—Maggie might have some luck sellin' her remedies and treating folk's aches and pains at the station down in Roundabout. Quite a crowd comes in to trade on Saturdays."

Naomi clapped her hands. "There's a fine idea! A peddler may be there with yardage for trade. We can make you some new clothes." Naomi turned to Maggie. "You can meet some of the other women as well. Many are a-childing and'll soon have need of a midwife."

"Hannah and I earned a good living catchin' babies," Maggie offered as added incentive.

"Aye . . ." Seth pondered the opportunity. "It would be good for Maggie to meet some of the other women, don't ye think, Tom?"

Tom searched through the contents of his pouch. "Can't seem to lay hand to my spoon . . . oh, never mind, here 'tis." He hunched over his food and put the horn spoon to use—shoveling up great mouthfuls of fried onion, scrambled egg, and spoonbread—pausing only to wash it down with great gulping swallows of milk.

"Can I go with, Da—to Roundabout?" Jack asked.

"Aye, lad . . . we'll all go."

"What about it, Tom?" Naomi said. "Stay on till Saturday and come along with us . . ."

"No!" Seth almost shouted. "Tom's a busy man, woman. He's but passin' through."

Tom eyed Seth while chewing a piece of crisp bacon. "That's true, I shouldn't linger. I'm goin' on a market hunt with De-Montforte overmountain. Quartermasters are paying good silver for wild beef tenders and tallow." He smiled at Maggie, leaned over, and helped himself to additional helpings of everything. "This all eats good, Maggie . . . sure hits the empty spot."

"You were away awful long, Tom. Did you have a good hunt?" Winnie asked.

"I'd say so. Came out with five hundred deer hides, three hundred beaver . . . sold the lot for over a thousand pound."

Jack whistled. "You're rich, Tom!"

"I might have killed three times as many if I had the means to bring it all out. I aim to head back there come fall—"

"Ah now, Tommy," Seth interrupted. "Shawnee and Cherokee willna take too kindly to trespass on their hunting ground. Yer like t' get yer hair lifted."

"They have to catch me afore they can skelp me." Tom shrugged. "Naw . . . there's nothin' that'll stop me from heading back to *Kenta-ke.*"

"Tell, Tom . . . tell Maggie 'bout *Kenta-ke,*" Winnie begged.

"*Kenta-ke,*" Maggie repeated. "Such an odd word."

"Shawnee word." Tom poured himself another mug full of buttermilk. "Means 'land of great meadows,' and I'm here to tell I've never been to a more beautiful place in my life."

Maggie leaned an elbow on the tabletop and rested her chin in her palm, enthralled.

"Tom has no time fer tales." Seth glared across the table at Tom. "He needs t' finish his breakfast and get back on the trail."

Tom ignored Seth. "In my mind *Kenta-ke* is akin to the Garden of Eden, a green place, full of life. Clear rivers—forests tall with chestnut, oak, and maple . . . and deer! Deer a-bounding—more beaver and turkey than I had lead t' shoot 'em with. I saw vast herds of wild beef and—"

"Seein' as how yer of a mind fer tellin' tales, lad," Seth interrupted, "why don't ye tell Maggie one o' those from the time when ye lived among the savages, ken?"

The two men stared at each other for a moment. Tom picked up his spoon and began eating again.

"Na . . . ye didna live among heathen Red Indians, did ye?" Maggie asked.

Tom nodded, and continued chewing.

Winnie piped in. "C'mon, Tom! Tell Maggie all 'bout how you were adopted . . ."

"Ye were *adopted* by Red Indians?" Maggie's eyes were wide.

"Tell about runnin' the gauntlet." Jack bounced in his seat.

"Hush your mouthing!" Naomi shot her husband a chilling look. "Can't y'all see Tom don't want t' be talkin' about all that . . ."

"Naw. I don't mind." Tom scraped up the last bits, spooned them into his mouth, and pushed back his plate. "Nothin' better than a tale, bold and true—right, Seth?"

"Aye. Nothin' better than the truth," Seth agreed.

Tom produced a small block of birchwood and a folding knife from his pouch. He took his time, whittled off a toothpick, installed it at one end of his smile, and began his story.

"Back in '55, unlike most of my Quaker brethren and much to the dismay of my father, I was more than eager to join the fight with the French. So, I ran off. Up and left my father's farm on the Susquehanna and signed on with Braddock's colonial militia. My oh my"—Tom smiled in recollection—"I was only just seventeen years, a foolish, pindling boy . . . not much bigger than Seth here." Everyone laughed.

"We set out with purpose. That old jackass Braddock didn't make much of us colonials as soldiers. He put most of us to work cutting a wagon road westward through the forest, from Fort Cumberland all the way to Fort Duquesne. I worked with an advance party of axmen—about a dozen of us—felling trees pretty far ahead of the regulars and artillery."

Tom slapped his hand down on the tabletop. "And that sudden-quick, a band of painted Indians sprang out of the brush, screamin' and shootin', and here we were with naught but one decrepit musket for defense. I dropped my ax and lit out. Yep, I did—I cut mud—runnin' with a fury back to the main column. One big, bull-strong Indian gave good chase and knocked me down. He dragged me back." Tom's face fell grim. "A grisly sight, that. All my comrades, save one young fella named Colby, kilt and skelpt. And poor Colby, standin' there a-shivering, so scared, he'd pissed himself."

Jack said. "But you weren't ascairt, were you, Tom?"

"I tell you what, Jack, I was never more scared than I was on that day. I had to work awful hard to put on a brave face, and made ready to part with my topknot. But a strange thing happened . . . you recall the big Indian fella what knocked me down?"

Maggie bobbed her head up and down along with Winnie and Jack.

"Why, he grinned at me and sheathed his tomahawk. He spoke a great lot of gibberish, all the while lashing my wrists together with a length of tug. He held tight the tug end and the whole band moved out at a smart rate to the northwest."

"An' the other lad?" Maggie wondered.

"Colby? He was taken prisoner by one of the others. We didn't stop till after dark and camped without fire. It was then I took heart—when I saw how they divided the rations—for Colby and I were given equal share of their provisions, and this I took for a fair sign."

"Why's that?" Maggie wondered.

"'Cause if they meant to torture and kill them, they wouldn't bother to feed them," Jack explained, impatient for the rest of Tom's story.

"So, we marched and camped four days and nights," Tom continued. "On the fifth day—"

"Why not run off when the Indians fell t' sleep?" Maggie interrupted. "That's what I'd do."

Tom shook his head. "Naw . . . there was no escape. At sleepin' time, Colby and I were bound tight with many lengths of buffalo tug and laid down with Indians on either side. At that point, I was of a hopeful mind that we were to be ransomed anyway." Tom removed the toothpick from his mouth and flicked it to smolder on the coals lingering from the breakfast fire.

"On the fifth day, we were marched into their village. My gut tangled into a knot. Coming into the village did not bode well for our survival, for if we were to be ransomed, they'd have brought us to a French post."

"Tell Maggie about the village," Winnie said.

"Not much to tell." Tom shrugged. "'Twere a small village, five timber longhouses, a council house, and some cleared acreage for growing sister crops—corn, beans, and squash. I recall the war party's homecoming was greeted with much hallooing and gunfire. The bloody scalps of my comrades dangled from their belts as the warriors marched in proud. Us being there, Colby and me, sure caused quite a stir. There was much merriment and the air of a frolic, which of course I did not share." Tom glanced into his empty cup. Maggie leaned over and filled it with milk.

"Then, without any prompting that I could see," Tom continued, "the people began to stretch themselves into two long lines from one end of the village to the other—'bout thirty yards in all. They faced each other with maybe a five-yard span atwixt them."

"My Indian released me from my bindings, and by gibberish and gesture made me understand I was to run this gauntlet.

Colby received the same instruction from his Indian. I looked up and down those lines and saw most of the men armed with stout clubs. Women, young and old, chattered like jaybirds, all the while gathering good-size stones in their aprons. Even the children ran about snapping willow withies in the air. I shed my tattered moccasins, stretched my muscles, and hopped about. I figured on runnin' very fast indeed!" Tom stopped for a sip of milk, relishing the moment with Maggie on the edge of her seat.

"An' then?" Maggie urged.

"Well, when my Indian gave me the signal, I tucked my head and ran with long strides—quicker'n a snake through a hollow log." Tom wriggled his arm through the air. "I ended up taking quite a few solid blows across my shoulders and back, but nothing too hurtful. My Indian met up with me at the end of the gauntlet very pleased and puffed proud. I had done well."

"And Colby?" Maggie asked.

Tom shook his head. "Poor, poor Colby—that boy didn't have the backbone of a fishworm, and not an ounce of mother wit about him. Given a shove, he stumble-bumbled along, flogged and clubbed the whole long way. In the end, he just lay there writhing while braves took turns with their muskets, discharging powder into the bare skin of his legs and arms. His Indian drug him away, burned, bloodied, and beaten. I never heard tell of him again."

"And you—what happened with you?"

Tom stood up and snatched his hat from Jack's head. "I think I'll leave that tale for another tellin' . . . next time we meet up."

"Aw, Tom!" the children wailed in unison, but Tom would not be so coerced. He donned his hat, retrieved his rifle, slung it over his shoulder, and the Martin family followed him out to the dooryard. Tom dawdled, making a pretense of searching for Friday, then fussing with the lashings on his packs, waiting to see if Maggie might come out to bid him farewell. She didn't.

"Take care, Tom." Naomi hugged him. "Stop by and see us on your way back."

Tom ruffled Jack's hair and reached out to shake hands with Seth. "Thank you, brother, for the breakfast and all."

"Aye, Tommy . . . have a good hunt . . . mind yer topknot."

Tom set off through the clearing, making for the path that led down to the stream. Upon reaching the forest edge, he heard his name called.

"Tom! Tom Roberts!"

He turned to see Maggie, skirts flying, running through the cornfield. Breathing hard when she caught up, she held out a knotted bundle of red flannel.

"I meant for ye to have these. Corn dodgers . . . hot off the griddle. And this . . ." She dug into her pocket, pulled out a small muslin packet, and offered it to him. "Willow bark tea—if yer head should ache."

Tom weighed the packet in his palm for a moment before slipping it into the front of his shirt. "You've been kind. I'm glad to have a chance to thank you for your care and concern."

How pretty she was—breathless and flushed. He moved in, intent on pulling her into his arms for a kiss, but Maggie shoved the flannel bundle into his hands and scampered back several steps, saying, "A good pinch of that tea steeped in boilt water if yer head aches." She swayed and fiddled with a tendril of hair.

Tom took a step forward. "I know you most probably think me a proper savage, but given a chance, I think we might become . . . better friends."

"Aye . . . well . . . we'll have t' see about that." She turned and ran back up the hill, calling over her shoulder, "Good luck t' ye, Tom! Fare well on yer hunt!"

Tom watched until she disappeared beyond the crest. He sat down on a tree stump and opened the bundle. The dodgers were crisp and still warm. He bit into one of the yellow circles, and with pensive thoroughness, chewed and swallowed his way through the lot.

Tom whistled sharp and his dog came tearing out of the cornfield. He wrapped Friday in a bear hug and scratched him behind the ears until he got the dog's rear leg to thumping.

"Friday, I will tell you I am flummoxed—*women!*" He stood and brushed crumbs from his shirt, shaking his head. "I read the sign and stalked her with care, but when I took aim, she caught my scent and hightailed it." Tom looped his hand through the gelding's lead and headed into the woods, his dog trotting alongside. "Probably a good thing, though—that was a hurried shot, and those never hit true."

9

Hitting the Nail on the Head

Streaming sunlight pierced through morning mist and the tangle of foliage overhead. Tall-tree silence was interrupted by the crunch of their footfalls and the skreel of a hawk on the hunt. Although not much more than a deer path, the overgrown ridge trail they followed was the quickest way to Roundabout Station.

"There's another!" Jack's sharp eye was the first to spy the triangular notch blazed into a big oak. "I count *six* for me!" Winnie and Jack galloped ahead, each hoping to win the game and find the most markers along the five-mile trek.

Maggie marched behind the children, lugging her basket, keen eyes scouring the forest floor for familiar plants. Seth followed, burdened by a basket of barrel staves strapped to his back. The cooper might be at the station that day and Seth planned to trade the set of planks for a ready-made barrel. Rifle gripped in his left hand, he tugged the mule's lead with the other. Pregnant Naomi sat a clumsy sidesaddle behind Battler, who rode quite content perched astride Ol' Mule's withers.

Seth drew Maggie's attention to every marker and landmark, stressing the importance of learning the way. "Mind, Maggie, if the Redmen rise and the alarm to fort up is called, ye may need t' find yer way to Roundabout."

"Come onto the overpeer," Winnie called. "You can see the station from here."

Maggie ducked through a thicket of laurel and stepped onto a limestone ledge jutting out from the ridgeline. "Look yonder." Winnie pointed. "Down in the clearing . . ."

Bony-hipped cattle grazed among the stubble of stumps that pocked the clearing. A timber wall crawled along the crest of a low-rising hill. Multiple strings of smoke slid up from behind the stockade, dissolving into a sheer blue sky.

"Megstie me! Ye canna mean tha' scraggle of timber there?" She expected her last refuge from berserk, savage Indians to be something more—something of greater magnitude.

"Aye . . ." Seth joined them on the outcropping. "When planting began, attentions turned elsewhere, and as ye can see, we've yet to complete the west wall. Dinna fash, lass." Seth gave her a pat on the back. "I ken it doesna compare to the stone fortresses back home, but even a wooden fort unfinished is better than naught."

The last steep mile switchbacking down to the valley required careful footing. Entering the clearing, they wound a path through the sea of stumps—some of them five and six feet in diameter— and Maggie developed a greater appreciation for the labor entailed in providing for the common defense.

Sounds and smells of fellow humanity caused a quickening in the pace the ring of iron on iron, children squealing at play, hickory smoke and roasting meat. Maggie startled with alarm at the sudden report of gunfire.

"Rifle frolic," Seth said with a smile. "When the lads gang thegither, it most always leads to a target shoot."

The structure loomed before her. Centered in the stockade, a huge pair of gates hinged and banded with iron hung open. The wall was constructed of uniform logs sunk close on the vertical, each one adzed to a menacing point at the top. Maggie judged it to be twelve feet high and almost fifty yards long. A double row of gun ports decorated the two-storied blockhouse straddling the southeast corner.

While Seth helped Naomi dismount, Winnie and Jack ran ahead to join the huddle of children at the gate. Battler clung tenaciously to the mule's stubby mane and Maggie wrestled to pull him down and set him on sturdy legs. She squeezed his sweaty little hand in hers and grabbed her basket. Seth hobbled and slapped his beast to pasture, and they passed through the gates to enter Roundabout Station.

The rectangular fortyard was also littered with tree stumps. On Maggie's left, the unfinished section of stockade wall opened to a view of field and forest beyond. Before her, lining the long side, she counted a row of ten miniature cabins—each sharing a common wall with its neighbor. A half-size chimney constructed of smooth river stones flanked every doorway, and the plank roofs pitched from front to back, sloping up to the stockade, which served as the back wall of every cabin.

"So folk live in the station?"

"Newcomers use the station till they build their own homeplace," Naomi explained.

"The cabins are meant to shelter all during a siege," Seth added. "In times like those, ye can imagine 'twill be close quarters."

A few squinting women emerged from dark doorways, shading their eyes. Naomi waved and wandered off to speak with her friends. Maggie continued with Seth and Battler, intrigued by the surroundings and new faces.

"Missus Buchanan! How d'ye fend this fine mornin'?" Seth waved to a wide woman sitting on a stump, her hands busy plucking dung-caked daglocks from a puff of wool fleece.

"I canna complain." Her response was barely audible, as the large wicker hamper at her feet was filled with peeping chicks.

A fire burned in a ring of stones that served as the central hearth. There, a young girl tended a ham roasting on a spit. Drippings plopped onto hot coals in a sputter of delicious smoke. A pair of daring boys ran up and plucked off strips of crisp fat before being shooed away, their ill-gotten gains stuffed into their mouths.

"Och, aye!" Seth exclaimed. "The cooper's come up."

To the left of the blockhouse and nested in a circle of finished barrels, piggins, and tubs, the cooper turned the crank, winding the cord of his windlass to draw a dozen staves up into a bulging barrel shape. Seth lingered, perusing the cooper's ready stock.

Maggie tightened her grip on Battler's hand as he strained to join a pack of older children and their game of tag. Billows of dust followed as they dodged and hopped over tree stumps, racing from one end of the station to the other.

Next to the cooper, the blacksmith occupied the most prominent position at the northeast corner, where an open-faced shed housed a chimneyed brick forge. There, a sweat-drenched, bare-chested young man worked the leather bellows whooshing and bulging from one end of the forge. At the other end, an older and more substantial version of the bellows-man bent a curve into a bar of iron with a bang of his hammer and a turn of the tongs.

The two Willies. Maggie recognized them. Naomi had told her all about the burly smith and his hulking son—Palatine Protestants forced from their German homeland. The Roundabout settlers had happily organized a mule train to haul the smith's tools and bricks for a forge. The services of a good blacksmith, favorably equipped with anvil, grinding wheel, and bar stock, were essential for survival on the edge of the wilderness. Especially a smith as skilled as Willie Wagner, who—according to Seth—was one of few able to forge a square iron rod into a perfect gun barrel, rifled with the spiral groove that provided the deadly accuracy frontiersmen depended upon.

Enamored by the din and clang, Battler slipped his hand from Maggie's and darted toward the forge. Maggie dropped her basket and scurried to scoop the boy up just as he tipped over a rack of tools. Elder Willie glanced up from his task, fleeting irritation replaced by a broken-toothed grin.

"Sorry fer the bother, sir, but this wee laddie's full o' th' devil." Maggie struggled to right the rack and keep Battler planted on her hip.

Elder Willie pounded in rhythm with his speech. "I betcha you be Martin's new bondvoman."

"Aye, sir. Maggie Duncan." She bobbed a shallow curtsy, hugging squirmy Battler to her chest, very uncomfortable with Younger Willie's suddenly slow pumping of the bellows and gape-mouth gaze upon her.

"*Vilhelm!*" the father barked. "*Vershwendete zeit ist verlorene zeit.*"

The son tore his eyes away and worked again with fervor. With a swift shift from stern to friendly, Elder Willie explained, "You see? I say him, 'Time vaste ist time lose.' He good boy, my Vilhelm. Good verker—so strong, like Papa." Willie punctuated this proclamation with one last bang of his hammer and dropped the bar into a cooling tub. Yellow-hot iron hit the water with a hiss and a pillow of steam rose to collect among the roof timbers. He stepped around the forge, massive arms akimbo, and looked Maggie up and down. "You strong girl. Good verker?"

"I'm no' afeart to dirty my hands, if that's what yer after."

"Yah, good vide hips I see . . ." He wagged his mastifflike head, smiled big, and gestured with a flip of his snaggle-nailed thumb. "My Vilhelm—he vant voman."

"What?" Maggie glanced over, catching Willie the younger engaged in open leering appreciation of her backside.

"Yah, yah." The father nodded, smiling. "Vilhelm needing voman—vife."

"Aye, well . . ."—Maggie took a step back—"good luck t' him." She turned on her heel and marched a quickstep back toward her basket, raucous man-laughter ringing in her ear.

Naomi had warned her about the scarcity of marriageable women on the frontier, but Maggie never expected such overt interest. She set the heavy toddler on his feet and retrieved her basket; not wanting to interrupt Seth, who was engaged in fierce barter with the cooper, she allowed Battler to take the lead. Tugging her hand, Battler pulled Maggie away from the Willies and toward the gunshots and applause coming from the unfinished end of the fort.

Just beyond the opening in the stockade wall, a group of men were gathered in a horseshoe around a rifleman. Skirting the periphery of the crowd, Maggie strained on tiptoes to see the man take aim. A shot rang out, resulting in cheers from a few, groans from most, and the busy exchange of curses, coins, and flasks. Battler whimpered and clutched at Maggie's skirt, trying to sclim squirrel-like into her arms.

Winnie and Jack waved to Maggie from a row of children perched like so many sparrows atop a huge felled pine tree. "C'mon up," Winnie called. "You can see best from here."

Maggie set her basket on the ground, swung Battler up, and scrambled onto the big log. She settled between Winnie and Jack with wiggle-worm Battler on her lap and enjoyed a clear view of the contest.

A smile crossed Maggie's lips when the next marksman stepped up to toe the line scratched in the dirt. The shooter's attire was an absurd combination of moccasins and fringed leggings topped by the scarlet jacket of a British infantryman. A sad periwig desperate for curl and powder sat askew on his head, while long black braids dangling with silver charms and feathers trailed down his back. The crowd hummed to quiet as the man leveled his weapon and took aim. He pulled the trigger ... *POW-thunk.*

Maggie peered downrange. "What's he shooting at?"

"See the girdled tree down yonder?" Jack pointed to a tree about fifty yards from where the shooter stood, a tree whose bark had been stripped midtrunk to deaden it for clearing.

"Aye . . . so they must hit th' tree . . ." Maggie was impressed.

"Not the tree, silly." Winnie laughed. "The nail—they aim to hit the nail that's pounded into the trunk."

"Yer jokin'!" Maggie could barely make out a black spot on the bare wood. "That's an impossible shot."

A man sprinted out to the tree with a claw-end hammer. He shouted back, *"Scant inch!"* and jerked a six-inch iron nail from the tree, and then banged it into a new position.

"The Indian hit less than an inch away," Winnie said.

"A Red Indian?" Maggie took a second look at the fair-skinned young man as he stepped aside to make way for the next shooter.

Jack said, "He ain't no Indian. Simon Peavey's naught but a white lad gone renegade."

"Well, Indian or no, so far Peavey's shot hit closest to the mark," Winnie said.

Jack gave his sister a shove. "Pah! Tom can beat that shot. If I had any, I'd put my money on Tom."

Tom Roberts stepped out from the crowd and Maggie's heart thumped into her throat. She drew a deep breath and blew it out slow. The flutter of Battler's cowlick tickled her nose.

There stands as pretty a man as ever I saw.

Several days' stubble and the slant of a broad-brimmed hat shadowed his face, diminishing any boyishness with considerable dash. Amid the backdrop of buckskin and walnut-dyed home-spun, Tom gleamed in a shirt of sun-bleached linen with a cravat of the same looped into a loose knot at his throat. Rather than breechclout and leggings, Tom sported black woolen breeches and leather boots polished to shine like British artillery.

Holding his rifle waist-high, pointing downrange, Tom pushed the hammer forward. He clicked open the frizzen and primed the pan with a slight measure of powder tapped with precision from a miniature horn procured from his pouch. He snapped the frizzen shut and stepped to the line. Pushing his hat back slightly, he turned into shooting stance and Maggie caught his eye. With a nod and a smile her way, he licked the tip of his thumb and swiped it across the sight. The crowd hushed to silence. Maggie gripped Battler tight. Tom fit the stock firm against his shoulder and squeezed the trigger—*POW-ponkk!*

Tense silence was maintained while the target man trotted down to the target. Cupping hand to mouth, he shouted, *"Hit the nail on the head!"*

The crowd huzzahed and swarmed Tom with handshakes and slaps on the back. One man, brandishing a fistful of winnings, shouted, "Yer an able man with that weapon, Roberts."

"Yep . . . that's what all the gals tell me, anyway," Tom retorted, much to the guffaw and delight of his comrades. He looked up at Maggie and winked. She bit her bottom lip and squirmed in her seat.

Tom stepped back to reload. He kept his eye and smile on Maggie, seating powder, ball, and patch down the rifle barrel with three hard strokes of his ramrod. An unbidden tremor twirled up from the base of Maggie's spine. She shivered and resisted fanning her face.

Simon Peavey stepped to the line. According to Winnie, he had one chance to either match or best Tom's shot. Peavey's nervous hands belied his stoic countenance. Priming the pan, he spilled a stream of powder onto the ground and seemed to rush his aim. The crowd was still engaged in a frenzy of wagering when he squeezed the trigger. The hammer fell, flint struck steel, igniting the powder to flash in the pan, but there was no report—no shot—a misfire.

"Merde!" Peavey swore, shifting the angle of his grip to pick with annoyance at the touchhole on the flintlock mechanism.

The gun discharged. Peavey yelped, dropped his weapon and his knees to the ground, his face and neck peppered with a fine spray of black powder that had exploded through the touchhole. Face in hands, he moaned. Blood dripped through his fingers, landing in the dirt like a scatter of soft buttons.

"Winnie, mind Battler." Maggie hopped down and pushed her way through the crowd. She knelt beside the wounded man. "Bring me some water!" Maggie placed a hand on his shoulder. He growled and shrugged her off, but she persisted. "Let's have a look, lad."

"Leave that renegade trash be, girlie. It'll soon scurry back to whar it come from."

Maggie glanced up at the sniggering crowd. She couldn't tell which of the anonymous faces had uttered the unkind remark and she had no time to remonstrate with them. Someone shoved a canteen in her hand. She doused the right side of Peavey's face with cool water. This brought immediate relief. His shoulders eased, and he dropped his hands and settled back on his haunches, eyeing Maggie with fierce distrust.

He was younger than she figured—twenty-five years at most— and his youth and her curiosity made it easy to ignore his glare. She had never before seen a powder burn.

The compound tang of sulfur, scorched flesh, and burned hair hung in the air—and no wonder—for his brows and a portion of the silly wig he wore were singed completely away. Bright blood continued to seep from a rent in his cheek. His forehead and eyelid were inflamed and stippled black with hot grains of powder embedded into his skin. Maggie reached out to gingerly pick at one. Simon Peavey sucked air and winced.

"And yer eyes?" she asked.

He shook his head and grunted, "Shet 'em in time."

"Yer lucky tha' . . ."

Jack pushed through the crowd with her basket. Maggie flipped it open and crinkled her forehead as she began poking through her things, studying Peavey's face and her remedies, mulling over the best course of treatment.

"Don't waste yer worry on that down-gone wastrel, missy," one man advised.

"A decent woman would never bother with that dirty, no-account—"

"Like buzzards on a carcass," Tom Roberts said, pushing through the crowd. "Y'all move along now—go on about your business and leave the girl to hers."

Tom stood glaring until the crowd muttered itself back into the fort. He turned and dropped a clump of uprooted greenery onto Maggie's lap and went down to one knee to examine Peavey's face.

"Why, you're as freckled as a turkey egg." Tom laughed.

"And you're an auger-eyed son of a bitch," Peavey replied with painful half smile. "Good shootin'."

"Poking and peering down the flash hole after a misfire." Tom tsked. "You ought know better, Simon."

Maggie said, "Spare him the sermon, Reverend, and lend the lad a scoof from yer flask."

Tom fished through his pouch and handed over a bottle. Peavey dosed himself while Maggie inspected the plants lying across her lap, clumps of dirt and clay still clinging to the roots. "Soldier's woundwort!"

"Naw, that there's yarrow," Tom corrected.

"Aye, 'tis called yarrow in the lowlands." She set the greens to the side and pulled her heavy mortar up from the bottom of her basket. "I couldna have wished for anything better to stanch and seal a bloody wound. 'Twill ease the burn as well." Maggie stripped the feathery leaves into the bowl. Kneeling in, working the pestle with the strength of her shoulder, she mashed the leaves into an oily paste, reciting:

> *"Thou pretty herb of Venus's tree,*
> *Thy true name is Yarrow;*
> *Now who my one true love must be,*
> *Pray show me thou tomorrow."*

Tom laughed, and this time it was Maggie's turn to wink. "Ol' wives claim a spray of yarrow under yer pillow and that verse aloud will bring a vision of yer true love." She scooped some salve onto two fingers and held them to Peavey's nose for a sniff and giggled. "Reeks a bit like an ol' wife, no?"

Simon shrank back, squinty with skepticism.

"Och, he's givin' me the gimlet eye." Maggie sighed, and turned to Tom. "Tell him, Tom. Tell the lad how I repaired yer cracked noggin."

With solemnity, Tom ran two fingers down the purple-and-white-beaded strap of his pouch. "On my honor, the gal has strong medicine."

Peavey pondered this statement for a long moment, then settled into a comfortable cross-legged position. Maggie applied the salve with a gentle touch and he bore the treatment in stony silence.

Maggie piled her things back into the basket, stood up, and wiped her hands on her skirt. "Mash yerself a salve when ye need relief. Keep the wounds clean, aye?" She handed him a muslin packet identical to the one she had given Tom several days before. "Willow bark tea—'twill ease the pain."

Tom hoisted the young man up to his feet. Peavey shouldered his weapon and, without a word, walked off.

Maggie watched Simon slip into the forest. "Now, that one's an oddling for certain."

"That fella's a crack shot and expert tracker."

Maggie brushed away toddicks of dirt clinging to her skirt. "The others dinna seem to care for him much."

Tom shrugged. "They suspect Indians."

"But the lad's white . . ."

"Naw." Tom leaned on his rifle, his hands rough against the slick oiled barrel. "Simon's an unfortunate caught atwixt two worlds and he can't seem to find a fit in either. He's had a hard life—younger than Jack when he witnessed all his folk massacred."

"Who massacred them? Th' English?"

"The English!" Tom laughed. "No . . . I'd say more likely the Huron by order of the French. A band of Shawnee found the boy and adopted him into their tribe. When I met up with Simon three years ago, he was scouting for the British. He'd been with the Shawnee so long he could only manage a few words in English. Even now, he blacks his hair with soot and bear grease, desperate to look Indian, at the same time mingling with whites." Tom shrugged. "Simon's a contrary. Makes folk uneasy." He picked up Maggie's basket and they strolled back into the station.

Seth rushed up, breathless and scowling. "Maggie! Where've ye been? Naomi has a gaggle of customers a-waitin' on ye." He pointed to a gathering of women and children standing near the cookfire.

"Losh!" Maggie took her basket from Tom, saying, "I might yet earn a penny or two." She bade the men good-bye with an excited smile and hurried away.

Tom leaned in on his rifle and watched her every step as she moved across the fortyard. "That Maggie is a prime article—a real up-headed gal."

"Hmmph." Seth slouched down to sit on a large stump. "I spied Bess Hawkins come through the gate not too long ago. Why don't ye seek her out? I'm sure she's willing t' sell ye a pair of socks."

Tom turned and considered Seth with narrow eyes. "Why don't you just outright tell me what's on your mind?" He settled onto the stump, laid his rifle across his lap, and drew a tiny copper pick from a compartment built into the stock of the weapon.

"Aye then, I will." Seth fumbled through his pouch for his flask. "Ye ken well our Maggie's far from home—on her own here with no kinsmen t' uphold fer her."

Tom stuck the pick through the touchhole on the flintlock, scraping away the powder residue built up around the edges. "Go on . . ."

"And, well . . ." Seth fiddled with the cork in his flask. "She's a good lass, aye? Like a sister t' me, she is—like the wee sister I lost at sea, and it's on me to see to her best interests."

Tom nodded, pulled a square of sueded leather from his pouch, and rubbed small circles into the walnut stock. "You're yammering, Seth. Line it out plain."

"I want ye t' stay away from Maggie, Tom. There ye have it." Seth gulped a swig.

Tom set his gun to the side. "I'm sorry t' hear you say that, for I have an inkling Maggie is of another mind."

"She doesn't know ye th' I way do. She sees ye starched into yer best Quaker-go-to-meetings, payin' her court—but I ken yer busked out for a hunt of a different sort. Aye, a wolf may lose his teeth, but never his nature."

Tom laughed. "What's that s'posed to mean?"

"Och, Tommy . . . scrape yer whiskers, comb yer hair, carry her basket . . ." Seth sighed and threw an arm across Tom's shoulders. "I love ye like a brother, lad, but at the end of the day, yer the sort who plants his corn without building a fence." He handed Tom the flask. "I willna stand for it. I paid twenty-three hard-earned pounds for th' lass to tend *my* bairns, not one o' yourn."

Tom took a long swallow from the flask and handed it back. "There's something you seem to have forgotten, Seth—you've contracted Maggie's labor, not her heart. Of all people, you ought be one to know the difference." He stood up and slung the rifle over his shoulder. "It was a pleasure sharing a drink with you—*brother.*"

❧

Maggie set up shop under a tarp on the long trestle table near the cookhearth. She spent the morning conducting a brisk trade, dispensing remedies, offering advice, and sharing recipes with the women who'd gathered there, all with a mind to forming a bond of trust, hoping the women would call upon her in their time of travail.

Eager customers, the frontier women were quick to trade for remedies. The paper twists filled with tooth-cleaning powder

Maggie concocted of white clay, salt, and peppermint proved most popular. Eileen Wallen exchanged a Luckenbooth brooch for a jar of comfrey ointment for her infant's rash. Susannah Bledsoe parted with a yard of blue ribbon for a packet of tansy tea to rid her twin boys of roundworm.

While the women worked together preparing a communal supper, Maggie saw to her last customer, examining a carbuncle the size of a robin's egg on the back of Ada Buchanan's neck.

"I'm afeart it must be drained, missus."

Ada heaved a sigh and settled her generous backside onto the stool Maggie offered. "Aye, then yid best have at it, lass."

Maggie put her pestle to work crushing equal handfuls of chamomile flowers and poppy seed. She poured half the mixture into a drawstring sack and dropped it into a bowl of steaming water. She heated her darning needle to red-hot in the candle's flame as the poultice steeped.

"Best keep an eagle eye on your men, ladies," Ada announced, "for I see Bess Hawkins is in station, totin' a basket full o' socks."

Maggie glanced up. Near the smithy, a woman wearing a broad-brimmed straw hat stood with her back to the cookhearth. With a large rush basket resting on one jutting hip, the woman entertained a semicircle of smiling men, Tom in the forefront among them.

"My Sam bought a pair last week." Very pregnant Susannah Bledsoe stirred the johnnycake batter. "Those socks are so badly fashioned I was hard-pressed to tell toe from heel. Not a total waste, though—I put 'em in the outhouse to use as bum fodder." Everyone laughed.

"There'll be a bit of a pinch now, missus," Maggie warned before she slipped the tip of the needle into the center of the boil. Ada scrunched her mobcap in her fists as Maggie squeezed yellow matter from the carbuncle onto a wad of cotton lint. "We'll poultice this once it's drained. That'll give ye some ease."

"If Bess'd but scour and card her wool properly," Naomi noted, "those socks wouldn't reek so and she'd not have near as many slubs in her yarn."

"Bess is no fool. Why should she bother with hard work?" Rachel Mulberry said as she hung a pot full of scrubbed potatoes to boil. "The woman never fails to sell every pair of socks she makes, slubs or no."

Bess Hawkins must have said something awfully funny, for the men she held in thrall burst into laughter. Tom pushed his hat back on his head.

Maggie stood with the chamomile poultice hot in the palm of her hand, transfixed by the scene—Tom's handsome smile and bright blue eyes focused on another. He delved into his pouch and handed the woman a coin. Bess boldly reached up, teased her finger along his jawline, and handed him a pair of socks. The other men began to digging in pockets. Amid a flurry of giggles, Bess Hawkins exchanged socks for silver, emptying her basket.

"Mr. Wallen deems buying Mistress Hawkins's wares a Christian kindness." Eileen Wallen hoisted her baby onto her shoulder for a burping. "After all, the woman's husband has gone missing, poor thing."

Smiling and waving gaily to her hapless customers, Bess turned and sauntered toward the cookhearth, well aware of the many eyes admiring her departure.

"She doesna look so bad off t' me," Maggie observed.

Bess wore a gray silk skirt cut so her ruby-red petticoat flashed with every step. A bright blue bodice set off a crisp white blouse fit tight to slender arms with flounced lace at the elbows. The straw hat pinned over a ruffled mobcap was trimmed with crimson ribbon roses. With one hand deep in the pocket tied to her slender waist, Bess jingled the coins just earned and greeted the women at the cookhearth with a hearty "Good day, good wives."

"Good day, Bess." Naomi was the first to return the greeting, spurring the others to chime in with halfhearted "good days" of their own. Maggie collected her wits and pressed the poultice to Ada's neck, securing it there with a strip of linen.

Ada sighed. "Och, Maggie-lass, that is pure heaven."

"I thought I heard tell of a midwife come to station . . ." Bess set her basket on the table and gave Maggie a good once-over.

Naomi beamed. "That'd be our new gal—Maggie."

Flustered under Bess's keen-eyed scrutiny, Maggie gathered her things into her basket. Acutely aware of her drab, threadbare attire and capless head, she couldn't help but compare herself to the woman.

Where Maggie was dark, Bess Hawkins was as bright as a new-struck coin, with fresh, fair skin she carefully kept shielded from the sun's ravage. Wisps of copper-red hair tickled the ruffled edge of her mobcap and she watched Maggie with confident blue eyes.

"Maggie, is it?" Bess Hawkins called with a tilt of her head. "Might we have a word?"

Surprised, Maggie took her basket and joined Bess at the far side of the hearth.

"They say you have a tooth powder . . ."

"Aye." Maggie set her basket down. Squat on haunches, she fished out a twist of the powder and held it up to Bess. "Mix a paste in the palm of yer hand. Use it with a birch twig t' give yer teeth a good scrub—one penny."

Bess dropped to a crouch and pressed a Spanish dollar into Maggie's hand.

"Ah, no, mistress." Maggie stared at the coin in her hand. "I dinna have the silver t' make change . . ."

Bess folded Maggie's fingers over the dollar. "Wild carrot—d'you have any?"

Maggie met Bess's eye with a curt nod and slipped the silver into her pocket. She dug through her basket and produced a bulging sack the size of her fist.

With a furtive glance over her shoulder, Bess snatched the sack and stuffed it into her pocket. Maggie laid a hand on the woman's forearm and whispered, "Chew it well afore ye swallow, aye? A generous spoonful—no more'n a day after ye correspond with a man."

"Mind your tongue," Bess rasped. Shrugging Maggie off, she stood upright and a smile blossomed on her heart-shaped face. She straightened her skirts and fluffed the lace at her sleeves. "Thank you ever so, Maggie. Such a nasty toothache . . ." She patted the bulge in her pocket. "I'm certain this will do the trick."

Maggie stood with folded arms, watching Bess Hawkins swing and sway her way over to where Tom, Seth, and a few men gathered at the smithy.

Ada came to stand beside Maggie. Issuing a Scottish snort, she muttered, "Toothache, mine arse."

⟨⊛⟩

Ada Buchanan paid in chicks. Maggie cradled the three peeping balls of fluff in her apron until Naomi came to the rescue with a borrowed egg basket in hand. The baby birds tumbled into the basket in stunned silence, offering a brief interlude before striking up the peep chorus anew.

"Well, they'll be good in the pot one day," Naomi said.

"Aye, but it's coin what buys cloth." Maggie jangled the silver in her pocket—six triangular bits lopped from Spanish dollars plus one whole dollar from the transaction with Bess Hawkins. Though the Martins had a legal right to her earnings, they insisted the proceeds were hers to keep. She closed her fist tight to the loose silver, relishing the bite of clipped pieces digging into her palm—her first profit in the New World—more than she'd ever earned before.

Something thumped into the dirt at her heels. Maggie turned to find the renegade lad, Simon Peavey, looking every inch a Red Indian brave. Shiny-chested and smelling strong of yarrow mash and bear grease, he'd discarded his silly wig and red coat for a striped blanket draped over one shoulder and belted at the waist. Silver trinkets decorating his long braids and ears flickered in the sunlight. He gestured with flat hand extended to the furry bundle at her feet. "For you, miss."

"For me?"

"A pair of beaver pelts." Simon pointed to his face. "For tendin' to my wound."

"Fine pelts like these are worth a pretty penny," Naomi noted. "At least three dollars apiece."

Maggie shook her head. "It's too much, lad . . ."

"'Tain't too much for me." Simon blinked green, guileless eyes and his features softened in a hopeful expression. "Please, miss— a gift—I'd be right shamed if you didn't keep 'em."

Maggie thought a moment and nodded. "Aye—a lovely gift, and I thank ye kindly."

Simon turned about-face so abrupt, she almost didn't catch the boyish smile he flashed. Maggie muscled the bundle up onto the stump, watching him stride straight-spined through the gates. "Truly an oddling, he is . . ."

"Poor boy was too long among them Injuns." Naomi ran a hand through the lush fur. "Try as he might, that one'll never shite a white man's turd."

The two of them were clipping the bindings to further inspect the pelts when Elder Willie marched from behind the forge, circling a hammer inside a triangle of iron. Everyone set aside their doings and moved toward Willie, who'd climbed onto a tree stump, clanging away.

About fifty men, half as many women, and again as many children assembled in the center of the fortyard. The women settled down on tree stumps, organizing small children to sit quiet at their feet. Men and adolescent boys stood on the periphery in loose cadres, leaning on rifles and muskets. Maggie and Naomi found a place beside Susannah Bledsoe. Both Tom and Seth stood not too far behind Willie. When it seemed the smith had drawn everyone's attention, he ceased his clanging and spoke.

"Our *gut* friend Tom Roberts brings *mit* him some news."

Tom seemed startled by the brief introduction. He paused to lay his rifle on the ground, then mounted the speaking stump and cleared his throat. "Out on the trail, I met up with a hunter. Some of you may know him—Guy DeMontforte—Frenchman from the Illinois. He told news of some consequence and I felt obliged to turkey-tail back and pass it along." Tom slipped his hat off and shifted his weight, uncomfortable without his rifle in hand. "I figure you've all heard talk of Pontiac, the Ottawa chief up north . . ."

Maggie glanced from side to side. Heads bobbed and a low murmur floated through the crowd. Naomi clutched her hand. Susannah's squabbling twins were shushed with a sharp smack to the back of each head.

"Well, it seems the talk has merit. Pontiac's been moving among the northern tribes, stirring up hell with a long spoon. He's managed to form an alliance—Ottawa, Wyandot, Chippewa, Miamis, Sauk, Seneca, Delaware, Mingo, Potawatomi— all banded together."

The string of odd words didn't mean much to Maggie, but the settlers grew stone-still as each exotic name tumbled from Tom's lips. Women leaned in, eyes wide, their mouths taut, thin lines. The men all stood ramrod stiff, white-knuckled fists gripping weapons tight.

"I'd as lief not be the bearer of bad tidings, but Pontiac has sounded the war cry. His message to his brethren is this—'lift the hatchet against the English and wipe them from the face of the earth.'" Tom's upraised palm quelled a wave of outraged muttering. "Listen up! Forts Detroit and Pitt are both under siege . . ." Tom paused. "Fort Sandusky on Lake Erie, Fort St. Joseph on Lake Huron, Fort Miamis, Forts Ouitenon, Michilimackinac, Venango, Presque Isle, Le Boeuf, Fort Edward—every British post along the Ohio and Great Lakes is taken."

A feminine moan rose up in harmony with a masculine groan, self-restraint broke, and everyone began speaking at once, rendering them all incoherent. Tom waited for the concert of voices to dim. Willie banged iron and attention was restored.

"There is some good news—this mayhem is confined to the garrisons up in the old French territory, and hopefully, it will go no further. Commander Henry Bouquet and a division of Regulars are dispatched to regain order. That's all I know." Tom stepped down.

Seth leaped up onto the stump. "I say we are verra lucky—lucky indeed to have a friend like Tom Roberts. We thank ye, Tom." A scattering of applause and a few feeble huzzahs pierced the tension left in the wake of Tom's announcement.

"I say . . ." Seth shouted louder to be heard above the agitated crowd. "I say this: forewarned is forearmed." He pointed toward the unfinished stockade wall. "Our task is clear. We need to fell at least twenty trees. A show of hands—who can stay on during the week as axmen?"

The Willies raised their hands, along with six of the younger men not burdened with families to care for. Willie the Elder joined Seth on the stump. "Ve must purchase stores—meat, meal, gunpowder, lead . . ."

"Aye," Seth agreed. "Let us hope for the best, but prepare for the worst. We will come thegither to finish the station and collect funds to prepare for siege. Spread the word—a gather-all, four days hence."

10

The Gather-All

"It's time, lassies," Seth announced. "Set yer baskets here and line up along the wall."

Maggie placed her basket with five others. She squinted up at the sun ball scorching a hole low in the early evening sky and found a shady spot near the new section of stockade wall.

The men had labored since sunup to enclose the station sturdy and safe. Roundabout women contributed a fair share, cooking meals and preparing foodstuffs to store for a possible siege. The setting sun signaled the time to relax and enjoy the camaraderie of good friends, food, and music—just reward for a hard day's work.

Maggie tugged at her stays. *That minikin Naomi had the strength of ten men when she tightened these laces.* The stiff corset ribbed with baleen drilled a painful hole beneath each armpit. She cursed her vanity, sorely regretting the three bits squandered on the stays. But that had been the only bad bargain she'd made, trading her silver and pelts for enough fabric and thread to outfit herself with a new wardrobe. Maggie had stitched like a demon into the wee hours to have new togs ready to wear to the gather-all.

She smoothed the pale gray-and-blue-striped dimity skirt with pleasure, never having owned anything so fine. Her blouse and petticoat were cut from an ell-wide length of crisp linen shirting, and she fashioned a bodice from a remnant of indigo twill the peddler man let her have for a song. Maggie pinned her hair into a sleek coil with two new silver hairpins, and Naomi gave her a pair of white cotton hose and garters to wear.

"Gather 'round! Gather 'round for the supper-basket auction!" Seth clanged a cowbell and hopped up onto a large tree stump in front of the row of young women. Maggie's fellow basketeers squealed and exchanged whispers in anticipation.

"Bachelors to the fore!" Seth encouraged a scrum of young men to congregate in a heap nearer his rostrum. Sitting and standing in a loose band around the core of single men were those too old, too married, or too young to partake in the auction, but still eager to enjoy the spectacle.

Maggie pulled a square of muslinet from her pocket and dabbed the puddle of sweat collected at the apex of her cleavage. She looked up to find at least two dozen pairs of man-eyes plastered on her bosom. Shaking her head, she sighed.

"Gentlemen, let the bidding begin." Seth held aloft a small basket tied with a bow of yellow ribbon that matched exactly the ribbon adorning petite Sally Anderson's soft brown hair. "Have I two bits?"

"For that puny meal I'll bid two cents." Charlie Pritchard drew a masculine laugh and a feminine scowl with his rude remark.

"Piggy-eyed, pimple-snout Pritchard, so concerned for the size of his meal," whispered Janet Wheeler, the girl to Maggie's left. "Him with a belly like a rain barrel."

Maggie snickered.

"Included with each supper basket, the pleasure of sharing a meal *in private* with one of the bonnie lassies ye see here." Seth waved his arm toward the girls with a courtly flourish. He glanced over his shoulder at tiny Sally Anderson. "They say good things come in small packages."

Sally blushed pretty, which compelled Billy Barlowe to bleat out a bid of two bits and the auction began in earnest. With only six baskets for sale, the competition grew fierce.

". . . SOLD to Hamish Macauley for three and a half dollars!" Seth rang the cowbell with vigor and handed the tiny basket to the fiery-haired Macaulay. Maggie stifled a giggle when the huge, thumping frontiersman encased Sally's hand in his paw and strolled gallantly out the gate.

The gang of single men watched the mismatched pair leave and collectively glanced back to the baskets sitting at the base of Seth's tree stump—but five left. Hamish's conquest seemed to steel the lads with new determination.

Maggie had been disappointed to learn Tom'd left Round-about days before, off on his summer hunt, she supposed. She perused the faces in the crowd of potential dinner mates and could put a name to only a few of them. Willie Wagner the younger stood at the edge of the crowd, gawking at the line of ladies, his moist mouth agape.

Maggie nudged Janet. "That Willie—carries his brains in his bollocks, na?"

Janet giggled into her hand. "But he has a good trade. Pa says he's plump in the pocket."

"What am I bid?" Seth held up a basket trimmed with a spray of laurel blossoms, and Alice Springer tilted her head for all to notice the matching pink flower tucked Spanish-lady style behind her right ear.

"Mr. Raeburn," Seth called. "What say ye? Two bits."

Jamie Raeburn obliged, opening the bidding with a shout of "Two bits."

Janet nudged Maggie and whispered, "The way I heard it, Alice let Jamie open her bid at the corn shucking."

Maggie absorbed this tidbit of gossip, eyeing Jamie Raeburn standing among the bidders, slender as lath with archangel good looks. "That one seems overaware of himself," she observed. "All vine and no potatoes."

"A-yep—thinks he hung the moon," Janet agreed. "I, for one, wouldn't have him if his hair were strung with gold."

Jamie Raeburn remained silent after his initial bid, and shadow-shy Will Russell won Miss Springer's basket for the sum of three dollars. Too timid to take his lady by the hand, Will traipsed after Alice like a lost sheep. As they passed through the gates, Maggie saw the renegade lad, Simon Peavey, coming into the station to join the auction crowd.

Simon had decked himself out British Regular–style for the gather-all, brass buttons glinting on his red wool coat. His bulky braids were tucked under his singed, cockeyed wig and he carried a large bale of hides lashed like a pack to his back. Maggie was happy to see the powder burns on his face looked to be healing well.

Simon created a bit of a stir, shoving and pushing his way to the front. He struggled free of the straps and dropped the bale on his back to rest at the base of Seth's tree stump. He glanced up and caught Maggie's eye with a look of such fierce intensity, she lost her smile and stumbled back a step. Janet pinched Maggie on the arm. "It's your turn."

Seth hefted Maggie's big basket, conspicuous by its lack of decoration. "Aye . . . plenty to eat in here, lads." Everyone laughed when Seth set the basket down, rubbing his arm as if to sooth sore muscles. "Who will open the bidding?"

"Two bits." Jamie Raeburn flashed Maggie a gorgeous smile.

"Four bits."

"Five bits!"

The bids came fast and furious. The price for her basket rose swiftly, and when the price grew too dear, many of the bidders— Jamie Raeburn included—dropped away.

"Four dollars!" Willie Wagner topped the last bid.

"Four dollars once . . ." Seth intoned. "Four dollars twice . . ."

"Five bucks!" Simon Peavey shouted.

Whistles and low-toned mutterings filtered through the crowd.

"Seth," Jamie Raeburn complained. "I don't see why we need allow this greasy Indian . . ."

Simon shifted his stance, and quick-slipping the rifle from his shoulder, he cocked the lock. Through gritted teeth he said, "I'm as white as any of you."

"No argument, lad." Seth kept a calm voice. "But I'll have ye lay that weapon aside, afore I continue with the auction."

Simon backed off glaring; the muscle at his jaw taut and twitching, he laid his rifle at Seth's feet. Seth heaved a sigh. "Peavey has the bid at five . . ."

"Five and half," Willie countered, agitated pink splotching his fair cheeks. "Silver."

Maggie was none too keen on having her basket acquired by either Simon or Willie, and she shot Seth a look that would have curdled a pail of milk.

"Five and a half dollars once . . ." Seth began.

"Eight." Grim-faced, Peavey crossed his arms over his chest. "Eight bucks."

With Maggie's sharp eyes boring two holes in the back of his head, poor Seth was desperate for another bidder. "Come now, lads," he pleaded. "A good cause, this—Young Willie, are ye bid nine?"

Shuffling backward, Willie shook his head and stove his hands into his pockets.

"*Waugh!*" Simon Peavey yelled, and tossed his wig into the air. He threw his head back and ululated a heathen yip that pierced eardrums and sent a cold stream down Maggie's spine. "*Coo-wigh-wigh-wigh!*"

"Now, just hold on there, Simon," Seth warned. "I've yet to close out the bidding. The bid is eight bucks to Peavey . . . eight bucks goin' once . . ." He raised the cowbell. "Eight bucks goin' twice . . ."

"Ten dollars!"

Standing far left of the crowd of bachelors, dusty and grimy Tom Roberts pushed his hat back, leaned on his rifle, and smiled through a scruffy beard. His faded blue shirt was ringed with salt stains and dark with sweat. In his right hand he cupped a leather sack heavy with coin. Maggie restrained an urge to run to him, happier at that moment than she could ever remember being in her whole life.

"Ten dollars once," Seth shouted, smiling. "Ten dollars twice . . ."

"Fifteen." Peavey shifted his ramrod stance to rest his foot on the bale of hides. "Fifteen bucks."

Maggie could not believe her ears. Simon's bid served to squash the air from her lungs. Fifteen buckskins—equal to fifteen silver dollars—a ridiculous amount to spend on a supper basket.

"Fifteen, lad," Seth cautioned. "Are ye certain?"

Renegade black braids dangled along the gold braid of his jacket. Simon squared his shoulders and nodded. Janet took hold of Maggie's hand.

Seth took up the cowbell. "Fifteen bucks once . . ."

Maggie squeezed Janet's hand, staring straight ahead.

"Fifteen twice . . ."

She fell back to lean against the wall.

"Fifteen thrice . . ."

Tom's leather sack landed with a jangle at Seth's feet.

"Thirty silver dollars."

The crowd gasped, choked, and coasted into utter silence. Tom stepped forward; sliding his rifle to rest in the crook of his arm, he pulled the hammer to click back. "That's ten more dollars than hides in your bale, Simon."

Peavey cast a wary glance at Tom's half-cocked weapon and held his hands out wide, showing empty palms open. With angry-arrow eyes shifting from Tom to Seth, he bent to hoist the bale onto his back, snatched up his rifle, and stormed away.

Seth clanged the cowbell with full fervor. "SOLD to Tom Roberts!"

⋰⋱

"*Hoy!* Tom! Hold up . . . yer supposed t' be enjoyin' the pleasure of my company." With skirts bunched over her arm, she struggled to keep up, picking her way through the thick brush. "There's no bloody path here. If my new togs get spoilt I'll . . ." Maggie trailed off, at a loss to come up with anything to threaten him with.

Sliding his rifle to hang over his shoulder, Tom turned to wait. Supper basket in his left hand, he offered Maggie his right. "C'mon—not too far now—just up ahead."

She slipped her hand into his, her knuckles grinding and rolling in his rough grip, and Tom helped her up a steep incline through a thick understory of mountain laurel. At the crest of the ridge they burst through the dense bramble to witness a sky aflame. Beneath the auburn sun tickling the horizon, the mountains ranged into a silent, undulating sea of purple and blue ribbons as far as the eye could see.

"Megstie me!" Maggie blew out a breath. "This is quite a sight . . ."

"A favorite spot of mine," Tom said, pleased by her reaction. "I call it the Stone Man Overlook—named it for that fella there." He pointed to a lone chunk of limestone jutting up near the edge. Nature had hewn a pensive face into the craggy stone, complete with hook nose and heavy brows.

Tom plunked the basket down and divested himself of hat, rifle, powder horn, and pouch. He sank to sit propped against a lichen-covered oak with long legs outstretched. "Break out the grub. I swear I'm so hungry, my gut's beginning to think my throat's cut."

Maggie laughed. She sat opposite Tom on the thick cushion of leaves, her legs folded and tucked to the side. She spread a square of worn calico between them and delved into her basket.

On the cloth she centered a blackberry cobbler, its crunchy

topping sweetened with muscovado sugar. Alongside the cobbler, she set eight pieces of fried chicken tied loose in a grease-stained scrap of flannel. Maggie also brought out a small wheel of cheese wrapped in fern leaves and a crock of bread-and-butter pickles, perfect with the cornbread and bottle of rose-hip tea she'd baked and brewed that morning.

Tom frowned, rummaging through his pouch. "Can't seem to lay hand to my . . . oh, never mind." He smiled and raised his horn spoon, triumphant. "Here 'tis."

Supper laid out, Maggie turned back to gaze at the sinking sun—the gloaming—her favorite time of day. The stunning vista drove home a bittersweet awareness of just how very far she'd come. The Blue Ridge—so vast and rich with color—quite different from the stark crags of the Grampians, half a world away in Scotland.

"Have ye been there? Beyond those mountains?" she asked, turning around to find Tom shoveling blackberry cobbler into his mouth. "Och!" Maggie snatched the tin from him. "The sweet's for the *end* and we're meant to *share* it."

Tom smiled a wicked smile, arched his eyebrows, and licked his spoon. He shifted to sit a bit closer to Maggie. "Naomi sure bakes a fine cobbler."

Annoyed he assumed—no matter rightly so—that Naomi had provided the cobbler, Maggie resented his willingness to gobble the whole of it without sharing a bite.

Good manners suffer bad manners. She took a deep breath and reminded herself—save for Tom, she would right now be suffering Simon Peavey's volatile heathen manners. She handed him a piece of chicken. "Would ye care fer some tea?" she asked, uncorking the bottle.

"No thanks." Tom dug into his pouch and offered up a flask of his own. "Seth's finest . . ." He proceeded to wolf his supper like a starved man, only interrupting his chewing to take gulps from his bottle. Maggie nibbled a chicken leg in silence. The picnic was not progressing quite as she had envisioned.

"Delicious." Tom groaned and tossed the bone from his seventh piece of chicken over his shoulder. "That sure smoothed the wrinkles from my belly. Worth every dollar."

"The way ye galloped yer meal, I'm surprised ye tasted any of it," Maggie muttered. "A deadly sin that—gluttony."

"Glutton! I've spent three days running news up and down the frontier—not taking time for much more than the jerky and johnnycakes in my pouch, and you label me a glutton?" Tom eyed the cobbler and cast Maggie a little lad look that once most probably melted the taut Quaker cords of his mother's heart.

She giggled and handed him the cobbler. "Aye, g'won then, have yer sweet."

He scooted to sit side by side with Maggie. Holding the tin between them, he grinned and offered her a sticky spoonful. "You said we are meant to share it . . ." Taking turns, he fed her a spoonful and then one to himself. As he scraped up the last of it, Tom leaned forward, pointing with the spoon to the corner of Maggie's mouth. "Thee's left a bit of berry there . . ."

Maggie caught the sweet morsel on the tip of her tongue, smiling at his slip into the Quaker informal. With his handsome face only inches from hers, Maggie held on to the smell of this man, a heady blend of leather, sweat, wood smoke, and whiskey. She restrained a strong urge to run a fingertip along his stubbly jaw.

"Three days on the run and ye havna shaved . . ."

"Or bathed . . ." Tom admitted with a crinkle of his nose. "I had to hustle to get back in time to save your bacon at the auction."

Maggie groaned. "I should have known better than let Seth and Naomi talk me into such foolishness. Thirty dollars is an awful lot of silver lost on my account."

"Like Seth says"—Tom reached up and tucked a tendril of hair back behind Maggie's ear, slipping his hand to trail down her neck and skim the honey-silk skin along the crest of her breast—"all for a good cause."

Jolted by the intimacy of his touch, Maggie shied back like a filly being broke to halter. She scooted sideways and began collecting the remains of the picnic into her basket. "We—we ought be gettin' back. Naomi and Seth will worry if I'm not back soon . . ."

"Naw, they've left for home." Tom, smiling at her skittishness, moved back to lean against the tree, bringing his bottle along for company. "Naomi was feeling out of sorts—tired—but she didn't want for you to worry or miss the frolic. I told Seth never mind, and promised I'd see you home." He took a deep swallow and wiped the top of the bottle on his sleeve. "Share a drink?"

Maggie skimmed a hand along her neck, retracing the warm trail his touch had impressed on her skin. "It's almost dark, the frolic's about to begin . . ."

Tom sat quiet beneath his tree. Twilight and a three-day beard cast a dangerous shadow across his features. Eyes filled with blatant yearning skimmed over Maggie's curves. A prickly ball of anxiety settled into the pit of her stomach, and she leaned forward to quick crumple the calico into her basket, anxious to get back to the station. She said, "Time to go, na?"

"Come sit . . ." He patted the ground with one hand and held up the whiskey in the other. "Sit beside me and share a sip."

Maggie hopped to her feet and stood over him. "I think I can hear the fiddler tunin' up . . . let's be off, or we'll miss the frolic."

Tom set the bottle aside, grabbed Maggie's hand, and pulled her down to land in a gasp and tumble across his lap. "Let's have a frolic of our own."

Maggie forced a halfhearted giggle. "Quit this foolishness—yer worse fer the drink . . ." She tried to stand, but he held her tight, folded in his arms. She felt the power of his need pressing up against her leg and knew he wasn't about to let her go.

Tom kissed her. Pushing his tongue into her mouth, he bent her back, his mouth pressed hard on hers. With one arm locked around her shoulders, he slid his free hand up the tangle of her skirts, endeavoring to force a passage between her thighs. The boning in her stays gouged painful ridges into her flesh, and Maggie couldn't catch a breath, trapped beneath Tom, his every muscle wound tight against her.

"Give us a little sugar, Maggie," he rasped in her ear.

"My knee t' yer bollocks is what I'll give ye!" Bracing both hands against his chest and shoving with all her might, she propelled herself free and scuttled away like a crab. "Brute!" Maggie swiped the sour combination of whiskey and berry cobbler from her lips. She jumped to her feet and swept debris from her skirt. "I'm no Bess Hawkins to fall back and spread my legs fer yer drunken pleasure, thirty dollars or no!"

Her hair tumbled loose over her shoulder. Crying, "Och, my pins! I've lost my pins," Maggie fell to her knees in a frantic search through the leaves.

Tom sat there blinking, looking much like he'd woken from a deep sleep. "Why're you in such a swither? I meant thee no harm . . ."

"Stiek yer whiskey-guzzling Quaker gob and help me find my pins afore it's too dark . . . they're silver plate and cost me a pretty penny."

"There's one." Tom crawled over and pulled a hairpin dangling precariously from the end of Maggie's waist-long curls, offering it to her.

She snatched it from him and plucked up the second pin, caught on the frayed edge of his shirt collar. "And here's the other." She sat back and twisted her hair into a knot. Tom scrambled to his feet and offered Maggie a hand up but she shrugged him off. She rose and arranged her skirts over her arm. "Bring the basket," she ordered.

Tom heaved a sigh and took up his gear and the basket. Punching a path through the bramble, he headed back to the station.

Maggie followed a few paces behind as the fiddler's melody wove its way up through the trees, clear and sweet in the silence between them.

❦

Sputtering pine-pitch torches jutting from the stockade illuminated a stumpless patch of ground that served as the dance floor. With bounce and expectation, the dancers faced one another in two parallel lines while the three musicians huddled beneath the blockhouse sharing a pint and a loud argument.

Phil Smillie put an abrupt end to the heated discussion and began blowing a tune on his flute. Brian Malloy shrugged. Resting his bodhran on his knee, he drew a heartbeat from the goatskin tacked taut to a circlet of birch with a stick that looked like a double-ended spoon. After a few measures, scowling John Springer braced his fiddle against his chest, set his foot tapping, and joined in on "The Blue Ribbon Reel."

Maggie linked hands with handsome Jamie Raeburn and the pair skipped between the two rows of dancers, stopping at center to meet another couple. Both couples disengaged and executed an intricate figure-eight maneuver. The pairs joined hands once again to foot it back and fall into their original places.

Tom loitered off to the side in the shadows of the stockade wall, his back pressed against its rough timber. Eyes a-squint, he swallowed back an overwhelming urge to smash his fist into Jamie Raeburn's smiling face.

Goddamn it, but isn't she lovely . . . Laughing and clapping with her hair all a-towsie and her tawny skin slick with perspiration, Maggie was by far the most beautiful girl at the gather-all—probably the most beautiful girl he'd ever seen.

Goddamn it! Tom banged a fist to the wall. Up to this day, he'd considered Raeburn a friend, but as he watched Maggie twirling under Jamie's arm, Tom wanted nothing more than to pound the man into the dirt. Then he would take Maggie in his arms and they would spin around and around and around, until everyone and everything faded into a whirling blur.

I mucked it up . . .

"A good lass," Seth called her. Tom snorted. He surely had no experience wooing one of those. How stiff, how absolutely frightened she'd been when he pulled her into his arms up on the ridge—shoving a hand between her legs as if she were no better than a two-shilling whore—he groaned to think of it. *Came at her like buck in rut . . .* Tom could almost hear his father's voice in his head. *That's what comes of living lax . . . too long away from family and proper society.* At the very least, Tom figured, he owed Maggie an apology.

The music ended with a whoop. Jamie tucked Maggie's arm under his and they sauntered to the smithy, where Ada Buchanan was busy pulling pints for a thirsty crowd. Raeburn abandoned Maggie and elbowed into the fray.

Tom pushed off the wall and rushed to catch her alone. She looked up to see him approach and he winced to see her happy exuberance devolve into wary apprehension. He swept the hat from his head. "Maggie, might I have a word with thee?"

Her jaw tensed. She nodded.

"It's like this." Tom drew a deep breath. "I truly regret the way I treated thee and I beg pardon."

Her features seemed to soften a bit and she met his eye direct. "Ye were quite rough, na?"

"Well . . ." Tom combed fingers back through his hair. "I know it's no excuse, but I was a bit worse for the drink . . ." He shifted from foot to foot, accordion-crunching his felt hat between his hands. "I just hope you can find it in your heart to forgive me, is all."

The light returned to Maggie's eye and she smiled a little. "Look at ye—hat in hand no less. Och, yer such a gowk." She sent him back a step with a two-handed shove.

He fit his hat onto his head and plowed onward. "While I'm

not much for dancing, maybe the next time the fellas strike up a tune, maybe you and me . . . maybe we could give it a go?"

Maggie tipped her head and her smile widened. "Aye—maybe."

The knot in Tom's chest loosened, and just as he relaxed enough to manage a reciprocal smile, Bess Hawkins rushed up in a swish of panniered brocade. Slipperier than a naked Iroquois, Bess wormed her way between them and clamped on to Tom's arm.

"Tom Roberts! I swan! Where have you been hiding?"

In a blink of the eye, each woman took the measure of the other, and Tom found himself caught in the massive wave of malevolent spite crashing between them. He struggled to extricate his arm from Bess's grip in a gentlemanly fashion and blathered introductions. "Ah . . . Maggie Duncan—Bess Hawkins."

"Aye," Maggie said, cocking her chin up a notch. "*Mrs.* Hawkins and I are well acquainted, na?"

"Martin's bondgirl . . ." Bess tossed a nod. "I didn't even notice her standing there." She tightened her grip, clinging to Tom's arm tighter than a tick to a running hound.

Maggie stepped back, folded her arms, and gave Tom a look that reminded him so much of his mother, it was all he could do to keep from squirming.

"Old friends, are ye?" she asked.

"Old friends? Naw . . . naw . . . I wouldn't say that." Tom shook his head and struggled to free his arm from Bess's iron grip. "Her husband, Bert—Bert and I have hunted together . . ."

"How you talk!" Bess gave him a bump with her hip. "Why, we go way back. Recall two summers ago? Up there on Stone Man?"

Maggie's face puddinged and she looked as if her bread had just fallen buttered side down into the dirt. Before Tom could utter another word, she gathered her skirts and barreled past him, joining up with Jamie Raeburn emerging from the crowd bearing a pair of pints. Tom slumped a bit to see Maggie reward Jamie with a soft kiss on the lips.

"Indentured." Bess sneered, triumphant. "Beggars, thieves, cutthroats, and whores—the lot of 'em." John Springer began to tune his fiddle and Bess squealed, tugging Tom toward the dance floor.

Tom dug in his heels and none too gently pried her fingers from his arm. "Leave off, Bess. You know damn well I'm not one for dancing." He folded his arms across his chest, looking over Bess's head to see Maggie and Jamie line up for the next reel. The musicians struck up a tune and the dance began.

Undaunted, Bess wound an arm about Tom's waist. "Truth is," she purred, resting her head against his shoulder, "I'd rather not waste time dancing." She dallied coy fingers along the hem of his breechclout.

It had been a long time since Tom had enjoyed the company of a willing woman, and here was Bess Hawkins—a toothsome piece—ready to oblige in exchange for a coin or two. He cast a fleeting glance to Maggie, having a grand time dancing with Jamie Raeburn, and allowed Bess to draw him deep into the shadows. She coaxed an expert hand inside his breechclout and cupped his parts. Tom heaved a sigh, closed his eyes, and leaned back against the wall to enjoy her ministrations.

But rather than pleasure, Tom found himself plagued by an onslaught of conscience. *A married woman,* he thought as Bess nuzzled his neck. *Another man's wife.* Tom slipped his hands around her slender waist and buried his nose in her neck, which smelled of elder flower. *Bert ought know better than to leave his wife unattended. Poor Bert . . .* Tom pulled away. "This is wrong, Bess."

"Um-hmm," she moaned, pressing forward, plump breasts crushed against his chest, her hand still tangled within his clout. "We are ever so wicked, aren't we?"

"I mean it, Bess." Tom tried to wheedle out from her embrace. "Bert's a friend of mine . . . and this ain't right." She grabbed his hand and placed it upon her breast.

Tom forced his arms to his sides, fists clenched. "I'm not going to do this."

Her warm palm inside his breechclout elicited a response quite contrary to his protestations. Firming her grip, she went up on tiptoe and whispered husky in his ear, "Ahh, but your man here begs to differ."

"Stop it—"

She continued to ignore his sudden fit of morality, heedless fingers working magic between his legs, her tongue and teeth nuzzling and nipping his neck. Fearful he was approaching the point of no return, Tom gritted his teeth. "I mean it." He grasped her rough by the upper arms and pushed her hard, causing her to stumble back a few paces. "I said STOP." Tom slumped back against the wall and drew a deep breath.

The music squealed to a rollicking finish, drawing a burst of applause. Tom could see Maggie in the torchlight, laughing and clapping, calling for another tune.

Stunned, Bess rubbed her arms. "What in the world has gotten into you?"

"It just ain't right." He tugged at the flap of his slack clout to fit it tight. "Bert being a friend of mine and all . . ."

"Fine time for you to develop a creed," Bess snapped, shaking out her skirts and smoothing the fabric.

"Sorry—you'll have t' find another dance partner."

He left Bess behind and slunk away. Avoiding the crowd of dancers surrounding the smithy, he sank down onto a tree stump—elbow to knee, chin to fist— absolutely flummoxed as to how and why he had spurned the favors of a beautiful, willing woman.

Bess wasted no time pining. She slithered off to prowl through the crowd. In no time at all, she latched onto Willie the elder, coiling around his arm like a copperhead ready to strike.

Alistair Buchanan came Tom's way, a tankard clenched in

each hamhock fist. "No loss there, lad," the old Scotsman said, following Tom's gaze. "Th' woman's a viper—her ear ever tuned to the amount of silver jangling in a man's pocket. I pity poor Bert. He hasna a clue."

Alistair handed Tom a pint and situated himself on the stump. At sixty years, the man cut an impressive figure dressed in his highlander finery. His kilt, patterned in red-and-black tartan, was gathered at one shoulder with a striking circular brooch—a silver dragon devouring its own tail. A badger-skin pouch, beady-eyed head intact, hung centered from his waist, and a soft, blue wool cap adorned with two slender pheasant feathers crowned his unruly silver hair.

Tom tipped his tankard to his benefactor and slugged down a healthy draught. "Compliments, Buchanan. Your missus brews the finest ale this side of the Rogue's Road."

"I dinna ken how she does it—lacking barley and hops, my woman works a miracle with maize and molasses. Tae th' wee wifie!"

"To th' wifie!"

Tom was happy for the company. The two men sat in silence, sipping ale and watching couples pair up for the next dance.

"Martin's bondgirl—" Alistair ventured with pheasant feathers bobbing. "Now, there's a bonnie lass—ye fancy her, na?"

Tom studied the inside of his cup. "Sure I fancy her, as do at least twenty other fellas."

"Aye, yiv th' right of it. Every man and his brother would like to dock a boat in that harbor—all the more reason t' not sit idle. G'won and ask her for a dance. Thirty silver pieces entitles ye t' one dance at least."

Tom shook his head, staring at his feet. "Dancing is not a talent within my compass."

"Pish. G'won . . ."

"I'm a product of a guarded education—music and dancing strictly proscribed."

"Hmmph, Quakers." Buchanan shot Tom an elbow to the ribs. "Tell me this—what's stoppin' ye from taking th' lass intae th' shadows for a kiss and cuddle?"

Tom picked up a stick and began scratching a series of chevrons into the hard-packed dirt at his feet. "Truth is, I've gormed it all up, Alistair. When it comes t' women—nice women anyway—I'm as caw-handed and cork-brained as any pimply boy."

"Truth is, all the while ye sit here like the butcher's dog, sniffin' but not eating the meat, yon Raeburn blazes a trail beneath yer lassie's skirt."

Tom took a sip from his tankard. Peering over the rim, he watched Jamie Raeburn settle his hand at the small of Maggie's back and steer her away from the yammering group of dancers. Old Alistair slammed his tankard down with a thunk and gave Tom a two-handed shove that sent him topsy-turvy, arse end into the dirt. The Scotsman loomed over Tom.

"Raeburn's naught but a prissy, pindling Englishman—he couldna wrest a tattie from a baby. Chase the poacher off and stake a claim."

Jamie Raeburn bent his golden head to Maggie's and whispered into her ear.

Tom sat in the dirt, jaw clenched. "Stake a claim, you say . . ."

"Fight for your lass. Show her how much ye care." Alistair offered him a hand up.

Slicker than a peeled onion, Raeburn twined an arm about Maggie's waist and steered her beyond bright torchlight, through the gates, into the dark.

Alistair continued to devil. "I'm tellin' ye true, Tommy—feather into the bastard."

"Feather into him . . ." Tom repeated, grinding a clenched fist in his palm.

"That's it. Sharp's the word, and quick's the motion." The old man brooked a solid stance, fiercely jabbing at empty air. "One clean blow to the belly and the lass is yourn."

Tom strode with purpose through the gates. Away from the glow of torch and lantern, he could barely make out his outstretched hand as he skirted along the wall. Glisks of yellow light and the twang and twee of the fiddler tuning his instrument keeked between the chinks in the stockade. Tom stopped dead at the scrunch of feet coming his way and called out, "Is that you Maggie? Maggie Duncan!"

"Quit yer gallie-hooin', Tom. There's no more'n three yards betwixt us." Maggie stepped out of the shadows, hand in hand with Jamie Raeburn.

The sight of her so casually comfortable with another man rankled worse than a full-blown blister on both heels. Like a bull on the charge, Tom rushed forward and gave Jamie a sharp shove to the shoulder. "And what are you after, out here in the dark?"

Maggie pushed between the two men. "None of yer concern, Tom Roberts."

"Time to go home, miss." Tom grabbed Maggie by the arm and pulled her along.

Maggie dragged two long furrows in the dirt. "*Let go!* Let go, ye brute! Ye hold no dominion over me."

"I promised your master I'd see you home." Tom resolutely jerked Maggie along with him. "And I aim t' keep my word."

Maggie wailed, flopped down to the ground, and flung one arm wide, imploring Jamie to save her. "*Jamie!*"

Jamie stepped forward. "She's with me, Tom. I'll be taking her home . . ."

Tom let Maggie loose and grabbed two handfuls of Jamie's shirtfront, lifting the man up onto his toes. Their faces but inches apart, he snarled, "I'm in a bad skin, Raeburn. Fool with me and there'll be a new face in hell tomorrow." He flung Jamie to land in a sprawl against the stockade.

"Get up! Get up, Jamie, and give him what for!" Maggie leaped and shouted as Raeburn rose to stand, brushing dirt from his hands.

Even in dim light, it was plain to see Jamie's fair face had gone as white as a freshly plastered wall. Tom cocked his elbows, clenched his fists, and moved forward. "Best make your feet your friends and scuttle off, for I intend to come down on you like an anchor chain!"

Inside the fortyard, the musicians struck up a rousing jig that happened to keep perfect time with Jamie's footfalls thudding off into the darkness. As Maggie's champion ran off, she cupped hands to her mouth, shouting, *"Bloody English COWARD! Tuck tail and run, that's all yer fit for!"* She kicked a clod of clay to smithereens. "I dinna need ye anyway, Jamie Raeburn!" Maggie turned and speared her finger into Tom's chest. "An' neither do I need you. I'll make my own way home in my own good time."

Smirking, Tom caught her by the arm as she tried to push past. "You go right ahead, miss, and the she-bear I was tracking this morning will be licking your tasty bones by day bust."

"*Why?*" Maggie put on a face like a mule eating briars. "Why do ye plague me so?"

"Fetch your things. I'm taking you home."

⸙

Carrying Maggie's big basket in one hand, Tom led her by the other along the ridge trail back to the Martin homeplace. That morning's dewy, shade-dappled path had transformed into a sinister tunnel, filled with the flap of winged predators and wisps of night webs strung across the path, sticking to faces and arms. Maggie held a lantern aloft, but the candle glim seeping through the pierced tin barely illuminated their path.

Tom's silence was the heavy lining to the cloak of night. He didn't speak but to offer Maggie a warning now and then to watch her step over one obstacle or under another. Plodding through menacing darkness, Maggie quickly developed a frontier sense for the worth of a man's protection. And although she bristled thinking on his behavior, she had to admit feeling very safe with her hand in his. After more than a mile with only night noise and the scrush of their moccasined feet on the forest floor for company, Maggie gave in. "Why're ye so quiet?"

"I figured you're vexed with me . . . have a care here," he warned. "Careful over this snarl."

"I am vexed. I'm unused to being treated like a fool."

"Well then, maybe you shouldn't act a fool."

"I suppose it's better to skulk, wallowing in a pint, glowering at one and all. Or strut about with that . . . that Bess Hawkins dangling from yer arm like snot from an old drunk's nose."

"You shouldn't be wandering into the dark with the likes of Jamie Raeburn," Tom countered. "You don't seem to understand, Maggie. A fella like that—hell, every fetchin' fella back at the station for that matter—they all have but one thing on their minds—and that thing dwells beneath that pretty striped skirt. Mind your reputation, miss."

"Ha! A sermon from a rogue who cavorts with a married woman . . ."

"Be quiet!" Tom ordered.

"Dinna dare speak so to me . . ."

Tom tossed her basket into the brush. He stepped behind Maggie, wrapped one arm about her waist, and clapped the other hand over her mouth. Maggie kicked, squirmed, and squealed.

He breathed in her ear, "Somethin's on our trail!"

Maggie ceased struggling and then she felt it, too—a muffled *thud-ump, thud-ump*—reverberating along the soft bottom of the trail. Tom put a finger to his lips. Maggie nodded, wide-eyed. He released his grip and took her by the hand. Slipping under boughs and through bracken, they left the trail to duck behind a large chestnut. Tom leaned around the tree, his every sense peeled sharp. Maggie crowded behind him, the tin lantern still lit in her hand.

"Dowse that light!" Tom snarled through clenched teeth.

Maggie fumbled to open the catch on the tiny door. The hot

metal scorched her fingertip and the lantern toppled to the ground, the flame snuffing itself in the process. As her eyes adjusted to the starlit night, emerging shadows settled in varying values of purple black and deep blue gray. Tom remained so statue-still and quiet, Maggie laid a hand on his shoulder to reassure herself that he was truly there.

"A bear, maybe?" she asked.

Tom drew several long breaths in through his nose. "I'm not nosin' any bear."

Maggie stretched to peer into the blackness beyond Tom's shoulder. A lonesome laurel-blossom breeze rustled in through the leaves, sweeping over the warm spot where her hand met his shoulder. "Probably naught but the wind playin' tricks with our ears," she whispered.

Tom's body shifted, and even though Maggie could not make out his features, she could feel the reproach of his gaze. "Can you hush?"

In absolute stillness, they continued to listen. Maggie slipped her hand to rest square between Tom's shoulder blades. She could feel his breath regular and steady as a bell tolling midnight. His muscle beneath her thumb twitched.

"There's nothing out there. Let's go." Maggie's impatient whisper hissed and cut the silence like cold water drizzled on a hot pan. She stepped around Tom to scramble back up to the trail. He caught Maggie by both arms and pushed her up against the tree trunk.

"Stay put—I'll be right back."

Before Maggie could squeak out a protest, he was gone.

She waited, shifting from one foot to the other, restless as the tip of a cow's tail. Startled by pinching tree-bark fingers grasping the hair she'd twisted into a loose knot at the base of her neck, she gulped back budding panic and squelched the urge to call out for Tom. Maggie loosened the two silver pins, freeing her tresses to spill over her shoulders and roll down to her hips.

She hugged her hair like a blanket, comforted by its smooth silk against her skin.

Then she heard them. Voices carried on the breeze. Male voices in concert with the slow drum of hooves hitting the dirt. A shadow loomed out from the black hole to her right and Maggie gasped as Tom stepped in front of her and placed two fingers to her lips. He leaned in and whispered, "Hush."

The travelers approached the point on the trail directly parallel with Maggie and Tom's position. The fecund smell of horse wafted on the breeze. Hoofbeats plodding forward grew distinct, accompanied by the clank of tin on tin, equine snorts and snuffles, and the random creak of leather tack. Tom settled a hand on Maggie's hip and bent his head to the place where the curve of her shoulder met her neck, his warm breath on her skin, saying, "Two on beastback."

The rhythm of predictable hoofbeats was interrupted by what sounded like a sack of buckshot being poured into a tin washtub, and suddenly the air was filled with the clatter of man and beast.

"*Whoa!*" both horsemen shouted at once. Their mounts reared squealing, snorting spurts of mucus and stamping agitated hooves. After a frantic moment spent calming the horses, a pair of heavy boots descended on the trail.

"*Thatch, thistle, thunder, and thump!*" one man cursed. "Goddamn it, Jeremiah! Your Gunter's chain has come undone again."

"All right, Geordie. I'm coming to lend a hand." Another pair of boots landed with a thud and crunched along the trail. "I do detest night riding."

"Then let's camp here," Geordie suggested with a noisy yawn. "I'm all drug out and saddle sick."

"Na . . . we can get a few miles in yet. You know as well as I, Cavendish will flay us alive if we fail to record the plats by week's end. Hand me the sack."

"Cavendish." Geordie spat out the name. "How I despise that nancy little bugger . . ."

"Aye, but bugger all, how you love his silver." Jeremiah chuckled.

"That I do, Jeremiah, that I do—but right now I would gladly trade it all for a tall pint of March beer and the company of a good-natured woman—the kind who, when you ask her to sit down, will lie down instead."

"I hear you, brother—and that in a nutshell is why we two will never be rich men." Jeremiah laughed in tune to the smooth sound of iron chain slinking its way back into a canvas sack. "There—grab ahold the other end. On the count of three . . ."

After securing their cargo, the two men remounted and continued up the trail. Maggie and Tom stayed quiet and still as the sounds of Geordie and Jeremiah dissipated in the wind.

"Surveyors plotting Portland's grant . . ." Tom mused.

"Surveyors, eh?" Maggie acknowledged. "I wondered what business drew Cavendish men here."

"Cavendish . . . isn't he the Englishman who offered Seth forty pounds for your contract?"

"Aye. He's the one."

"He's Portland's agent?"

"He's Portland's son, the ne'er-do-well they shipped off to the Colonies. Aboard the *Good Intent*, he fancied me and I blacked his eye with my fist, drunken lout. I had to spend the better part of the journey hiding down in the tween—" Maggie sighed. "I was certain he'd win my contract at auction—he's a man of means, ye ken? Och, I shudder t' think . . ."

Tom leaned down, his mouth at her ear, so close his three-day beard rasped the soft skin on her jawbone. "I'll allow no harm come to thee, Maggie Duncan."

Those spare words whispered in the dark loosened the taut wire of wariness she'd strung from her brain to her heart. Maggie wrapped her arms around Tom's waist and pressed a cheek to his chest. Tom found her lips in the dark. He kissed her once, twice—tender and warm.

Twining one hand in her hair, his other at her hip, he pulled

Maggie in, kissing her deep and long—a kiss that made her moan and feel as if as a stream of liquid silver had slipped through her and pooled molten between her legs. Maggie rose up on tiptoes, feeling his full length pressing hard against her thigh. Tom broke the kiss with a growl and took a step back.

"What's th' matter?" Maggie reached out.

Heaving a huge sigh, Tom took her by the hand.

"I'd best get you home. Danger lies on this trail."

11

Fences Are Down

The thud of Seth's maul echoed from behind the stable and kept company with the clack of split logs being tossed onto the woodpile. Naomi gazed up at the sun, which seemed like an angry fist pounding the bright blue sky—a hot, still day, without even the slightest puff of a breeze to cleanse the heat from the back of her neck.

Naomi sat on a rag rug centered in a smidge of shade under the lone tulipwood in the dooryard, her legs tucked tailor style. Six long strings of beans dried in the pod were piled on one side. Battler, sprawled on his back, lay asleep on the other. After shooing a horsefly from the boy's face, she continued stripping the leathery pods, beans plinking into the small kettle held on her lap.

The baby inside began a languorous roll across her midriff. Naomi set the pot aside and slipped two hands under her loose blouse, smoothing callused fingers over skin stretched thin and tight. Keeping a hold on the life waking in her belly helped ease the niggling fear always pecking at the base of her hopes and dreams. She shifted her seat and moved one hand around to rub the ache at the small of her back. The last weeks always proved to be the hardest to endure. Soon, if all went well, she would live to hold this baby healthy and alive in her arms.

Winnie came from around the cabin toting a sloshing bucket, their two dogs crowding her heels, pink tongues lolling. She poured water into their trough.

"Move over, Patch—there's enough for both." Winnie wrapped her arms about the brindled hound, pulling him back. "Git in there, Little Black. Have a drink." But Little Black ignored Winnie, turning instead to strike a stance staring out at the cornfield. A ridge of bristly hair crawled upright along his backbone and he flew off like a dry leaf in a windstorm. Patch broke from Winnie and lit a shuck after Little Black. Both dogs dashed into the waist-high corn, barking like mad.

Naomi braced against the tree trunk and struggled to her feet. A man, filmy and faded in the brilliant sunlight, loped toward her, dodging around cornstalks and tree stumps. Naomi took two steps forward, dogs barking, a fistful of blouse clutched at the hollow of her throat. The midday heat shimmered above the field and she shaded her eyes, squinting.

Black hat.

Blue shirt.

White man.

It was Tom—Tom Roberts.

"*Winnie!* Run fetch Jackie and your da. *Hurry!*" Naomi watched Tom tearing across the field in full stride, her jaw clenched. News carried swift-foot in the blaze of a summer day could not bode well.

Tom, Seth, Winnie, Jack, the Martin dogs, and Tom's dog, Friday, all met in the dooryard, kicking up a chaos of dust and noise. Battler woke snuffling, coughing, and screaming, and Naomi sank down to gather him up on her lap.

Red-faced Tom doubled over, panting hard, hands pressed to his knees. He went to the trough, got down on his hunkers, shoved the dogs aside, and filled his hat with water. Tom took three long gulps and dumped the remainder over his head. "War party . . ." he finally gasped, standing tall. "Shawnee . . . movin' fast . . . coming along the streambed . . ."

Winnie clasped Jack by the hand and Naomi's children stood together in the dooryard, stiff and pallid as the French porcelain figures in her old master's china hutch. Desperate to stanch the onslaught of sick horror wrenched up from her gut and throbbing in her throat, Naomi closed her eyes and pulled Battler tight to her breast, squeezing the squawking toddler into silence. She drew in one long, deep breath and set Battler down on his rump on the rug. "Winnie, mind your brother." She hoisted herself up to her feet. "I'll go gather the bedding."

"Help yer mam," Seth directed Jack. "Sclim up to the loft, and toss down a bag o' meal, a side of bacon . . . I'm goin' to saddle the mule . . ."

"Where's Maggie?" Tom asked, stopping the Martins in their tracks. Seth looked to his wife, who turned to her daughter.

"Where is she? Where's Maggie?" Seth demanded.

Winnie blurted, "I told her not to, but she said she needed cherry bark to make syrup for Battler's croup . . ."

"SYRUP!" Seth shouted.

"She said she'd not be long . . ."

"AYE-GOD! Does anyone ever mind a word I say?" Seth stomped about the yard, finger piercing the air. "Stay close, I tolt yiz. Nae wanderin', I tolt yiz. Perilous times, I tolt yiz all . . ."

"Maggie means well," Naomi interjected. "Battler's been awful poorly . . ."

"A snotty nose isnae worth a body's scalp, woman!"

Tom grabbed Seth by the shoulder. "Hell ain't but a mile away, brother, and the fences are all down. Tuck tail and get your family to the station *now*." Tom flattened his felt hat and wedged it under his belt. "I'll find Maggie. We'll meet up with you in Roundabout."

Seth nodded to the sense of Tom's solution. "Ye dinna need Friday underfoot. We'll take him with us."

Tom nodded and pulled a knife from the sheath at his side. Propping his right foot on an overturned bucket, he bent over and secured the blade under the red wool garter at his right knee. "Did anyone take notice which way she headed?"

Winnie pointed to the northwest. "The cherry grove, near the Berry Hell . . ."

Naomi ran to Tom and hugged him about the waist. "Bring her in safe but be wary—she's gone upstream."

"Upstream," Tom repeated with a chuckle. "Now, don't that just figure?"

Seth stepped forward. "Mind yer topknot, Tommy."

"And you mind yourn." The men clasped forearms, and Tom lit out.

⊂𝓮✦𝓼⊃

At last Maggie was free from Jack stalking her heels, Winnie jabbering in her ear, and Seth recounting yet another horrific tale of the Redman's cruelty. Her worries seemed to fly from her shoulders and perch high up in the treetops. She skipped into the cool, clean silence of the forest, singing her favorite ballad.

> *"In Scarlet town where I was born,*
> *There was a fair maid dwellin'*
> *Made every youth cry well-a-day,*
> *Her name was Barbara Allen."*

Seth's strict orders held them all but tethered to the cabin. Even the two cows, usually belled and allowed to roam free to forage, were penned behind the stable. Hunting and trapping fresh meat for the table was curtailed, forcing the Martins to depend on depleted winter stores of salt pork and jerked venison.

Maggie and Winnie only were allowed to leave the dooryard

to collect water, or to see to the dairy chores—and even then, only if accompanied by Jack and his ancient musket. Their boundaries were stringent, the times, grim.

"Stay well within earshot." In this, Seth was firm. No one was allowed to wander alone. And absolutely no one was allowed to wander beyond the cleared field to the north or the springhouse to the south.

Maggie scooted alone and defiant down the steep path toward the Berry Hell, swinging a hatchet in her hand and singing her song.

> " 'Twas in the merry month of May
> The green buds were a-swellin'
> Sweet William on his deathbed lay
> For love of Barbara Allen."

What began as a stuffy nose had settled thick in Battler's chest. Maggie worried when her standard mustard plaster and hyssop-flower tea seemed to give him little ease. His pitiful crying and coughing made it almost impossible for anyone in the Martin household to find sleep. Sick baby and dire threat of Indian attack combined with exhaustion to concoct a stressful brew of frayed nerves and short tempers.

Early morning, while braiding her hair, Maggie noticed Battler's odd color and rapid breathing. She pressed an ear to his laboring chest and heard the crackling rattle that signaled lung fever. Not wanting to alarm Naomi or deal with contentious Seth, Maggie determined to violate restrictions and take swift steps to treat Battler's illness.

The Berry Hell crept alongside the stream, a good twenty square yards of thick, thick briar protected by a tall stand of wild cherry trees. Maggie entered the grove and strode up to the largest tree—one whose trunk was wider than her outstretched arms—its lateral roots growing close to the surface. Resolute in her task, she fell to her knees and used her hatchet to scrape away hard-packed earth, exposing a good portion of meaty root.

Battler's congested lungs required a strong tonic obtained from macerated root bark. Although difficult to harvest, the soft inner bark of black-cherry root would yield a very potent syrup, much more effective than what she could distill from trunk or branch bark. She attacked the tough root with rabid fervor and chopped it through.

Using the hatchet as a lever, she pried the cut root end to jut out from the earth. Maggie rolled her sleeves up past her elbows and straddled the root. She planted bare feet, spit on her palms, grabbed solid hold, and began tugging and twisting with all her might. The tree root creaked, crunched, and stuttered out of the ground, popping up a spray of dirt, ripping free to send Maggie flying backward, square on her bum.

"Och, aye!" She caught her breath, staring in stunned triumph at the five-foot length of black-cherry root lying between her splayed limbs. She stood, tucked the hems of her everyday brown skirt into her waistband, and dragged the root down into the stream.

"Now, that's quick harvest," she praised herself, with a self-satisfied smile. Seth would never even know she had disobeyed him. Maggie picked up her song as she rinsed away the clumps of dirt and clay clinging to her prize.

> *"He sent his servant to her door*
> *To town where she was dwellin'*
> *Haste come ye now, to my master's bed,*
> *If your name be Barbara Allen."*

"*Maggie!* Stop that singing!"

Startled, she looked up to see Tom circling around the Berry Hell, blue eyes intent on her. Hatless, his long hair was tied loose with a leather lace and two angry furrows were drawn between his brows. With his rifle in a two-fisted grip, Tom's shoulders sat rigid in his chambray shirt patched dark with sweat.

"Thee must come with me—*now*." His voice was quiet and low.

She had not laid eyes on Tom Roberts since the night of the gather-all two weeks before, when he bade her farewell in the dark with a chaste kiss on the cheek and a promise. "I'll call on you soon."

Every day from that day on, she watched for him—waited for him to stride smiling through the waist-high corn and take her up in his arms. But he never came.

Probably for the best, she figured, as her life was not her own—not for four years anyway—and Seth had warned her to steer clear of Tom. "An unfettered man like tha'," Seth said. "Lord only knows where he goes, where he spends his nights . . ."

Maggie tossed and turned some nights, envisioning Tom in Bess Hawkins's bed. But most nights, she tossed and turned envisioning herself in his arms, in his bed, only to remind herself that other than a rude blanket on the dirt, Tom did not even have a bed to call his own.

Now Tom appeared suddenly, creeping through the brush like an irate phantom, and Maggie found herself struck dumb, clutching the tree root dripping in her hands.

"Quick . . ." he implored, his hand outstretched. "Shawnee war party comin' upon us."

Maggie clambered up the bank. "What of Naomi . . . the children . . . ?"

"On their way to the station. I've come for you." Tom wrested the root from her hands and tossed it into the water.

"I—I need that . . ." she stuttered, taking a step back.

He seized Maggie by the arm and pushed her along. *"Move!"*

She stopped short. "My hatchet . . ." she said, pointing to where she'd left it lying beneath the cherry tree.

Tom cocked a woodsman's ear, listening. Maggie heard it, too. The subtle sound of bodies traveling through the underbrush, murmuring voices harmonizing with the tone of water rushing over smooth stones—a steady movement of many, most assuredly coming their way. With Maggie by the arm, Tom snatched up the hatchet and slipped it into his belt. "We have to hide."

"*Hide?* We have to run!" Maggie struggled to pull free.

The crisp sound of brittle wood snapping underfoot cracked through the trees. Maggie twisted away and ran scrambling up a steep incline to the ridge trail. Tom followed with three long steps. Clutching a fistful of skirt, he yanked her down. Maggie flailed about like a trout tossed up on a bank. Tom clapped a hand over her mouth and whispered in her ear. "God's eye on it, Maggie—you will not outrun a Shawnee brave."

Tom half carried, half dragged her to the Berry Hell. He slid his rifle into a low opening in the briars—a brambly tunnel not more than two feet across, formed by hogs rooting for fallen fruit. "Scoot in, push your way to the center. I'll be right back."

Maggie clutched him by the arm, tears springing hot to her eyes. A smile played across Tom's lips. "I have to wipe our tracks," he explained, prying Maggie's fingers from his wrist. "I'll come right back . . . I promise."

A shot rang out, followed by deep wing thumping as a pair of turkeys flapped cackling over the treetops. "Get in there." Tom shoved Maggie to her knees and went to disguise their trail.

She threw herself on her belly, snake-crawling through loose loam and over rotting berry pulp, tugging Tom's rifle along. Prickles and thorns tore at her hair, caught on her clothes, and gouged the flesh on her arms as she wriggled deep into the dim leafy innards of the Berry Hell.

"Hurry." Tom's gruff whisper accompanied by a two-handed shove to her behind gave Maggie cause for relief. She shifted over. He shimmied in alongside her, pulling bramble down to disguise the entry to their hiding place.

Tom flipped over to lie flat on his back. Maggie nestled against him, her head on his shoulder. She draped her free arm over his belly, fitting her fingers into the spaces between his ribs. Tom squeezed her tight, caught her eye, and pressed a finger to his lips.

Distinct voices drew close and closer, speaking throaty, complicated words, reminding Maggie of the Welsh tinkers that traveled through Glen Spean. Soft-soled moccasins scrunched the earth accompanied by a rhythmic, silvery jangle—sounding like the tinker's cart bumping along a rough road.

Maggie dug her fingers into Tom's flesh. She turned to breathe in the comfort of his strong body. The smell of him blending with the sweet scent of ripening fruit helped to quell the hysterical scream rising up into her throat.

The grove seemed thick with savages talking and, surprisingly, laughing with one another. Through a thinning in the bramble she spied tawny buckskin—a hank of Irish-red hair curled along one fringed legging. She squeezed her eyes tight, heart thumping, the brambles quivering as the Indian gathered handfuls of berries before running off to catch up with his comrades.

The war party continued to move past, unaware of the man and woman entangled in the tangle beneath their very noses. Voices and footfalls moved into the distance, fading . . . fading . . . gone. Maggie opened her eyes and her breath escaped in a soft *whoosh.* Tom pressed his lips to her forehead and whispered, "Hush now . . . there may be stragglers."

Overhead, clusters of ripe berries dangled beneath furry green-gray leaves. Tom plucked a particularly large beauty. Maggie opened her mouth like a hatchling in the nest and he dropped the juicy morsel in. They lay there quiet, feeding each other berries for some time.

"I think we're safe," Maggie ventured.

"Safe for now," Tom said as he rolled to lie atop her, bread-and-butter fashion, propped on his elbows. "But you won't be truly safe until I get you inside the station." He smiled into her eyes, then kissed her handsomely on the mouth.

Maggie moaned and, wriggling her hips, arched up against him. Tom shifted to the side.

"I'd better shuckle on out this squirrel hole afore you get a notion t' plant a knee t' my parts." He took his gun and scrambled backward. Maggie crawled out after him, a knee to his bollocks the furthest thing from her mind.

She fished the tree root from the stream and concluded she could get by with just the thick end. Maggie called to Tom, who accommodated her request, whacking off a goodly chunk with three well-placed blows.

"Arm yourself." He handed her the two-foot cherry-root club and the hatchet. She slipped the hatchet handle into her skirt, hanging the blade end on the waistband. Maggie trailed on Tom's heels as he wandered around the bramble, studying the jumble of tracks in the dirt.

"Thick as dog hair." Tom whistled and shook his head. "At least fifty warriors . . . we sure don't want to run into these fellas again."

Maggie wagged her head in vigorous agreement.

"I think we'd best climb up over the saddle of Humpback Ridge." Tom pointed to the steep hill sloping up beyond the Berry Hell. "Then we'll double back, skirt Tuggle Mountain, and come upon Roundabout from the rear. All right?"

Maggie nodded. This man did not hesitate to put his life at risk for hers—a solid man of action he was. Save for Tom Roberts, her black hair would now be a bloody prize dangling from the belt of a Shawnee brave. She rubbed the top of her head and settled down on a stone to watch Tom make ready for the trail.

Before shouldering his weapon, he checked it thoroughly. He adjusted himself within his breechclout and tightened the knee garters on his leggings and laces on his moccasins. He fooled with his felt hat, shaping the crown and bending the brim until it rested just so on his head.

"Ye are a winnin' lad. What I mean is . . . yer a brave man, Tom. And I thank ye for saving my hide."

Tom grinned. "Well, I seem to find myself partial to that hide of yours." He headed toward the trackless slope with long strides, raising his eyes to study the dark clouds massing in the eastern sky. "Better get a move on. Looks like it's going to weather soon. Are you comin' or no?"

"Aye . . . I'm comin'!" Cradling her cherry root like a newborn in one arm, she hiked her skirts and ran to catch up.

Tom took the first difficult steps up the steep slope. "It's a hard go. A tough trail lies ahead . . ."

"Tell me what to do, Tom Roberts, and I'll do it. Just show me the path, an' I'll follow ye straight down intae th' middle pits o' hell."

Tom held a hand out, a wry smile crinkling the corners of his eyes. "For now, Maggie, just give me less with your jaw, and more with your feet."

She put her hand in his.

PART TWO

꧁ꕥ꧂

My brothers! My friends! My children! Hear me now:
We must now, from this time forward, cast out of us the anger for
whatever ill has risen up between us in the past. We must cast it
away from us and we must let ourselves become one people, whose
common purpose it must be to drive from among us the English dogs
who seek to destroy us and take our lands!

> PONTIAC, OTTAWA CHIEF,
> ADDRESSING THE COUNCIL
> GATHERED ON THE RIVER
> ECORCES, APRIL 27, 1763

Could it not be contrived to send the Small Pox among those
disaffected tribes of Indians? We must on this occasion use every
stratagem in our power to reduce them.

> POSTSCRIPT IN A LETTER TO
> COLONEL BOUQUET,
> SIGNED, SIR JEFFREY AMHERST,
> GOVERNOR GENERAL,
> BRITISH NORTH AMERICA, 1763

In 1763, the tribes unite to commence the deadliest and most successful
of all Native American uprisings.

12

Forting Up

Maggie flipped from back to belly, and then she flipped from belly to back. Shifting hip bones and shoulder blades, she laced fingers to rest her hands on her stomach as she pondered the ceiling above. Dusty gloaming light—the tail end of a long summer day—seeped quiet through the chinks between the roof shingles. A pair of yellow flies buzzed in tight circles, dangerously close to a huge web spanning two roof timbers.

The straw-stuffed palliasse, diligently shaken, aired, and beaten with a stout stick that morning, was pressed thin as a flapjack by her turbulence. Maggie bent her knees and scrubbed the callused soles of her dirty feet against the osnaburg canvas. She could feel the fabric, rougher than a cow's tongue, prickling her skin right through her sweaty shift. Maggie heaved a sigh, wistful for her goose-down tick left behind at the Martin homeplace.

Upon the alarm to fort up ten days ago, over one hundred souls crowded through the gates with what they could carry, seeking refuge behind the station's sturdy walls. The ten cabins lining the long palisade wall were reserved for women and children, each cabin crowded with bodies, bedding, and personal belongings.

Maggie turned to her right side and leaned up on one elbow. Battler, deep asleep, lay sprawled between herself and Naomi. She pressed the back of her hand to his sweaty, flushed face. Smiling, she rested her head on one bent arm. Battler's fever, broken three days before, had not returned.

The cabin was thick with evening damp and the hot breath of the others sharing the dirt floor. Even with an open doorway, the rank miasma of a dozen unwashed bodies combined with a half-filled night soil bucket and the odor of sour baby spittle to hover over them like a dense swarm of no-see-ums. Across the room, a cabinmate broke wind.

Maggie's eyes popped open. Rivulets of sweat tickled along her hairline. She squirmed on her spartan bed, struggling for air, feeling as if she were drowning. "Bloody hell!' She scrambled to her feet and plucked her skirt and bodice hanging from a peg jammed between two logs.

Naomi blinked and bolted upright. "What? What is it? Injuns . . ."

"Nooo . . . no Indians. Dinna fash, lass." Maggie stopped tightening the laces on her bodice to lay a hand on Naomi's shoulder. "I've got a bad case of the allover fidgets. I'm off for a breath of air." Naomi sank back into her pillow. Maggie didn't bother to pin up her hair, leaving it to swing in one heavy plait. She tugged on her skirt and picked a path between prone bodies and out the door.

Maggie dipped her kerchief in the water barrel strategically placed to catch the runoff from the roofline and wiped her face. Water collected from the stream once a day by an armed bucket brigade was strictly rationed for cooking and drinking use only. *One never kens the worth of water till the well goes dry*, she mused, tying the damp kerchief about her neck.

Mid-June, true nightfall was long in coming. Only a handful of bright stars showed scattered across the slate-blue sky as she headed to join the small group maintaining sentry at the blockhouse. Maggie stopped dead in her tracks when she spied Bess Hawkins sitting among them.

By mutual unspoken agreement, Maggie and Bess avoided each other's company—no mean feat when confined within stockade walls. Just as Maggie was about to turn and head back to her cabin, she spied Ada Buchanan leaving the cookhearth, juggling a cloth-covered basket and a heavy jug.

Ada called out, "Maggie! Can ye carry this jug for me? A treat for the lads on watch."

Scant twenty men had stayed behind to defend the fort—the men and boys who were too old or too young to join Round-about's able-bodied. Tom and Seth were counted among the forty who mustered as militia to drive off the marauding Shawnee. The militiamen marched out the gate nine days before and had not been heard from since.

The half-dozen souls gathered around a small fire cheered and broke into applause when Ada and Maggie joined them, armed with fresh-baked raisin scones and the jug of sweet metheglin. Alistair scooted over on his log to make room for the newcomers. "Have a seat, lass."

"I only came t' give Ada a helping hand," Maggie said, handing Alistair the jug.

"Och, sit a spell." Alistair patted the seat beside him. "Ada's metheglin is akin to the nectar of the gods—not to be missed— and John's getting ready t' play us a tune."

The recollection of her sweltering bed and the promise of honey wine overshadowed her distaste for Bess's company. Maggie settled next to Alistair.

John Springer sat across the way with his fiddle on his lap, re-placing a broken sheep-gut string. Like a king's consort, Bess sat in a semi-recline on the stump beside John's. With her auburn hair glinting copper in the firelight, she cooled herself, waving a painted parchment folding fan.

Smoking a clay pipe, Bess's father-in-law, old Henry Hawkins, shared the neighboring log with young Jacob Mulberry and Will Falconer. Captain Duncan Moon, a grizzled old veteran of the French Indian wars, hobbled about on his peg leg, igniting torches and lights. He handed Will Falconer a bright lantern. Young Will slung an ancient musket over his shoulder and scrambled up the ladder to the blockhouse roof to take his turn on lookout.

"Keep those eyes peeled, lad," Duncan admonished.

Ada Buchanan orbited the circle with her basket. She served lanky Jacob Mulberry three scones. "Eat up, lad. Ye need put some meat on those sharp bones."

"That's true, boy," Bess Hawkins piped in. "You'll never get a woman in your bed looking like a death's head mounted to a mop stick."

Jacob accepted the advice with good humor, and falling to his knees, he tugged at Ada's skirt. "A woman in my bed! Please, missus, stuff me with scones." Everyone laughed.

Maggie sipped a cup of honey wine. "Hellish hot in those cabins. I'm bone tired and canna find sleep."

"Can't sleep?" John Springer hoisted his fiddle to his chin. "Here, I'll play you a lullaby."

"And I'll rock you," young Jacob Mulberry teased with a freckle-faced grin. He tucked a greasy strand of hair behind one protruding ear, held his skinny arms wide, and moved in on Maggie. On cue, John Springer began sawing a soft, sweet melody.

"Bugger off!" Maggie giggled and pushed Jacob away. "I'd sooner sleep out in the pasture and pick corn from horse droppings than share a bed with any o' you lot."

"That's not what I heard," Bess Hawkins said, fanning her face with a languid motion.

Ada said, "Now, Bess, slander is equal to murder in the eyes of the Lord."

Bess's fan fluttered. "It's only truth I speak, Ada. You don't really think a man like Tom Roberts paid thirty dollars for chicken supper and a chat, do you?"

"Yid best mind that vile tongue, Bess Hawkins, for I've a truth or two to tell as well," Maggie warned. "I'm no gossip, but ye sorely tempt my good nature."

Bess sat upright, snapped her fan shut, and smacked it to the palm of her hand. "I don't take kindly to threats from indentured trash."

"How would ye take to yon fan shoved down yer throat?"

"*Whore!*"

"BITCH!" Maggie jumped to her feet.

"Ladies . . ." Alistair grabbed Maggie by the shoulders.

Henry Hawkins shook a finger at Bess. "There is strife abundant, without the two of you going at it like a pair of polecats."

"Aye, well . . ." Maggie sat down, clenched fists on her knees. She took a deep breath. "That one tries my patience with her lies."

"Aye, well," Bess mocked. "That one's still a whore . . ."

"Enough, Bess!" Henry barked. "Shet yer trap or I'll shet it for ye."

Bess settled back into a relaxed pose, pleased to have gotten in the last word. She slowly passed the closed fan through her half fist. Unfurling it with a practiced flick, she opened her fan and glared at Maggie over the arched edge with spitting eyes.

Alistair handed Maggie the jug and she poured herself a generous scoof, trying very hard to ignore Bess Hawkins. John Springer began to saw a soft, mournful version of Maggie's favorite, "Barbara Allen." With fellow musicians out hunting the Shawnee, John's fiddling seemed especially woebegone this evening, missing the heartbeat of Brian Malloy's bodhran and the trill of Phil Smillie's flute.

The music did much to calm her ire and brought Maggie back to the cherry grove. Only ten days had passed since her arduous flight to the fort with Tom, but it all seemed so long ago. She certainly did not relish her present lot, safely penned in, cheek by jowl, carefully measuring out dwindling stores of salt meat, dried beans, and meal—waiting, waiting, and then waiting some more. John Springer ended the tune on a sweet, warbling note.

Maggie sighed. "I wonder how they fare . . . our lads . . ."

"Aye, we've been overlong without word." Alistair shook his shaggy head. "I confess, I'm uneasy for our friends. Let us hope that they are only in danger."

"*Only!*" The whimper tumbled from Maggie's lips. "What d' ye mean, Mr. Buchanan?" The panic that she daily plucked and discarded like a weed in the corn patch began to sprout anew, its tendrils twining tightly up the stalk of her spine. "D'ye suppose them . . . dead?"

"Ye auld goat! D' ye even ken how t' keep that potato hole of yers shet?" Mrs. Buchanan snatched the bottle of metheglin from her husband and handed it to Duncan.

"Tell me true." Maggie's voice dropped to a whisper. "Can they be murdered?"

"Of course they can be murdered," Bess said, matter-of-fact. "The Shawnee can steal up in the dark of night and cut their throats—every one. Or most likely, the savages will ambush them on the trail—mow 'em down without a warning . . ."

"Ah now—I'm sure the fellas are fine." Henry tugged on his pipe. "No point in scarin' the girl."

"She should be scared," Bess countered. "She better learn—being scared is a woman's lot on the frontier. I'm scared every night I lay my head on my pillow without my Bert beside me. Marry a hunter and you marry uncertainty."

Ada clucked in true sympathy. "Aye, that must be trying, lass, never knowing for months on end whether yer man's alive or dead."

Bess sniffed and shrugged. "Every time Bert goes overmountain I worry and worry till the worry wears me down so's I don't feel much of anything anymore." There was a lonesome quality in her voice, like that of a morning dove calling to her mate. Maggie almost felt sorry for her.

"Ah, you always figure Bert for dead," Henry said. "And my boy always comes home, his horses heavy with pelts—enough t' keep ye busked nicely in Frenchy fans and fancy beebaws. It wouldn't hurt you none to have a little faith in yer man."

Bess folded her fan and sat up. "What would you know of a woman's plight, old man?"

"Woman's plight!" Henry spit into the fire. "If ye had a baby or two pullin' at yer apron strings, ye wouldn't have so much time to complain about a good man."

"You might become a grandsire one day if your boy would linger long enough to plant a baby in my belly." Bess glanced briefly Maggie's way.

Duncan Moon sank down next to Maggie. Propping his peg leg on his knee, he broke the awkward silence. "Common sense tells us our boys have not been massacred. If they had been, the Shawnee would have come knockin' at our door by now. Never fear." He gave Maggie a little pat on the back. "The militia is busy keepin' that war party far from us."

"Captain Moon's got the right of it, Maggie," Henry said, with a slap to his knee. "Our boys have them Injuns on the run . . . chasin' 'em all the way back to the Ohio country. Lord, don't I wish I were with 'em!"

Alistair was contrite for having opened a Pandora's box with his misgivings. "Aye . . . worry tends to give a wee thing a big shadow. We need to be patient and hold fast."

Bess fluttered her fan. "Sam Bledsoe couldn't be bothered to wallow here in the station. He labeled you all a pack of frightened fools for stayin' put."

"The poltroon!" John Springer set his instrument aside to join in the conversation. "You'll notice Bledsoe also couldn't be bothered to join the militia. Truth is, he's a rank coward."

Three days earlier, Sam Bledsoe, itching to return to his hold-ing and the six cows he'd recently driven up from Richmond, de-clared the Shawnee scare over. Against all advice and entreaties to the contrary, Sam packed up his very pregnant wife and their five children and left the station. Maggie had to admit, she envied Susannah Bledsoe that day as she passed through the gates.

Alistair harrumphed. "Samuel Bledsoe is a malingerer and a tightfist. It beggars belief that the man's concern for corn and cattle would cause him to be so reckless with the lives of his wife and weans."

"I s'pose Bledsoe's right in his thinking, though. It's nigh on ten days since those Shawnee meandered through our valley." Henry Hawkins passed the jug to young Jacob. "On the other hand, it wouldn't have hurt Sam nor his cattle none to take the advice of those who've lived through Indian scare. Always best to wait on solid word from the militia."

"Ye ken what they say, Henry," Ada offered. "Givin' advice to a fool is much like givin' cherries to a pig—a waste."

"*Cap'n Moon!*" Will Falconer shouted down from his post on top of the blockhouse. "I think maybe . . . yep, maybe I see some-thin' out there . . ."

Duncan rose up and limped closer to the ladder. "What is it?"

"Not sure . . . maybe it's just fireflies." Will shuttered his lan-tern and studied the western horizon.

Henry gave Jacob a shove to the shoulder. "Sclim up the lad-der and put another pair of eyes on it."

They all waited quiet while Jacob clambered up to join Will. "I'd say they're torchlights for certain." Maggie winced at the squeaky hitch in Jacob's almost-man voice. "And they're moving quick, down the switchback trail."

"You two, keep your look out. Torches—awful brazen, even for Shawnee . . ." Duncan pondered a moment. "Henry—sound the alarm. Have the men ready weapons and gather ammunition."

Maggie turned to Ada. "It might be our militia come home . . ."

"Aye . . . and it might not." Ada's apple-cheek grin had crumpled into a glum crease in her fleshy face. Bess sat stone-still, her face gone very pale and wan.

Henry Hawkins wandered the fortyard, banging a hammer to an iron bar. The defenders bounded up from their bedrolls, tugging on footwear, strapping on belts, snatching up guns, powder, and shot, shouting direction, and running to take position at the gun ports.

Women and children roused by the clatter filtered out the cabin doors like pale wraiths in the moonlight. Battler on her hip, and Winnie and Jack close behind, Naomi joined the growing crowd murmuring beneath the blockhouse.

"The lights have broken free of the forest!" And just as Will finished this proclamation, the crack of musket fire rang across the valley. The rooftop lookouts plopped down on their bellies and the settlers were further jolted by a steady tattoo beaten on a skin drum.

"Children into the cabins!" Alistair boomed.

In a sudden screaming hubbub, alarmed mothers ran, snatching up toddlers, slapping, scolding, and herding children.

Will shouted, "They're moving through the clearing now!"

Every infant seemed at that moment squalling. Every dog barking, howling, and tearing about in mad circles. Maggie grabbed Battler from Naomi. Winnie and Jack linked hands with their mother, all of them caught in the current of the screaming melee.

"At the ready, boys!" Duncan shouted.

Sounding like fistfuls of pebbles cast hard at an iron cauldron, the hammers of twenty-odd muskets clacked back in staccato response.

"Roundabout! *Roundabout!* Hold your fire!" shouted a voice from afar.

And within, the forted population stopped, shocked into stillness, listening.

"Halloo the station!" The call was accompanied by another spat of drum thrumming.

"That's my Brian!" Sally Malloy announced with a laugh.

"Malloy and his bodhran!" John Springer shouted.

A relieved huzzah rose up. Mothers hugged their children and wiped their tears. Men and boys relaxed their posts, uncocking weapons and slapping shoulders. Will Falconer, still atop the blockhouse, opened his lantern and waved it over his head, while Jacob Mulberry leaped whooping wildly at his side, "Open the gates! Open the gates!"

It took four boys to lift the timber latch and push them open. The heavy doors rode in smiling grooves swung deep in the hard-packed earth. Soon, militiamen spilled into the station yard. The fort-bound settlers crowded close, straining to see, searching faces illuminated by scattered pools of sputtering torchlight.

"I see Seth!" Maggie pointed.

And Seth saw them. The Martin family ran and collided in a clutch of hugs and kisses. Maggie joined to give Seth a fervent welcome.

"Are there many wounded?" she asked, eyeing a bloody tear on his shirtsleeve.

"We've all a scratch here and scrape there, but we're all come home."

"Tom?"

"Bringing up the rear." Seth took Battler from her arms. "There . . . see him? Comin' through the gate along with the litter bearers . . ."

Dodging around and through groups of friends and families welcoming loved ones home, Maggie ran shouting, *"Tom!"* He caught her in his arms, swinging her high to fly feet up from the ground. "I'm so glad t' see ye back safe," she sobbed into his chest.

"I have to admit"—Tom wrapped his arms tight about her and nuzzled his nose in her hair—"it's awful nice to have someone to come back to."

"Welcome back, Tom." Bess was beside them, looking lonely

in the happy confusion of families reunited. "It is good t' see you safe returned."

Tom broke his embrace from Maggie to greet Bess with a happy handshake. "Yep. It's good to be back."

"Hoy, Tom!" Hamish Macauley bellowed. He and his fellow litter bearers stood waiting. "Where should we put 'em?"

"The blockhouse. Get some of the boys to clear it out . . . and gather torches. We'll be needing the light."

The bearers trundled off with two litters, a blanketed bundle centered on each.

"Let's get your basket." Tom took Maggie by the hand. "We caught up to the Shawnee at the Bledsoe place."

Tom offered up his trencher. Janet Wheeler ladled venison stew into it. Alice Springer plopped a steaming slab of cornbread on top and he shuffled over to join the men clumped around Ada Buchanan's ale barrel.

"Sorry, lads, but I've only small beer to offer." Ada dipped tankards two at a time into the keg, handing one to Tom and one to Brian Malloy.

Brian slurped up the froth spilling over the brim. "MM-mm! Thick as porridge—I dare not trust my arse with a fart after downing a cup or two of this brew, missus."

With tankard and trencher in hand, Tom steered toward a large tree stump across from the blockhouse and settled down next to Alistair. "It's been so long since last I et," he said, setting his drink at his feet, "that I swear my great guts are ready to eat my little ones." Tom balanced the trencher on his knees and rifled through the chaos of his pouch. "Can't seem to lay hand to my—oh . . . never mind . . . here 'tis."

Tom crumbled the cornbread into the stew, hunched over his plate, and shoveled the food into his mouth. He gulped his beer, belched soundly, and rose to his feet to fetch another cupful.

Alistair caught Tom by the shirttail and pulled him to sit back.

"Enough of that pap. Time for a man's drink." He held up a leathern flask. "*Uisquebaugh.* Carried over ocean and land twenty-three years ago. *Slàinte.*" The old man took a goodly swallow and handed it to Tom. "Savor that—cask-strength, lad. Pure malt."

Tasting of mellow scorched earth, the whiskey furred Tom's mouth, slithered down his throat, and burrowed into his belly to glow like a mound of embers pulsing red under the bellows. Tom handed Alistair back his bottle. "I'm privileged, sir—profoundly grand stuff."

"Na, laddie. Keep it. Yiv earned it." The old man reached into his shirt with an evil grin and produced another flask.

Tom sipped whiskey in companionable silence with Alistair, keeping his eye on the blockhouse, hoping to catch a glimpse of Maggie.

Furnished with a bolted door and a proper puncheon wood floor, the blockhouse was normally used to guarantee storage of the station's most vital supplies—munitions and ale. It had been cleared earlier that evening. Sloshing, open tubs filled with fermenting wort were carefully transported to the smithy. Bunged firkins of ale, kegs of gunpowder, and crates of lead bar were passed from hand to hand and stacked just outside the door. Maggie worked inside the makeshift hospital, and every so often she bustled past the open doorway, her white blouse agleam in the lantern light.

Alistair also watched the hospital. "Och, but I'm sorry in my heart for th' Bledsoes."

"Damn wily Shawnee." Tom spat. "With a knowance that we were coursing their trail, they confused the sign. Then the buggers split in two. One half led us a merry chase north while the other snuck off sideways and wormed its way back here."

"The clever devils surely have an instinct for skulduggery. I've seen where they have tread exactly upon one another's tracks to hide their numbers."

"Or double back along their own tracks to increase their numbers. When I lived with the Ojibwe hunting in Iroquois territory, we would hike a ridiculous course, walking along fallen logs, leaping from boulder to boulder, anything to confuse the sign." Tom straightened his spine and stretched his arms up over his head. "There are those who make the mistake of thinking that Indians are a stupid people. But stupid people would not be such fatal enemies. I for one should have known better."

"And I should never have allowed the Bledsoes leave . . . but th' stubborn eidgit just refused to listen to reason." Alistair pounded a fist into his palm. "Good Lord forgive me, t' think I was happy to see th' hind end of Samuel Bledsoe and his complaints . . ."

"Sam's past complaining now. No use fretting over what thee cannot change."

"Aye, Tommy." Alistair corked his flask. "But tonight, even the finest *uisquebaugh* in the land cannot quell my fractious conscience." Hands on knees, he levered himself to stand. "I bid ye good night, lad."

"Good night, Alistair."

Tom slipped down to sit rump in the dirt, legs outstretched. He scratched his back against the stump bark, closed his eyes, and wondered, like Alistair, what could have been done differently to alter the course of the tragic day.

Earlier that afternoon he had marched along with the militia en route back to the station, looking forward to a hot meal and a cup of beer, secure in having driven the war party far to the northwest, when a black cloud belled up beyond Tuggle Mountain, darkening the southern sky like a flock of migrating pigeons. The company turned and made for the smoke, many of his fellows praying to find that it was not his home afire.

Having left the Bledsoe family safely ensconced behind the gates of Roundabout Station, the militiamen approached slowly; with great stealth they half encircled the Bledsoe holding. Lurking in the thick brush east of the cabin, they surveyed the raucous scene and waited for the best opportunity—the opportunity to kill as many Indians as possible.

A pair of cows lay haphazardly butchered in a puddle of syrupy red blood. Beyond the cabin, the barn collapsed in flames. Tom counted at least ten Shawnee going in and out the cabin door. A few warriors tossed cookware and tools to clank in one big pile in the dooryard. Others emerged with armloads of linens, blankets, and clothing, which they stacked next to the tools.

Still more came with sacks of meal slung over shoulders, clutching smoked hams and strings of sausages. A trio of Indians made a great yowling game of chasing flapping chickens and honking geese, wringing the birds' squawking necks when captured. Poultry carcasses and other provender became the third pile of plunder.

When the Indians prepared to set torches to the cabin, a silent signal was passed along the militia firing line. The frontiersmen drew careful aim and let loose a volley of ball, killing or wounding almost every one of the marauders. Tossing spent weapons aside, the militia charged in with tomahawks raised and longknives unsheathed.

A dozen more Redmen ran out from behind the burning barn, whooping, shooting wild, swinging war clubs, thirsting for vengeance. The two sides clashed in a clatter of wood and metal. The Shawnee were outnumbered by more than two to one, and the hand-to-hand combat resulted in violent annihilation. The dust settled. All the Roundabout men stood panting and twenty-two Shawnee warriors lay dead in the Bledsoe dooryard.

Hamish Macauley was the first to grab hold of the bear-greased topknot on the closest dead Indian. Hunting knife in hand, he carved a circular incision around the crown of the head. Planting his large foot between the warrior's shoulder blades, Hamish gave a sharp yank. The trophy pulled free from the skull with a pop, sounding much like a bung plug knocked free from a firkin of fizzy ale. Others joined in, rifling corpses, pulling scalps.

Collecting such booty held no interest for Tom. He wandered back to the brush to retrieve and reload his weapon. Intent on ramming a charge of powder, ball, and patch down the barrel, Tom startled when a cow broke from the trees, its bell clanking a riot as the panicked animal quick-trotted into the cornfield. He ran after the valuable beast, calling, "Seth! Help me get her into the cow pen."

Seth ran over. Without a twist of rope for a lead, each man grabbed a horn, pulling the smoke-shy cow toward the pen near the smoldering barn.

Tom should have known by the droning blowfly buzz and the harsh caw of crows feeding. He should have known by the raw stench growing stronger with every step—a noxious combination of burned hair, spilled entrails, and sickening-sweet rot in humid heat. Through the fog of gray smoke, an odd movement caught his eye—a body swinging from the low-slung limb of a big sycamore. The cow lowed miserably and wrenched away to wander back into the forest.

Slit open from gullet to brisket, Sam Bledsoe's naked, scorched body hung suspended by a tangle of his own intestines. Seth flung a stone to disperse the covey of carrion pecking at the gaping wound. This first horror led them to the others.

Tossed helter-skelter amid a slurry of guts, blood, and brain jelly, all five Bledsoe children lay at the base of the sycamore, each child clubbed and scalped.

Tom scouted the area, to make certain no Indians skulked about. Seth fell to his knees and scrambled from one body to the next, desperate for life signs.

Twelve-year-old Billy lay facedown, his wrists bound back with a strip of tug. Shiny green-and-blue flies clustered writhing over the oldest boy's skull, cracked open like a goose egg. The twins lay side by side, young Josh's mangled head resting on his brother Jeb's shoulder. Biting his lip to quash the gorge rising up his throat, Seth untied the kerchief at his neck and used it to cover the broken, pulpy mass of two-year-old Suzy's face.

He moved to Winnie's friend, Mary. Seth gasped, a finger pressed to the base of her throat. "This one's breathing." He put his ear to the girl's chest. Encouraged by a steady heartbeat, he gathered her up.

Tom ran over. Unconscious, Mary hung in Seth's arms like a load of sopping-wet linen, the smooth bare crown of exposed bone streaming brilliant crimson over what remained of her golden curls.

"Get her into the cabin, Seth. Press cobweb to her skull t' stanch the bleeding. I'll fetch more."

Tom sprinted into the woods to find a series of funnel webs strung cross the gap between two fallen trees. He bent to collect the web and spied a scrap of cobalt-blue calico caught on a laurel branch.

Tom studied the sign and found evidence of a chase—broken cane and beaten-down brush trailing deeper into the woods. Now and then he found a distinct bare footprint running along with larger, moccasin-clad feet. He crept carefully, following erratic footprints down toward the creek. He raised his rifle and continued forward with the hammer back, finger light on the trigger and the stock solid at his shoulder.

Tom found them creekside.

A burly Shawnee warrior sprawled on his back, centered on a dark ellipse of blood-soaked leaves, cleaved unto the neck, his head near severed.

Susannah Bledsoe sat slumped next to a large mossy stone. The Indian's knife lodged in her left side, stove in clean up to the haft. Though she was splattered and stained with gore from head to toe, Tom could see she was alive. Eyes wide open, she held the handle of a bloody ax loose in one hand and the other fist clutched the corner of a flannel blanket to her cheek. Her gaze was fixed not on Tom with his rifle upraised, but on the pale, blue-tinged body of her newborn, who'd tumbled free from his swaddling blanket to rest curled on a soft mound of green cress, his downy head dashed in on jagged rock.

Tom lowered his rifle and stepped toward her. She tilted her face and met him with bland expression and eyes dulled from enduring the unendurable. Fingers streaked red closed tight on the ax and Susannah whispered, "Leave me be."

13

Turds and Primroses

"Maggie?"

She'd drifted to sleep sitting hunched with elbows on knees, her face cupped in her hands. The voice called quiet, but Maggie startled nonetheless and near fell from her stool. She eased up slow, the segments of her backbone piling one atop the other to sit poker straight. Squinting in dim light cast by a near-spent lantern, she scrubbed her eyes with the heels of her palms.

"Maggie?" The heavy door scraped inward on creaky buffalo-strap hinges. Framed in a blue rectangle of new day, Mrs. Buchanan stood in the open doorway, her fleshy arms embracing a wooden bowl of steaming water, her ruddy face glossy with sweat. "Yiv had a long, hard night, dearie. I came t' spell ye."

"No need to whisper." Maggie waved Mrs. Buchanan in. "They're dosed and deep asleep." Shaking stiff limbs to life, she walked to and fro between the beds on either side of the room.

Maggie could not have patients so severely wounded lying on the floor. Right off, she enlisted Hamish and Tom to rig raised platforms using thick planks laid across kegs of salt pork. Mattressed with ticks stuffed with raw wool, the two bedsteads were tucked into opposite corners of the square, windowless room.

Tom used the same slapdash method to set up a table between the makeshift beds. The tools of Maggie's trade were laid out on this work surface. Ordered like soldiers on parade, bottled tinctures, oils, and potted unguents were arranged in neat formation at one end; a tin basin of rusty water and a hummock of blood-besmirched towels occupied the other. Linen strips, rolled tight as tickled potato bugs, were stacked in a pyramid next to a muslin sack bursting with a cloud of cotton lint. The big stone mortar was anchored at center in a scatter of paper packets and belladonna sprigs. The rest of Maggie's collection, more packets and bundles of herbs, roots, and barks, was stuffed in jumbled disarray inside her big basket under the table.

Ada Buchanan strode into the sickroom. She swept a space clear and squeezed her bowl onto the counter. From the copious pocket dangling over her apron, she produced a snow-white towel, a stiff-bristled brush, and an ivory oblong of soap.

"I'll just tidy a bit." Bending to grip the handle of the brimming chamber pot, Ada poured its content to the left of the threshold. At the quickstep, she returned for the water basin and let the bloody water fly in a sheet to land splash in the fortyard. A pair of hounds ran up to lap at the puddle. Ada made a quick about-face, marched back to the counter, and plopped the pile of soggy linens into the empty basin. "We're boilin' the wash today, so give up yer duds," she ordered, her arm curled around the bowl of dirty towels. "A soak in stale piss and a good salt rub will have yer blouse as good as new."

Maggie stood blinking, still not quite awake. Her blouse was smeared and daubed ocher red—her wool skirt dark with stiff patches of Bledsoe blood. "I must look a fright, na? But I've no other . . ."

"Sweet Jesus, Maggie, ye look like Saint Perpetua after she'd been mauled by wild beasts; hand over yer duds." Ada extended an arm. "Bide a wee, and I'll find ye something to wear for the meantime."

Maggie pulled her blouse over her head and stepped from her skirt, handing the garments over with a smirk. "Yid best hurry back. I'm awful hungry. I'm liable to go and breakfast in naught but my shift."

"G'won. I dare ye. Stroll about in yer shift, and young Mulberry, among others, will be certain to grow the third leg. Tom's having his breakfast. I'm certain he'd enjoy a peek at your pretty make." Brows waggling, Ada added, "I'll be back in a tic." Leaving Maggie giggling.

The mention of Tom made Maggie anxious for a wash. She slipped arms through sleeve holes to let her muslinet shift pool in a soft puddle at her feet.

Maggie soaked the towel and lathered it with Ada's soap, the source of its fragrance eluding her for a moment. *Linden flower*, she finally decided with a self-satisfied smile. She started with her face, moving down quickly to wash the rest, and wriggled back into her shift.

She studied her hands for a moment. *I've the hands of a butcher boy . . .*

Maggie took up the brush to scour away the coagulated clots caught under her fingernails and crusted around her cuticles, then sank onto her stool. The single braid hanging over her shoulder looked like a length of badly frayed rope. Tugging free the lace, she finger-combed snarls from the braid-crimped tresses. *Almost human again.*

A tap on the door, and Ada Buchanan reentered, breathing heavy and brandishing a dark blue skirt. "On loan from Janet Wheeler." Grinning, she draped a creamy-silk blouse across Maggie's lap. "A gift from Eileen Wallen. Yers to keep."

"Och, na! She must be daft."

"Eileen's grateful t' ye for stitchin' the gash in her husband's arm."

"Aye, well." Maggie fingered the dense weave and admired the splash of Irish lace at the neckline. "This is much too fine for the likes of me. I'll wear it for the now, but only till my own things dry."

As Maggie dressed, Ada went to adjust and smooth Susannah's bed linen. "At least the poor thing is resting peaceful . . . yer a rock, Maggie—a solid rock. I couldna bear it last night—had to stop my ears with my fingers—the way she screamed and clutched, beggin' ye to put an end t' her with a fatal dose."

"Aye, good thing Duncan had the laudanum." Maggie pulled the blouse over her head. "Even at that, it took near a fatal dose to get her to quiet." She joined Ada at the bedside. Curled on her right, Susannah faced away, huddled up to the timber wall.

Ada tsked. "Poor, poor mother . . . it's no wonder she has no will to live. She's lost them all, she has."

"Not all, Ada—there's still Mary." Maggie turned to the other bed.

Mary Bledsoe lay flat on her belly, a tiny snore bussing in and out her nostrils. Her head, completely bandaged in linen strips, rested on a goose-down pillow.

"Does she no resemble a wee papist nun, swaddled in winding, waiting for the veil?" Ada took Maggie by the hand. "Take my advice, dearie. Dinna pin any hope on her survival. The Good Lord slipped our bones intae a hide for good reason, and a piece of Mary's hide has gone missing."

Maggie knew Ada had the right of it. Mary's ghastly wound could not be stitched or cauterized. In time, the naked bone would mortify, rot away in blackened patches, and expose the delicate brains within Mary's skull to every element. By not dealing a mortal blow, the Indian who so haphazardly scalped Mary guaranteed her slow, painful, and certain death. Maggie turned to hide the tears sprung to her eyes, and she fumbled trying to tie her hair into a tail at the nape of her neck.

Ada rattled on. "Aye, the poor wee lassie would have been better off if she had gone the way of her brothers—"

"Ada!"

"I say so out of good pity. Susannah kens. When you tolt her how her daughter survived—I saw it in her eye. She's no fool. She kens well what lies ahead, aye? Insufferable pain and yet another wee grave to tend."

Maggie cast her eyes down into her basket on the floor. It held no cure for this mother and child. At best, she could keep the girl comfortable with painkilling decoctions and develop the fortitude to do for little Mary what she'd done for her own Hannah, and ease her along with a fatal dose. She kicked the basket, smacking it into the wall, spilling its content over the floor.

"Come now, lass. Yiv done yer best. The rest is up to the Almighty." With a chubby arm hugging Maggie's shoulders, Ada steered her out the door. "Mrs. Mulberry has a pot of black Bohea a-brewin'. Can you imagine? Real tea! G'won now—I'll stay on here till ye return."

Maggie stepped through the sickroom door, filled her lungs with a gulp of fresh air, and let it out with a breathy sigh. Stomach clamoring, she wandered through the fortyard tracking the smell of fried bacon.

Since the militia returned, Roundabout Station buzzed with industry. A column of smoke churned up from the smithy chimney, and Maggie waved, happy to see old Willie back stoking his forge. A gaggle of girls hovered nearby to gape at bare-chested young Willie working the bellows with sweaty, muscle-bound fury.

For the first time in many days, the gates stood wide open, the ominous timber wall interrupted by a view of fresh green field, trees, and hills. Women bustled in and out of the cabins, packing goods into panniers and packs, readying for the trip back to their homesteads. Maggie strolled along, dodging a gang of boys racing between tree stumps who were fighting a mock battle with stick guns.

It was late in the morning, and few congregated near the plume of smoke screwing upward from the communal cookhearth where Rachel Mulberry stood duty, spoon in hand, serving all comers.

Ada spoke true. There, bright as a beacon on a stormy night, resting precariously on an upended hogshead—a porcelain teapot decorated with a delicate spray of blue posies. Equally miraculous, on a square of indigo paper alongside the elegant pot sat a cone of white shop sugar.

"In celebration," Rachel explained as she poured Maggie a mugful.

"Of course!" Maggie smiled. Mired in Bledsoe misery, she'd almost forgotten—beloved husbands, fathers, and sons had all returned safe to their families—just cause for celebration.

She used Rachel's sugar shears to pinch a chunk from the brittle cone, and stirred it into the Bohea with a splash of cream. Maggie held the cup to her nose, drawing Chinese luxury into her head. Rachel handed her a bowl of mush sweetened with molasses and a plop of clotted cream. "There's a platter of bacon on the table."

Flanked by split-log benches, a trestle dining table sat tented beneath a tarp of oiled sailcloth. Tom, Seth, Alistair, and Duncan sat together at one end of the otherwise empty table. Tom waved Maggie over. She slipped in to sit beside him and Seth, across from Alistair and Duncan.

Seth took note of Maggie's new wardrobe. "Yer busked out fine this morn, lass . . . tha's a fancy piece of goods yer wearing."

"On loan from Eileen Wallen. My own things needed a wash." She took a sip from her cup and moaned with pleasure. "Mmmm . . . I canna even rub up a memory of the last time I drank a cup of proper tea with real sugar! Rachel Mulberry is an angel to share with us."

"And yer our bonnie angel, Maggie, gracing our table with yer beauty." Old Alistair waxed poetic. "Fine silk and lace become ye."

"Thank ye, kind sir." Maggie smiled and fingered the lace tickling her collarbone. "But truly, after th' night I had last, I'm feeling more like a mushy turd decorated with primroses."

Seth snickered. "Our angel has a mouth like a Billingsgate fishwife."

"Rough night?" Tom laid his hand on Maggie's back and massaged the space between her shoulder blades.

"Aye." Maggie looked up at Tom with weary eyes. "Rough and still rougher ahead."

Alistair edged forward. "Will Susannah live, at least?"

"She will, and I figure that's the worst of it." Maggie set her spoon down. "Her stab wound bled freely—good, clean blood— nae bile there. No damage to her guts. I'm certain the knife didna pierce a lung, her breathing is clear and steady. I put in some stitches dressed with honey to quell any festering. With proper care, that wound will heal . . ."—Maggie picked up her spoon and scraped furrows into the glop congealing at the bottom of her bowl—"but I've no such confidence or cure for the deep rents to Susannah's soul. It took twenty drops of laudanum to get her to quiet."

Duncan whistled. "Twenty drops!"

"And Mary?" Seth almost whispered.

"Wee Mary's wound is beyond my ken. She will linger, but she canna survive." Maggie sighed and pushed her bowl away. "Susannah will lose her last child and most likely her mind as well. Megstie me! D'yiz ken th' woman gave birth only yesterday morning? And what has she today? Och! The whole sad story gives me a spoilt spleen."

Tom said, "Mary doesn't have to die, Maggie. I remember once—"

"No, Tom." Maggie shook her head. "Bare bone is bound t' rot . . ."

"Listen to me, Maggie—I know this French trader who'd been caught filching game from a Huron trapline—"

"Pierre Labiche!" Duncan interrupted.

"Um-hmm. You know what I'm talking about, Duncan. Well, I was there, at Fort Le Boeuf when they drug Labiche in. He'd been whole-head scalped—nape to brow, ear to ear—a bloody mess, but he was breathing. The Frenchy surgeon, he fixed Pierre's skull and the scalp grew back. He's as bald as a turnip, but Labiche traps and trades to this very day."

"Fixed it?" Maggie snorted. "How'd he fix it?"

"I must admit, I wouldn't have believed it unless I'd seen it. To my mind, it made no sense. But I did see it, and it worked." Tom held up an index finger. "First, the surgeon drilled Pierre's skull full of bitty holes with a fine pegging awl. Matter oozed up through the holes, and after a day or two, the scalp mark scabbed over with dark scales. When the scabs lifted, ol' Pierre's noggin was covered from stem to stern with shiny pink skin."

∗∗∗

Ada rushed along behind Maggie and Alistair, bearing an armload of linen, following them to the cookhearth. "I beg ye t' think twice, Maggie . . ."

"Ada! Please! Enough of yer clishmaclaver—we're doin' this thing." Upon reaching the dining table, Maggie set her basket onto the bench. Alistair set the kettle of water he carried on the gridiron over hot coals.

"Pokin' holes in a body's head." Ada snapped a sheet out over the long table. "It's not right. The Good Lord has provided us all the holes we need—"

"And it's time t' shut the hole he provided you, wife," Alistair added.

Ada ignored her husband with practiced ease. "Maggie, you young folk tend t' rush ahead without ken to God's boundaries. I canna help but believe yer fiddling with what is His will."

Maggie fluffed a pillow and laid it at the head of the table. "If we do naught, Mary surely dies. This is her best chance. Her onliest chance. A chance provided by God, maybe."

Ada struck a stance with arms akimbo. "Still, the poor thing has already suffered much."

Maggie pulled an amber glass bottle from her basket. "A wee

drop or two of henbane will keep her in deep sleep. Mary will not feel a thing." She measured a careful dose of the potent tincture into a tin cup and held the bottle up to the sunlight.

An' there's plenty left if things dinna go well . . .

⸺

Seth laid Mary Bledsoe carefully onto the sheeted tabletop. Her blue eyes were wide open. "Susannah's awake as well—" he told Maggie. "Dinna fash, she's in good company. Ada's spoonin' a bit of broth intae her and Eileen is reading lovely poetry aloud. Naomi and Winnie are keeping company as well."

Disoriented, Mary looked up at Maggie and Seth hovering over her and began to whimper, clutching fistfuls of linen, mewling like a newborn lamb. "Sha, dearie." Seth stroked the bit of Mary's cheek not swathed in bandage with his grimy forefinger. "Maggie's goin' to give ye medicine to make ye feel better."

Maggie passed her arm under Mary's narrow shoulders, angled the girl up, and held a tin cup to her mouth. "Drink up, darlin' . . ." she crooned. The little girl swallowed then sputtered, pursed her lips, and turned away.

"I ken it's vile." Maggie pressed the cup to her mouth. "Finish the lot and I've a nice sweetie for ye . . ." The bribe parted Mary's lips and Maggie was able to get the sedative down her throat. "There's a good, good lass." She fished a lump of shop sugar from her pocket and slipped it into the child's mouth. A smile passed over Mary's face and her eyes fluttered shut. Maggie laid her patient down, turning the girl to lie on her stomach, her injured head positioned comfortable on the pillow.

Carrying a thick leather roll like a stout stick in one hand, Tom crossed the fortyard from the smithy with a skip in his stride. "We're in luck," he announced upon reaching the makeshift surgery. "Willie had one, the cordwainer had two in his kit, and the cooper had one as well." Tom unrolled the leather onto the table, displaying four stubby pegging awls. He gripped one knobby handle in his fist. Jutting from between his fingers like a stinger, the two-inch triangular blade tapered to a fine, needle point. Maggie pressed the pad of her index finger to the tip, drawing a bright bead of blood.

"Careful," Tom said. "I had Willie hone them extra sharp."

Alistair called from the cookhearth, "Maggie! Water's on the boil . . ."

"Unwind her bandage for me, Tom, while I fix a wash for the wound." She fished a muslin sack from her basket and tossed two handfuls of dried marigold flowers into the rolling boil. The blossoms swirled into an instant sunburst. Maggie used a pothook to set the kettle to the side and ladled half the yellow infusion into a tin bowl.

At tableside, she found a crowd gathered and offering unsolicited commentary as Tom peeled back the last bloodstained linen pad. Maggie set her bowl on the table and leaned in close to examine Mary's scalped head. Crusty around its ragged edge, a rude five-inch circle of skin had been carved away—exposing a crown of smooth skull stained rusty with blood.

"This wound has calmed considerable. Not near as angry as last night." Maggie sniffed, fearful she'd find infection's moldy goat cheese smell. Instead her nostrils met the tang of raw meat. "Smells right. No corruption there."

"She's fast asleep," Seth said. "Oughtn't we be gettin' started?"

"Bide a wee." Maggie pinched off a handful of cotton lint and dipped it into the marigold tea. "I want to clean the bone."

Tom looked around. "I'll need something sturdy to sit upon . . ."

"I'll go fetch a stool," Seth volunteered.

Maggie swabbed Mary's wound. Tom and Alistair chatted with the audience. John Springer settled on a nearby stump, tuning his fiddle.

Most of the settlers were on the trail heading back to their homesteads, but some stragglers and the population who called the station home—tradesmen and newcomers seeking a claim—

formed a curious crowd jostling for position under the tarp. Some even began to seat themselves at the benches flanking the table, as if ready to dish up their supper.

Jamie Raeburn and Willie the younger tussled over the seat closest to the head of the table. Catching everyone by surprise, they moved swiftly from angry words to shoves and then to blows. The occupants of the benches scattered; Jamie and Willie fell to the ground, rolling, grappling, grunting, and swearing.

Maggie skittered out of the way, catching her basket by the handle before it hit the dirt. Her tin bowl toppled, splashing brilliant yellow over the combatants. Mary's poor head bounced on her pillow as the wrestlers smashed into the table trestles. Maggie rushed back and held on to Mary to keep her from being bumped from the tabletop.

Fiddle tuned, John Springer sawed the strings with a lively reel; the boisterous crowd chimed in with a raucous chorus, encouraging either Willie or Jamie to give the other "hell." Alistair insinuated an iron pothook between the squabblers to pry them apart while Tom clapped Willie by the collar and pulled him off.

Maggie let fly the soggy wad still in her hand, striking Willie splat on the forehead. "BUGGER OFF! All of yiz!" She moved around the table like a rabid sheepdog, shoving and poking everyone back to a comfortable distance, some three feet away.

"But I canna see a thing," big Hamish complained from the back row.

"Ye can see just fine," Maggie insisted.

"Let up, Maggie . . ." Jacob Mulberry whined. "None of us ain't never seen a hole put to anyone's head . . ."

"Stiek yer gobs," she growled. "Yer bound t' wake the lass."

"I'm amazed she didn't wake," Tom said. "That is strong medicine you dosed her with."

"Aye, well, she needs strong medicine to get through what we have planned for her."

Chubby Charlie Pritchard said, "Why all the bother anyway? Even if she survives havin' her noggin bored through, the gal still ends up living her life with a head lookin' like a burst melon—"

"Shet yer hole, ye great gallumpus!" Maggie came flying around the table, wagging her finger an inch from Charlie's nose. "Have ye not an ounce o' pity for poor Susannah? We're trying t' save her only child here. Look at ye—" She poked her finger into his paunch. "More guts than brains and a face like th' south end of a northbound ox to boot, but I wager yer mother loves ye regardless, na?"

Properly chastened by mention of his mother, Charlie sank back to stand as a silent observer while his fellows howled and hooted. Maggie marched to the hearth to collect the rest of the marigold tea and came back brandishing the pothook. "Pipe down—th' lot of yiz! This is a serious business, aye? Yiz want t' see a hole put to a head? Well, th' next man who rankles me gets a clout on the nob."

Seth returned to find a passive and orderly audience. He set a three-legged stool at the head of the table. "There ye go, Tom . . . best get started."

"Um-hmm . . . time t' get started." Tom tested the strength of the stool. He rolled his sleeves. He paced around the table, glancing at the sun. He stopped to toy with the awls arranged on the leather swath, and then he studied the little girl's butchered skull. "I don't know, Maggie . . . it may be that thy hand is better suited to this task."

Maggie slapped an awl into his palm and gave him a shove. "Like it or no, this task has fallen plump upon ye, Tom. Yiv seen it done, now have at it."

Resigned, he sat down, adjusted the stool, and gingerly turned Mary's head to face his left. "Well . . . I guess I'll just aim for center and then work my way 'round."

Seth and Maggie crouched next to him, watching as he

centered the awl tip in the field of bare bone. Cupping Mary's chin with his left hand and the knobby handle in his right, Tom twisted the sharp steel into her skull. A thin corkscrew of bone spiraled up from the site and he was surprised by the faint smell of burned hair.

"Mind, dinna bore too deep . . ."

Tom stopped and let out a breath. "It feels like I've drilled through." He pulled the awl out with a counterclockwise twist. A pink pearl of jelly oozed up from the hole, no bigger than a mustard seed. Everyone closed in for a better look-see. Young Willie standing in prime front-row position gagged, doubled over, and retched on his neighbor's boots. Tom scrunched a face at the sour smell. Seth ran over to kick dirt over the sick, offering the general announcement, "Anyone else wi' a pukey stomach—try and cast up yer accounts a ways from the table."

"Tha's a lovely hole, Tom." Maggie clapped her hands.

Tom sat back, satisfied. "It went easier that I expected."

"Like drilling a piece of maple?" Alistair asked.

"Probably more like oak," Seth suggested.

Tom scratched his head. "Oak . . . no . . . I suppose it felt more like ash—"

Maggie interrupted the inane comparison, rapping Tom and Seth on their heads with her knuckles. "Imagine how long it would take to drill through yer thick skulls. Mary's wee head bone is not fully hardened an' that's why the drillin' goes easy. Quit bletherin' and finish the job whilst she sleeps."

Tom continued to drill holes, developing a gridlike pattern, each hole approximately one inch away from the next. He stopped, set down the tool, and massaged his hand.

Seth took up a sharp awl. "Move over—I'll spell ye."

Alistair also offered to take a turn, as did Maggie. Two hours later, between the four of them, they had bored thirty-seven tiny holes into the sleeping girl's head. Per Tom's recollection of the operation he had witnessed, Maggie simply dressed the wound with a swaddling of fresh linen strips.

"We've done our best by ye, lass," Maggie whispered as Seth carried Mary back to the blockhouse. She gathered her things, tucking the amber bottle of henbane into the deepest corner of her basket.

14

Both Human and Divine

Tom glanced up at the sun melting a hole in the sky and dragged the sack of barley to a rare piece of shade near the blockhouse. Laying his kit to the side, he tossed his hat on the pile and sank down to sit, too tired to bother with the knots on his leggings and moccasins. Using the barley for a backrest, he stretched his legs and wriggled back, molding the grain into a comfortable support. Friday moseyed over with tongue lolling, turned around three times, and flopped down in a snort, laying his muzzle to rest on his master's lap.

Tom pulled two books from his pouch, thanking his lucky stars Eileen Wallen had been willing to part with them for ten Spanish dollars. *Worth every penny*, Tom thought, the written word and Friday often his sole companions in the wilderness.

He examined the larger of the two volumes purchased. Leather bound in tooled black morocco with gilt titles, this book was undoubtedly the finest he had ever owned. He opened to the first page, admiring the marbled endpapers. Running callused fingers across the illustration on the engraved frontispiece, he read the title: *The Life and Strange and Surprising Adventures of Robinson Crusoe.*

He reached for his second acquisition. The cracked spine and loose binding strings on the thinner volume barely held the paste-board cover boards attached. Paging through worn, finger-stained leaves, Tom could tell it'd been well enjoyed by its previous readers.

"Hullo." Maggie stood at his feet, basket in hand, the sun glowing a halo around her head. Tom noticed she'd exchanged the borrowed silk and lace finery for her everyday clothes—plain blouse, brown skirt, front-laced bodice. He regretted to see her black tresses once again pulled and twisted in a utilitarian knot at the nape of her neck.

Tom put his books aside. "How's Mary faring?"

"She's cleverly—sittin' up as we speak, being spoon-fed a pos-set by her mam." Maggie came to kneel beside him, opposite Friday. "What've ye got there?"

Tom showed Maggie his books. "I'm surprised Eileen parted with them."

"Eileen told me herself, when the alarm sounds, she first gath-ers her children, then gathers her books, so dear they are to her." Maggie shifted hips to sit with her legs curled to the side and picked up the smaller book. "How I wish that I could read . . . I've never been schooled—lassies weren't allowed t' attend."

"Eileen hales from Pennsylvania, not far from my family farm. Among Friends . . ."—he clarified—"among Quakers, both boys and girls are taught to read and write." He showed Maggie the novel. "This prize is a boyhood favorite of mine, *Robinson Cru-soe*."

"*Robinson Crusoe*!" Maggie exclaimed. "MacGregor read it aboard the *Good Intent*—'twas such a long crossing, he read it through twice. The best bit was when Crusoe spied the footprint in the sand . . ." She paused, and smiled. "Now I ken . . ." Maggie reached to scratch Friday behind the ear. "Did ye find this wild heathen on a Friday?"

"More like he found me."

She handed the book back and rose to her feet. "Maybe one day ye can read to me, eh?"

"How about right now?" He held up the book she'd just handed him. "*Hesperides, or Works both Human and Divine of Robert Herrick. Poetry.*"

Holding up the basket, she said, "I need to gather some lady's mantle. I spied some by the river. For Susannah—her milk's come in and she needs relief." Friday whimpered with sad eyes blinking. Maggie bent down to give the dog a farewell scratch on the snout.

Tom's senses were suddenly racked by the smell of scented soap clinging to summer-warm woman-flesh and the glorious sight of golden breasts poised to almost, but not quite overflow the bounds of a tightly laced bodice. He resisted a devilish urge to bend forward and touch his tongue to the chocolate half-moon of her nipple peeking from above her neckline.

"I'll be back soon, Friday-lad," Maggie murmured.

Her voice, an erotic whir in his ear, set Tom's heart to pounding. Her fingers, stroking the length of Friday's nose resting in his lap, sent muscles twitching. Tortured, Tom clenched fists, squirmed in his seat, and raised one knee to disguise the growing evidence of his ardor. The flap of his red breechclout slipped to the side and Maggie inadvertently brushed a molten streak along the taut muscle of his inner thigh with the back of her hand. He groaned.

As if scorched by a pot boiling on the grate, Maggie snatched her hand back and popped up erect, cheeks blazing. "I—I'll leave ye t' yer books . . ." Turning on bare foot, she all but ran away.

Her scent lingered in a sweet, soapy cloud. And with much more than tender regard, Tom sank into his barley backrest, watching her every step, spellbound by the sway of her hips as she passed through the station gates and disappeared.

With his index finger, he drew a narrow rectangle on his leg, outlining every inch of skin she'd touched. He then uncorked his flask, swallowed two big gulps, set the flask aside, flipped open the volume of poetry, and read the first lines on that page:

A sweet disorder in the dress
Kindles in clothes a wantonness.

Tom laughed, and read on.

❧

Maggie ran through the clearing till she reached the shade of the canopy. Gulping for breath, she dropped her basket and fell back to rest against the corky trunk of a sweet-gum tree, slapping herself on the forehead. "Eidgit! Reachin' between a man's legs . . . och!"

'Twere mischance . . . I only meant to pet Friday . . . She stamped her foot.

But the simple touch that lit the spark in Tom's eye had also set her own blood aflame. Hands flew to cheeks. She took several deep breaths to quash the clamor in her head. She was innocent. Her intent had been pure. He was the guilty one.

"Aye . . . Him," she muttered, snatching up her basket. "He's at fault here. He's a rascal. He was the one wrigglin' 'round like a worm on a fishhook." Satisfied with laying blame for the incident upon Tom, she flounced down the path.

The woodlands opened to a lush meadow flanking the river. Maggie stood at riverside, eyeing the cluster of lady's mantle growing on the opposite bank, more than twenty feet away. The current ran strong here and seemed much deeper than the branch back at the Martins'.

But Susannah's milk had come in, and without a baby to nurse, her breasts would become engorged, painful, and susceptible to corruption. She glanced across the river where lady's mantle teased, leaves bobbing on a breeze. A tea brewed from those leaves combined with cabbage-leaf compresses would offer Susannah much relief.

Maggie stripped to her shift and left her togs folded in a neat pile. She waded in with arms extended, her collecting basket plopped on her head like a hat, glad to find the water never higher than hip-deep.

Struggling up the steep grassy bank, Maggie disturbed a host of biting midgies to swarm about her sweaty face. She yanked up three clumps—roots and all—dumped them into her basket, and sloshed back into the river. She slogged against a strong crosscurrent, full basket in one hand, the other busy swatting tiny flies flitting into eyes and ears and feeding on tiny chunks bitten from shoulders and neck.

"Fiech!" She jerked to slap a bloodthirsty predator on her arm, slipped, and fell arse backward into the water. Maggie emerged sputtering, basket in hand, sopping wet but happily rid of the midgies. Rivulets trickled down her legs and arms as she ran up the bank. She plopped into the grass, dropping her basket next to her dry clothes.

"Whew!" She removed the pins in her wet hair, and let it fall like a satin drape to her waist. Maggie rolled back to lie in sweetgrass, sodden muslin clinging like a second skin. With hands cradling her head and ankles crossed, she closed her eyes and emptied her brain, baking in the hot sun like a corn dodger on a griddle.

The meadow hummed with the pitched pulse of cicada bugs, and every so often, a fly buzzed loud past her ear. In the distance, a woodpecker drummed in starts and stops. And just when the sun blazed too hot to bear, a river breeze swept across the field, cooled her instantly, and allowed her to wallow a few moments more.

She couldn't be bothered to open her eyes to see whatever had landed, tickling on her nose, and she just shooed it away with lazy fingers. She brushed it away from her ear, and the persistent bug moved to the hollow of her throat to scurry down the neckline of her shift between her breasts.

Maggie jerked up squealing, plucking at her shift, to find Tom crouched on hunkers next to her, grinning mischievous, waving a tufted stalk of sedge grass.

"Away wi' ye, rascal!" Blushing, she fumbled for clothes. Knees hunched to her chest, she struggled to put on her bodice.

"Caught me nappin' in naught but my shift . . ." She paused, noticing he was unarmed, encumbered only by his pouch hanging over one shoulder. In sudden realization, Maggie snatched up a clump of lady's mantle and whipped it at his head.

"*Ow!*"

"Yiv been skulkin' about, haven't ye? Sneaking 'round like a Red Indian . . ."

Tom brushed dirt from his shirt, a wry smile on his face. "I came to lend a hand . . ."

"Lend a hand . . . hmmph!" Maggie sneered, tightening the laces on her bodice with a firm tug.

"C'mon, Maggie . . ." Pulling *Hesperides* from his pouch, he said, "I brought a book to read."

He seemed contrite, and for some reason she was happy he had followed after her. "Well, all right," Maggie relented, patting the grass. "Read to me, then."

Tom reclined beside her. Up on one elbow, he opened to a page marked with a finger length of blue ribbon. "Lie down . . ." He gave her a gentle shove to the shoulder. Stretching back to lie with arms tucked under her head, Maggie closed her eyes. Tom cleared his throat, and read:

> "*Bid me to live, and I will live*
> *Thy protestant to be;*
> *Or bid me love, and I will give*
> *A loving heart to thee.*
> *A heart as soft, a heart as kind,*
> *A heart as sound and free,*
> *As in the whole world thou canst find,*
> *That heart I'll give to thee.*
> *Bid that heart stay, and it will stay,*
> *To honour thy decree;*
> *Or bid it languish quite away,*
> *And 't shall do so for thee.*

Bid me to weep, and I will weep,
While I have eyes to see;
And having none, yet I will keep
A heart to weep for thee.
Bid me despair, and I'll despair,
Under that cypress tree;
Or bid me die, and I will dare
E'en death, to die for thee.
Thou art my life, my love, my heart,
The very eyes of me;
And hast command of every part,
To live and die for thee."

"Oh, Tom . . ." Maggie sighed, turning toward him. One hand slipped about his neck, she grabbed his leather belt tight with the other hand and pulled him close.

Tom tossed the book aside and wrapped her in his arms. Their hungry mouths blundered then met in an urgent, deep kiss. Arms and legs entwined, they rolled slowly and Maggie found herself flat beneath him, legs parted.

With one arm entangled in her hair, Tom buried his face in her neck. He groaned, pressing large and hot, a forged iron rod straining against damp muslin and soft belly. A tiny, wobbly whimper escaped Maggie's lips and she pushed against his chest.

Tom pulled up on elbows, his hair hanging wild, distressed brow furrowed. Breathing heavy, he hovered there.

Maggie bit her lip, hands still pressed to Tom's chest. She looked into his eyes for a moment, then smiled and slipped her hands down to unbuckle the belt about his waist.

Tom laughed and rolled to lie beside her. He kissed her soft on the lips. Sky blue eyes intent on hers, he loosened the bow and tugged, one by one, the laces from the eyelets on her bodice. "Maggie Duncan, I mean to ravish thee . . ."

"Aye, lad . . ." she breathed. ". . . Get on with it."

Strands of rosy-gold light wove a horizontal pattern across the twilight sky. Down on one knee, Tom fiddled with the laces on his moccasins while Maggie waited at his side, swinging her basket, shifting weight from one bare foot to the other.

Maggie studied the sky. "The gloaming's comin' quick upon us. We tarried overlong."

"I like 'tarrying' with you." Tom glanced up with a wicked smirk. "And I think we ought 'tarry' more often."

Blushing, Maggie gave him a playful bump with her hip. "Och, but yer a cheeky lad!" She turned on heel and marched a quick-step toward the trailhead.

Tom hopped to his feet, scurried to pluck a fistful of flowers, and ran to catch up. "Maggie, I'll carry that . . ." He pried the basket from her hand and offered her the nosegay. "None-so-pretties—like you."

Tickling fingertips over the petals, Maggie buried her nose in the cluster of purple flowers, pleased by the offering. "What a clever name, none-so-pretty . . ."

"That's what my mother called them, anyway." Tom slid his arm about Maggie's waist and she slipped her arm about his. Together they strolled down the woodland path toward Round-about.

"You know, back home in Glen Spean, I could put a name to almost every growing thing—wood or field. But here . . ." Maggie heaved a sigh.

Tom held up the basket filled with lady's mantle. "I've seen this flower growing along streambeds my whole life long and never knew its name till today. I'd say you know more'n most folk."

"Aye, what I know best is I've still much to learn."

"I can show you some—" Tom stopped short and veered off the trail, pulling Maggie by the hand to stand at the base of a tall tree. "I learned this from my time with the Ojibwe. They called it a medicine tree—*ozhaashigob*."

"Ohh-gaa-shkee-bob . . ." Maggie giggled.

"*O-zhaa-shi-gob*. White folk call it slippery elm."

Maggie reached out and touched the tree. "It's no verra slippery . . ."

Tom tugged the tomahawk from his belt, carved off a gritty, gray strip of bark, and turned it over to show Maggie the pale, viscous inner bark. "See—it's slick on the inside. You peel the smooth part free from the rough and grind it to a flour. I always try to keep a sackful in my kit. Comes in handy."

Maggie took the bark from Tom and sniffed. "Smells like celery, na? What's it good for?"

Tom continued to work the tomahawk, efficiently stripping the trunk clean. "I mix the flour with a few drops of water. Slippery-elm plaster heals sores and wounds better than anything. See this?" He showed Maggie a shiny scar the size of a Spanish dollar located midthigh, just above his leather legging. "Stopped a Mohawk musket ball. Pried it out, packed the hole with slippery elm . . ." Tom slapped his leg. "Good as new."

"Mohawk? A Red Indian shot ye?"

"Um-hmm. Ambushed hunting their ground with the Ojibwe." Tom hunkered down and began peeling curls of inner bark from the pile he'd harvested. "Mohawk and Ojibwe are sworn enemies."

Maggie knelt to help, repeating the odd word. "Oh-jib-way."

"Um-hmm. Ojibwe women fix slippery-elm tea for a flux in the belly or gut . . ."

Ojibwe women! Maggie's heart jerked and danced a jealous jig in her chest. *Aye . . . where else would he have learned those things . . .*

A flush rushed to her cheeks and a shiver coursed her spine, recalling the past hours spent in his arms. Tom Roberts had proved to be more than ably skilled in the art of love. Maggie could only guess at the countless women he'd pleasured in acquiring those skills, and she cringed a bit, recalling her own awkwardness. Maggie kept her hands busy peeling bark, covert eyes watching Tom. She could never hope to compare to the likes of pretty Bess Hawkins or wild Indian maidens.

"You can eat slippery elm," he rambled on. "Cooked, it tastes kind of like walnuts. Ojibwe women use the flour to make a wholesome gruel for weaning babies or to feed the infirm. It's good food . . ."

Aye . . . I'll wager he's lain atop many a wanton Indess . . . Maggie shook her head to banish the image from her mind.

". . . I swear it's the truth, Maggie. When game was scarce and corn run out, our whole clan ate it. Many a time we had naught but *ozhaashigob* porridge to hold pinching hunger at bay." Tom stood. "We have enough here. We'd better get going."

Basket in one hand, he hoisted Maggie up to her feet. Gathering her in a one-armed embrace, he pressed a sweet kiss to her lips, saying simply, "I am that happy." Taking Maggie by the hand, Tom led her back onto the trail.

Maggie's mind slipped back to their time in the meadow. *Live and die for thee.* That's what he whispered in her ear the moment they had joined flesh. As she walked alongside Tom, his seed mingling with virgin blood seeped sticky between her legs; she gripped his hand tight, and tried hard to shove her doubts aside. Tom Roberts was her man now and she was determined to know him well. "How long did ye live among Red Indians?"

"Oh, a little more'n three years."

"Three years! It must've been awful for ye, livin' among the fearsome brutes . . ."

Tom stiffened and squared his shoulders. They walked for a stretch in uneasy silence.

As suddenly contrite as she was jealous, Maggie blurted, "I didna mean to pry—it's no wonder ye never speak on it . . ."

"Naw—it ain't that. I guess I spend so much time on the trail alone, I've just grown accustomed to keeping things close to my own heart." He met her eyes smiling and squeezed her hand slightly. "Truth is, it weren't awful. As a matter of fact, I found the Ojibwe people lived a more Christian life than most whites who profess the faith."

"What yer sayin' runs contrary to everything tolt t' me about Indians."

"Yep. I speak hard truths, and when I returned, I didn't hesitate to tell others what I thought. But I learned quick—it's much easier for white folk to believe all Indians are devils. Makes it easy to push them aside. Easy to take advantage. Tends to rub the conscience less when you steal from a heathen."

"But they *are* heathens—savages."

"All men are savages when at war. The Ojibwe are fierce warriors, but they are also kind, generous, and honorable people. From the moment they washed the white out of me, I was always treated with fairness and respect, an equal to any true son of the clan."

"Washed the white out of ye?"

Tom laughed. "You remember how I was captured and ran the gauntlet?"

Maggie nodded.

"After that I was traded off to a band of Ojibwe. I left with my new captors, thinking I'd gain an opportunity to make good an escape. But we traveled to the north country by canoe, and it was days and days afore they discarded my bindings. By that time there were hundreds of miles between me and Braddock's army. I began to despair of ever getting back."

"Could ye no sneak off into the night?"

"A green boy, just seventeen, unarmed in hostile territory with winter comin' on?" Tom shook his head. "It would have been the end of me for sure. Winter up north is harsh, like nothin' you've ever seen.

"When we arrived at the village I was lickety-split stripped of my clothes. They dressed me Indian fashion—a buckskin shirt and leggings heavy with bead and quillwork. My ears were bored and hung with silver ornaments—"

"No!" Maggie looked close. Sure enough, though unadorned, Tom's ears were pierced.

"And an old woman pulled almost every hair from my head—plucked me like a Christmas goose—bald but for a greased and befeathered topknot. I must have been quite a sight to see.

"They brought me to the river where the multitude had gathered. I began to fidget a bit, feeling more and more like that Christmas goose. I figured they'd trussed me up for some grand entertainment—like being roasted on a spit.

"Then a very old man—the chief—stood and spoke a great lot of what at the time was gibberish to me. When he finished, I was seized by a gaggle of young women. They pushed and pulled me to the water. I was sure they meant to drown me, so you can imagine, I kicked up quite a fuss. I struggled, hollerin' loud, swinging elbows and fists until I heard one woman say, 'No hurt you.' I stopped struggling then. The women took me into the river and scrubbed every inch of me." Tom winked at Maggie. "It weren't so bad after all."

Imagining the scene, Maggie suppressed another wave of sickening self-doubt from overcoming her reason. She would have to grow a thick skin if she really meant to become a true friend to this man. "And the Indians," she asked, "they truly believed they washed the white from you?"

"A baptism of sorts I s'pose. After that, I was considered one of them."

"But ye aren't one of them. Ye shouldered yer rifle and marched off with the militia eager to kill Redmen. Ye saw firsthand what the devils did to the Bledsoes . . . to wee Mary . . ."

"And I've also seen many terrible things white men have done to Indian women and children as well. It's a quandary—I know they're heathen people and have seen with mine own eyes that they're quite capable of the worst savagery, but still, I find much to admire in them."

"Admire!"

"They're the best hunters, Maggie." There was a curious sparkle in his eye as he spoke. "They live close to the land. Almost everything I know about tracking, trapping, and woodcraft, I learned in the three years spent with the Bear Clan."

"Hmmph! If it were all so grand, why'd ye ever leave?"

Tom stopped and faced Maggie. "I left because I came to know that thee can never wash the white out. It don't work that way—not for me anyhow."

"*Maaaggieeee!*"

The two turned in tandem to see Jack Martin, kicking up a whirlwind tearing along the trail toward them. He skidded to a cataclysmic stop and leaned one scrawny arm against the trunk of a honey-locust tree, his cheeks painted bright with exertion, gulping air.

"Da sent me t' fetch y' back . . . Mam's havin' the baby!"

15

Old Clothes and Comfort

"Ada . . ." Maggie shook the dozing woman by the shoulder. "Ada, wake. The head's crowning."

Ada Buchanan stirred from her stool in the corner, rubbing sandy eyes with fists and stretching to stand upright. Maggie opened the blockhouse door, drinking in a quick breath of almost dawn before striding with purpose to her worktable.

Squinting in the dim light, Ada surveyed the room. "Where's Eileen?"

"She's gone to fetch more water." Maggie looked up from pinning a bib-style apron to her bodice and laughed. "Yer cap's all cockeyed . . ."

Ada straightened the mobcap awry on her head, rolled sleeves up over fleshy forearms, and glanced out the open door. "Not quite daybreak—we need more light."

"Aye." Maggie dropped several items into the large pocket on her hip. "There's another lantern outside the door."

The sleepy, windowless room was now alive with activity. Ada hung the lantern from the center ceiling rafter, bathing the crowded sickroom in bright, swinging light. Sharing the bed opposite the birthing bed with her daughter Mary, Susannah Bledsoe woke and rose up on one elbow. Eileen trounced in and set a brass kettle under the table, its plume of steam adding to the swelter of close quarters. Maggie unfurled a frayed bedsheet and snapped it out to cover the narrow floor space between the two beds.

Naomi moaned, her thin face pinched in pain. She pushed up to sit and swung her legs over the bedside, her toes barely grazing the floorboards. Panting, sweating, gripping the edge of the makeshift bed, Naomi struggled to stand. "This baby's a-comin' Maggie . . . this baby's comin' NOW!"

Ada and Eileen scurried around. Flanking the laboring woman like stalwart sentry soldiers, each looped a strong arm about Naomi's waist and helped hoist her to her feet. Maggie knelt down, centered and facing the linked trio of women.

"Hike up her shift . . ." Maggie ordered. The women obeyed, each yanking a fistful of sweat-soaked muslin, hip-high. "Now bear down, Naomi . . ."

Tossing her head like a mare shy of the halter, Naomi moaned, "I'm so tired."

"Bear down!"

"I can't do it . . . I can't."

Maggie locked eyes with Naomi. "Dinna give up now. Yiv endured hours of grinding pains. These are the forcing pains, lass. Take a good breath and bear down."

Naomi nodded. Drawing in a deep breath, she swiped away the tears and strands of auburn hair plastered to her ruddy cheeks. Bracing herself between the two solid columns of women, she crouched down into a semisquat, scrunched her eyes tight, and pushed.

"*Uuurrrrgghh!*"

Maggie reached up between the laboring woman's straining thighs, cradling the murky little head as it squeezed its way into the world.

"This babe's wearing its caul!" Maggie grinned, peeling off a piece of thin, translucent membrane that clung to the knob of the newborn's skull like a sailor's cap.

"Save the caul for a charm, Maggie," Ada advised.

"A good sign." Eileen spoke soft into Naomi's ear. "Thee's birthing a lucky one, dearie."

Gasping for breath as she slumped between the two women, Naomi could only nod. She planted her feet to make ready as muscles bunched and a wave of pain rode over her distended abdomen, crashing full force at the nexus between her legs.

"Hold fast, Naomi," Maggie encouraged. "Bear down . . ."

Fingers digging ridges into Ada and Eileen's steady shoulders, Naomi crouched down once more, growling like a wounded she-bear.

"Gggrrrraauuughhh!"

With one hand Maggie supported the tiny neck and shoulders as they popped free of the birth canal. Ready, and with expert ease, she caught the baby as it slipped out in a sloppy rush of membranes, blood, and birth water. "A son!"

Naomi went limp; exhausted, she was lowered to sit.

Working with quick deliberation, Maggie laid the newborn belly down onto the sheet and carefully unwound the knobby gray cord tangled about his torso and limbs.

Ada and Eileen hugged and petted the new mother, but Naomi shrugged them off and leaned forward, suddenly stiff with anxiety. "He's not breathing . . ." Her whimper rose to a panic. "Maggie, he's not breathing!"

Too busy to do aught but glance up with an assuring smile, Maggie said, "He's just fine . . ."

Eileen pointed to the pulsating umbilical cord trailing out from between Naomi's legs and still attached to the newborn. "Remember, thee harbors his life whilst the navel string is uncut."

Relieved, Naomi watched Maggie slip her pinkie finger into the baby's tiny mouth to scoop out a globule of mucus. She flipped him onto his back and the boy sucked his first breath. Pixie chest heaved and he allover blossomed in an instant, turning from sickly lavender gray to healthy pink. Sputtering, minuscule features screwed into an angry scowl, he screamed with annoyance, flailing wee arms and fists, extended limbs taut and trembling.

Naomi laughed, tears streaming down her face. "Oh, but isn't he the spit of his da!"

Cupping the squalling baby by the head and behind, Maggie hefted the boy, judging his weight. "A great chunk of a boy. I wager he's at least half a stone, if not more."

Susannah said, "He's got a strong pair of lungs, God bless him."

Naomi smiled at her friend across the aisle. "He does, doesn't he?"

Maggie's heart lurched at the sound of Susannah's voice. *How difficult this must be for her.* She glanced over her shoulder and could see that Susannah wore a bittersweet smile, and her eyes glistened with sad tears.

"Eileen, ready water for the bath." Maggie reached into her pocket and drew out three items, laying them side by side to her right—a sharp paring knife, a twist of twine, and a slender, green glass bottle. She unraveled the twine and snipped off two foot-long pieces. "I'd like to tie off and cut the cord now," she told Naomi. "It's barely throbbing."

Maggie wound the string very tight, a knuckle length away from the baby's navel, tying it firmly in place. She repeated the task, tying the second string two inches from the first. Taking up the knife, she sliced through the umbilicus between the two knots, leaving a two-inch protruding stump tied off.

"Here's clean swaddling." Eileen set a folded blanket and a tin basin at Maggie's left.

Maggie moved the baby into the basin, rinsing away blood and the layer of cheesy coating that protected delicate skin in the womb. The warm water calmed Baby Martin, and he found his thumb and dozed off.

"Mind," Ada warned. "Keep the lad's palms dry—ye dinna want to wash away his good fortune."

"Dinna fash. I've bathed many a bairn and have yet to rinse a fortune away." As always, Maggie had been careful to keep the newborn's hands from touching water, rubbing them clean with a dry towel. She laid him with his head positioned at the corner of the clean receiving blanket and dabbed him dry. "Ada." Maggie uncorked the green bottle and drizzled a few drops onto the cut end of the umbilical cord. "Hand me that roll of bandage there and the penny."

Eileen sat down next to Maggie. Three months pregnant herself, she had a vested interest in evaluating the new midwife's method. "What did thee drip onto the lad?"

"Oil of cloves. It helps the stump t' dry and fall off quick." Maggie placed the penny near the baby's navel and wound a soft band of flannel firmly about his middle, tucking the loose end in. "Makes for a nice neat belly button." The midwife flipped the blanket up and crossed over both sides. She gathered the swaddled baby and handed him up into his mother's eager arms. "Here ye go, Mammy. Give yer bairnie a lick and a nuzzle."

"He's lovely!" Naomi shrugged off the shoulder of her shift to expose her breast. She stroked the sleeping baby lips with the tip of her nipple pinched between two fingers. Eyes still shut, her baby snuffled, rooted, and latched on. The women broke into applause.

Naomi toyed with the fluff of red hair on her baby's head, "He's ginger . . ."

"He's the loveliest baby boy . . ." Eileen said.

"And so quick to the breast . . ." Susannah observed.

"Dinna forespeak th' bairn, ladies," Ada admonished. "Praise will only draw the attention of the faeries."

Naomi bit her tongue, but practical Eileen Wallen laughed at the notion. "Faeries! Ada, thee does not hold truck with all that old-country nonsense?"

"'Tis no nonsense," Ada insisted. "Faeries are known t' steal a newborn and leave a changeling in its place. It's best to take steps and keep the faeries at a distance. Maggie kens. Aye. Did ye no see her slip the penny intae the bairn's belly band?"

꧁❦꧂

Brilliant orange light keeked between the chinks and drizzled over the top of the stockade wall. A scrawny leghorn rooster flapped up onto the trestle table and crowed in the new day.

Tom shooed the rude bird off the tabletop with a swipe of one arm, and continued to transfer crisp slices of fried salt pork from the griddle to the platter.

Armed with a wooden paddle, Alistair sat crouched on his haunches beside the cookfire, tending a skillet of scrambled eggs. A cauldron of cornmeal mush hanging from a tripod over the flames bubbled and popped. Seth sat droopy-headed opposite Alistair. Using the long wooden spoon meant for stirring the porridge, he aimlessly poked at the embers, arranging the glowing coals into meaningless patterns.

Alistair said, "Here comes Maggie . . ."

Maggie trudged across the fortyard, the tin pail she carried glinting rose in the morning light. Seth scrambled to his feet, absentmindedly tossing the wooden spoon to burn in the fire. He skirted the cooking pit in three long strides and met Maggie just as she reached the dining table under the tarp, his bloodshot eyes rimmed with worry.

"Naomi's safe delivered . . ."—Maggie plunked her pail onto the tabletop—"and yiv a son! A fine, banging boy!" Seth whooped and swept Maggie into a big bear hug.

Tom and Alistair huddled around and the three men met in a manly exchange of shoulder slaps, handshakes, and cheers of "Well done!"

"I'm fair puggled." Maggie laughed, hands on hips. "Would ye look who's cock of the walk? Why, it must have been Seth who labored through the night."

Seth sobered. "But ye swear Naomi's well, Maggie?"

"Aye. Though she canna abide straddling a mule just yet, she's cleverly tucked into fresh linen wi' yer son at her breast . . ." Maggie gave Seth a two-handed shove. "Away wi' ye, now. G'won. Off to yer woman . . ."

Seth stumbled a few steps, turned, flashed a grin, and took off in full gallop toward the blockhouse.

Maggie linked fingers, stretched her arms over her head, and yawned. "I'm off as well."

"Off?" Tom asked. "You haven't had your breakfast yet."

"I've one task left me." She tipped the tin pail slightly to show him the umbilical cord coiled like a bumpy snake atop a veiny, liver-red mass squashed at the bottom. "This afterbirth willna bury itself." She gripped the wire bale handle in her fist and swung the pail from the table.

"Aye, bury it straightaway, lass." Alistair grimaced with a shake of his shaggy white head. "We dinna want the wee bairnie cursed with ill luck."

Tom tried to prize the pail away from Maggie. "Let me take care of this for you. It's plain to me that thee is worn thin."

"No, Tom." Maggie maintained firm hold on her responsibilities. "This is a midwife's duty. But dinna fash, I intend to find my pillow with speed."

"Well, at least take a moment and have a bite to eat . . ." Tom and Alistair both turned to face the cookfire. Black smoke spiraled up from eggs burned and crusted in the bottom of the skillet. Glops of porridge boiled over the pot's brim, landing plop and hiss in the fire below.

Maggie giggled and snicked a crisp piece of bacon from the platter to munch as she headed toward the open gates.

⟨❧⟩

Hugging her pillow tight, Maggie woke, blinking at the dark. She lay quiet, listening to John Springer tune his fiddle, producing random notes sounding like smooth, round stones dropped one by one into still water. *Plunk . . . plunk . . . plunk-plunk.*

The odd music was cushioned by soft voices and laughter gathered around a crackling fire. Maggie sat up, mildly amazed she'd slept the day away. As her eyes adjusted to the night, she was glad to see the Martin children had managed to find their beds without her urging. Winnie lay on her back, sapling straight between her two brothers, curled at either side. She tiptoed a path around the sleeping children.

The smell of venison roasted over hickory coals teased in the moonlight. The rumble in Maggie's belly put a spring in her step. Making her way to the cookfire, she crossed her fingers and prayed for leftovers.

Roundabout's regulars and a few lingerers sat within the bounds of bonfire light in loose clusters of twos and threes. As Maggie drew nearer, she was able to discern faces flickering in the glow. Eileen Wallen sat on the hard-packed earth, leaning back to rest against her husband, Fletcher. Next to the Wallens, Janet Wheeler sat holding hands with Young Willie, and Janet's father kept an eagle eye on the courting couple from across the fire, where he shared a log seat with Bess and old Henry. Like a row of roosting chickens, Seth, Alistair, and Duncan Moon were perched side by side on a log at the opposite end of the fire pit, passing a bottle between them. Lanky John Springer stood off to the side with one foot propped on an upended log, fussing with his instrument.

Maggie greeted everyone as she wound her way around to the dining table where Ada Buchanan pulled a frothy pint of ale from a tapped keg. She pressed a full cup into Maggie's hand. "Did ye have a good rest, dearie?"

"Can ye believe I snored the day away? I'm starved. Is there anything left t' eat?"

"I put a bit by for ye, figurin' ye were bound t' wake hungry." Ada produced a trencher groaning with hefty hunks of buttered cornbread, slices of cold roast, half a garlic pickle, and a triangle of yellow cheese.

"Maggie!" Seth called to her with a wave. She settled next to him, juggling her meal in her lap. He eyed the pile of food on her plate. "Hungry, eh?"

"Hollow. My backbone's rubbin' up against my belly." Maggie chewed a bite of pickle. "I dinna see Tom anywhere . . ."

"He left earlier—on a hunt, I s'pose."

"Oh." Disappointed, Maggie centered a piece of venison on a slice of bread. "Naomi and the bairnie are doin' well?"

"Aye." Seth smiled proud. "He's a lively lad."

She tore a bite off and chewed on her bread and meat for a while before asking, "Have yiz settled on a name?"

"Alexander—after my da."

"Now, there's a fine Scots name—Alexander Martin—a name a lad can grow into. As soon as I finish my dinner, I'll go and see t' yer wife and son."

Maggie headed to the sickroom, feeling much the better for the supper in her belly. She stepped into the lantern-lit blockhouse and found Susannah Bledsoe sitting Indian style on her bed, nursing Naomi's newborn.

"Och, Susannah!"

"Shhh." Susannah touched the tip of her finger to her lips then gestured to Naomi asleep in her bed across the aisle. "The poor girl didn't get a wink of sleep the whole day. She's only just now slipped into her dreams."

Maggie moved to the bedside, disapproval firm on her face. Susannah held up her palm. "Don't fret so." Her whisper was oddly forceful. "Naomi asked me to feed him."

"Why? Is she ill?"

"Naw, just tuckered out after suffering the day with a headache and a fussy baby."

Maggie glanced over her shoulder to Naomi sleeping soundly. "A headache?"

Susannah nodded. "And you know how she worries. Poor Naomi has but little for him, yet this fella squalls so . . . she was at wit's end." Exhibiting the expertise of a woman who'd nursed five children, Susannah poked a finger into the corner of the infant's mouth. Breaking the suction, she swiftly switched the baby to nurse at her left breast, giving him no time to sputter even the tiniest protest. "Naomi's my good friend," Susannah went on. "I don't know what it's like over the water where you come from, but here on the frontier, we do for one another. It's how we survive."

"Still, Susannah, ye ken it's best not to make a habit of feeding Naomi's son." Maggie stepped to her worktable, poured a dose of lady's-mantle tisane, and offered it to Susannah. "Drink this and bind yer breasts with cabbage leaves like I tolt ye. As much as it may ease ye for the now, nursing Naomi's bairn will only prolong yer discomfort."

Susannah looked up; a tear rolled down her cheek and fell, absorbed in the swaddled bundle clutched to her breast. "Nursing him eases my pain, Maggie . . . the pain you've no medicine for . . . the awful pain in my heart."

Maggie sat on the bed beside Susannah and wound an arm around her shoulders. "I've no children of my own, but I think I ken what ye mean. Sometimes comfort comes in old clothes, na?"

Susannah leaned into Maggie's embrace and together they shared the peace gleaned from watching a baby suckle to sleepy contentment. Afterward, Maggie changed his nappy and bundled him to lie beside his mother.

"How's wee Mary?" Maggie gestured to the little lump curled beside Susannah.

"Ada made Mary a doll and she played the day long." Susannah pointed to the rag doll nestled in the crook of the little girl's arm. "She calls it Baby Alexander."

"Has she pain?"

"My Mary's a strong spirit. She's not one to complain." Susannah lay back and gathered her daughter in a cuddle in her arms.

Maggie straightened the bedclothes. "I'd say Mary's much like her mother in that. Now try hard to find some sleep." She dimmed the lantern and closed the door.

Maggie rejoined the circle of friends making merry around the campfire in time to see Ada pulling Duncan and Alistair front and center. After the threesome joined heads in whispered consultation, Duncan swaggered around the fire on his peg leg, addressing the audience.

"The Roundabout Players will regale you with 'The Tale of the Trooper's Horse.'"

A rousing cheer rose up in anticipation of the bawdy favorite. Maggie jumped to her feet, skirting around to better her view. The fiddler struck up the familiar tune and Ada sang the first few lines in a fine, clear voice:

> "'Tis a landlady's daughter and her name was Nelly,
> And she took to bed sick with a pain in her belly.
> It was then a bold trooper rode up to the inn,
> He's perishing cold and wet to the skin.
> The landlady put 'em in bed together
> To see if the one couldn't cure th' other."

Alistair stepped forward with Ada's beribboned mobcap perched silly on his head. He struck a girlish pose and warbled Nelly's part in falsetto:

> "Oh my, what is this, so stiff and so warm?"

Duncan, as the Bold Trooper, draped an arm around "Nelly" and responded in baritone:

"'Tis Bald, my Nag, he will do you no harm."

And to the delight of the spectators, they continued on with the song, each man taking a turn singing his part in comical fashion.

"'But my! What is this that hangs under his chin?'
'Tis the bag that he puts his Provender in.'
Quoth he, 'What is this?'
Quoth she, "'Tis a well, where Bald, your Nag, can drink
*   his fill.'*
'But what if my Nag should chance to slip in?'
'Then catch hold of the grass that grows on the brim.'
'But what if the grass should chance to fail?'
'Shove him in by the head, pull him out by the tail.'
'But how can you tell when your Nag's had his fill?'
'He'll hang down his head and turn from the well.'
'How can you tell when your Nag wants some more?'
'He'll rear up his head and paw 'round the door!'"

The crowd clapped and howled with laughter. Duncan bowed like a courtier and Alistair, at his side, bobbed and curtsied like a maid. Ada retrieved her cap and herded her fellow players back to their seats.

"Enough ribaldry . . ." Ada scanned the faces gathered and pointed. "The Wallens! C'mon up and give us a ballad."

Eileen demurred but was pulled to her feet by her husband, Fletcher. "All right . . ." she said, "how 'bout 'Over the Hill and Far Away'? Everyone can join in on the chorus."

A resounding cheer served to seal the bargain with the audience. The fiddler sawed the melody, Eileen's soft soprano melded in close harmony with her husband's strong tenor, and the duo sang the first stanza of the well-known love song. With arms folded across her chest, Maggie swayed from side to side and joined in singing the chorus along with everyone else:

"And I would love you all the day,
Every night would kiss and play,
If with me you'd fondly stray,
Over the hills and far away."

A strong hand wound around Maggie's waist and the refrain caught in her throat. Tom came to stand behind her, his palm flat and fingers splayed just beneath her belly, pulling her back—a cushion pressed against his hardness. She sighed and leaned back. Nuzzling the curve of her neck, he breathed warm in her ear, "Stray with me . . . beyond the gate." And then he let her loose.

Maggie turned to catch the last of his shadow as it blended into inky darkness beyond the bonfire—only his scent lingered, a distillation of hard work, leather, and green woods. She pressed a hand to her forehead. *Such a strange affliction.* The man held a tether on her heart and one tug of the rope left her fevered, wobble-kneed, with heart a-pounding.

The Wallens finished their song and drew a round of applause. Seth stood, staggering slightly, more than a bit pickled after a long night of celebration. Ada handed him a full tankard and he raised it high. "A toast!" he said, with brogue extra thick. "Tae ma wee wifie, an ma bonnie wee laddie—tae Alexander!"

"To Alexander!"

John Springer tapped his foot and tore into a rollicking rendition of "Red-haired Boy." Seth got hold of Ada and the pair launched into an energetic, two-person reel around the bonfire.

Maggie cheered and clapped along, all the while inching backward, until breaking free the bounds of fire glow, she headed toward the open gates at the quickstep. The full moon, briefly enveloped in cloud cover, cast a dark face on her escape, and she slowed her pace, carefully navigating the tree stumps that littered the fortyard. Just as she breached the palisade, Tom reached out from the dark and grabbed Maggie by the arm. She squeaked in surprise and spun into his arms. Grappling, groping, and giggling, the lovers staggered back and fell against the stockade wall.

"I'm hungry for thee." Tom drove his tongue in deep to occupy her mouth. Maggie's fingers fumbled with the buckle at his waist. Tom's arms flailed like a whirligig through yards of brown wool and muslin.

Suddenly an odd voice sang out, "*Oh Tom, vas is dis, so stiff and so varm . . .*" Young Willie and Janet Wheeler poked their heads around the gate.

Maggie jerked away and backed into the shadows. Flustered, she smoothed her skirt, tucked stray wisps of hair behind her ears, and tried to catch a breath. Panting, Tom stood with fists clenched, looking much like a young lad whose wagon had shed a wheel. Laughing aloud, Willie and Janet scampered off, hand in hand, disappearing into the dark.

"Willie Wagner . . ." Tom growled, snatching up his rifle. "Sorry shall be his sops when I get ahold of him tomorrow . . ."

"Ah, now, Tommy . . . just a bit of fun. No harm done."

Tom shouldered his weapon and grabbed Maggie by the hand. "Come with me . . ."

Song and fiddle strains grew faint on a gathering breeze. Maggie tripped after Tom, walk-running to keep up with his determined stride as he cut across the cleared field surrounding the fort. "Where're we going?"

"My camp," he said, pointing to the tree line where the dark forest began.

"Yer camp? Why d'ye camp in the open with the station right there?"

"Station's too crowded for me," he said, and Maggie laughed.

The wind picked up; racing across the open field, it tore through the treetops with a rumble akin to a coach and six rolling along a cobbled street. Ahead, the black wall of trees loomed, swaying from side to side—giant hands warning them to stay away.

Maggie hesitated. "D'ye think a storm's brewin'?"

"Just windy, is all." Tom's hand tightened on hers. "Camp's just ahead." He tugged her forward, into the woods.

The breeze, in concert with the moonlight keeking through the veil of silver leaves, cast a mottled pattern of moving shadows on their path. Friday trotted up to greet them with tail wagging as Tom led Maggie to the spartan camp he'd pitched on a level patch within a crown of white birch. A pale wool blanket banded with three black stripes lay in a rumple near a ring of stones containing chunky embers throbbing red on the breeze. Tom's possibles pouch, leather panniers, and half a dozen birch logs were piled next to the fire ring. Hobbled in the shadows, the gelding huffed and shuffled his hooves.

Tom let go of Maggie's hand and slipped his rifle from his shoulder, propping it barrel end up on the firewood. Maggie ruffled Friday's ears and held him rapt with a good scratch.

"Go 'n lie down now!" Tom commanded.

Maggie startled, and for a ridiculous instant, she thought Tom's terse order had been directed at her. But Friday knew better; breaking away from Maggie, he spun in three tight circles and flopped down with a grunt.

Tom hefted a pair of logs onto the embers, sending a brilliant *whoosh* of sparks to swirl up like a host of fireflies into the night. He smiled at Maggie and unbuckled his waist belt, dropping it in a muffled clank with the rest of his gear.

A gust of wind twirled in through the trees, fanning the embers to flames. Maggie stood a bit uneasy, fumbling with her laces, awkward in the brighter light. Exasperated, she turned her back to Tom's wry smile and slipped free her bodice, carefully hanging it from a nearby birch branch. She reached back to undo her hair.

"Let me." Tom came up from behind. He pulled the pins from the knot she'd twisted at the base of her neck, sending her hair tumbling over her shoulders like a freshet over a cliff after a hard rain. His fingers traveled through her hair down to untie the knot at her waistband. Pushing her skirt down past her hips, Tom bent his head, nosed her hair aside, and sang soft in her ear:

"And I would love you all the day,
Every night would kiss and play,
If with me you'd fondly stray,
Over the hills and far away."

Maggie turned in to his embrace. Dressed in nothing but her muslin shift, she pulled him close, his full measure pressing a warm ridge into her belly. She slipped tentative hands under his frock shirt. He pulled back and tugged the shirt off over his head.

Tom stood before her in the flickering firelight in naught but breechclout and doeskin leggings, his moccasined feet planted as if ready to spring—exuding a raw force Maggie found both fascinating and frightening. A breeze coursed the treetops with a whistling moan and she shuffled back a step, irrational dismay welling up in her throat.

"Maggie . . ." Tom reached out to her with one open hand. "I couldn't sleep for hurtin' t' have thee naked in my bed."

The stark, rough hunger of his admission stole her breath away. Maggie's shift drifted into a puddle at her feet and she stepped into his arms, molding to him like wet linen laid to dry on a sun-warmed stone.

They sank to the ground and he covered her body with his own, pressing her into the cloud of crumbly humus carpeting the forest floor—their whispers and moans lost to the crackling blaze and the rustle of birch leaves trembling on the breeze.

16

A Nice Cup of Tea

Tom slipped out from under the leg and arm she'd thrown over him and trotted, stark naked, to a huge oak ten yards from camp. Piss-proud member in his right hand, feet spread wide, he propped his left hand against the tree trunk, leaned in, and aimed his stream to burn a hole in the soft loam at the base of the oak. *Sweet relief!*

Streamers of fuzzy daylight penetrated the canopy of leaves overhead. Tom watched a doe and her speckled twin fawns grazing on greenery in the misty distance. *August already*. Knee-deep in summer and he had yet to acquire a single pelt for trade.

Tom shook the last draibles of urine into the dirt and scampered back to his bed. Maggie turned on her side, cuddled under the wool skirt they'd used for a blanket. Tom curled up behind her so they fit together like two spoons in a tinker's basket. He closed his eyes and breathed deep the wonderful smell of warm woman and fornication—a fine way to start any day.

The night spent between Maggie's legs had left him more than well sated. She groaned and wriggled her backside, squishing up against him. Tom closed his eyes and ticked off the days left for a summer hunt.

No sense goin' for deer this late, but I can yet deliver one good-size cargo of beef . . . DeMontforte's set up near the lick at Sweet Salt Creek. Tom could still catch up with the Frenchman. He rolled onto his back and kicked off the wool skirt. *At war with Pontiac, the British are bound to pay top dollar for wild beef, tongues, and tallow . . .*

"Time to wake, Maggie." He ran a finger down the buttons of her spine and tickled the two dimples at the small of her back. Maggie batted his hand away.

Buffalo are fattest at summer's end anyway. Low on lead and powder, though—I'll talk to Duncan. Tom pinched Maggie on the bum. "Wake now, laze-a-bed."

"Ow!" She elbowed up, blinking through a storm cloud of hair hanging over her face.

"Day's a-wastin'." Tom pecked her on the cheek and jumped to his feet. Scurrying around to gather the clothing strewn about the campsite, he tossed Maggie her shift. It floated down to land draped over her head.

He laughed. "C'mon, Maggie, get dressed."

But Maggie didn't budge. She just sat under her shift in a sleepy daze, much like a little muslin ghost on a morning haunt.

"Really, Maggie." Tom gave her a nudge. "We ought t' get back afore they all wake."

Maggie tugged at the fabric, her head popped through the neck hole of her shift, and she slipped her arms into the sleeves. Tom tied a soft leather strap around his waist. He tucked one end of his breechclout up through the back, pulled the loose end between his legs, and threaded it under the strap at the front, adjusting flaps front and back. He liked for his clout to fit snug in the straddle.

Maggie stood and gingerly picked her way across the campsite to retrieve her bodice hanging in a tree, wincing at every step. Tom bent to pull on his leggings. He glanced up grinning and waggled his brows. "Sore?"

"Aye . . ." Maggie blushed a bit. "Yer enough to wear a woman out after one round, much less three . . ." She smiled and smoothed wrinkly, dew-damp muslin over her flat stomach. "I'll not be surprised t' find ye planted a babe in me."

Tom shot upright. "Naw . . . you think?"

"Ye never know—we've been awful busy . . ."

"I hope not." Tom pulled his shirt over his head and maneuvered arms through voluminous sleeves. "Seth would have me hunted, flayed, and nailed to the stockade wall for target practice if I up and left you with a bellyful."

Maggie slipped into her bodice, looking at him as if he had just licked all the butter from her bread. "Yer leavin'?"

"Yep—summer hunt—I've put it off far too long." He strapped the tooled leather belt over his shirt, sliding the sheaths for knife and tomahawk to sit comfortably on his hips. "There's no coin to be made lollygaggin' in Roundabout."

Maggie stepped into her skirt and pulled it up over her shift. "I've been thinkin', Tom . . ." She kept her eyes downcast, tying a slow knot at her waistline. "Seth might be inclined to sell ye my paper, now that Naomi's birthed her baby . . ."

"Yep." Tom gathered his moccasins and sat on the ground. "I've been reckless—thoughtless." He shook his head and tugged a moccasin onto each foot. "Next time we lie together I'll be certain to pull out before—" He looked up. Maggie stood over him with her bodice half laced, tears welling up in angry eyes.

"*Next time!*" Pulling hard on her bodice strings and securing them firmly in a double knot, she added, "There willna be a 'next time'—and dinna fash over my belly—if I need to, just like yer old friend Bess, I can stop a thing afore it has a chance to start." She marched off toward the clearing.

"Bess Hawkins? Now, what's that s'posed to mean?" Tom hurried to secure his moccasins and leaped to his feet. He loped after her, catching her by the arm at the forest edge. "Maggie! Wait! If Bess has fed you some nonsense about me . . ."

She jerked from him and swiped at the tears spilling down her cheeks. "Nae worries, Tommy, for a midwife kens the ways . . . just as Bess willna be fettered with yer by-blow, neither will I."

"Come now, Maggie . . ." Tom tried pulling her into his arms. "You don't believe . . ."

"Bugger off!" Fierce as a gut-shot she-bear, Maggie pummeled and slapped him away. She rapped herself on the head with fisted knuckles. "I'm such an addlepated eidgit. Ye but crooked yer finger and I came a-runnin'—fell flat on my back with legs spread—no better than a prostitute. Worse—for I wager Bess at least gains a shilling or two for her trouble."

Tom groaned. "Ahh, Maggie, you know it's not like that between us."

"Then tell me, Tom—g'won an' tell me what is there betwixt us"—she poked a finger into his chest—"other than yer ready cock!"

Tom winced at her crude assessment. "Don't talk like that."

"Why not? If I'm t' play whore for ye, I should speak like one."

Two deep furrows formed at the bridge of his nose. "You know damn well why I can't buy your contract. I've no home—how am I supposed to keep a wife and children in fire and corn when I'm off on a hunt eleven months o' the year?"

"Aye—yer nobody's fool, are ye?" Maggie sniffed and folded her arms. "Yer a canny fella . . . aye . . . why bother *buyin'* the cow, when ye can sup the milk for free?"

Tom's blue eyes narrowed. *"Goddamn it, Maggie.* I care for you and you know it."

Maggie's face crumpled. "Then why're ye so eager to leave?"

"Summer's almost over." His shoulders rose and fell in an exasperated shrug. "Prime deer season's passed me by and I've naught to show for it."

Her shoulders slumped and she could not stifle her tears. "I will miss ye so."

"Ah, Maggie," he soothed. "I promise thee, I'll be back as

soon as I earn a bit." Tom took her by the hands and tugged her into an embrace. They stood for a long moment entwined in each other's arms.

In a voice quiet and small Maggie said, "I could go with ye on yer hunt—be yer helpmate—cook, tend t' the camp . . ."

Tom pulled back and looked down at her as if someone had poured a horse dose of vinegar down his throat. "A woman on a hunt? Are you daft?"

Maggie pulled him tight and pressed her cheek to his heartbeat. "I dinna ken if I can bear the worry, not knowin' if yer dead or alive . . ."

Tom heaved a sigh and rested his chin atop her head. "I'll be back soon. You'll see."

"I've a notion." Maggie spoke into his chest. "Seein' how summer's almost spent as it is, why not claim acres—like men do—claim yer cabin right . . ."

"*Oh no!*" Tom threw up his hands and took a step back.

"But we wouldna need much." Maggie stepped toward him, hands outstretched. "Clear a bit of land, build a small cabin—a cow—I could keep a garden . . . earn some coin catchin' babies."

"No, no, no . . ." Tom shook his head with vehemence. "I'm no settler. I wander the wilderness to earn my living. That's how it is—that's just how it is."

"Aye . . ." Maggie sucked a deep breath through clenched teeth. "Well, ye can wander intae hell and fry in yer own lard for all I care." She doubled over with fists to her middle as if she'd been kicked in the gut and ran to the station.

⊙❀⊙

"*Och, Maggie!* Ye gave me such a start. Yer like t' give a body a fit of apoplexy." Ada clutched her bulging apron with one hand, and calmed her palpitating heart with the other, and unloaded the breakfast fixings carried in her apron onto the table. "What are ye after anyway, hunkered there like a fox at the henhouse door?"

Maggie looked up from where she sat on the ground next to

the cookhearth, knees bunched to her chest. "Sorry . . ." She swiped her snotty nose on her sleeve, planted her chin on her knees, and continued to stare at the smoldering ashes.

Ada tossed a few sticks of fat pine on embers left from the night's bonfire, fanned them to a blaze with her apron, and added a pair of split logs. She settled a hand on Maggie's shoulder. "Ye appear poorly—are ye comin' on yer courses?"

For a moment Maggie thought to throw herself into Ada's arms and weep into her comfy bosom. Ada could stroke her hair and curse all men, and Maggie could cry and cry and cry. She shook her head. "I've a wambly stomach is all."

"Poor dearie. I woke a bit sour as well—tipped one tankard too many—we'll both feel better with a bit of breakfast in our bellies, aye?"

Maggie wasn't sure how long she had been sitting alone in the empty fortyard, hugging her knees, rocking and sobbing—long enough for her head to ache from having no tears left to spill—long enough for Tom to come and find her.

But he didn't.

Too long. She pushed up to stand on her feet. "Can ye use a hand, Ada?"

"Aye. Fetch a kettle of water for tea."

Maggie traversed the distance to the water barrel on rickety legs. She had danced on the wind for a few wonderful days, only to be slammed into a storm-tossed sea, to struggle with all her might to keep from being pulled into its murky depths. The only way to survive was to forget. She must forget about the life she imagined sharing with Tom. Those dreams were lost to her.

Lost.

The kettle in her hand swung to and fro in halted momentum as she stalled in her tracks—immobilized by the impossibility of it all. She would never be able to forget the pure rapture of her body joined with Tom's, moving in concert.

Never.

Heart filled with woe, Maggie lurched forward. She peered with tear-swollen eyes into the near-empty water barrel and was struck by her dark reflection. She didn't recognize that bitter face nested in a nasty frizz of hair. She dipped the kettle into the water to disperse the ugly specter.

What a complete and utter fool she'd been to give herself over to a man like Tom Roberts. She hung the kettle over the fire and flopped down at tableside. Ada handed her a thick chunk of toasted bread slathered with honey. Maggie gobbled it down.

"Better, aye?"

"Aye," Maggie lied, still feeling as hollow and brittle as the long-necked gourd Ada used to ladle chamomile tea into her cup.

"Aye, a nice cup of tea will work wonders."

While Maggie sipped her tea, one by one, cabin doors scraped open. The fort dwellers staggered out, lured from their beds by the smell of bacon sizzling on the griddle. Maggie helped Ada dish up bowls of porridge and pour cups of tea. It did her good to busy her hands—helped to keep her mind from her troubles. They served breakfast to an ever-shifting group. The Willies, the Wallens, the Wheelers, and sundry bachelors came and went.

When Duncan Moon, their lone customer, scraped the last bit of porridge from his bowl, the women began to clear the breakfast mess away. Maggie gathered dirty trenchers, bowls, and cups. Ada heated a large tin basin of water into which she dropped a scoop of soft soap.

The door to the Buchanans' cabin creaked open. Arm in arm, Seth and Alistair stumbled forth. Shuffling to the far end of the table, they sat across from Duncan in a mutual crabbed squint, like a pair of hobgoblins caught out in the light of day.

"For shame, Seth Martin." Ada dealt a stern tongue-lashing. "Knee-walkin' drunk ye were last night—as pissed as a mattress." She shook a spoon in her husband's direction. "And you, auld man. Ye ken where I found ye? Behind the smithy! Aye.

Drunker than ten Indians ye were—lyin' there bung upward—britches scootched 'round yer ankles. Not a pleasant sight, that. Ye can thank me for draggin' yer hairy arse intae bed."

"Ada," Alistair moaned, cradling his shaggy silver head in his hands. "Cull an ounce of pity from tha' withered black nubbin ye call a heart, and fix us lads a nice cup of tea."

"Hmmph," Ada snorted.

"I'll get it," Maggie volunteered.

Duncan called, "Tea for me as well, Maggie."

Bess Hawkins was the last to join the breakfast table. She emerged from her cabin overdressed as usual, in a summer gown made of sprigged lawn trimmed with Belgian lace. Her auburn hair was covered with a frilly edged mobcap from which she'd drawn several curls to frame her face and tickle the nape of her neck. She twirled the long handle of a white silk parasol on one shoulder. Bess closed her parasol with great ceremony and propped it against the table edge. She settled next to Duncan at the end of the bench, fussing with the arrangement of her skirts as Maggie circled around to serve the men their tea.

"Aye, yer a true saint, Maggie." Alistair reached inside his shirt and produced his flask. "What d'ye say, Seth? Duncan? A hair from the dog what bit us?" Duncan nodded, Seth grunted in assent, and Alistair added a splash of whiskey to each cup.

"Hmmph," Ada snorted.

"Speaking of hair, Seth," Bess piped up, pointedly eyeing Maggie's ill-kempt, bedraggled appearance. "I must say, your servant girl looks about as pleasant as the pains of death this morning."

Seth was never one to pay much mind to Bess and he had no problem ignoring her that morning, but Maggie had to bite back the remark that flew to her tongue. Her head was pounding, her throat ached from choking back tears, and she was in no mood for Bess Hawkins.

"He's gone, isn't he?" Bess simpered in her seat. "Tom has up and left you—it was bound to happen sooner rather than later."

Itching to grab her by the roots and slap the smirk from her face, Maggie snapped, "Sod off!"

"So Tom HAS left you! HA!"

Alistair winced. "There's no call t' shout."

"Aye," Seth agreed, massaging his temples. "For here's Tom now."

Maggie's stomach lurched at the sight of him. Tom came through the gate fully accoutred for the trail, leading his pack-horse with Friday trotting at his side. After securing the gelding's lead to the hitching post at the blockhouse, he headed straight to the cookhearth.

Casting about for something to do other than gawk at him, Maggie hefted the washbasin onto the end of the table closest to the hearth and dove in, madly scrubbing cups and crusty trenchers with a stiff bristle brush.

"Mornin'," he called.

"Good mornin', Tom," Bess singsonged.

"Porridge, lad?" Ada asked, spoon in hand.

"Naw . . . I'm just about ready to head out."

"Summer hunt?" Seth asked.

"Yep—meetin' up with the Frenchman." Tom laid a hand on Duncan's shoulder. "Can you fix me in powder, lead, and flint?"

Duncan nodded. "As soon as I finish my tea."

Slipping hat from head, Tom shuffled sideways to stand opposite Maggie and her basin. He leaned in, one hand on the table-top, his voice low. "Might I have a word with thee?"

She was afraid to look up—afraid he'd see the longing in her eyes. She took a deep breath but could not mask the quaver in her voice. "So yer taking off right now?"

Tom nodded. "I have to."

Elbow-deep in warm water, she bent her head to her task. A teardrop plopped into the basin.

"Aw, Maggie . . . You've got to hear me out . . . I *have* to go."

Maggie cringed with wanting to stop her ears and cover her

eyes—blot out his voice, his eyes, his smile. She was so afraid—petrified she would not be able to keep from falling at his feet to beg him to stay, or worse, that she would promise to wait till kingdom come to lie in his arms once again. She fought to erase all expression from her face and forced herself to meet his eyes—eyes that matched exactly the summer sky overhead. "Good riddance t' ye," she said.

Tom flinched and she was glad to see she'd caused him to suffer a small measure of the awful pain enveloping her own heart.

His face went hard. "There's naught for me to do if you won't listen to reason. I won't beg, Maggie." He fit his hat on his head. "Duncan, I'll meet up with you at the smithy." He stalked off. Duncan gulped his tea and limped after Tom.

Maggie hugged the edge of the basin to keep herself from running after Tom as well. *I love him so.* Every step he took was a hard blow to her chest. How easy it was for him to leave her behind. *I hate him.*

"Maggie!" Bess called sweetly. "Can you give me a nice cup of tea?"

Her head spun and Maggie snarled. "What I'd like t' give ye is the back of my hand." She gritted her teeth and tossed a stack of wooden bowls into the washbasin.

"Leave Maggie be." Ada handed Bess a cup. "Ye can see how she's in a thin skin today."

Bess aped wonderment. "Oh . . . what with her being sweet on Tom, and Tom leaving and all . . ."

"Keep yer pug nose out of my business, Bess Hawkins," Maggie warned.

"Don't lose heart, Maggie." Bess's tone was ever so cloying. "There are plenty of fish in the sea. I heard tell Charlie Pritchard's mama was lookin' t' buy him a wife. Hoy, Seth! You might be able to get a good price."

Seth looked up from his tea and slid sideways, away from Bess, scooting closer to the end of the table where Maggie had stationed herself. Clutching his cup with both hands, Alistair followed suit. Maggie refused to rise to the bait; biting her lip, she churned up suds with her vigorous scrubbing.

Bess did not let up. "You didn't really expect a night or two between your legs would serve to tame a man like Tom, did you? Why, you're as common as a penny—Tom's bedded a score better'n you."

Maggie scrubbed harder. "Yid better just shut yer sorry hole . . ."

Bess tsked. "Such ire! It's true what they say—hell hath no fury like a woman—"

Maggie whipped the scrub brush across the table, hitting Bess with a thunk, square on the head.

"Ha!" Seth slapped his knee.

Bess popped to her feet, greasy dishwater sprayed over the fine lawn of her gown and dribbling from her cap. Maggie rushed around the table with murder in her eye, fists clenched.

Screaming, "Stay away from me, you filthy slut!" Bess snatched up her parasol like a club and scrambled backward. Tripping on her skirts, she toppled arse end into the dirt.

Seth said, "I'll stake three to one Maggie knocks the snot out o' Bess."

Shaking his head, Alistair took a gulp from his flask. "Two to one we'll sight a pair o' bubbies afore it's over."

"Bedlam!" For a large woman, Ada proved quick to react; insinuating herself between the two women, she pushed sleeves to elbows. "Draw in yer horns, ladies. I willna allow yiz t' brawl like mongrels after the same bone."

"Keep that madwoman away from me, Ada." Bess scrambled to her feet, batting at the debris clinging to her rear end. She unfurled her parasol and flounced off.

Ada wound an arm around Maggie's heaving shoulders.

Maggie sputtered, "She wouldna stiek her gob—"

"Aye, she's a knack for pokin' at raw wounds. But Bess

Hawkins is not the root of yer trouble. Take my advice, lass—
make peace with Tom afore he makes for the mountain, otherwise ye'll be miserable for months."

Maggie shook her head. "I canna . . . he . . ."

"Swallow yer pride, lass."

"It's too late," Maggie sobbed.

"Nonsense. Open yer eyes. A careless watch invites a thief."
Ada grabbed Maggie by the shoulders and gave her a little shove
toward the blockhouse. Bess Hawkins was standing there with
Tom.

"Aye." The sight put a bad taste in Maggie's mouth and a rod
in her spine. She swiped the tears from her cheeks, smoothed
back her hair, and marched a beeline for the blockhouse.

◖❈◗

Tom held a translucent amber flint up to the light.

"French," Duncan said. "You'll find none finer."

Tom nodded. "Give me a dozen . . . and a quarter barrel of
powder, and two dozen bars of lead." The small lead bars weighed
in at half a pound each. Tom would melt the bars down once he
reached the hunting camp, and mold a supply of round ball to the
precise caliber required by his weapon.

Duncan peered over Tom's shoulder. "Seems to be some sort
of a fracas among the women . . ."

Tom turned to see Ada planted like a bulwark between
Maggie—who stood with fists raised to do damage—and a
shrieking Bess. Snapping open her parasol, Bess turned on her
heel and headed straight for the smithy.

"Hurry and count out those bars, Duncan, and meet me by
my horse." Tom tucked the packet of flints into his shirtfront and
hoisted the cask of gunpowder onto his shoulder. "Goddamn it!"
he swore, seeing Bess alter her course to match his.

"Tom!" she called, meeting him at the hitching post.

Tom found a length of rope in one of the panniers. "I'm busy,
Bess." He lashed the cask to one side of the packsaddle. He

looked up from tying a sloppy knot to see Duncan hobbling along with the crate of lead bars.

Bess closed her parasol and leaned it against the post. "I know you're in a hurry." She glanced over her shoulder and stepped close. "But I wanted to bid you farewell and wish you luck on your hunt." Quicker than a finger snap, she laced her hands at the back of his neck, jerked him down, and pressed her mouth to his.

Caught off guard, Tom floundered for a moment, but she clung tenacious, like a possum in a peach tree. He grasped her about the waist. At once pushing her away and pulling himself back, he broke free, and swiped his mouth with the back of his hand. "What's gotten into you?"

Bess didn't answer. Standing with her hands on her hips and a grin on her face, she watched Maggie run into one of the empty cabins.

"Thee's an evil bitch, Bess Hawkins." Tom grabbed the crate from Duncan and whistled for Friday.

⟨✦⟩

Though it was only a glimpse—for a glimpse was all her eyes could bear—Maggie could not shake the image from her mind's eye. Tom's hands caressing Bess's tiny waist. Bess pressing to Tom's hard body—his lips on hers . . . Maggie sat at the table with her head cradled on her arms, suffering the mother of all headaches.

Ada bustled around the hearth preparing the evening meal. "I've allowed ye t' wallow in despair the day long, but ye must set yer heartache aside now and be about yer business." She dropped a full tray on the tabletop. "Naomi and Susannah need their tea and wee Mary's pate needs tending."

Maggie lugged the tray to the blockhouse and pushed open the door. Naomi was trudging back and forth across the room, jostling her screaming baby. "He's so fussy, Maggie . . ." she complained. "I'm at wit's end. He's been nursing in fits and starts for hours."

Maggie was surprised to see little Mary fully dressed, wriggling like a worm on a fishhook while Susannah braided the hair that had escaped the scalping knife into two golden plaits. Blue eyes clear and bright, Mary announced, "Ma says enough lyin' about, Maggie. We're gonna have our tea at a proper table today."

"I coated her head with the balm y' give me," Susannah explained, "and changed the dressing. It's scabbin' over nicely, so's I saw no harm . . ."

"It's a fine idea." Maggie set the tray down on the worktable and wrinkled her nose at the fetid air of the windowless room. "It is a mite close in here . . ." She gathered the writhing baby into her arms and sniffed his bottom.

Naomi sighed in relief and dropped to sit on her bed. "He's hungry all the time and I've so little for him . . . I'm deep bone tired and my head aches so . . ."

Maggie offered Susannah the screaming baby. "Would ye mind givin' th' lad suck one time more?"

Susannah glanced down at the wet patches staining the front of her bodice and loosened her laces. "We'd sure rather feed the little fella than listen t' him squawk, right, Mary?" Mary huddled close to watch the baby nurse.

His eyes squeezed tight, red-faced Alexander worried his fists, snorting and rooting for his breakfast. Susannah brushed her nipple to his cheek. With the instinct born in every babe, he turned to food and latched on. Muscles relaxed and the boy pulled and grunted with a steady rhythm, nursing with greedy ease from Susannah's abundant supply.

Maggie tied the strings of a clean linen cap under Mary's chin, happy to see this patient run off to be with the other children. She considered perhaps Naomi should be up and about today as well, for Seth was eager to get back to the homeplace, but as she poured a cup of tepid tea for each woman, she thought twice on that plan.

Susannah said, "You look under the weather, Maggie."

"Bad stomach—bad head." Maggie shrugged and poured a cup for herself.

"Making too merry 'round the fire, eh?"

"Aye." Maggie poked through her supplies neatly organized on the worktable and found the last of her wild carrot seed. She dosed herself, chewing a heaping teaspoon to a pulp. Tears stung her eyes as she choked it down. She tipped a good ration of willow bark powder into her tea to ease her throbbing head.

Susannah drank every drop in her cup, and asked for more. Naomi sat slumped on the edge of her bed, holding her full cup in loose fingers, staring at the wall, glazed, pink-rimmed eyes set in circles of deep lavender.

"Drink up, drink up, Naomi," Maggie urged. "How d'ye expect t' make the milk yer bairn craves if ye dinna drink?"

Naomi struggled to lever her legs up onto the bed; she sucked air and winced, her features contorted at the effort. Maggie rushed to take the tea from her. She lifted Naomi's legs and settled her back onto the pillows. A loud, rancid stench assailed the midwife's nose. She shot a glance at the chamber pot sitting beneath the bed, but it was clean and empty. Naomi shifted her hips and stifled a groan.

"Pain?" Maggie asked.

"My head—and just then, a bit of pain in the gut." Naomi drew a deep breath. "Overlong on my feet, is all." She flashed Maggie a desperate smile.

Maggie pressed her hand to Naomi's pale cheek. "Yer a tad feverish . . ." She slid fingers down to the base of her neck and counted a pulse beating too rapid. With both hands, she gently probed Naomi's soft abdomen, causing her to cry out in pain. The malevolent smell enveloped them, thick as a misling fog.

"Let's get ye cleaned up. I want t' change the clout between yer legs." She reached under Naomi's shift and slipped loose the double-thick pad of flannel bound, breechclout style, to a soft strap around Naomi's middle. Maggie held her breath, not surprised to find the clout reeking with a pungent yellow discharge. Naomi whimpered and began to shiver as Maggie quickly bundled the cloth into a tight roll and set it outside the doorway.

"Dinna fash, sweeting." Maggie floated a blanket over her. "After I get a fresh rag on ye, I'll fix something for the headache and fever." She worked to keep her tone smooth and even, simultaneously sorting through an array of treatments in her mind. Maggie took Naomi by the hand and met her limpid blue eyes.

"We'll start with a warm linseed poultice on your belly. Yer goin' to rest, gather strength, and get well." Heart pounding in her chest, Maggie glanced over her shoulder at Susannah. "Ye ken we need ye t' wetnurse the lad a few days yet . . ."

Susannah bit her lip and nodded.

17

Dispossessed

Maggie crossed from the cookhearth to the blockhouse with Winnie, Jack, and Battler in tow. Ada had prepared a basket of good eating for the trail. Maggie added it to the bundles piled outside the blockhouse door.

"We'll wait here till everyone's ready to go."

Diffused light seeped through morning fog still clinging like cotton lint to the treetops. She shaded her eyes, squinting to see Seth bring Ol' Mule in from pasture.

"Move yer bleedin' arse!" Seth shouted, and slapped Mule's hindquarters with the hobble strop. Mule laid his ears down, curled his lip back, and brayed. Carnaptious Ol' Mule, for reasons unknown, balked at entering the fortyard. Equally carnaptious Seth tugged and pushed.

"Megstie me." Maggie sank down to sit on a tree stump. "This might take a while." Battler crawled up onto her lap and Jack and Winnie plunked down on either side to watch the contest of wills.

"Da better mind so's he don't get a kick in the head," Jack said, slipping his scrawny arm around Maggie's waist and tipping his head against her shoulder. "Ol' Mule don't take t' being whipped or shouted at."

Seth spat on his hands, dug moccasins into the earth, and pulled with all his might on the mule's lead. *"Moooooove . . . ye fuckin' stupid bag o' shite!"*

Head hanging low and long ears flopped, Mule did not budge.

Seth tossed the lead and his arms into the air. He paced to and fro, rapping out an endless string of vile curses.

Maggie fished in the lunch basket and handed each child a raisin scone. "I'm goin' to help yer da." She came up on the mule and stroked his withers with the flat of her hand. Long ears shot up and twitched. "D' ye mind, Seth, if I give a try?"

His face screwed in an awful pucker, Seth welcomed her effort with a wild sweep of his arm. "Fuck-all if I care . . . have at it."

Maggie positioned herself between man and mule. "C'mon, laddie . . . nothin's goin' to harm ye . . . come along with Maggie," she cooed. The mule sniffed then munched the bit of scone she held out, his nose fuzzy and squishy, like a half-eaten peach in her palm. She tugged on his halter and he moved forward, slow and steady, right through the gate.

"Huzzah for Maggie!" Winnie and Jack cheered.

"Hmmph," Seth grunted, and followed behind Maggie as she led the mule to the blockhouse. He clapped his hands together and the children hopped to their feet.

"All right, let's load up. I thought to be halfway home by now . . ." He snatched up a pair of wicker panniers and slung them over the animal's rump, looping the hanger strap under Mule's twitchy tail. "I canna believe I wasted most of the morning chasing after this pasture-spoilt beast. Winnie—bring the saddle pad."

"He didn't mean no harm." Jack stroked the length of Mule's velvet nose. "He's just cautious, is all."

"Cautious!" Seth snorted.

"And we've plenty morning left, Da." Winnie handed her father a woolly sheepskin. "Most everyone else is still abed."

Seth knit his brows into a dark wing. "I dinna give a tinker's fart what most are doin', miss. Stiek yer gob and fasten those straps." He positioned the sheepskin over the mule's back and set the saddle atop it. Winnie chewed on the end of her braid and ducked under to buckle the cinches snug around the mule's belly and across his chest.

Arms akimbo, Seth pondered the pile of gear waiting to be packed. "By God's blood and the nails they nailed Him to the cross with—all this lot onto one lone beast?"

"Ye needna be such a crosspatch." Maggie sorted through the pile and separated out the small bundles that would fit inside the panniers. "We're all of us anxious t' get home and willin' to tote 'n carry if needs be."

"Winnie—" Seth turned to see Winnie wandering away, heading toward the gate. He hollered, "Winnie! Where are you off to, miss?"

Bold as can be, Winnie paid her father no mind and continued forward.

"*Winnie!* Answer when I call ye."

She halted, hunched shoulders up to her ears, and shouted with terse deliberation, "I'm goin' to pick flowers for Mam!" With that, she took off, braids flying around the corner to disappear behind the stockade wall.

"Mam!" The scone tumbled from Battler's chubby fist. He clambered down from the tree stump and toddled after Winnie, a huge grin on his crumb-covered face.

"Och, bloody hell." Seth's shoulders slumped. "Jack—fetch yer brother."

Jack heaved an annoyed sigh, tossed aside the twig he'd been poking into an anthill, and scooted after his brother, halting Battler's escape none too gently, jerking him rough by the tail of his smock shirt. "C'mon back, y' ninny."

Twirling around and around as frantic as a puppy after his own tail, Battler chased Jack, clawing and slapping at the hand gripping his shirt. "No, Jackie—let go!"

Jack tugged Battler inch by inch, back to the tree stump. "C'mon—quit bein' such a baby."

"Not a BABYYYY!" Battler screamed, threw himself to the ground, and stretched his arms out, wriggling chubby fingers. "*Mam!* Want Mam!"

"Mam's dead! She's dead an' in the hole," Jack shouted, and pulled Battler by the ankles, dragging him through the dirt.

Seth ran over and grabbed Jack by the upper arm, clenching tight through muscle and tendon down to thin bone, shaking the boy hard. "What's gotten intae ye? By God, if I had a switch I'd wear out yer tail end . . ."

Jack wrenched away and staggered back two steps. "You shout at us all the time . . . we didn't do nothin' wrong. We didn't die!" The boy fisted the air and kicked a tree root, bloodying his bare foot.

Freed from his brother's grasp, Battler leaped up and collided with Maggie, hugging her around the legs. He buried his cherub face in her skirt and let loose a mournful dirge of a wail. Maggie stood mute, bewildered as to which of the Martin males she should comfort first—shrieking Battler; teary-eyed Jack, defiantly taking a stand against his father; or poor Seth, looking like Ol' Mule had indeed just kicked him upside the head.

The stoic shell in which Seth had encased himself since the night Naomi died crumbled away, his face and limbs suddenly slack. He stumble-stepped forward, his voice pinched and pained. "I'm so, so sorry, Jackie."

Jack fell into his father's arms. "'S awright, Da."

"No. We're havin' rough times, one and all . . . I've no call t' . . ."

"Yer just angry Mam's gone and died," Jack lamented, pressing up against his father's chest. "I'm angry, too. We're all of us, out o' heart."

Maggie hoisted Battler onto her hip and rubbed his back. He snuffled snotty into her neck. She sat down with him on her lap, fighting to squelch her own tears, rocking the sobbing boy quiet. "Sha, laddie . . . sha now . . ."

Seth pulled back and looked straight into Jack's eye. "Yer mam surely wouldna like for us to be so cross and sad—I'm goin' t' try hard t' be better."

"I'll try too, Da."

"We'll all feel better once we get home," Maggie said.

"Aye—" Seth draped an arm around Jack's shoulders. "And if we mean t' make it home with daylight to spare, we best get on with the packing. Ye g'won lad, fetch yer sister back." Seth clapped his boy on the back. Jack tore off, kicking up a dust trail as he raced through the gate.

Seth sank down beside Maggie, legs encased in filthy deerskin breeches splayed out in an exhausted V. He laced his free arm through to link with hers. "My Jack's but ten years old and he kens well the way of this sorrowful world. I *am* angry, Maggie. Angry my Winnie has a grave t' pick flowers for . . . angry Battler willna recall his mam's face . . . angry Naomi's no longer crowding me in my bed . . ."

"It all takes time, Seth. Only time will tame yer grief."

"She was gone from me afore I had time t' wrap my mind around the notion of her dying . . . gone . . ."

"When corruption settles in the womb, it moves awful quick," Maggie explained, just as she had the night Naomi died. "There's naught but the will of God to stop it. It's a rare thing for a woman to survive a bout with childbed fever."

Water welled up in Seth's doleful, bloodshot eyes. "I miss her so, Maggie . . . I do miss her so . . ." He swiped a hand over his face and stared at the wet on his fingers. "An' here I thought I was past tears . . ."

Maggie took Seth's rough hand in hers and she sat with him, and he cried the odd way men do, stifled and stiff and silent, tears coursing a ragged path down his stubbly face.

"Yiv lovin' children and many good friends t' help ye get

through these tryin' times." Maggie regretted mouthing another of the tired platitudes she knew he'd been hearing for days—wanting for something more to say—something to make his anguish less.

"Aye . . . children and friends"—Seth reached over and ruffled his fingers through Battler's sun-blond curls—"in that I am a wealthy man." He scoured his face with his sleeve. "I sorely wish Tom hadn't taken to the hunt. It would've done me good t' have him 'round."

Tom's name aloud hit Maggie like a thwack on the back. Her heart tripped and knocked against her breastbone and a pocket of air pushed from her lungs in a soft *unghh.*

Seth didn't seem to notice. "Naomi's passing will be an awful shock for him when he comes back."

"If he comes back."

"Och, Tommy always comes back."

"Aye . . ."—Maggie tucked a tendril behind Battler's ear—"but maybe not this time."

"Ahhh, Maggie." Seth straightened his spine. "What d'ye do?"

For a moment she cursed herself for opening the door to her problems, burdening overburdened Seth with even more worry. But she could see he seemed to perk up, his face suddenly not so dour. *Tendin' t' other people's troubles can free ye from yer own.* That's what Hannah used to say. Maggie had to admit, living over the last seven days, dealing with Naomi's illness, death, and burial, she'd had scant time to give Tom Roberts any deep thought, other than to wish him back.

"Why don't ye tell me what happened." Seth squeezed her hand.

"Ye ken we had a terrible row the morning after celebrating Alexander's birthing . . ."

Seth nodded. "'Twere but a sennight ago, but it seems like ages and ages, na?"

Battler shifted in Maggie's lap, leaning his damp cheek to rest against her bosom. "I was awful harsh with Tom tha' day."

"A wee quarrel willna keep Tom away." Seth attempted a smile. "I've never seen a man so lovestruck. He'll be back. Tom lives for the chase and he's determined t' have ye."

"Aye—and he did—" Maggie peeked through lashes at Seth. "Ye ken what I'm sayin'?"

"Och, lass . . . I warned ye . . ."

Maggie held up her hand. "The deed is done."

"Aye. True . . . water under the bridge, eh? Tell me, what did yiz quarrel over?"

"Well . . ." Maggie wound and unwound one of Battler's curls about her index finger. "I took it hard when he balked at the notion of our havin' a baby together . . ."

"Baby! Yer not . . . ?"

"Na . . . but when I suggested he should buy my contract from ye . . ."

"Och! Ye didna?"

"Aye—I did. Then I mentioned he might claim acres and build us a cabin, and he lit up like a pine-pitch torch."

"A cabin!" Seth groaned. "Sweet-talkin' a man who pants for the hunt with visions of being harnessed to a plow . . . what on earth were ye thinkin'?"

Maggie tapped her forefinger hard against her head. *Dop-dop-dop.* "Thick as a church door."

"Listen to me, Maggie, I've followed in his tracks and I ken better than you the life he leads. Tom has no fear of going beyond maps to live in the open-uncertain for months on end, but when the bed's too soft and food's too regular, he grows uneasy. Babies and cabins!" Seth shook his head. "Yiv sent him intae the hills for a good, long time."

"Wait, I have yet t' tell ye the worst of it." Tears bubbled over. "I saw them—him and Bess Hawkins—together."

"Together?" Seth waggled his brow.

"Aye—well, kissing." The telling was as painful as the seeing. Maggie felt as if she might vomit.

"Och, Maggie, if ye ask me, Bess Hawkins is not the least of yer troubles with Tom. She means nothing to him. She never did. At best, she was handy."

"Handy . . . I was handy as well. It was verra easy for him to leave me behind, and that's truly what put the ache in my heart. The bastard. But no matter how hard I try t' hate the man, I know I'll never love none but him. I love him."

Seth pulled Maggie under his arm and she bent her head to rest on his bony shoulder. "Taming a man like Tom to the marriage bed is like training a wolf to eat from the palm of yer hand— possible, aye—but takes yards of time and gallons of patience."

"Ye think?"

"Naomi always thought Tom'd leave off his wild tracks for the right woman." Seth gave her a squeeze. "I'm certain he loves ye true, and in the end, true love tends to overcome reason of the mind."

The blockhouse door creaked open. Susannah stepped out, her wooden cup gripped in one hand, sleepy Alexander nestled in the crook of her arm. Wearing a crisp linen cap, Mary followed along carrying her rag-doll baby in the exact fashion.

"Good mornin'." Susannah transferred the baby into his father's eager arms. "See if you can get him to bring up a bubble— I need to slake my thirst. Do you think there's any o' that sweet-balm tea left, Maggie?"

"Aye . . . but it's bound t' be cold by now . . ."

"No matter." Susannah took her daughter by the hand and they strolled to the cookhearth.

Seth dabbed the corner of the blanket to the drop of bluish milk trickling from Alexander's mouth. He hoisted the baby to his shoulder and pressed his nose to the newborn's copper-downy head and breathed deep. "Susannah's got the right of it. A baby is a tonic—the very smell of him fills my heart with hope."

Maggie smiled. "Lucky ye dinna have to send him away t' be nursed. Susannah's misfortune is yer son's saving."

Susannah and Seth had bartered a mutually beneficial arrangement. She agreed to move into the Martin homeplace and wet-nurse Alexander. In exchange for this costly service, Seth agreed to harvest the Bledsoe corn and round up the remaining Bledsoe livestock to pasture in his field. In the fall he would butcher and process a Bledsoe hog in addition to his own. Susannah and her daughter were thus guaranteed sustenance and the protection of a man for the time it took to wean Alexander to cup and soft food.

Seth watched Susannah circumnavigating the hearth in her quest for tea, the knife wound in her side giving her cause to take care. "That woman is a rock, is she no? She suffers my sorrow times five. How does she bear it?"

"She may seem rock solid, but mind, every night, when the lantern's dimmed, I hear her weep into her pillow and whisper her children's names one by one. Like t' break yer heart."

Seth shifted the baby to cradle in his arms. "He's the spit of Naomi, na?"

"Alexander has his mam's ginger hair for certain and her sweet features as well," Maggie agreed. The baby suddenly belched loud. "But he definitely has the Martin forthright disposition."

Battler giggled, slipped down from Maggie's lap, and sidled in to stand beside his father. He pressed endless smacky kisses on his sleeping brother's cheek and jostled him by the hand. "Zander's a baby," Battler said with a knowing nod. "I'm no baby. I'm a great big lad."

"Ah no, ye wee rascal—Jackie's a great big lad—Winnie's a great big lass, and Battler"—Maggie reached around and poked a finger into his soft keg of a belly—"is our wee laddie."

"An' Zander's a wee, wee baby," Battler asserted, satisfied with his move up in the pecking order.

"I'd best get back t' packin'." Seth passed the infant to Maggie.

"Moo cows." Battler blinked.

Maggie heard it, too—the dissonance of multiple bells clanging in the distance. She took a few steps toward the gate. The clanging grew louder.

"What in the . . . ?" Seth stood beside her and they both shaded their eyes to see Winnie and Jack with windmill arms awhirl charging across the cleared field, shouting, *"Da! Maggie!"* The siblings ran up, gulping for breath.

"Indians?" Seth asked.

Winnie shook her head no. "The Mulberries—the whole lot of 'em—comin' down the ridge trail."

"Miz Mulberry's driving beasts . . ." Jack added.

"Mister's trailing far behind—he looks bad hurt, Da—bloodied and limpin' along . . ."

Seth cast a glance back, spotting his rifle atop the pile of gear. "Jack, run tell Cap'n Moon. Maggie! Dinna shilly-shally—come with me." He grabbed his rifle and lit out. Winnie took the baby. Maggie tucked the tails of her skirts into her apron string and chased after Seth through the field. She could see the Mulberry family enter the clearing.

Peculiarly capless, with her waist-length hair unbound and skirts kilted up, prim-proper Rachel Mulberry marched to the cacophony of cow and goat bells at the head of a ragtag column. Long brown strands of hair caught on the breeze, flowing about her head like so many silken ribbons. As Maggie drew closer, she noticed an angry welt raking a plum-colored stripe across Rachel's left cheek.

With a rifle as long as she was tall strapped over one shoulder, Rachel carried her delft teapot like a baby and led a string of four cows tailed to one another. Her two youngest sons sat astride the bony spine of the lead cow. Not far behind, twelve-year-old Jem and his younger brother Will whistled and whipped the air with long switches, herding a trio of uncooperative goats and one large sow.

When Seth and Maggie met with Rachel, the woman did not pause in her course. She continued marching stalwart toward the station. "Don't bother with me, Maggie." She gestured to the rear. "Go help my Joe."

Trailing some twenty yards behind, the eldest Mulberry boy, fifteen-year-old Jacob, acted as crutch, helping his father limp along. Joe's shirt was bloodied so it looked like a full goblet of Burgundy had been spilled onto it. Leaning heavy on his son's not-yet-man shoulders, Joe clutched his side.

"Rachel, what's happened?" Maggie asked.

"They near beat him to death."

Maggie ran to help Joe.

Seth fell in alongside Rachel. "Shawnee?"

"No . . ." She shook her head. "Dispossessed."

Seth stopped cold in his tracks. *"Dispossessed?"*

"Removed from the land." Rachel plodded forward. "He's come to stake his claim." She looked over her shoulder with weary eyes. "Portland."

❦

The breeze picked up, causing the oilcloth overhead to snap on its framework. Joe Mulberry lay in its shade, flat on his back on the communal dining table. "There's the last stitch." Maggie snipped the thread with her shears and dabbed at the gash in his scalp with a puff of raw wool soaked with a tincture of arnica. She secured a linen bandage around Joe's head and together with Rachel helped him to sit with his legs dangling over the edge of the table.

"It hurts to breathe," he gasped.

"I suspect yiv busted a rib or two," Maggie diagnosed. "Though it pains ye to breathe deep, ye must. Yer lungs are liable to collapse with shallow breaths, and collapsed lungs are easily stricken with lung fever."

Rachel stroked her husband's arm. "Listen to what Maggie says, Joe—breathe deep."

"Mm-hmm," he grunted.

Winnie and Jacob Mulberry came carrying a bushel basket of

greens between them. "We did like you tolt us, Maggie," Winnie said. "Cut the stalks and left the roots."

"Is it enough?" Jacob asked. "I can get more . . . Winnie showed me where . . ."

"This is plenty." Maggie dumped the comfrey greens onto the tabletop. "Go and fetch me the kettle of boilt water." She cast a glance over her shoulder at the snarl of men muttering around the cookhearth, glaring her way. Now that her patient's head wound was stitched and dressed, she would not be able to hold them off any longer.

"D'ye feel able?" she asked Joe, jerking her thumb toward the hearth. "That bunch is chompin' at the bit t' have a word with ye."

Joe winced and nodded.

"All right!" Maggie called them with a wave of her hand. Alistair and Seth strode over, along with Duncan Moon and Fletcher Wallen, to form a loose semicircle around Joe.

"I still need to poultice and bind his ribs," she warned, "so I'll thank yiz all to keep out from underfoot, aye?" The men nodded in agreement.

"How d'ye fend, Joe?" Alistair asked.

Maggie said, "I just put fourteen stitches in the man's noggin and ye wonder how he fends? Break out the *uisquebaugh*, ye ol' miser—let him benefit from a scoof from yer flask."

They all laughed while Alistair fished a flask from inside his shirt. "Yiv the right of it, Maggie—what whiskey canna cure there's no cure for."

Joe dosed himself with a gulp and Maggie attacked the comfrey with a heavy cleaver, chopping the large leaves and thick stems to bits, tossing them into the kettle of hot water. "Help Joe off with his shirt."

It took some doing in cooperative effort—Joe could barely lift his left arm, so stiff and sore he was—but Seth and Alistair managed to slip the bloodied shirt over his head. A whimper escaped

Rachel's lips, and Maggie looked up upon hearing a collective indrawn breath.

Alistair whistled low. "Who did this t' ye, Joe?"

"Portland's hired men . . ." Joe panted and pulled another gulp from the flask.

Maggie set the cleaver aside and elbowed her way in for a good close look. Joe's torso was riddled with injuries. His left side—from armpit to hip—was a mass of sickening purple-blue bruises overlayered with a curious pattern of small circular welts. Maggie crouched to study the worst of it, tracing fingertips over the welts. "Hobnail boots?"

Joe nodded. She scooped up a cup of the water the comfrey was steeping in and added a generous pinch of willow bark powder to it and gave it to Joe. "Drink this down." Maggie handed Rachel a small clay pot. "Rub this salve onto the scrapes and bruises across his back and on his face."

Seth propped one foot up on the bench and leaned in. "Tell us what happened, Joe."

"Ambushed," Rachel answered as she smoothed the ointment onto her husband's wounds. "Stepped out the door to see to his chores and they ambushed him."

Joe fingered the bandage on his head. "Walloped me acrost the pate . . ."

". . . with a spade," Rachel finished. "I heard a commotion and stepped out to find a red-haired giant of a man standing over him, spade in his hand. There were others in the dooryard with guns trained on Joe."

"How many, all together?" Fletcher asked.

"Four," Joe answered.

"Five," Rachel corrected, "if you count Portland, prancing and curveting about on his fancy steed. Never dismounted, that one—had his henchmen do his dirty work while he sat gloating in the saddle."

"That drunken Brady Moffat," Jacob squeaked. "He was one of 'em."

"Brady Moffat," Duncan snorted. "Can't say as I'm surprised. He's as rotten as a turd and not worth a fart—so desperate for the drink he'd hog-tie his own mother for a ha'penny."

"That renegade Simon Peavey was there as well . . ." Joe clutched his ribs. "*Ooahh!*"

Maggie came around the table. "Ye havna drunk yer tea, Joe."

He cast a dubious glance at the still-full cup sitting beside him on the table. "That seems a vile ooze, Maggie . . ."

"'Tis vile, but 'twill ease yer pain—now drink!" She held the cup to his lips. He drew in a measured breath and took a swallow. She handed him the cup and stood there with a baleful glare until he finished the dose.

"What about the other two?" Seth continued. "Did ye recognize either o' them?"

Joe breathed deep and slow. "There was Moffat, Peavey, the redheaded giant, and a withy little Irishman . . ."

"Scrawnier than a plucked chicken," Jacob chimed in.

"'Connor' they called him—he's the one did the talking," Rachel expounded. "A face like a bag of nails on that one."

"The giant man was called 'Figg,'" Jacob recalled.

Rachel shook her head. "I've never seen a man as big—but even with a head the size of a muskmelon, he must have been standing behind the door the day they passed out the brains. 'Twere clear he's a simpleminded fella."

"I've seen wiser eatin' grass . . ." Joe wheezed.

"Figg was the only one unarmed." Jacob noted.

Maggie unrolled half a yard of flannel onto the tabletop. She scooped the blanched greens from the kettle and plopped the gelatinous goo onto the rag. Using a wooden paddle, she spread it in an even, steaming layer over the cloth.

"Did ye offer to pay a quitrent on the land?" Seth asked.

Joe nodded. "I asked to parlay—" He stopped, closed his eyes, and drew in a deep breath.

"Take it easy, Joe." Rachel wiped her hands on her apron. "Portland refused to speak with us. Connor said proper surveys had been filed on the land grant from the king—"

"He showed us a writ from the governor in Williamsburg ordering us dispossessed," Joe continued. "Connor said Portland meant to plant tobacco and we must abide by the writ."

"Hmmph." Fletcher tightened his grip on the barrel of the rifle he leaned upon. "*Must* is a king's word."

"I read the order with guns trained on me," Rachel pointed out. "We had no recourse or means to resist."

"It's no wonder ye were the first they preyed upon, Mulberry." Alistair tugged on his whiskers. "Yiv the best access to the river . . . necessary for a tobacco plantation."

Maggie pressed her palm into the comfrey on the cloth. Satisfied it had cooled sufficiently, she peeled the poulticed rag from the tabletop. "Raise yer arm as high as ye can." She applied the flannel, mushy side against his battered skin, plastering the worst of his bruises with the warm remedy.

"Ahhh . . ." Heat and comfrey brought instant relief. The lines etched in Joe's sweat-slicked forehead disappeared. Maggie wrapped lengths of linen stripping around and around his torso to secure the poultice in place. "What on earth did ye do, Joe, to cause them t' beat ye this bad?"

"I-it wasn't Joe's fault, Maggie," Rachel stuttered. "It was me . . ."

"Now, darlin' . . ." Joe took his wife by the hand.

"You know it was all my fault, Ma," Jacob insisted.

Rachel wound an arm about her son's shoulders. "We've been on pins and needles since we heard about our surveys bein' bad." She sighed. "Seeing the court order—ink on paper—it almost came as a relief. Just as I set my mind to packing, everything went awry . . ."

Joe nodded. "Our Jacob here bust out from the cabin swingin' my rifle . . ."

"I got off a hurried shot." Jacob punched a fist to his palm. "Missed the duke fella by but an inch or two. Sent his mount on hind legs."

"Lucky that, ye wee fool." Alistair shook a finger at Jacob. "Yer mother doesna need t' see ye dangling by the neck, branded murderer."

"Moffat drew a bead on Jacob. I lunged and knocked his gun aside so's his shot flew wide." Rachel touched fingertips to the welt marring her face. "Then he struck me . . ."

"I leaped on Moffat," Joe added, "and Figg fell on me."

"Figg took Joe down with fists and kept him down with boots—kicking and stomping." Rachel's eyes welled up in recollection. "I pleaded and screamed for him to stop—finally Connor called the brute off."

"Portland then barred us from taking much more than the clothes on our backs." Joe gripped his wife's hand and smiled. "But my Rachel managed to come away with her teapot and my rifle."

"Thank the Lord the boys were able to find most of our stock foraging in the forest." Rachel pushed her hair back from her face. "We're hoping to trade the cows and goats for enough provisions to get us back to my folks up in New York."

Duncan said, "Whatever you need, Rachel—we're all sorry for your trouble."

"I didn't think he'd be so swift to evict," Fletcher said, brooding. "Thought at least we'd be able to buy time to harvest our crops and winter over . . . the Duke of Portland's surely a cold-hearted, cruel bastard."

"This man yiz call Portland—" Maggie spoke up. "I know him, and he's no the duke."

Seth shot Maggie a look. "Ye know him?"

"We sailed on the same ship." She pulled at her apron strings to loose the bow. "Viscount Julian Cavendish, th' youngest son to the Duke of Portland. Ye must have seen him at the auction, Seth—all silk and lace and walking stick—he had one o' those black spotties pasted onto his cheek. *Feich!*" She bundled her apron into a ball.

Seth pinched the bridge of his nose between his fingers. "Not the periwigged fop what bid against me on yer contract?"

"Aye, one and the same." Maggie sponged the sweat from her face and neck with her wadded apron. "Och, he made the voyage a living hell for me. Drunken sot dogged my steps so, I had to hide in the tween to keep safe from him." She shimmied up to sit on the tabletop. "I surely never fancied layin' eyes on him again . . ."

"Neither did I." Seth shouldered his weapon. "Pack yer things, Maggie. We need to get home."

PART THREE

My Answer is, that I Wish there was not an Indian Settlement within a Thousand Miles of our Country; for they are only fit to Live with the Inhabitants of the Woods, being more nearly Allied to the Brute than the Human Creation.

SIR JEFFREY AMHERST,
GOVERNOR GENERAL, BRITISH
NORTH AMERICA

. . . you can well see that they are seeking our ruin. Therefore, my brothers, we must all swear their destruction and wait no longer. Nothing prevents us; they are few in numbers, and we can accomplish it. All the nations who are our brothers attack them—why should we not attack? Are we not men like them?

PONTIAC,
OTTAWA CHIEF

18

A Dreadful Wind

Seth loosed the knot on the kerchief about his neck and used it to swab dusty, gummy sweat from his face. He was grateful for the shade provided by the broad brim of his hat, for it was the only bit to be had out in the middle of the cornfield. Snapping an ear of corn from its stalk, he peeled back the husk and cut into a kernel with his thumbnail. A pearl of milky starch oozed up.

Too green.

This early in the harvest season the pickings were slim. Seth sought hard, ripe corn ready to shell for grinding and most of his corn was still in the silk. He dropped the green ear over his shoulder into the collecting basket strapped on his back and picked a dozen more to roast for supper.

Without much tending at all, his corn had grown tall—horse-high and higher—the result of a fine growing season, a perfect balance of sun and rain. Riddled with stones and stumps, Seth's fields were unplowable and he was obliged to forgo straight, old-world style furrows and plant his crops Indian style. Mounding the rich soil into small hills, he had planted each hummock with three varieties—corn, beans, and squash. *Three sister crops.*

The Indian method was ingenious. Corn grew sturdy and tall

enough to support a bean vine twining up its stalk. The bean vines anchored the cornstalks to the ground and prevented erosion. The squash plant's broad leaves hunkered at the base of every cornstalk, retaining moisture in the soil, hindering weeds from flourishing.

Seth trod between the mounds and tree stumps, suddenly proud to think he'd chopped down every tree and planted each seed with his own hands. *Did it once, and I can do it again.*

He stopped for a moment to slip the carry strap of his rifle from right shoulder to left. He was resigned to the fact that they'd be soon moving on, but he could not afford to be caught unprepared, like Joe Mulberry. For unlike the Mulberrys, the Martins had no family to turn to. It was up to Seth alone to provide for the seven souls that depended on him, and as a result, from before daybreak to past nightfall he worried and planned, worked and worried.

He stepped up onto a tree stump, arms akimbo, and looked out over tassel tops waving on the breeze to survey this holding. *Two years toiling—breaking our backs—all for naught.*

If the Irish surveyor he'd hired had filed the claims proper, they would have found out right off they had no right to claim this land. He hopped from the stump.

Drunken bastard! Seth kicked a clod of dirt into smithereens. *Never pays to truck with the Irish.*

The Bledsoe holding was lost to Portland's grant as well, but Seth was still bound to provide for Susannah and her daughter for as long as Alexander required a wet nurse. They'd traveled to her farm the day before to recover valuables, but the place had been ransacked—tools, weapons, livestock—all gone. Susannah came away with a bit of clothing and a few odds and ends. Seth gleaned her fields for ripe ears with small return on the effort.

At the very least, I have t' figure on one bushel a month each for Maggie, Susannah, and meself . . . Seth ciphered in his head as he worked the field. *Three-quarter rations for Winnie and Jack. Half rations for Mary and Battler.* He tapped out calculations on his thigh, fingers ticking off an allotment of provender for each person in the household. *That comes t' five and a half bushels a month—November through April* . . . Fingers tapping . . . *Thirty-three bushels!* To survive the winter, they'd need to harvest, shuck, and shell thirty-three bushels of grain before Cavendish came along with his writ and his henchmen to boot them from the land.

Seth added and multiplied the figures once again, hoping for some miracle in miscalculation that would make this impossible task seem manageable. But the numbers did not lie. Thirty-three bushels—subsistence rations needed to ward off starvation.

I've but days, when what I need is weeks.

Finding a ripe ear here and a ripe ear there, he moved from cornstalk to cornstalk, stepping in time to a late-afternoon cicada chorus echoing through the field. *Zhing-zhing-zhing-zhing*—the surrounding woods sounded as if filled with men shaking pocketfuls of coin.

A whole pocket full of silver . . . wouldna tha' be fine? Seth's mind leaped easy from worry to wish and then to remorse. And for the first time, a twinge of regret for the money spent on Maggie's contract twisted in his chest. It was the most coin he'd ever had in his pocket at one time—earned it selling four kegs of his corn whiskey and his best mule.

I meant to save Naomi, but Death came determined and spared no questions.

A wave of nausea staggered Seth, his stomach suddenly soured as if he'd swallowed a cup of turned milk. He headed back to the cabin. Basket dragging heavy on his back, he could see Susannah in the distance, sitting alone in the shade of the tulip tree, shelling corn.

The drop edge of the world . . . That's what Naomi called it the first time she saw the piece of land he'd claimed. He should have known right then it was all too much for her.

Swallowed her whole. Such a wee slip was never meant for

this harsh life. If only she were stronger . . . if only I hadna brung her here . . . With a shake of his head, he said aloud, "No time to waste pondering ifs and mights."

More time. That's what he needed—or something of value to trade for corn. He hashed over the situation once again as he broke clear of the cornfield.

Seth passed Ol' Mule munching the goosefoot weed sprouting on the manure pile. *There's value in that mule, but a man canna hope t' clear a field or build a cabin without a mule.* Trading the mule was not an option. Seth skirted past the hog snuffling in a makeshift pen near the smokehouse. *Have to keep the hog.*

Corn alone would not get them through the winter. A body depended on fat to survive. Seth might get lucky and track a bear this winter, but in truth he'd have little time to spare for hunting. The hog was a sure thing and he planned to spend the next day building a makeshift pen in the woods to cache the beast beyond Cavendish's reach.

Seth wanted to leave as soon as they were supplied. *Hug the Blue Ridge and head south—careful to steer clear of Cherokee country.* It would be warmer longer down south, give him time to find a place to settle. Over winter he'd work the ax and clear acreage for planting . . .

Seedcorn!

Seth stopped in his tracks. *At least two bushels.* He had to plant a crop in the spring, or they'd face an even grimmer winter next season. *Thirty-FIVE bushels of corn . . .*

He glanced over his shoulder at the sun scratching the rim of purple hills on the western horizon. Seth drew a deep breath, adjusted the basket so the burden lay square between his shoulders, and shuffled forward. *No . . . not near enough hours in a day . . .*

The solitary tulip tree in the clearing cast a long shadow across the dooryard. Susannah had dragged a bench from the cabin and sat in the shade. She wore a triangular shawl looped with the narrow points knotted at one shoulder. Alexander slept sound in the pocket of this sling she'd positioned diagonally across her back.

She took an ear from the pile of shucked corn sitting to her right, leaned forward, knees spread, and rubbed an old corncob against the ripe ear, forcing the kernels to drop *tat-a-lat-a-lat* into the willow-withy basket between her feet. When every kernel had been rubbed free, she flipped the spent cob into a growing pile to her left and took another ear.

Seth propped his weapon against the tree, slipped free the basket on his back, and spilled the ears he'd just picked onto the ground to create a third pile—corn that needed to be shucked. "There's little out there what's ripe." He looked around. "Where's Maggie—the children? They ought t' be helpin' out . . ."

"Found 'em underfoot." *Tat-a-lat-a-lat.* "Battler's a hellion and Maggie's not much of a hand at shellin' . . ."

"Aye that. The lass's an able midwife, but when it comes to farm chores, she's as—"

Susannah cut Seth short. "Maggie saved my Mary and I'd be happy to shuck and shell her corn from now till forever." *Tat-a-lat-a-lat. Tat-a-lat-a-lat.* "I sent 'em all into the field for beans. Figured it wouldn't hurt us none to come away with a sack or two."

Seth nodded, chastised. "Aye, wouldna hurt." He glanced into Susannah's basket.

"Almost a bushel here," she said. "I've four full bushels inside."

"Well, make room—I'll lend a hand."

Susannah wriggled over; Seth sat beside her and began peeling and twisting husks from the corn. Working together in silence, intent on their tasks, they both heard it before they felt it—a dreadful wind, droning like the monotone skirl of a bagpipe, louder and louder as it scoured the field, cornstalks rattling in its wake. It swooped in and washed over them, raising the hairs on the back of Seth's neck.

He clapped a hand to his hat to keep it from flying off and walked to where he could see thunderheads massing on the eastern horizon. Another fierce gust rushed in to sweep through the pile of discarded cornhusks, launching them up to rustle in the sky.

Seth rubbed the back of his neck. "Eastlin' wind . . . boding wind."

Susannah came to stand beside Seth. Her skirts slapped her legs and she tussled with her apron flapping about her face. "I figured it were set to rain hard when I spied those horsetail clouds in the sky this morn."

Little Black and Patch darted in from the field and tore around the dooryard in mad circles, barking and leaping after the cornhusks caught in the whirlwind. Seth crushed his hat between his hands, stuffed it under his belt, and cupped his mouth. "*Maaggggiieee!*"

Bursting out of the cornfield, Maggie raced into the dooryard bumping a single-wheeled barrow. Little Mary and Battler sat inside laughing, screeching, and holding tight to the sides. Jack and Winnie trotted after, each lugging a canvas sack filled with just-picked beans. Maggie skittered to a raucous stop at the bench, breathless. "There's an evil storm a-brewin' . . ."

Seth barked orders as he swung Mary and Battler from the barrow onto their feet. "Jack—you go and stable Ol' Mule. Winnie—get th' wee ones intae the cabin . . ."

Susannah undid the knot on her shawl. "Take the baby in as well . . ."

Winnie dropped her sack and gathered Alexander into her arms. Little Mary took Battler by the hand and the children did as they were told.

Seth gazed skyward. A gray slurry of clouds churned above the hills. "Comin' straight at us—best get the corn inside afore this landlash lets loose."

The wind grew wild and continued to incite the dogs to bark incessantly. Seth, Maggie, and Susannah scrambled, tossing armfuls of corn into the barrow. Seth pushed the first load through the cabin door and was busy dumping it into the corner when the room was suddenly thrown into darkness. Winnie cried out, *"Da!"*

"Dinna fash, just the wind blown the door shut . . ." Seth maneuvered the barrow around in dim light and turned to find a great, huge man filling almost every square inch of the open doorway, obscuring all light.

Battler yelped and scuttled across the room. Seth caught him up and the boy buried his face in his father's neck.

The enormous pair of shoulders bowed, torso bent at thick waist, and a prodigious head covered in wiry, carrot-red hair cleared the lintel piece. Hobnail boots clacked on the floorboards as the giant man clomped into the cabin. Seth's eyes moved helpless to the empty rifle pegs near the door, the image of his gun leaning against the tulip tree flashing through his mind.

In order to avoid banging his head on the ceiling rafters, the giant was forced to stand awkward, with knees slightly bent and head tilted. He gripped a stout oaken cudgel in one hamlike fist and slapped it to a palm the size of a two-egg skillet.

"Aw' out, sez I," he bellowed, his voice thick and creamy with phlegm.

"Ooohhhh, Da!" Winnie whimpered.

Never taking his eyes off the giant, Seth slowly sidestepped around the table. "I'm coming for yiz, lass."

Winnie didn't wait. With Alexander asleep in the crook of her arm, she took Mary by the hand and scurried to her father's side.

"FIGG!" a man's voice hollered from outside.

The giant seemed to swell and he boomed, "Out, sez I! Out, or I be crackin' heads!"

Battler squeaked and clung tight. Seth placed his free hand on Winnie's shoulder. "We're goin' to do just as the man says, lass, so hang on to Alexander and take hold of wee Mary . . ." He could feel Winnie beneath his hand, trembling like a leaf on an aspen, but he moved forward, steering the group past the large man, through the door, and into the yard.

Beneath an angry sky flashing lightning in the distance, Maggie and Susannah sat stiffly on the bench. Brady Moffat stood a scant ten yards away with his rifle trained on the twosome. Patch and Little Black—bristling and barking bundles of fury—stood between the women and the armed man. Weapon cocked, finger on the trigger, Moffat spat a brown stream of tobacco juice that arced through the air, lifting on the wind. "Call off your dogs, Martin, or I will shoot 'em dead."

Seth whistled and slapped his leg. The dogs stopped barking and ran to sit at his side. Jack was not in the dooryard. Seth hoped the lad had hidden himself somewhere safe. He lowered Battler to stand on his own. The toddler hugged his father's legs.

"I've nae quarrel wi' ye, Brady Moffat." Seth raised his arms, palms open. "Ye can see I am unarmed. Put by yer weapon and let us settle this thing like thinkin' men."

Moffat smiled a friendly smile and kept his gun trained on the women. The wad of tobacco shifted from his left cheek and he spat the chaw splat into the dirt. "You need t' talk t' that fella there . . ." Brady jerked his curly brown head toward the cabin, his grin sardonic. "That there's our thinkin' man."

Seth hadn't noticed, but a little man leaned against the cabin wall with one booted foot propped up on the water trough. His rawboned, sinewy frame banged around in shirt and breeches so loose, the fabric snapped and buckled in the wind. The brace of pistols stuck in the man's belt in combination with Seth's rifle weighing heavy on his bony shoulder seemed to be the only things keeping him from being whisked away like a cornhusk on the breeze.

"Ye have my weapon, sir," Seth noted.

An Adam's apple the size of a baby's fist bobbed on the stalk of the little man's neck. Brushing windblown strands of raggedly cropped ginger hair from his face, he shouted in a thick Irish brogue, "Jaysus, would ye stand down, Moffat?"

"Aye aye, Cap'n Connor." Moffat dropped his weapon to cradle in the crook of his arm and offered a mock salute. Slumping against the tulip tree, he fished in his pocket, came up with a pigtail of tobacco, and pinched off a bite to tuck under his lip.

Bane of my existence . . . Seth ran his hand through his hair and muttered under his breath, "Drunks and the fuckin' Irish."

Encumbered by the weight and length of the rifle strapped to his shoulder, Connor swaggered over to where Seth stood with the girls. The skin of his face was scathed with pockmarks and clung tight to his skull. Blue eyes bulged buglike from dark circles. "That bollocks Moffat has the right of it. I'm the man t' talk to."

"G'won now," Seth told the girls as he disengaged Battler from his leg. "Take yer brother and go to the women." Battler ran to crawl onto Maggie's lap. Susannah took the baby. Mary and Winnie sat on the ground at her feet. Just then, Simon Peavey came around the cabin dragging angry Jack by the arm.

"Let go!" Jack struggled, swinging and kicking air. "Poxy Injun bugger—let go!" Peavey released the boy and Jack tumbled off to join the others.

Seth barely recognized Peavey with his long braids cropped off and his hair clean of grease and soot. The renegade still sported the regimental red coat, but he'd replaced moccasins and deerskin leggings with boots and breeches. Simon Peavey had not relinquished all of his Indian trappings—a clutch of bright feathers and silver charms dangled from the stock of his rifle. Seth could not help but sneer. "Yer lookin' almost white, lad."

Staying true to his Shawnee upbringing, Simon registered no reaction. He looked beyond Seth as if he did not exist and announced, "There's a good mule and pig back there."

"Handle this." Connor slipped the rifle from his shoulder and handed it to Peavey. "It's puttin' a crick in my neck. Find Figg and have him tether the beasts—"

"NO!" In three strides Seth stood toe-to-toe with Connor. "Ye willna take my beasts." Not a big man, Seth still stood taller and heavier than the tiny Irishman.

"FIGG!" Connor squawked, and fumbled to extricate a flat leather wallet from the front of his baggy shirt. *"Fiiiggg!!"*

Moffat and Peavey stood passive while Connor tugged papers free from the wallet, sputtering and waving the documents in the air. "We've a charter . . . granted by King George himself. A writ of dispossession . . . signed by the governor in Williamsburg . . ."

Seth snatched the papers from Connor. Unable to read any of the flowing, official-looking script, he ran a callused finger over the green wax impression that bonded a loop of scarlet ribbon to the parchment. "Seal of the Realm," he said, shaking his head.

"FIGG!" Connor shouted. *"Fiiigggg!"*

Figg appeared at the cabin door and performed a series of contortions to fit his huge shoulders through the opening. He'd abandoned his menacing club and in his right hand carried a round loaf of bread, clutched like a biscuit. His left fist strangled the neck of Seth's last bottle of whiskey and his happy smile was bedaubed with yellow globs of half-chewed cornbread plastering the gaps between his stained teeth.

Brady Moffat moved in quick to snatch the bottle from the giant, thumping him on the back. "You done good, Figgy. Real good."

In a spray of crumbs and spittle, Figg giggled. "Amen to that, sez I."

Connor marched over and slapped the bread from Figg's hand, sending it rolling in the dirt. "Ye great gobshite! Where are ye when I need ye? I'll tell ye where—stuffin' yer piehole—*Jaysus!*" The little man gave the giant a shove. "Arrah now, fetch the mule and the pig from the byre."

"STOP!" Seth ran to where big and little stood near the cabin door. He handed Connor the documents. "We'll leave th' land, no quarrel," he offered, trying to stay the panic rising in his throat, "but ye canna have the hog—I beg ye, man—that hog is the difference between life and death for us."

"Are ye dim?" Connor rattled the parchment in Seth's face and jerked a thumb over his shoulder. "Yer man there takes what he wants, and he wants it all."

Seth followed Connor's thumb. The wind had calmed a bit— the tall cornstalks moving but gently, to and fro, creating a soothing, undulating backdrop to Seth's worst fears realized. Mounted on a jet-black Andalusian, Julian Cavendish sat still as a military statue at the edge of the cornfield, monitoring his hirelings from afar.

Seth could hear his heart drumming in his head. "All I need's a bit more time—can ye ask him t' give me but a day or two?"

"Give ye?" Connor scrunched his face and snorted. "That bastard wouldn't give ye the steam off'n his piss." The Irishman folded and returned the documents to the wallet. "Na, yiv been cast adrift, boyo. The price ye must pay for squatting on what belongs t' another."

The sight of the king's seal and Cavendish aloof on horseback served to sap all strength from Seth. There was no beating a man who had the means to purchase the power of the law and the lawless. Seth turned his back on Connor, shuffled away, and dropped down to sit between Maggie and Susannah. "Everyone intae the cabin," he droned. "Gather your things."

Winnie and Jack took the little ones by the hand and did as they were told, but Susannah and Maggie did not budge. The women stayed at his side. Seth buried his face in his hands. He was beat—beat hollow and thin as a tin cup. A thick torpor of hopelessness clouded his brain.

Lightning cut the clouds, soon followed by rolling thunder,

and Alexander woke squalling. After a momentary discreet fidget, Susannah began nursing him under the shawl draped over her shoulder and the infant quieted.

Lightning flashed again. "We better get a move on," Moffat advised. "You know how his lordship hates the wet."

Connor glanced over his shoulder at Cavendish and barked, "Figg! Would ye g'won now an' fetch those beasts so we can be on our way?"

Figg veered off the path to the stable and wandered toward the tulip tree. Squatting on haunches in front of Susannah, he tilted his huge head in slack-jawed fascination, trying to catch a glimpse beneath the shawl.

Bristling like an angry hedgehog, Maggie leaped to her feet and gave the big man a two-handed shove that sent Figg sprawling bung end into a pile of corncobs. "Away wi' ye—ye great gallumpus. Leave the woman nurse the babe in peace."

Seth groaned. "Maggie . . . have a care . . ."

Connor ran over. "Jaysus, Figg! Get up—get up, I tell ye!"

Figg struggled mightily to draw his massive frame upright. "But, Connie, I want to see th' wee baby . . ."

"Never mind the baby! Go fetch the bleedin' beasts like I told ya." Connor brushed the dust from him, gave him a push, and Figg lumbered away.

Connor turned to the women. "Can ye believe it?" Shrugging, he offered a half grin. "The big oaf fancies babies."

"Fancies babies?" Maggie plopped back onto the bench. "For what? His breakfast?"

"He meant no harm," Connor defended staunchly. "He's simple."

"Aye, *he* may be simple," Maggie retorted, "but what's yer excuse?"

Brady Moffat burst out laughing.

Pink-faced, Connor grabbed Maggie by the hair and snarled, "Yer a fuckin' mouthy cunt! On yer prayer bones and beg mercy . . ." Pulling hard, he bent her head back at an unnatural angle, forcing her down to knees in the dirt.

Quicker than a hawk's talon snatching up prey, Susannah reached out and clamped her hand between Connor's legs. "Let Maggie go," she said.

A fistful of Maggie's hair in his right hand, Connor fumbled unsuccessfully to draw a pistol snagged on his belt with his left.

Seth leaped to his feet. "Susannah! Stop!"

A sweet smile curled the corners of Susannah's mouth; her grip tight and steady as a vise, she continued to nurse Alexander without interruption.

As shrill as a choirboy on Easter morning, Connor squeaked, "*MOF*-fat! *PEA*-vey!"

Leaning on their rifles, Brady Moffat and Simon Peavey stood by, much amused. Moffat called out, "Take care, Connor. That one chopped the head clean off'n a Shawnee brave—she may well pinch off your prick."

"Susannah," Seth pleaded, "dinna be sae reckless . . ."

Susannah blinked once and gave Connor's parts a twist.

The wee man's beet-red eyes near bugged out of his skull. "Awright!" he yelped, and released Maggie.

Susannah let loose. Connor stumbled backward, doubled over, gasping in pain.

"It wouldn't be hard at all, pinchin' off a nubbins like his," Susannah said blithely, pinkie finger extended.

"Woo-hoo!" Moffat hooted, slapping his thigh. Maggie giggled and even stoic Simon Peavey cracked a smile.

Connor turned and kicked Susannah's bushel basket, sending kernels of corn flying through the air like a spray of bird shot, screaming, "Drive them off! *Do it!* DO IT!"

Moffat sighed. "C'mon, Peavey. Let's finish this up." The gunmen moved in, rifles raised, herding Seth, Maggie, and Susannah to the center of the dooryard.

Seth grabbed Brady Moffat by the arm. "Can ye let us gather a few things first?"

Moffat jerked away and slugged Seth upside the head with the butt end of his rifle.

Slumping to his knees, Seth saw double and fingered the knot rising near his temple. Maggie pushed past Moffat and knelt at Seth's side.

"There was no need to wallop him . . . yiv no right . . ."

Connor stormed in with pistol drawn and pressed the barrel end to the back of Maggie's head. "Yer the one with no rights, missie." *Clack-clack,* the tumbler notched into fully cocked.

"Mr. Connor! Holster that weapon!" The viscount trotted into the dooryard, ordering his henchman in a voice as clipped as the Andalusian's iron-shod hooves on the sunbaked soil. Displaying expert horsemanship, the nobleman maneuvered his stamping and snorting mount to dance a tight circle around the group.

Mouth agape, Connor flinched under his master's scrutiny. Immediately uncocking the lock on his pistol, he stuffed the gun back into his belt, stuttering, "N-no need for concern, m-m'lord . . ." The little Irishman scuttled like a roach exposed to the light of day, hurrying to be the first to grab the stallion's halter and aid the viscount in his dismount.

Brady Moffat's slack posture stiffened and he shouldered his weapon infantry style. "Everything under control here, sir," he hiccuped, and scurried with Connor to curry favor.

Peavey's eyes narrowed at the nobleman's uncharacteristic intrusion. He tipped his head sideways much like a curious hound, took three long, slow steps back, and dropped his rifle to rest in his elbow.

The hog came snuffling and grunting into the dooryard, followed by Figg, besmeared with and reeking of pig muck. The giant man held tight the lead he'd tied to the hog and he tugged Ol' Mule along by the harness. Cavendish grimaced; pulling a lace-edged handkerchief from his voluminous sleeve, he held it to his nose.

Connor waved Figg away. "Stay downwind of his lordship, hear?"

Amid this shabby company, the viscount gleamed like a looking glass tossed on a refuse pile. Wigless and simply dressed in a brilliant white shirt tucked into fawn-colored breeches, this man was quite different from the powdered fop Seth had encountered aboard the *Good Intent*. With his sleek dark hair queued in a red satin ribbon that fluttered on the breeze, Julian Cavendish looked every bit the country lord.

Maggie and Susannah helped Seth up onto his feet. "Take his offer." Maggie spoke quick in his ear.

"What?" Seth swayed, knees buckling. The women on either side propped him up. He steadied and rubbed his head, trying to recover his wits and the ability to depend on his legs.

"He's come to make an offer—take it!" Maggie said.

"She's right," Susannah hissed. "Look at him—he wants her bad."

Seth blinked and focused. The viscount brushed past his obsequious henchmen, tapping his riding quirt against the burnished leather of his boot. Much like a man judging the fitness of a horse, he paced to and fro with deliberate regard, attention riveted on Maggie.

"The bastard . . ." Seth muttered.

Maggie urged. "My contract . . . trade it for corn."

"No!"

"Dinna be a fool. Strike a bargain."

"Sign ye over to tha' fiend?" Seth shook his head.

Maggie squeezed his arm. "Send me word when yiv harvested the corn . . . I'll run and meet up wi' yiz . . ."

"Too risky—I willna—"

"Ye must, Seth," Maggie rasped in his ear. "Yiv no choice."

Cavendish approached their group slowly. Maggie stood beside Seth, staring straight ahead with eyes hard as flint. Her waist-length hair had long since tumbled free and the braid-crimped strands writhed about on the wind like beckoning arms.

Connor simpered after his master. "You've a good eye, yer grace. She's a fine piece of goods."

"Yes . . . she is quite the thing, isn't she?" Cavendish stepped close to catch a tendril of Maggie's hair. He held it to his nose and breathed deep. He turned to Seth. "You seem inordinately blessed with a preponderance of females, yeoman."

Seth did not respond immediately, and Moffat prodded him between shoulder blades with the barrel end of his rifle. "His lordship's talkin' to you . . ."

"Leave me be, ye kiss-arse." Seth shrugged Moffat off with a glare.

"I've not forgotten the last time we met," Cavendish continued. "As I recall, you declined the generous offer I made on this girl's contract. Perhaps today you are . . . inclined?"

Random spits of rain began blowing in on the wind and Seth stood quiet for a moment, weighing his options before speaking. "It's true ye find me in desperate straits, sir, but dinna assume I'm sae eager to sign away th' only asset to which I hold clear title."

"Two weeks." Cavendish tossed out his offer casually. "You wanted time? You may have two weeks and the right to keep your harvest in exchange for the girl."

Maggie leaned into Seth and dug her thumb into his leg.

"Och." Seth shrugged, equally casual. "I'm reconciled to bein' dispossessed. The lass is a skilled midwife, and I wager there's muckle silver to be earned if I put her out t' work in Richmond-town . . ."

"Scots!" Cavendish rolled his eyes at Connor and heaved a sigh. "Very well, I will sweeten the pot—two weeks *and*"—he pointed his riding crop to the hog rooting for spilled corn at the base of the tulip tree—"the pig you so desire."

"Aye . . . a good offer." Seth worried the stubble on his chin. "But as ye must ken by now—a young, fine-lookin' white woman on th' frontier is scarcer than a preacher in paradise. I'll want both the pig *and* the mule," he countered, smiling. "One must pay dearly for a scarce commodity, na?"

Maggie pulled her shoulders back. In her best imitation of Bess Hawkins, she breathed deep, forcing her breasts to plump up beyond the constraints of bodice and blouse.

The muscle in the viscount's jaw twitched. "I am not one to dicker over picayune details. Keep the beasts—both of them."

Maggie double-jabbed Seth with her elbow, but he had caught whiff of the upper hand. Seth bounced on the balls of his moccasined feet as if he were getting set to run a race. "Let me be certain we understand one another, sir. In exchange for the lass's paper, I'll have two weeks—unhindered—the harvest, the hog, and the mule"—he glanced behind to where Peavey leaned against the cabin wall—"*and* my flintlock returned to me."

Cavendish rapped the leather quirt to the palm of his hand. "Your tenacity has ceased to amuse, yeoman . . ."

Connor bristled. "The Scotman's a canny devil, m'lord."

"And yer a wee Irish catch-fart." Seth sneered.

Moffat butted in. "This man's a crack shot, m'lord. Give him that gun and he'll have a ball lodged in the nape of your neck afore we reach the tree line."

Seth placed a hand over his heart and intoned, "I swear on the lives of my children and the grave of my dear wife, I willna seek violent retribution against you"—he paused to cast a derisive glance Connor's way—"or yer flunkies. Ye have my word on it."

"His *word*!" Connor sputtered.

Cavendish silenced Connor with a wave of his hand. "And I should trust in your word?"

"The only thing I've left to give and keep is my word, sir. Those are my terms—have we a bargain?"

Cavendish looked Maggie over once again. She tilted her chin and tucked a curl behind her ear; the pink tip of her tongue darted out for an instant to touch the corner of her mouth.

"Two weeks, corn, hog, mule, and rifle." Cavendish rapped out the terms. "Agreed?"

"Agreed. I'll fetch the paper." Seth gave Maggie's hand a squeeze before turning to run into the cabin.

"Mr. Moffat, go and bring the horses so we can be on our way."

Raindrops began to patter a random rhythm on the leaves of the tulip tree. Seth returned shortly to hand the contract to Connor. "I've signed my mark to it."

Connor examined the document. "All in order," he informed the viscount, and added the sheet to the others in his wallet. "Will the lass be riding with you, m'lord?"

"I think not." Cavendish mounted and leaned forward to stroke his Andalusian's neck. "I'd rather not tax my boy in the rain . . . bind her hands and have Figg lead her afoot."

Connor grabbed Maggie by both wrists. "Figg! Bring rope."

"Let go, ye grubshite!" Maggie twisted and tried to jerk away from his grasp.

"Ye needna bind the lass," Seth exclaimed. "She goes willing . . ."

"Mind yer business—she's his now. FIGG!" Connor struggled to hold on to Maggie, scrunching his nose as Figg came near. "*Phew!* Th' smell of ye, man . . . yer funkin'!"

Maggie stopped thrashing at the sight of Figg. The giant's wide face mushed from smile to frown and back to smile in an instant. He took her hands and stroked one palm with his sausage finger—a sound like the purr of a cat resonated from his massive chest. "Soft and sweet's yer hand, sez I . . ."

Connor gave Figg a shove. "Arrah now—shut yer potato trap and get busy."

Figg bound her wrists with a length of fuzzy rope. Maggie nodded to the children, who'd come out from the cabin, clustering around Susannah in tears, and called out with a brave smile, "Dinna fash for me—I'll be fine."

"That's the best feather in yer wing, lass—yer strength." Seth opened wide his arms. "I'll not forget what ye did here for us, Maggie Duncan." Maggie stepped into the bear hug and he whispered, "Be strong—be ready—two weeks at most, sooner if I can." She buried her face in his neck and nodded.

Connor came between them and pushed Seth away. Moffat brought out the three horses they had hidden in the woods. As the men began to mount, Seth called out, "Mr. Cavendish! My weapon, sir—as agreed—"

"Of course." Cavendish smiled. "Mr. Peavey—the man's rifle—*à tout de suite* . . ."

Simon slipped Seth's rifle from his shoulder. He snapped open the frizzen and blew the powder out the pan. He twisted the flint from the jaws on the cock and dropped it into his pocket. After jamming the rifle, muzzle first, straight down into the dirt, he strode over and dropped the weapon—lock, stock, and barrel— into the water trough.

"Your rifle, Mr. Martin—as agreed." Cavendish turned his steed and headed out.

Thunder rumbled through the hills, sounding like a brewer's cart on a cobblestone street. Cavendish led the string of horsemen toward the cornfield. Figg trailed at the end, pulling Maggie along by her tether. She stumbled to keep up with his long strides, struggling against the wind. She did not look back.

Heavy rain arrived in a *whoosh*, sheets of water driven by strong gusts of wind. Seth leaped up onto the bench and watched Maggie being led off like a sheep to slaughter. Suddenly Simon Peavey broke away from the orderly column. Turning his mount, the renegade backtracked past the others, to meet with Figg and Maggie in the rear.

Cavendish continued into the cornfield, but Connor turned, shouting, "Peavey! What are ye doin'? Get back here, ye heathen!"

Simon did not suffer a glance back. He leaned over and said something to Maggie that Seth could not hear over the wind.

Maggie lifted her bound wrists; the renegade drew his knife and freed her hands. With Figg's aid, Maggie mounted to ride pillion behind Peavey and they rejoined the column. Clutching the dangling rope in his hand, Figg leaned into the wind and ran to catch up.

Two weeks . . . Seth thought, watching Figg's bobbing head disappear in the cornfield. As soon as the party of horsemen progressed beyond his sight, he jumped down and ran to fish his gun from the water trough. He peered down the barrel. *There's a half a day's work* . . .

Seth yanked hard on the latchstring and swung open the cabin door.

19

No Man's Slave

Simon Peavey leaned from his saddle, reaching out to her with one hand. "Ride with me."

Maggie stood in the pouring rain, bound hands raised like a supplicant at an altar. "I canna—"

He freed her hands with a flick of the sharp knife drawn from his belt. Verdant-green eyes locked on hers as he took firm hold of her upper arm. "Ready?"

Maggie leaped and swung her leg over; her free arm flailing, she could not get a good grasp on the horse's round, wet rump. Caught midmount, she dangled by one heel hooked at the gelding's tail and one arm held in the renegade's grip. The horse lost patience with her clumsiness and balked. Maggie's arm slipped through Simon's fingers and she fell, landing flat on her back.

"Figg!" Peavey worked the reins to control his skittish mount. "Help the gal up."

The giant loomed over Maggie. Before she could even utter a gasp, Figg pulled at the waistband of her skirt and propped her up to stand in the morass churned by thrashing hooves.

Peavey maneuvered his mount closer and offered his hand once again. "C'mon . . ."

Wringing wet, covered with mud, hair dripping, Maggie threw her arms in the air and sobbed, "It's no use . . ."

Heedless, Figg spanned her waist with his hands and hoisted her astride the dapple-gray gelding as if she weighed no more than a gunnysack full of plucked goose feathers. She clutched Peavey by the shoulders and wriggled to find a secure seat.

Bare legs dangled from sodden skirts bunched thick and lumpy around her. Bristly horsehair scoured the skin on her thighs and she squirmed, wishing for a bit more padding between her parts and the horse's rump. Maggie had never ridden beastback in her life, and this perch so very high off the ground seemed extremely precarious.

Peavey reached back and tugged her arms, pulling them to wrap about his waist. "Hold tight." He clicked his tongue, kicked heels to horse, and they cantered forward. Pelted by wind and rain, Maggie hunkered close to Simon's back, pressing her cheek to the wet wool of his regimental red coat, glad for something warm to cling to.

They entered the forest and the storm instantly lost its fury under the trees. Only the most determined raindrops breached the thick canopy churning overhead. Driving rain diminished into a rhythmic drumming on the leaves and soft forest floor.

Maggie sat back a bit. "Where we headin'?"

"Roundabout."

"*Roundabout!*" Maggie breathed easier. The prospect of a familiar place and friendly faces did much to cheer her.

Simon glanced over his shoulder. "They ain't there no more."

"Who?"

"All of 'em—they took off."

"Took off?"

"Yep—took off afore he could run 'em off."

He. Him. Cavendish. In a few short days the world had gone so suddenly mad, lives irreparably altered by the coming of this one man. She felt heavy, saturated with dread. Maggie sagged against Simon and they bounced along the narrow footpath, her anguish a hard, sharp thing caught in her throat, as if she'd swallowed a shard of glass.

Worry saps strength an' dulls th' wits. Maggie drew herself upright and sucked in a great lungful of air. She could ill afford to dwell on dread and could hear Hannah's voice in her ear. *What canna be cured must be endured.* Maggie would not be undone by the likes of Julian Cavendish. She'd survived much in her young life, and she was determined to survive the next two weeks. *Then I'm off . . .*

"I know you're gonna run."

Maggie jerked. "What?"

"I heard you whisperin' with Seth—you're set to run once the corn's in."

It was as if he had read her thoughts. Maggie's heart tumbled topsy-turvy in her chest. "Ye heard *wrong*."

"I'm glad you're gonna run." He turned around in the saddle and smiled. "Don't fret. I'm no snitch."

She'd always been so distracted by Peavey's rather frightening Indian regalia and stern countenance, she never noticed he was quite a winning lad. Simon's genuine smile—the first she'd ever seen on him—eased many misgivings. She said with a wry grin, "Aye, maybe yer no snitch—well and good—but I'm no runaway."

"Well, from what I seen, you sure ain't no man's slave."

The shadow of several days' growth strengthened the line of his angular jaw and darkened his upper lip, providing a bit of roughness to counter pleasing features that bordered on pretty. Soaking wet, his cropped hair curled and framed a lean, sunbrowned face, marred only by the scar of black powder freckles burned into his right temple. Maggie reached up and Simon flinched. She ran a finger over the tiny black specks and felt the muscles across his back draw taut as a bowstring.

"Yer burn healed fine, na?"

He turned in to her touch, thick dark brows arched over wary green eyes flecked with bits of gold. *Hannah had eyes like that.*

"Hang on now—" he advised, attention drawn back to the trail. Maggie clinched him tight. Simon steered the gelding between two lichen-spattered boulders and down a steep, slippery incline. Pointing out a patch of blue sky through the trees, he said, "Looks like the weather's fairin' up."

The storm had abated, reduced to sporadic raindrops shaken free by the wind and the rustle of emerging birds and squirrels. Sunshine penetrated the overstory and the trees began to glisten. The air was rich with a savory blend of fresh-washed leaves and sweet, wet decay crushed beneath hooves.

"Mind your head," Simon warned. In tandem they ducked beneath a low-slung limb. He snapped off a branchlet in passing, plucked a shiny green leaf to chew, and offered the rest to Maggie. "Sourwood—slakes your thirst. G'won—it's good medicine."

She took one of the smaller leaves and popped it into her mouth, surprised by the refreshing flavor, likening it to the crisp bite of not-quite-ripe apple. She held the branch to her nose and sniffed. "What kind of medicine?"

"They say sourwood makes for a strong heart."

"Who says? Red Indians? The Indians what raised ye?"

He didn't answer, and but for the low thud of hoofbeats on the forest floor, they rode out the stretch of flat trail that curved along the top of the ridge in silence. She chewed sourwood leaves and wondered what to make of the friendship Simon Peavey seemed to be offering. She could use an ally where she was heading. Maggie leaned forward.

"So why does a likely lad as yerself pander to that devil of an Englishman?"

"The devil pays in Dutch silver." Simon kept his eyes on the forward trail.

"Aye, but turnin' folk from their homes at gunpoint—"

"It's Cavendish what's turnin' 'em out, not me."

"Och, what blether!"

"I do what I have to, t' git by," Peavey said, turning slightly to face her. "No different than Seth."

"Och, ye saw how it was. Seth had no choice . . . we'd have all starved otherwise."

"I'd sure never trade your paper to that devil of an Englishman—an' I sure as hell would never have left you behind, like Tom did."

Maggie smiled. "Och, lad, ye ken we've a thing or two in common. When I was but a wee lass back in Scotland, my folk were all massacred—like they tell me yer folk were. On that awful day I learned it's most likely not my fortune t' live life happily ever after." She tried hard to put on a brave face. "So I'll do what I always do and make the best of a bad bargain. I figure a body can stomach just about anythin' for two weeks."

Simon leaned left and dug into his saddlebag. He twisted around, a bone-handled dagger lying across the flat of his hand. "Take it."

"*Wheesht!*" Maggie pushed his hand away. "Tha' nasty wee Irishman'll see ye . . ." She leaned sideways to peer up trail. Connor rode a scant twenty yards ahead.

"Take it." The blade, no more than six inches long, was encased in a rigid leather sheath. He pressed it into her hand. "It'll do some damage in a pinch."

"Are ye daft?" Maggie pushed him away. "I've nowhere t' keep a knife."

"Tie it to your leg—up high." Simon tugged at the red silk kerchief looped around his neck and offered it together with the knife. "I've seen what he does to the other slave girl. You best take it." His gaze was so fierce and honest, he didn't need to say any more.

Maggie took a deep breath. "Awright. Keep yer eye on Connor." She hid the knife in the tangle of her skirt and checked the back trail. A stone's throw away, Figg gallumped along, breathing heavy, his ponderous arms swinging to and fro before him.

"Pay no mind t' Figg." Simon tapped a finger to his head. "A lackwit—wouldn't know to wipe his own arse if Connor didn't tell him to. Hurry an' fix that knife t' your leg."

Maggie's hands trembled. She struggled to keep her balance while twisting the kerchief into a rope and tying it onto her right leg. She slipped the sheath under the silk to lie flat along her outer thigh and pulled skirts down to cloak the weapon. She laid a hand on Simon's shoulder. "I'm grateful t' ye."

They traveled down the switchback trail in silence. The pace quickened when they passed Naomi's grave at forest edge and entered the clearing surrounding Roundabout Station. The sight of the bouquet Winnie had laid on her mother's grave, wilted and strewn, stung Maggie's heart worse than vinegar poured on an open sore.

Even from a distance, the station seemed much changed. The field that had been littered with tree stumps was being cleared. A team of Negro men dressed in rough hempen shirts and loose trousers worked a pair of chained oxen, pulling and prying up one of the few stumps remaining. Another black man steered a plow and mule, gouging great gashes into the earth.

"Tobacco beds," Simon explained.

Maggie found it strange to approach the fort with the stockade gates closed shut. Two menacing fellows sat atop the blockhouse, guns in hand. As the riders approached, the sentries rose to their feet, giving shout. One gate creaked open and the party of outriders clip-clopped through.

Within the stockade, a gang of blackamoors dressed in the same loose shirts and trousers formed a human chain, unloading one of several wagons filled with cargo. They chanted a rhythmic song while passing crates, heavy sacks, and casks from one to another, storing the goods in the first of the small cabins that lined the back palisade.

Four white men sat around the table beneath the tarp—hunters,

Maggie surmised by their garb. They set aside their playing cards to meet the party.

The familiar clang of hammer on steel and the *whoosh* of the bellows drew Maggie's attention to Willie's forge. But instead of the hearty German, a powerfully built man as black as the bar of iron he worked wielded the hammer. Distracted by the newcomers, the skinny young Negro pumping the bellows paused to gawk. A brilliant smile flashed across the smith's face and he did not miss a beat as he chastised the lad in a rich baritone, "Achilles! You best keep my coals white-hot or I will take a switch t' your bony behind." The boy resumed pumping with vigor.

Against a backdrop of ruffled shirts and bedsheets hanging on a line strung between the smithy and the cabins, a slender woman used a long paddle to fish steaming linen from a cauldron. Maggie would classify the woman as half-caste—her skin the golden brown of muscovado sugar. A riotous mass of shoulder-length kinked curls exploded from the white scarf she wore on her head. The laundress looked up from her work. She and Maggie exchanged nods.

Moffat and Connor dismounted. Simon helped Maggie down. The door of the blockhouse banged open and two boys scurried out to stand at attention, one boy on either side of the doorway. Their identical faces stared blankly, straight ahead.

Maggie tried to sort one twin from the other, but the brothers were as alike as the brass buttons on their crimson jackets. The outlandish costumes came complete with blue satin pantaloons, white knee hose, and silver-buckled shoes. From each neck dangled a brass key on a golden chain, and their twin faces—as black as India ink—were crowned by red, befeathered turbans.

Connor rushed to quiet the Andalusian while Cavendish swung down from the saddle, riding quirt in hand. With furious gaze focused square on Simon and Maggie, he shouted, "A word, Mr. Peavey!"

Maggie shuffled back, putting the horse's rump between herself and Cavendish. Simon outright ignored his employer. He pulled his rifle from the saddle holster and untied the leather cuff that protected the lock mechanism from the weather.

"Mr. Peavey," Cavendish called again, snapping the quirt to his boot as he approached. "I ordered the servant girl bound. She was meant to travel afoot with Figg."

Simon flipped open the frizzen and scrutinized the condition of the prime in the pan before responding. "I saw no harm in her ridin' with me."

"The harm, Mr. Peavey, stems from your willful disobedience of my direct order."

Simon clapped the pan shut and clicked the cock half open. Resting his weapon in the crook of his arm, he glared at Cavendish through narrow eyes. "I'll try and keep that in mind for next time." He turned and ambled toward the hearth.

"See to it, sir," Cavendish blustered.

Grim-faced, one of the card-playing men stepped forward and muttered something into Cavendish's ear. The viscount did not seem pleased. He shouted, "Mr. Connor—have the girl wait in my quarters," dismissing Maggie to the blockhouse with a double flick of the hand.

Connor grabbed Maggie by the arm. She shook him off. "Keep yer filthy mitts t' yerself, ye wee sack o' shite. I'll go on my own speed." The leather sheath strapped to her leg bit into her skin as she marched past the twin sentinels at the door. Maggie crossed over the threshold and stepped into another world.

The makeshift keg-and-board beds where she'd nursed Susannah and Naomi were gone. An ornate, four-posted bed done up with crisp linens, damask bed curtains, and an array of pillows occupied the far corner of the room. An iron-banded chest rested at the foot of the bed, and in the corner opposite stood a tall cabinet with gleaming brass hardware.

A long writing table was pushed up against the wall, one end of its polished mahogany top cluttered with papers and ledgers, the other end graced with a silver tray on which was arranged a china tea service. A pair of four-branched silver candelabra flanked the tray, beeswax tapers lit, steady flames bathing the room in clean bright light. Maggie had seen things as fine as these in shop windows back in Glasgow.

Two fringed woolen carpets—one lapped over the other—covered the width and breadth of the rough wood floor. She wandered about the room, curling her toes into exotic ruby-red and sapphire-blue patterns, soft and lush on the soles of her feet.

Maggie studied the faces in the pair of gilt-frame portraits hanging above an overstuffed wing chair—a stern man wearing an ermine-trimmed cape; a lovely lady in pearls and powdered hair. Longing to sink into the comfortable chair, she ran a hand over the upholstered armrest and noticed a book marked with a trailing blue ribbon sitting on the small table beside the chair. Maggie sighed, and caught the silken ribbon between her fingers.

Tom . . .

It seemed so long ago—that hot day by the river when he had read poetry and loved her so well. *Thou art my life, my love, my heart . . .* She closed her eyes and pressed both hands to her stomach, wondering for the thousandth time—where was he? Did he think of her? Was he ever coming back?

"Here he comes!" The twins rushed in, their faces set serious.

Maggie quelled a flutter of excitement, a momentary irrational hope that it might be Tom. She knew exactly who it was. She inched around the chair to melt into the corner.

The boys said not a word, not even to each other. Using the key hanging around his neck, one boy unlocked the corner cabinet, removed a crystal decanter along with two goblets. He filled them both with tawny liquid.

The other boy unlocked the chest. He whisked out a silk dressing gown and draped it at the foot of the bed. The two of them scurried to stand soldier stiff, shoulder to shoulder near the open door, each bearing a goblet centered on a small lacquered tray.

Cavendish stormed in. He snatched up a glass and drank the spirits in one swallow. After gulping down the second serving, he growled and let the goblet fly. It bounced off the face of the man in the portrait and crashed into bits on the floor. Throwing his head back, Cavendish railed to the rafters, "Ye gods! How long must I be banished to this eighth circle of hell?"

The twins stood stoic, barely blinking. One stepped forward. "Tea, sir?"

The viscount composed himself with a deep breath. "Thank you, but no, Pollux. More port, I think."

Pollux refilled the surviving goblet. His master made quick work of the third and fourth glassfuls poured. At last, Cavendish smiled. Sufficiently inoculated, he tugged shirttails from breeches, pulled his wet shirt over his head, and tossed it on the floor.

Accustomed to seeing men shirtless, toiling the day long under the hot sun, Maggie was shocked by the nobleman's unhealthy pallor. It was as if the man's skin had never been exposed to the sun—his hairless chest an eerie, opaque expanse.

Cavendish preened in the center of the room and took a sip from yet another glass of port before slipping his arms into the robe offered by the other brother. "Thank you, Castor—see my shirt delivered to the laundress."

Castor scooped up the shirt. He and Pollux arranged themselves side by side and waited.

"Dismissed." The viscount waved the twins away. The boys beat a path out the door, and Maggie hurried to follow. Cavendish stepped between Maggie and the open door.

"I do not recall giving you leave."

He belched. A rank blend of bilious sputum and sour port hung in the air. Maggie took a step back. Cavendish kicked the door shut, shot the bolt home, seized her by the wrist, and pulled her across the room. Exhibiting a strength that belied his frail pallor, the viscount flung her onto the bed.

Maggie scuttled back on elbows to hug the bedpost in the far corner. Pale blue eyes, bloodshot and tinged yellow, tracked her every movement. His cold appraisal chilled Maggie to the bone. "Please, sir . . . ye seem worse for th' drink . . ."

"*La, mademoiselle*"—his accent precise—"intemperate I may be, but I shall perform admirably nonetheless. According to *Papa*"—Cavendish gestured with a flourish to the portrait on the wall—"drunkenness and debauch are the areas in which I excel." Strutting like a crow that had just scavenged a shred of meat from a bone, he unfastened the buttons on his drop-front breeches and groped between his legs to produce a sad, limp member.

Too drunk to do the deed! Maggie felt like clapping. She silently blessed Pollux and his bottomless bottle of port.

With scowling brow Cavendish assessed his organ, flaccid as a stalk of rotting celery. He looked up at Maggie and smiled, almost apologetic. "But a moment . . ." Spitting into the palm of his hand, the viscount attempted to propel himself to erection.

The sight of him encouraging his vile flesh to life acted upon Maggie like a violent purgative, vanquishing all selfless reason and resolve from her mind. She choked back the bitter bile snaking up from her belly. She clung helpless to the bed curtains, her heart thumping like a military drum, beating a call to quarters in her brain.

The man's mouth was moving and Maggie knew he must be speaking to her, but she could not hear his words for the blood that rushed screaming into her head. She covered her ears, for the noise was deafening—screams, drums, and the clatter and clank of soldiers at the quickstep—heavy boots scuffling along the loose scree of the village road.

Maggie squeezed her eyes tight and could see it all just as she had so many years ago. Red jackets running from croft to croft with torches set. Thatched roofs alight—crimson and orange tongues licking billowing black smoke. She clung to her mother's skirt—fabric slipping through her desperate, little fingers as the trooper dragged her mother away—Mam's stricken face and the terror in her voice as she shouted, *"RUITH! Ruith, Magaigh!"*

RUN. Run, Maggie.

A growl gathered in the pit of Maggie's being, balled up, and burst from her lips as she sprang from the bed. Mindless of where she was going—knowing only that she had to be away— Maggie pushed past Cavendish and ran to the door.

He was right behind her as she fumbled with the bolt. Cavendish pressed one hand to the door to prohibit her escape. "You've not been dismissed."

Ruith, Magaigh! Her mother's voice echoed in her head. A bolus of rabid fury burned in her throat. She turned and feathered into the man like a wild thing, clawing, kicking, screaming, and biting.

"Mad bitch!" Cavendish caught her by the left arm and pulled her toward the bed. Maggie dug her heels in and flopped to the floor—carpets rolling and bunching as he dragged her along. She fumbled under her skirts for the knife and freed the blade from its sheath.

"UP! Up, on your feet!" Cavendish jerked hard on her arm.

And she complied, jumping to her feet brandishing honed steel.

He let loose her arm in time to leap back and evade the full force of her attack. Swinging the blade wild, Maggie slashed through his silken robe and sliced a red pinstripe across his chest. They both froze—immobilized by the sight of bright blood beading, then trickling scarlet tendrils down the viscount's white chest.

"You wretched *cunt*!" Cavendish pounced and wrested the dagger from her hand, flinging it to hit the wall and fall clattering behind the bed. In an instant, his enraged fist came full force to her face, knocking Maggie to the floor.

A blazing rod of pain pierced her skull and set her ears to ringing. Maggie rolled from side to side, moaning and sobbing.

"Get up." He prodded her with his foot like one would nudge a dog lying in his path. Maggie struggled to hands and knees.

"On your feet."

Threads of bloody spittle linked her aching mouth to the carpet. She turned her head slow and looked up with one eye already swollen shut.

Cavendish stood over her, his part erect and quivering. Maggie hawked up a glob of red-tinged mucus to land on the toe of his boot.

The savage kick he delivered to her gut lifted Maggie inches from the floor and sent her sprawling—gulping for air. Cavendish wound a hand around her hair and yanked her to her feet, wrenching her right arm behind her back.

Every feeble struggle she offered was now met with a furious ratchet of her arm and tearing at her scalp. She was racked and rendered helpless with pain. Cavendish drove her forward, slamming Maggie to bend face down over the writing table.

"Please, I beg ye . . ." She flailed with her free arm. "Please. Stop."

He answered her plea with a brutal twist to her arm, stretching tendons and muscles in agony. The man laughed in triumph as a sickening pop sounded and Maggie's shoulder dislocated from its socket. The viscount tossed muddy skirts over her back and kicked her feet apart. Pinning her to the table with one hand planted between her shoulder blades, he rammed himself into her.

Maggie arched her neck and cried out, writhing to escape his onslaught.

Grinding in deep, Cavendish leaned close. Mouth to her ear, he hissed, "An angry, snapping cunt makes for a nice, tight ride."

Maggie caught her sobs in her throat and lowered her head to the table. Her cheek pressed to the smooth polished wood slid back and forth in a slick of blood and tears. She forced herself to lie lifeless, chewing the flesh inside her lip to keep from moving or making any noise.

An eternity passed. Candle flames wavered and wavered as he pounded and pounded into her body. She shut her eyes but could not close her ears to the teacups and silver spoons tinkling in alarm with his every thrust.

A grunt. A shudder. He slumped forward and pushed off. Maggie lay still and listened to the scuffle of erratic footfalls as he skinked away—the bed cords creaking with sudden strain as he flung himself onto the mattress.

She tugged at her skirts with her good arm, drew a shuddered breath, and slowly stood upright. Her right arm hung painfully useless at her side. Picking at strands of hair plastered over her mouth and eyes and without a backward glance for her attacker, Maggie staggered out the door. She braced her good hand to the door frame and vomited, hacking and heaving till empty. Cavendish's seed seeped gummy between her thighs. Maggie hugged her battered ribs, retching anew, gagging up dry, painful spasms of air.

The guard peered down from the blockhouse roof, snickering. "Looks like his lordship treated you t' a ride, missy . . ."

Maggie shuffled forward and lowered to sit on a wide tree stump. She squinted one eye at the last rosy light of awful day. A small, striped lizard ran up her skirt, danced for a moment in the upturned palm of her useless hand, then scurried away to disappear in the scrub carpeting the fortyard.

Would that she could, like a lizard, slip her wretched skin . . . she'd leave it to dry paper thin in the hot sun, and wait for a strong breeze to come along and blow the battered, empty husk far, far away. Then like the wee lizard, she'd scurry away to disappear and blend into the bark of the world, new and whole again.

A gentle arm wrapped around her shoulders and urged Maggie to her feet. "Come along now, baby . . . we need care for those bruises."

Maggie yelped and winced, squinching eyes tight against the pain shooting down her arm to her fingertips.

"Oooh, sugar . . . I'm sorry," a soft voice soothed, and a gentle hand smoothed her hair. "That devil-man sure done beat you bad . . . real bad."

"Devil-man . . . aye." Maggie leaned her head to rest on the shoulder of her Samaritan. Wiry curls tickled her cheek and she was comforted by wholesome, good smells—lye soap and sun-dried linen pressed with a hot flatiron.

The laundress . . .

20

Better to Bend Than Break

If Maggie lay perfectly still—kept her head straight, fingers laced over her middle—the racking pain in her shoulder melded with the ache in her head and the soreness between her legs, forming an overall pulsing throb that was somehow . . . tolerable.

She lay on one of three straw-stuffed pallets lined up along the wall of the very same cabin she had shared with so many others during the Shawnee uprising. One eye swollen shut, Maggie fixed her good eye on the ceiling. Gloaming light keeked between the same chinks in the same roof shingles and she watched the same brown spider repair the web spanning the same pair of rafter beams.

Everything the same, yet everything so different . . .

The recollection of the viscount's hand planted between her shoulder blades, pinning her helpless to the table, caused her to shudder, then cringe with the sudden pain radiating out from her shoulder to the tips of fingers and toes.

To keep from being drawn into the abyss of self-pity and self-loathing yawning at the back of her mind, Maggie closed her good eye and concentrated on drawing deep controlled breaths. Never in her life had she been brought so low, to a position so tenuous—so reliant on the whim of strangers. She lay still and quiet, straining to hear the voices muttered outside the door.

A swoosh of skirts and a whiff of lye soap. Maggie opened her eye and leaned her head to the left, not surprised to see the slender laundress framed by the open doorway. The woman's honey skin was aglow with perspiration and the dusky light filtering through her wispy curls. She asked, "What they call you, sugar?"

It took forever to force her lips to form the words. "Mm-Maggie . . . Maggie Duncan."

The laundress settled her skirts so she could sit comfortably on Maggie's left. "My name's Aurelia, an' this here's Tempie—th' root doctor. She gonna make you good as new."

Maggie tipped her head to the right. A very small, very odd woman stood there, like a pixie come to life from the faerie tales. She was dressed in a brilliant saffron blouse and a clover-green skirt, her thin neck strung with many strands of multicolored seed beads. Tempie looked as though she'd sprung from the earth, her complexion as dark and smooth as the glazed umber cup she held in her delicate hands.

The tiny root doctor set the cup on the dirt floor. She sat down, tailor style, all the while considering Maggie with a wise smile and merry eyes bright and black as two jet buttons. Laying her little hands on Maggie's injured shoulder, she probed gently with knowing fingers. Teeth clenched, Maggie focused on the woman.

Tempie's hair was cropped short. Dense as a sea sponge, it clung to her head like a fleecy black cap. A salting of gray at the temples and the stamp of crow's-feet at the corners of her eyes were the only indications of any maturity. The woman seemed ageless—neither young nor old.

Aurelia loosened the laces on Maggie's bodice. "Tempie say she got to get yo' arm fixed quick or it won't never be right. You understand, Maggie Duncan?"

Maggie hadn't noticed Tempie say anything, but if she did say that, she was spot-on. The longer the muscles were left inflamed and stretched with bones out of joint, the harder the injury would be to repair. Maggie slid her good hand up to her shoulder to feel the odd mushy place left where hard bone should be. Putting a shoulder right was a tricky business, requiring know-how and considerable strength. Maggie shot a look at the diminutive root doctor and sucked air between her teeth. "An' this wee Tempie can set a bone?"

"Don't you fret none." Tempie spoke for the first time, her melodic voice sweet and tiny as her body. "I've coaxed many a ball joint back into they sockets. Help her set upright, Aurelia honey. I'se a draught for dis chile t' drink." Aurelia slipped her arm around Maggie's shoulders and levered her up. Tempie held the cup to Maggie's lips.

Wincing, Maggie sniffed the offering. Alcohol. Rum—and something else—something unfamiliar, sharp and peppery. "What's in tha'?"

Aurelia said, "Never you mind, you just drink up. Tempie's been doctorin' folk since afore you an' I was borned—do as she say, and you be awright."

Maggie turned her face away from the cup. "I willna drink it, lest I ken what's in it."

"Lawsy, Massa sho didn't beat th' stubborn from you, did he?" Aurelia shook her head. "That Simon feller tolt us you's some kind of a healer-woman. That so?"

Maggie nodded. "Midwife."

Tempie scooched in closer. "Seein' as how we's sisters in medicine, I can share my recipe with you." Her voice dropped to a whisper. "Two good-size chunks of black haw bark, ground to a fine dust and mixed wi' a measure of Jamaica rum." She dipped an index finger into the inky brew and stirred. "Black haw serves t' loosen th' muscles, but I also added a tiddy bit o' jimsonweed for pain." Tempie scrinched her pixie face, wide, flat nose crinkling at the bridge. "But don't you go foolin' with jimsonweed now—powerful stuff that—like t' kill a body if'n you don't know how t' use it proper."

Maggie'd never heard of "black haw" or "jimsonweed," but the woman had chosen herbs with properties Maggie would have sought herself—something to relax the muscles in her shoulder and something very, very strong to ease the excruciating pain of having a bone relocated. She gulped down the entire dose, the rum immediately washing over her like a warm rising tide in her belly. Tempie spread a small wool blanket across the pallet, and Aurelia carefully lowered Maggie to lie across it.

"We have t' wait for th' medicine t' take," Tempie said to Aurelia. "Bring me my sack o' simples, then go an' fetch Justice. I'll be needin' him soon."

Aurelia popped to her feet, set a sturdy canvas satchel at Tempie's side, and skipped out the door.

"See that gal run?" Tempie giggled, glass bottles clinking as she searched through her sack. "Aurelia sho' is sweet on that man, mmmm-hmm . . ."

"Swee' on wha' mon?" Maggie words slurred, her brogue suddenly thicker.

"She sweet on Justice—that new smith come from Williamsburg. Aurelia fancies him. Caught 'em spoonin' in the shadows last night. Mm-hmm, she is sweet on him—an' no wonder—big and pretty as he is." The root doctor moistened a handful of cotton lint with liquid from a blue glass bottle and dabbed gently at the bruising around Maggie's eye. "I be thinkin' Justice be a good match for Aurelia. Strong man. Man with a trade."

Maggie sniffed the air. "Arnica?"

"Naw . . . this here's mountain daisy." Tempie applied the tincture to the inflamed, battered skin along Maggie's jaw. "When you ain't so poorly, I can teach you some."

"Aye . . . teach me . . ." Maggie's legs felt heavy. Her mouth, parched. Without asking, Tempie leaned forward and moistened Maggie's lips with a wet cloth.

"That jimsonweed—dry you up drier than an ol' woman's cooch."

Maggie half laughed and squinted, her eyes suddenly sensitive to the minimal light coming through the open door. The screaming pain in her shoulder was dulling to a faint echo of what it had been, as if it were being muffled under layers and layers of cotton batting. Tempie tucked two pillows under Maggie's injured arm, positioning the limb to angle away from her body.

"Miz Tempie? Aurelia says you need my help." The big voice sounded skeptical.

"You c'mon in here, Justice." Tempie's small voice a sweet contrast to the deep baritone that rolled through the room when Justice spoke.

"Yes'm." The man ducked his head to clear the lintel piece and came to loom over Maggie. Muscular and imposing, the blacksmith seemed to have been forged of solid iron.

"I want you t' kneel on th' gal's left." Tempie flipped the excess portion of the blanket Maggie lay atop over her, encasing her torso in a loop of wool. "Aurelia, you set beside Justice, nearer to this gal's shoulder." The helpers jostled into their positions.

Of the few Negroes Maggie'd ever seen in her lifetime, Justice was by far the darkest, his skin the deep blue black of a moonless night. He crouched down at Maggie's side. Rolling the sleeves of his chambray shirt to expose his massive forearms, Justice flashed her a charming smile.

Maggie sighed. "He *is* preddy, Tem-pie! Big an' preddy."

Aurelia sputtered a giggle into her hand. Justice demurred, his eyes downcast.

"Why, Justice." Tempie laughed. "I believe that's the closest you'll get to blushin'."

"Tha' draught ye giv' me, Tempie . . ." Maggie waved her good hand erratically through the air. "Black haw an' weedsome-jim . . . I thing it's made me a wee bit dipsy." She turned to Justice. "D'ye ken, Justice? *D'ye ken?*" Her voice rose. "Root doctor! Yer med-cine has took. Let's have at it, aye?"

"That's fine, chile. Jest fine . . ." Tempie grew serious. "Justice, you grab an' hold that blanket tight. When I say *ready*, I'se goin' to pull on her arm one way, you keep her body in place by pullin' the other way—understand?"

"Mm-hmm, I can do that." Justice gathered the edges of the blanket in big fists and pulled it taut. Maggie smiled, snug and happy like a baby in a sling.

"Aurelia—you mind her head and left shoulder. She's apt t' draw up. You keep her down, hear?" Then Tempie fixed her grasp—right hand on Maggie's forearm, left on Maggie's upper arm.

"*Ready!*" she announced, and began to pull.

Rum, black haw, and jimsonweed notwithstanding, Maggie's whole body twitched in a massive spasm of pain, her breath caught on a scream clogged in her throat.

Tempie did not relent. Ignoring Maggie's strangled moan, she continued to pull, slow, steady, and controlled. Her thin arms strained with the effort, the spare muscles in her forearms tightened to ropes as she held firm. Justice hung on to the blanket, leaning back to provide the opposing traction Tempie required. Aurelia kept Maggie down, cooing soft into her ear, "Not too long now, sugar . . . almost there . . . almost there . . ."

After pulling the arm straight out, Tempie maneuvered it up. Dark patches of sweat stained her blouse, her brow beetled and dripped with exertion—then there it was—the gritty creak and grind of bone against bone as the ball joint seated back into its socket, where it belonged.

Maggie coughed a gasp and passed out.

◦⊱✦⊰◦

Stars began to gather in a sky not quite dark enough to mask the twin plumes of smoke rising from Guy DeMontforte's camp. The aroma of roast beef carried up on a breeze. Tom stood at the ridgetop with his stomach grumbling like a bear rousted from its winter den. Spurred by three days living on jerky and parched corn, he and Friday clambered down the steep incline, more than ready to consume an entire buffalo, hoof to horn.

The hunting camp nestled in a bald spot at the foot of a craggy limestone cliff. Two stone-circle hearths were centered on the clearing—one for cooking, the other for smoking meat and rendering tallow. In the shadow of the limestone wall, an open-faced framework draped with buffalo skins provided shelter and dry storage for supplies. Opposite the shelter, a large log stripped of its bark was propped with one end up on a boulder—the perfect angle and smooth work surface for fleshing and beaming hides.

Acknowledging his hunting partner with a nod and a desultory wave, Tom trudged back into camp empty-handed yet again.

Guy DeMontforte was busy at the far hearth, setting a green-wood rack over slow-burning coals. Shaking his head of shaggy black hair, Guy threw his arms in the air and sighed. "So it goes, *mon ami . . .*"

Dressed more like a pirate than a hunter, the Frenchman wore a ruffled red silk shirt with deerskin breeches and moccasins. Along with tomahawk and knife, he kept a fancy pearl-handled pistol tucked into the satin sash tied about his waist. Blue-black stubble ever present on his face cast a sinister shadow on handsome Gallic features. Gold rings on his fingers and dangling from one ear flashed the embers' gleam while he laid strips of buffalo meat in ordered rows across the rack. Friday darted in and snicked a piece of meat, at once gobbling it down and dodging the stone DeMontforte whipped his way. *"Sacré chien!"*

Tom slipped his gear; laying pouch, bedroll, and rifle to the side, he sank down to sit on a log situated near the cooking hearth. "I had a five-point buck in my sights this morning, but afore I could get a shot off he caught wind of me and took off— and that was the *best* part of my day." He leaned forward, elbows on knees, dropping chin onto fists. Friday circled three times and settled in a huff at Tom's feet.

"No worries, *mon frère*. Tonight we feast like kings!" The Frenchman waved a blousy-sleeved arm. "*Les boeufs sauvages.* Two fat cows crossed my path," he said with a smile missing one front tooth.

Guy paused and sniffed the air. "*Merde!*" He scampered to the hearth where Tom sat. Using his knife, he poked and rolled two scorched buffalo tongues out from the flames. With a deft hand, he peeled away the blackened skin, then skewered the tongues on sassafras sticks, impaling the twig ends into the ground so the seared tongues leaned forward, gently licked by flames.

"I'll fix a batch of dodgers." Tom pushed a skillet atop a pile of embers. In no time he combined cornmeal, bear oil, and maple sugar into a thick paste and plopped goodly size dollops of dough onto the hot pan. He watched the dodgers sizzle and snap, wondering for perhaps the hundredth time that day what Maggie might be doing. Wondering if she missed him as much as he missed her.

When Tom had hustled out of Roundabout three weeks before, cursing all women and the trouble they wrought, he never considered that he might miss Maggie. Never figured he'd wake every morning wishing for the weight of her leg thrown over him. Never figured he'd crave the smell of the nape of her neck like a Chinaman craved opium smoke.

I should have made things right with her afore takin' off.

Longing—it had fallen on him sudden, like a tree limb in a windstorm, and he was crushed under the weight of it. Tom tramped the woodlands distracted by the raw ache in his heart, unable to focus, unable to react quick enough. His despair had become a cumbersome burden, like dragging a loaded sledge through thick brambles, the tumpline cutting taut across his chest.

Good riddance, she said.

At night he tossed and turned, desolate under his blanket. He longed for her fingers clutching his shoulders, her wild moan in his ear, and the utter and complete contentment found slipping out from between her legs to fold himself around her warm, soft body.

I should not have left her like that.

The Frenchman came to squat at the fire and he gave marrowbones roasting on the coals a quarter turn. "I wish I knew, *mon ami*, what causes ze sadness in your face."

Tom shrugged. Suddenly Friday scrabbled up to his feet, barking like mad. DeMontforte pulled his pistol. Tom grabbed his rifle.

"Halloo, Tom Roberts! Halloo, ye outlandish French bastard!"

Shoulders eased, but weapons were kept at the ready until they saw Duncan Moon hobble out from the trees on his peg leg, leading two mules loaded with goods. Tom and Guy rushed over to greet the old trader with handshakes and slaps on the back.

"Saw the smoke. This close to the lick I figured it must be the two o' yiz."

They helped Duncan unload and hobble his mules and invited him to share their fire.

"I'd like t' contribute," he said, rifling through his packs.

Guy stood over him, clutching the crucifix hanging around his neck, muttering, "Brandy and tobacco . . . brandy and tobacco . . ."

Duncan tossed them each a pigtail of tobacco. From a second pack he drew forth three onion-shaped bottles and lined them up in the dirt. "Peach brandy."

Guy dropped to his knees, eyes squeezed tight, hands clasped in prayer. *"Merci beaucoup, Sainte Solange!* I swear to you—no less than three rosaries—once I am sober."

"What the hell kind of Frenchy-papist hoodoo is this?" Duncan planted his hands on hips. "I'm the one what fixed you in brandy and smoke. Who's this sansolange feller?"

"Sainte Solange—ze patron saint against ze drought. She answered my prayer." Guy hopped to his feet and gleefully gathered the bottles as if he were plucking posies in a garden.

Tom flipped crispy dodgers onto a piece of birch bark. Guy passed each man a tin plate and a bottle. The trio sat on a log and pulled the bones from the fire. They split them open with tomahawks and used the corn dodgers to scoop up steamy, rich marrow. They shaved tender slices from the roasting tongues with hunting knives and washed it all down with glugs of peach brandy. Guy was the first to finish. Producing a clay stem pipe, he slid down to sit on the ground, his back against the log.

Tom tossed Friday the remains of his meal and settled next to his partner in a well-fed stupor. "To the providers of the feast." He hoisted his bottle in toast.

"Here, here!" Duncan maintained his seat on the log and tapped his bottle to Tom's. The trader lit his pipe with a brand from the fire.

Guy puffed on his pipe. "*Ahhh . . . c'est une bonne vie, mes amis . . .*"

"So, Duncan," Tom said, loosening his belt a notch. "Tell me, how does Maggie fare?"

Before Duncan could answer, DeMontforte sat up and smacked himself on the forehead. "*Bien sûr*—of course, only women can cause such crazy in ze head."

Tom groaned. "I am not crazy in the head."

"*Mais oui*, you are crazy." Guy twisted around to address Duncan. "He cannot hunt. He cannot sleep. He is angry. He is sad." The Frenchman ticked off symptoms and jabbed Tom with his elbow. "He is in love!"

Duncan puffed out a perfect smoke ring. "Yep. He was sure lovestruck back at Roundabout—paid thirty silver dollars for Maggie's lunch basket at the gather-all. Can you imagine?"

Tom cursed under his breath and took a deep swig from his bottle.

Duncan lifted his bottle. "'Tis woman makes us love, 'tis love. that makes us sad. 'Tis sadness makes us drink, and drinking makes us mad!"

"*Bravo!*" Guy tapped his pipe to clink against his tin plate. "*Écoutez*, Tommy—you should have told me about zis woman. I am expert in love, and I—"

Tom cut the Frenchman short. "I'll warn ye right now, friend, you'd do well to mind your own snake. My love life stays none of your concern."

Guy tsked and threw his arm around Tom's shoulder. "Since you are like a brother to me, I will share with you ze wisdom of *mon père* . . ." The Frenchman paused, hand darting in the sign of the cross. He then raised his voice in oratory.

"Women, *mon ami*, are like ze perfect snowflakes falling from ze sky." Guy's fingers fluttered through the air. "Each one, unique. Each one, beautiful. Why limit yourself to one when there are so many? They all will melt when they land on your face . . ."

Duncan sprayed a mouthful of brandy into the fire, punctuating Guy's philosophy with a *whoosh* of flames and a raucous guffaw. He shook a finger at DeMontforte. "Sure, you and your Frenchy-parlay-voo will take up with anyone's dog that'll hunt with ye, but Tom here pines after a good woman, and he's gone out o' heart 'cause he knows he's most likely left his best fortune behind."

Tom shrugged Guy off, growling, "Blast your eyes, both of you—I wish t' fuck yid both leave it alone."

They sat quiet, but for the crackling of the fire and the crickets chirping in the trees, until Duncan braved the silence. "Bert Hawkins showed the day after you left. Came in with four big bales of buckskin."

Tom grunted. "Good for Bert. Bess must be happy."

"Yep. Good time t' find yourself with a pocket full o' silver what with that English feller running everyone off'n their claims."

Tom looked up. "You mean Portland?"

"Yep. Him and his gang of toughs beat Joe Mulberry to a pulp. I packed my goods and hit the trail to avoid any mischief done to me. Ada and Alistair went to their daughter in Richmond. The two Willies left with the Wheelers, up to Pennsylvania."

Tom couldn't help himself. "What about Maggie?"

"Last I saw, she headed back with Seth. He was in an awful swither, poor fella, everything tumbling onto his shoulders just days after buryin' Naomi."

"Naomi's *dead*?" Tom sat upright. "How?"

"Childbed fever, poor thing." Duncan shook his head. "Trouble rides a fast horse, it surely does."

Tom stoppered his bottle and set it in Guy's lap. "I have to go . . ." He jumped to his feet and began gathering his gear.

"Go?" Guy scrambled to stand. "Go where?"

"To Maggie. To Seth—I have to go."

"*Mon ami.*" Guy grabbed Tom by the forearm. "Wait for daylight . . ."

"Moon's on the rise, brother, and I can get a few miles under me yet tonight." Tom jerked free and disappeared inside the shelter.

"It's been more'n a week since I last saw Seth," Duncan shouted after Tom. "Said he was goin' to head out soon as he gathered provender. They're most likely on the road by now . . ."

Tom emerged with arms full. "Don't fret—I'll find 'em." He stuffed a sack of jerky into his shirtfront, extra powder and shot into his pouch. "You keep Friday for me," he said, slapping the speechless Frenchman on the shoulder. Tom slipped his arm through the rope that kept his bedroll tied, grabbed his pouch, shouldered his rifle, and turned to shake Duncan by the hand. "You understand, don't you, Duncan? My best fortune, you said."

He bid farewell to firelight and friends and climbed the steep path to the top of the ridge. Once there, he stopped to get a fix on the North Star and turned eastward.

The light cast by the star-strewn sky filtered through the leaves.

Tom coursed his trail through the dark, wondering, for perhaps the hundredth time that night, what Maggie might be doing. Wondering if she missed him as much as he missed her . . .

⎝€✦϶⎠

. . . *Twenty-two and twenty-three.*

Twenty-three spokes in the spider's orbed web. Maggie lay on her pallet with her right arm trussed in a soft flannel sling. She wasted the day doing naught but watch her spider spin the endless filament, connecting the spokes of her web with an ever-widening spiral of silk.

At daybreak, Justice had brought Achilles to the cabin. The smith's gangly apprentice dripped blood from a two-inch gash in his shin, the result of falling onto a just-sharpened hoe blade. Saying, "Sorry, Miz Spider," Tempie stepped up onto her stool and tore down the vast web and used it to pack Achilles' wound.

Nothing helped to stanch a bloody wound faster than spiderweb. Maggie always tried to keep a packet of the sticky stuff ready in her basket. Wounds dressed with web seldom festered and always seemed to heal quickly. Even Tom knew to gather spiderweb to pack wee Mary's scalp wound.

"Oh, Tom . . ." She felt as if someone had reached into her chest with both hands to wring her heart dry. Maggie swiped at the tears sprung to her eyes, once again caught off guard by the intensity of her heartache. These days, Tom never trailed too far from her thoughts. "Daft is what I am," she whispered to her spider. Beaten and raped by one man, and all she could do was yearn for another.

"Plain daft." She chided herself for her foolishness, but still could not keep her mind from wandering back to Tom. The pleasant memories of the time they spent together crowded out the awful reality of her brutal encounter with Cavendish. Turning her thoughts to Tom was the only thing that kept her from rending her garments and tearing at her hair. This worried Maggie, but Tempie said it made perfect sense.

"They ain't no wonder in you wishin' for th' man you love in trouble times. No wonder in that at all."

Maggie turned onto her left side, her right hand extended out from the sling, and she rested it on her belly. She closed her eyes, splayed her fingers wide, and pressed them into her soft flesh, calling up the recollection of lying curled in Tom's strong arms, his big hand pulling her close . . .

The dissonant tumbled rhythm of a hammer bouncing the inside of an iron triangle rang out, calling the slaves to their dinner. On this signal, Maggie roused from her pallet on the floor, a guilty glance cast at the basket of beans Tempie had asked her to shell, still sitting there untouched in their leathery pods.

She moved slow from one corner of the small cabin to the other, dipped a battered kettle into the water barrel, and shuffled to the fireplace to put the pot on the boil for their tea. Not a single ember glowed bright in the pile of ashes on the limestone hearth. Her eyes shifted from the cold ashes to the firewood stacked exactly as Castor and Pollux had left it early that morning.

"Feich!" She'd neglected to tend the fire properly—again. Maggie set the pot down and sank onto Tempie's three-legged stool, clenching the wool of her skirt in her sweaty fist. The notion of stepping out into the fortyard to fetch a bucket of hot coals from Tempie's cookhearth served to shrivel her belly into a tight prune. With eyes darting, she followed the ashes on the hearthstone, swirling with the ebb and tide of the evening breeze blowing down the chimney. It had been four days since Aurelia brought her into the cabin to see to her injuries, and Maggie had yet to step out over the threshold.

"Supper time." Aurelia appeared in the open doorway, her arms akimbo. "Why don't you c'mon on out today and git yo'self somethin' t' eat?"

Maggie looked up. "I'm not verra hungry."

"C'mon, sugar, a body gots to eat." Aurelia came to put her arm around Maggie's shoulders. Her voice dropped to an encouraging whisper. "You be needin' yo' strength if you's fixin' t' run off to your ol' massa, like you said you was."

Unbidden tears fell one by one, absorbed into the bunched fabric in Maggie's lap. "I canna go out *there*. *He* might be out there."

Aurelia rubbed soothing circles between Maggie's shoulder blades. "'S awright girl, no matter. I'll brang somethin' by for you." With that, she sailed out the door, her starched apron snapping on the breeze.

Hard times and shared burdens make for true fast friends. Maggie understood this now more than ever. She counted herself specially blessed for having these caring strangers take her in hand at her hour of dire need, just as Alan and Hannah Cameron had so long ago. Aurelia and Tempie were both so good to her. They listened to her rambling worries, their knowing heads nodding, pointing no fingers, placing no blame or shame.

When Maggie first woke from her jimsonweed-induced sleep, she found Aurelia had taken her clothes and scrubbed and salted away every speck of mud, blood, and rape. The laundress handed back a stack of fresh-pressed garments, unpleasant reminders tossed away with the wash water.

And though Tempie was as short and black as Hannah had been tall and white, Maggie thought them much alike. Tempie was gifted with the same rare wisdom and an intuitive empathy that Hannah had—the ability to know exactly what to say and what to do to make a body feel better.

The day before, Tempie managed to have the master's tin tub installed in their cabin. The slave women toted in buckets and buckets of hot water. Aurelia gave the lend of a stiff boar-bristle brush and her last sliver of lavender soap. Maggie benefited from the long soak in steamy water enriched with a sprinkling of aromatic herbs from Tempie's satchel and she scoured away every bit of Cavendish detritus—real or imagined—that might be clinging to her skin.

Maggie stood and wandered to the doorway. She looked out

onto the fortyard. Amber light from the setting sun was shining through the row of gun ports in the stockade wall.

Gloamin' time. Her favorite time. The time when the sky changed with every blink of the eye—shades of gold and pink blending into purple—when the stars began to show their faces, one by one. She scanned the fortyard.

The line of fieldhands dressed in their loose hempen shirts and trousers moved forward step-by-step to where Tempie doled out the evening fare. Each man took his portion of beans, salt pork, and cornbread, then retreated to find a tree stump where he could rest from the day's toil and eat his dinner in peace.

The door to the blockhouse hung open, framing a yellow rectangle of candle glow, and Maggie could see red-jacketed Castor and Pollux bustling within. The viscount was nowhere in sight.

Maggie hadn't laid eyes on the man since she passed through that same door the day he raped her, and if her luck held, Seth would send word soon and she would never have to see Cavendish again. She leaned against the door frame, chewing her thumb where flesh met nail. *But how will Seth send word?*

Armed guards stood sentry atop the blockhouse, and the stockade gates were bolted shut every evening as a matter of course. To further discourage slaves from escaping into the wilderness, horsemen patrolled outside the gates, and Connor oversaw the prominent installation of a whipping post, centered in the fortyard.

Castor had come to their cabin the day before, soon after nightfall. "Massa sends for Aurelia," he said, with eyes downcast.

Aurelia set her mending aside. In an instant her beautiful face had turned grim, her lovely green eyes, hard as glass. Without a word, she followed the bobbing feather on Castor's turban out the door. Tempie acted as though nothing untoward had occurred, and Maggie sat dumbstruck by her new friend's meek obedience.

It wasn't long before Aurelia came skipping back into the room. She lifted her skirts to show her ankles and danced a jig, singsonging, "Massa cain't git his pecker up. Massa cain't git his pecker up."

Maggie flashed a smile, recalling Aurelia's happy dance. *If only he were so afflicted for the rest of his days.* She never wished so hard for anything in her life. The mere thought of having to answer a similar call set her heart to pounding a wild tattoo in her chest, and she stepped back into the cloister of the cabin to catch her breath, startling the spider to scurry on silken threads and hide in the smidgen space between shingle and rafter.

If I dinna hear from Seth in ten days' time, I must run on my own.

"Run!" Maggie snorted aloud. She couldn't even muster the courage to step out the cabin door. She settled back on her stool. *I have to contrive a way . . .*

Tempie came bustling into the cabin. She set a laden trencher in Maggie's lap and thrust a spoon into her good hand. "I made this hoppin' john special for you, chile, and I 'spect you t' finish every bit of it." She glanced at the cold hearth and sighed. "I'll fetch some coals—you eat up!"

Awkwardly wielding the spoon with her left hand, Maggie forced herself to eat a few mouthfuls before falling into the habit of separating the beans from the grains of rice on her plate. Tempie soon returned with the coals to mend the fire. She frowned, seeing Maggie nudging the black-eyed peas into a precise pile in the center of her trencher. Tempie set the bucket down, took the whisk broom from its hook, and swept the ashes into the corner of the fireplace.

Maggie blurted, "I tell ye true, Tempie, if that monster calls for me . . . I swear, I will *kill* him! I will kill th' man afore he ever lays hands on me again—it'll be the end of him, tha's certain!"

"Keep on with that kind of foolish talk and more'n likely it'll be the end o' *you*." Tempie spilled the coals onto the hearth. "You ain't the first woman ever ill-used by a man, and you sho' won't be th' last."

Maggie set her plate aside. "But how can Aurelia just go to him, Tempie?"

"Aurelia know she'd be the first strapped to that new whippin' post if she refuse Massa's call." Tempie sat on the edge of the hearthstone and delicately arranged sticks of fat pine kindling over the glowing embers. "Pretty slave girl like Aurelia learnt long ago how to bend so's she don't break." The tiny woman stood and used her skirt to fan the coals into flames. "And that's what you need to learn. In this you ought take heart—that what don't break you, serves t' make you strong."

"*Maggie!*" Aurelia popped her head in the doorway. "Castor and Pollux say Marse Cavendish passed out—dead drunk! Won't you come on out now? It's a fine soft evenin'—Justice is comin' t' call, and Achilles is bringing his *banjar*!"

"C'mon, girl." Tempie offered a hand. "Fresh air will do you good—blow the cobwebs from your head." Maggie took Tempie's tiny hand and followed her out the door.

Although this was Maggie's first foray into the fortyard after nightfall, she understood the station's new population maintained a strict hierarchy. The white men—Connor, Moffat, Figg, and the like—occupied the cookhearth in the evenings, sitting around the fire passing a bottle from one to another, as men will.

Servants and skilled slaves, like the smith, cook, and laundress, gathered in front of Tempie's cabin to sing songs and tell stories. Field slaves were wont to seek their beds after a hard day's toil, but this night a dozen or so huddled around a small fire at the farthest end of the fortyard, roasting ears of green corn on the coals.

Maggie sat with Tempie on a wide stump not too far from the cabin door. Aurelia and Justice sat together on a tree stump opposite. Castor and Pollux, off duty and dressed comfortably in slave-standard loose shirts and trousers, sat together on a length of log arranged to form a rough triangle with the tree stumps. As promised, Achilles joined them, his *banjar* in hand. To Maggie's surprise, Simon Peavey, dressed in a long belted shirt and breeches, came up swinging a lantern. "Room for another?" he asked.

Maggie scooted to her right and patted the space. Simon set the lantern at her feet and sat down. His big green eyes were filled with concern. "How you been?"

Maggie glanced at her arm in its sling. "Tempie has me on the mend."

Achilles propped one foot on the log and began tuning his instrument.

"So that's the famous *banjar*," Maggie said. "Like a mandolin of sorts, na?"

"Achilles made that *banjar* himself," Justice boasted, proud of his talented apprentice.

"See them scars on th' boy's cheeks?" Tempie pointed out the vertical lines embossed beneath Achilles' eyes. "Those be his tribe marks. He the only one of us true Africa-born."

Justice nodded. "The boy didn't speak much English when my ol' massa brought him to me, back in Williamsburg. One day I found him tackin' a coonskin over a calabash gourd he'd cut in two and hollowed out." The smith leaned back on his muscular arms. "At first I figured he was makin' a small drum and I tried to warn him—Marse James didn't allow us no drums. The boy paid me no mind. He fit the gourd with that wooden neck and strung it with four catgut strings. I ain't ever seen such a thing, but it shore does make pretty music."

Instrument in tune, Achilles began plucking a pleasant melody. Aurelia hummed along in a rich contralto. Justice joined in, improvising a harmony with his deep baritone.

"I worried for you, Maggie. I'm real happy t' see you about." Simon reached into his pouch, pulled out a pair of moccasins, and set them on her lap. "I made these special for you."

"Och, but aren't they lovely things!" Maggie admired the

moccasins, showing the shoes first to Tempie then Aurelia. Much more elaborate than the utilitarian pair Seth had made for her on the trail, the elkskin slippers Simon had fashioned were double-soled, lined with rabbit fur, and decorated with fringe around the ankles and a pattern of colorful beads on the toes.

"I had to guess at the size," Simon said. "Try 'em—see how they fit."

Maggie slipped the mocassins on, squishing her toes in the soft fur. "They're perfect. Thank you." She squeezed him with her good arm around his shoulders and planted a peck on his forehead. He seemed very pleased.

"I'll sing a tune," Aurelia proposed, "and Achilles, you try an' follow along." Achilles nodded, and Aurelia began to sing a slow ballad.

> *"The blackest crow that ever flew will surely turn to white,*
> *If ever I prove false to you, bright day will turn to night.*
> *Bright day will turn to night my love, the elements will mourn,*
> *If ever I prove false to you, the seas will rage and burn.*
> *Oh, don't you see that lonesome dove, he flies from pine to pine.*
> *He's mourning for his own true love just like I mourn for mine.*
> *Just like I mourn for mine, my love, believe me when I say,*
> *You are the only one I'll love until my dying day."*

Maggie's throat ached, and she fought to choke back pesky tears as she listened to Aurelia sing the haunting melody accompanied by the melancholy strumming of the *banjar*.

> *"I wish my heart were made of glass, wherein you might behold,*
> *That there your name is written, dear, in letters made of gold.*
> *In letters made of gold my dear, believe me when I say,*
> *You are the only one for me, until my dying day."*

"That was beautiful." Maggie swiped her eyes on the back of her hand. "Where d'ye ever learn such a song?"

"The granny woman at my ol' place, she taught it to me." Aurelia snuggled close to Justice and he didn't appear to mind. "'Lover's Lament,' she called it."

"Sad old songs. I don't like 'em." Simon picked up a stone and tossed it hard against the cabin wall.

"That song *was* too sad," Castor complained, and Pollux added, "It made Maggie cry."

"I'm not crying. I'm all right—g'won an' sing another."

"Naw . . ." Castor protested. "How 'bout you tell us a tale instead, Auntie?"

"A tale 'bout Brother Rabbit," Pollux specified. *"Please!"*

Evenings past, Maggie had lain on her pallet inside the cabin, listening to the many adventures Tempie spun to entertain them all. The root doctor called upon an endless store of tales based on a variety of animal characters like Brother Rabbit and Brother Fox.

Tempie acquiesced to the beseeching twins, closed her eyes, thought for a moment, then began her tale as she always did. "Once upon a time, was a very good time . . ."

Castor and Pollux scooted closer to sit at Tempie's feet, and she continued: "Yep, once upon a time was a very good time, and Brer Rabbit had a nice fat trout hooked on his line."

"Huzzah!" Castor exclaimed, and Pollux added, "Brer Rabbit is my favorite fo' sho'."

Tempie leaned back in her seat. "Now mind, our friend Brer Rabbit was so pleased with the fine fish he'd just landed, he didn't notice ol' Brer Wolf hidin' in the bresh."

"Uh-oh," Pollux worried.

"Brer Wolf, he don't waste no time. In nary a blink of the eye he cotched Brer Rabbit up by the collar. 'I'se got you now,' says Brer Wolf, his teeth all shiny white an' sharp."

Tempie cast a spell over her audience, changing the timbre of her voice from low and gruff when speaking for the wolf to spry and youthful when speaking for the rabbit.

"Brer Rabbit, he wriggled and squirmed and kicked up a fuss with his big ol' feet, but Brer Wolf hung tight and carried his prey off. Brer Rabbit began to blubberin', 'Where you takin' me?'

"'Why, I'se takin' you to my cabin up yonder.'

"'What for?'

"'Cuz that's where I keeps my stew pot,' says Brer Wolf, lickin' his chops. 'I ain't et in two days and I am sore, sore hungry.'"

"Ooooo-ooooh," Aurelia piped in. "Brer Rabbit done fo' sure . . ."

"Hush, Aurelia," Justice warned. "Let Aunt Tempie finish her tale."

"Don't you worry, Justice," Castor asserted. "Brer Rabbit is th' cleverest."

"Mm-hmm," Pollux added. "He'll get away from that ol' wolf."

Tempie went on. "Now, Brer Rabbit thought to hisself as he dangled there in Brer Wolf's grip, 'I must gather my wits and contrive a way to stay out ol' Brer Wolf's stew pot.'"

Maggie leaned forward, as caught up in the tale as the rest of them. "Th' rabbit has no chance. Th' wolf is bigger and stronger . . ."

"Shhhh!"

"The first thing Brer Rabbit thought to do was quit his strugglin'. Instead o' strugglin', he set his clever mind to *thinkin'*." Tempie tapped her index finger to her temple. "Just then, Brer Rabbit spied a buckthorn bush filled with berries ripe for the pickin' and that's when he hatched himself a scheme."

"A buckthorn bush," Simon snorted. "That's trouble."

"Brer Rabbit said to Brer Wolf, 'Why, would you look at those purty berries? So ripe an' juicy—mmmmMMMM—don't everyone know nothin' goes better with rabbit stew than a great big bowl of juicy, delicious buckthorn berries.'"

"Buckthorn berries!" Castor and Pollux fell into a fit of giggles.

"What?" Maggie whispered to Simon. "What's wrong with buckthorn berries?"

Tempie ignored the interruptions. "Now, most folk know, eatin' buckthorn berries will have you squitterin' from your hind end with a bad case of the trots in no time. But Brer Wolf is a natural-born meat-eater, dim to the ways of things that grow. Those berries tempted him, hangin' on that bush, a-gleamin' red like jewels in the sunshine. He held on to Brer Rabbit's long floppy ears and set him to pickin'." Tempie began picking imaginary berries from an imaginary bush.

"As fast as Brer Rabbit picked those berries, greedy ol' Brer Wolf ate 'em. He took to those berries like a mule to millet. Soon there warn't a single berry left on that bush. With Brer Rabbit by the ears, Brer Wolf set back onto the path to his cabin. They walked quite a ways, and Brer Rabbit got to worryin' that maybe all his schemin' went for naught, when he heard a deep rumblin', grumblin' sound. 'Sounds like they's a storm a-brewin',' Brer Rabbit said, 'But they ain't a cloud in the sky.'"

"Brer Rabbit." Justice laughed, slapping his knee. "He *is* a caution!"

"Then a mighty queer look come over Brer Wolf. He let loose Brer Rabbit and grabbed himself 'round the belly. 'Oooohhh, lawsy . . .' says he, fiddling with the buttons on his britches.

"Brer Rabbit got to snickering with delight, 'Is you feelin' poorly, Brer Wolf?'

"And Brer Wolf took off like a blue streak, into the bresh. And Brer Rabbit laughed and laughed, then he lit out, hippity-hoppity, back to his briar patch."

Everyone clapped, happy Brer Rabbit had succeeded. Using his wits and cunning, he beat Brer Wolf once again.

"That was a good trick he played," Simon said. "Getting the wolf to eat those berries."

Tempie nodded. "Brer Rabbit, he never ever gives up." With

that, she sent the twins to their beds. Achilles got back to pluck-ing his *banjar* and the adults sat quiet for a moment, savoring a tale well told.

"Tha's the way . . ." Maggie murmured, sitting upright. "We can do it, too." She turned to Aurelia. "*We* can stay out o' th' wolf's pot as well."

"What are you talkin' 'bout, Maggie?" Aurelia leaned back against Justice. "There ain't no wolves 'round here."

"I mean him." Maggie waved her hand toward the block-house. "Cavendish. We can do like Brer Rabbit did to th' wolf— fix him so he doesna want either of us in his bed."

"Feed Marse Cavendish buckthorn berries?" Aurelia gig-gled.

"Aye. Or rub his smallclothes with stinging nettle leaves." Maggie laughed. "Between us cookin' his food and tendin' to his linen, we can keep him awful busy—him in a quandary as to whether he should scratch, spew, shite, or fart!"

"And in such a predicament, havin' his puny cock polished will be the last thing on his mind!" Aurelia clapped her hands with glee.

Justice's whisper was harsh. "Hush this foolishness, Aurelia. Pay no mind to this white woman and her crazy talk."

"Ye wouldna think it crazy, Justice," Maggie spat back, "if ye had to answer his call—bend t' tha' devil's will as we must."

"I been bending to the will of men like him my life long, and I've stripes on my back to show when I didn't."

"I'd rather be whipped than go t' his bed willing," Maggie hissed.

"Hmmph. That what you two are talkin' 'bout don't lead t' the whippin' post," Justice countered. "Slaves caught poisoning their master be burned alive at the stake."

"We ain't fixin' to poison Massa so's he die," Aurelia whis-pered. "We'll just make him a little uncomfortable, is all. Just so he keep to himself long enough for Maggie t' heal up an' run off to her ol' massa."

Simon added, "It'd serve us all to have that bastard laid low for a few days. He's been drivin' everybody hard."

Justice turned to Tempie, his voice dropping to an exasperated rumbling rasp. "You may be no bigger than a skeeter wing, Miz Tempie, but you are the mother of this mischief. Make these fools come to they senses. This kind o' talk is bound to get somebody killed, or worse."

"Justice is right—this kind o' talk is best left for the light o' day." Tempie stood, linked her fingers behind her head, and stretched catlike. "Th' day has eyes, but the night has ears. Everyone ought just button up now and find their bed."

21

A Deadly Web

It was very dark when Maggie startled awake. Barely able to see her hand before her face, she rubbed the sleep from her eyes, pressed up to a stand, and tiptoed around two blanketed gray mounds lying on their darker gray pallets. Aurelia rustled in her bed and moaned, "It daybreak already?"

Maggie whispered, "Shhha . . . back t' yer dreams, lass . . . I'm just off t' pee."

Fingers skimming over the rough timber wall, she felt her way to the corner where they kept the night bucket. Maggie fumbled gathering her shift and positioning the bucket—urinating being one among many things made more difficult with her arm en-slinged.

At last squatting over the bucket, she released her water to shush into the pisspot. Maggie scrinched her nose at the strong smell, like that of stewed celery root. Regretting having added to the funk of their close quarters, she picked up the bucket with her good left hand and headed out to discard its noxious content. The door latch pushed up with a loud thunk. Wincing at the noise, Maggie eased the door open.

The bucket's bale handle cut into the fleshy mounds on her

fingers. She padded on bare feet past the long row of cabins, down to the far end, where several large collecting barrels sat at the base of the stockade wall. Aurelia used the stale urine as a detergent to launder woolens. Tempie used it to set bright dyes in her fabric. The hunters used it as well when tanning hides.

Maggie spilled her bucket into the barrel. The fortyard was ghostly still—no cricket's chirp or owl's eerie trill interrupted the silence—that brief pure moment in time when it seemed all living things waited with bated breath for daylight to arrive.

The damp hem of her shift tickled her ankles as she ambled back to her cabin. Against the blueing eastern sky, Maggie could make out the lone silhouette of a sentryman posted atop the blockhouse. The blinking orange glow as he tugged on his pipe almost illuminated his face. She quickened her pace.

Back inside, she found Tempie awake and fully dressed, feeding wood to the fire she'd coaxed from the banked coals. Still in her thin shift, Aurelia hopped from one foot to the other.

"Where you been with that pisspot?" She snatched the bucket from Maggie and scurried into the dark corner.

Maggie sat on the stool and slipped her arm out of the sling. With elbow bent, she tested her injured shoulder joint, raising her arm up and down like a bird flapping one wing. Tempie turned from tending the fire. The ruffled mobcap she wore glowed like a golden halo in the firelight as she laid hands on Maggie's shoulder. "Swelling's gone down. How's it feel?"

"A bit tender, but I can do without the sling, I think."

"Just mind you don't overdo—heavy liftin' and suchlike." Tempie filled the kettle at the water barrel by the door and hung it from the lugpole over the fire. "Get dressed. I'll fix tea and we can have us a talk." She tossed several chunks of red sassafras root into the kettle.

Maggie retrieved her clothes, stepping into her skirt and lacing up her bodice lickety-split. She settled with legs folded in front of the fire and tied a kerchief around her head to hide sleep-mussed braids.

"Aurelia honey," Tempie called, her voice almost childlike. "Come an' have yo' tea afore the overseer rings the call."

Aurelia stumbled into the light cast by the fire, properly dressed save for the massive explosion of curls haloing her head. "I hate my hair!" she moaned.

"Sit here." Maggie patted the floor beside her. "I can fix it." Maggie smoothed and tugged Aurelia's wild locks into a thick, fuzzy braid trailing down her neck.

Sassafras tea brewing in the kettle filled the cabin with its clean, spicy scent. Tempie poured them each a noggin of hot tea sweetened with dogwood honey and sat on her stool with cup in lap, steam-dampened skin glistening in the firelight.

Aurelia ventured to begin. "Justice was sho' agitated last night . . ."

"Justice ain't nobody's fool. When contemplatin' dangerous doin's, wise folk plan it out careful, an' that's what we's about t' do. Agreed?" Both of the young women nodded, and Tempie continued: "The twins tol' me Marse Cavendish drank himself beyond useless—pecker-wavin' drunk he was last night. He is bound t' be sick as a dog when he wake today—"

Maggie interrupted, deep ridges furrowed in her brow. "Was Justice tellin' true? That what he said about slaves poisoning their masters an' burnin' at the stake?"

"What? You think you is th' onliest slave ever wished her massa ill?" Tempie shrugged. "Those burned were stupid enough to get caught. But I've lived this long, and I ain't been caught yet." She winked. "Now, when Marse Cavendish wakes poorly and calls for me today—"

Maggie interrupted once again. "Are ye certain he'll call?"

"Oh, Massa always call for Tempie the day after he dead drunk," Aurelia affirmed.

Tempie continued, "When I go to him—"

"No, Tempie." Maggie placed a hand on the woman's knee. "When th' devil calls, I will be the one who goes to him. Seeing as how I'm th' one who benefits, it is only fitting and fair that I shoulder the risk. I willna have ye put in any danger on my account. If we're caught out, 'twill be me who's burned at the stake."

Tempie sat quiet for a moment. She slipped her hand over Maggie's and grasped it tight. "All right, chile. When Marse Cavendish call for me, I'll send you in my stead."

"They won't burn you." Aurelia wound an arm around Maggie's shoulders. "They'll most likely only hang you—you bein' white an' all."

"Aye . . . well . . ." Maggie smiled. "I suppose that's a comfort of sorts."

"We haven't much time." Tempie demanded their full attention. "When Marse Cavendish calls for aid, you'll go to him . . ."

"He might send me away. I did draw a knife to him . . ."

Tempie shook her head. "Naw . . . white man desperate enough t' call for the nigger doctor don't rightly care who doses him. He just want relief. After rapin' you, he figures you is tame. If'n he seem suspicious, set him at ease by actin' contrite, all meek and mild."

"Aye, then I'll dose him." Maggie relished the thought. "I'll put a purge through him that will leave him green-faced and squirtin' fire from a red-hot arsehole for days on end."

Aurelia burst out laughing.

Irritated, Tempie stood and stirred the fire with the poker. Sending a shower of sparks up the chimney, she tossed the poker in a clatter, turned to stand before them with hands on hips. "You are either a fool, Maggie Duncan, or you is lookin' t' swing from the gibbet. Set aside yo' pride. Set aside yo' vengeful thoughts. You got to use yo' wits." She drilled her sharp fingertip into Maggie's temple. "When you answer Massa's call, you *will* give him sweet relief. Willow bark tea for the ache in his head. Slippery-elm porridge to soothe his stomach. Cool compresses laid over his eyes, an' th' like."

Tempie sat back on her stool and smoothed her skirt, smiling a wee, wicked smile. "An' just when he gets to feeling better, you give him somethin' to bring him low—but not too low—and it all begins again, the cossetin' with remedies and so forth."

"Yer brilliant." Maggie concurred with the elegant cunning of Tempie's clearly superior plan. Though satisfying to her soul, she would certainly be suspect if Cavendish were felled by a violent bout of diarrhea under her watch. "I will heed t' yer wisdom."

Tempie sipped her tea. "As much as it will gall you, chile, today you spend the day helpin' that man to feel good. Gain his trust."

A hammer beating iron rang out, calling the slaves to work. Tempie gulped her tea, and tied a red-checked apron over her green skirt. "We'll talk more later. When the two of you finish tidying here, come out an' lend me a hand gettin' breakfast out." She propped the door wide open with the stone kept for that purpose and headed for the cookhearth.

The sun ball peeked over the spiked ends of the stockade wall and dusty daylight streamed through the open doorway, brightening the room. While Maggie helped Aurelia store the bedding, she noticed Miz Spider had worked hard through the night to complete her task.

The new web stretched over the corner where the canted rafters met the wall—beautiful, taut, and deadly. Maggie watched a bluebottle fly buzz in with the daylight and bumble right into the sticky trap. The fly's pitiful struggle to free himself vibrated along the fine strands, and Miz Spider danced to her hapless victim over silken threads, ready to feed.

⚜

I will do this thing, Maggie resolved as she crossed the fortyard. The crockery arranged on the tray she carried rattled in rhythm to her step, keeping pace with her heart thrumming in her chest.

She came to a halt before the blockhouse door and her knee joints went to pudding. Maggie filled her lungs and released the breath slowly through puckered lips. The laden tray began to slip in her grip. She shouldered the door to creak open on its leather hinges.

The windowless room reeked of vomit and urine. Castor and Pollux sat cross-legged on the rug in the center of the room with heads bent, intent over a game of jackstraws, the silly feathers on their red turbans touching. They looked up as Maggie set her tray down onto the writing table near the door.

"Massa's asleep now," the twins whispered.

She forced her gaze to the four-posted bed in the far corner. Cavendish lay atop the coverlet, propped on a wedge of large pillows, one arm hugging an empty chamber pot—features drawn, eyes closed shut—a funny black velvet cap on his head. His complexion was as ghostly and wan as the sun-bleached linen pillow-slips he slept upon. The violet-gray half-moons beneath his eyes complemented the purple silk dressing gown he wore.

The viscount's eyes fluttered open, blinking and squinting at the bright light streaming into the room. He questioned in a voice dry and raspy, "Is that you, Tempie?"

The sound of him, combined with the malodor of rum-laced puke, caused Maggie to turn and gag back a stream of sick that'd rushed up her throat. She took a moment to tuck stray wisps of hair beneath her kerchief, pinch her cheeks, and knit her fingers beneath her breasts as if in prayer, before stepping forward to face him.

Cavendish shaded his eyes with his hand. His brow furrowed, then rose in surprise as he recognized her.

"Aid was sent for, m'lord." Her voice trembled slightly. "They say yer ill."

A smile played across his pale visage and the hand over his eyes slipped weakly to his side. "Not ill, per se." He curled his finger and beckoned her closer. "A case of *nimus bibendo appo-tus* at most."

"Sorry, m'lord." Maggie bobbed a curtsy. "I dinna ken the French tongue."

Her apology drew a laugh, followed by a wince and a sigh. "I but suffer once again from an overdose of ardent spirits." Cavendish attempted to raise his head from the pillows, only to drop back and pinch the bridge of his nose. "Oh, misery . . ." he groaned. "The brains pulse."

"I've brought remedy for such."

"Then be quick and apply it." Cavendish threw an arm over his face. "It stinks confoundedly in here!"

"He nastied the bed," Castor whispered, and Pollux pointed. Maggie followed the finger to a mound of soiled bed linen shoved beneath the writing table. She touched a toe to the bundle. "Lads, get this mess to Aurelia." The twins hopped to their feet and asked Cavendish for leave. He dismissed them with a feeble wave of his hand.

Maggie returned to her tray. She poured hot water over the powdered willow bark she'd spooned into a big clay mug, added a pinch of belladonna, a splash of rum, and a good penny's worth of honey. Stirring the hot drink with a shard of cinnamon bark, she carried the toddy to bedside.

Cavendish pushed himself to sit upright, heavy dark brows knit and lax spine suddenly rigid. He took the steaming cup in both hands and sniffed. "This concoction differs from Tempie's brew."

Maggie met his suspect squint with a level gaze. "'Tis mine own receipt, m'lord—an auld Scots remedy."

"Scots, eh?" Cavendish sniffed the brew again. "One might presume skulduggery after our last encounter. List your ingredients."

"Boilt water. Willow bark powder for th' ache in yer head." She skipped over the sleep-inducing belladonna powder. "Honey—t' cut th' bitterness." The burr in her accent intensified. "An' a wee bit o' the hair o' the dog that bit ye."

An eyebrow rose. The viscount took a small sip. "Rum?"

"For lack of good whiskey—aye."

"To the Scots!" Cavendish raised the cup in toast and drank freely. His features instantly relaxed as he leaned back in bed. Maggie began to fuss with straightening the bedclothes.

"Keep a distance," the viscount ordered curtly, and she stepped back. "My suspicious nature is not entirely at ease in the company of women prone to wielding daggers."

Cavendish proved himself no fool with this remark, and Maggie determined she must abandon her meek and mild demeanor for a more honest approach—an approach a man like Cavendish might be willing to accept.

"I willna feign a liking for ye, m'lord," Maggie said, "but I've come t' ken such is my loathsome lot in life—to serve ye. Should I risk my neck to twist from a hempen necklet in order to do ye some harm? Na . . ." She shook her head. "On that account, ye need no help from me." She strode over to the table and came back carrying a plate of toasted cornbread.

"Take that rubbish away." Cavendish turned his head in disgust. "This slave fare I am forced to consume has ravaged my gut. If I never see another kernel of Indian maize, I will die a happy man."

"Leave it, then, if yid rather be heavin' into yon pisspot." Maggie set the plate on the mattress next to him. "Willow bark can be caustic on an empty belly," she warned, "and from the stench of this place, I'd say yiv emptied yer belly."

Cavendish relented, took a piece of toast, and nibbled. "This harm I do myself—you refer to my intemperance?" He held out his empty cup to be refilled.

"Drunkenness—aye—'twill be th' end of ye." Maggie took the cup back to the table.

Cavendish sighed, gesturing with toast to the portrait of the beautiful woman hanging on the wall opposite. "My dear *maman*, she ofttimes worried the same for me."

"Ye can list me as one more hopeful than worried," Maggie boldly retorted as she measured another dose of powders into the cup. "I doubt yer mam will cheer huzzah as I will on the day yer carried off on six men's shoulders."

"My doom!" Cavendish laughed. "And when do you estimate that day to arrive?"

"By th' look of ye, within the year I'd say."

"A cold calculation that has been foretold by others. But to contemplate the alternative," he said with a shake of his head. ". . . to abandon spirits . . ." He shrugged and reached for another piece of toast. "Since my dear father has seen fit to banish me to this back of beyond, I find in drink my only solace."

"Solace!" Maggie picked up a hand mirror lying on a small table near the easy chair and handed it to him. "Look . . . pasty as a floured dumpling, ye are—the white of yer eye as yellow as old ivory. Yer no more'n five and thirty with veins webbed about yer nose like a man of sixty . . ."

"I'm but eight and twenty," Cavendish clarified with injured vanity.

"Eight an' twenty!" Maggie exclaimed, then clucked her tongue. "Youth is wasted on ye. I'd wager yer bowels are costive most days. Yer loath t' take nourishment—ye seem much fatigued . . ."

"You've left off the worst of it," Cavendish reminded with an evil grin and an obscene up-and-down movement of his hand that sent Maggie's heart to her throat. "My manly functions are compromised at times . . ."

"Aye." Maggie cast her eyes down to the tea she prepared. "That as well."

"Your diagnosis?"

She turned and looked him straight in the eye. "Yiv a bilious, fatty liver, overcharged with liquor, and if ye dinna effect a cure, ye'll die sooner rather than later."

"And the cure?" Cavendish sat up.

Maggie poured a double measure of rum into his tea. "They say the drinking of yer own piss—at least two cups a day . . ."

"Pah!" Cavendish fell back against the pillows. "If that is the cure, then I must die."

"One thing's certain, naught will cure ye unless ye abstain from activities taxing t' the humors—such as drunkenness and debauch."

"Abstain from quaff *and* quim?" he said, incredulous. "That suits your purpose."

"Aye." Maggie handed him a second cup of tea. "Ye must also partake in bed rest and sound diet. I think a good purge to cleanse yer organs, followed by a series of healthful tonics to restore strength t' the blood. Heal yer liver, sir, and in time ye can pick up yer habits once again, in moderation."

Cavendish raised his cup to the portrait of the bewigged man hanging beside his mother. "A toast to my dear father—God rot you, you hard-hearted blackguard." He guzzled down his tea in one long gulp, then leaned back against the pillows, thoughtful for a moment. His eyes seemed heavy, and he yawned. Maggie stood by with hands clasped until at last he pulled to sit upright and speak.

"Let us summarize. One—" Cavendish looked Maggie straight in the eye and ticked off on his fingers. "I am mortally ill with but a Scots midwife for succor—a woman more apt to plunge a knife in my heart than effect a cure."

Maggie laughed. "Yer a canny devil, I'll give ye that."

"Two—I should drink of my own piss and set aside the only two things in life what give me any pleasure in this pestilent hellhole to which I've been assigned."

Maggie shrugged. "There's aye a-somethin' . . ."

"Three—I must then be *purged*." He yawned again and rubbed his eyes. "I suppose I should be grateful there has been no mention of bloodletting."

"Ye asked for a cure. Bloodletting is the tool of butchers."

"Well, there's our silver lining. The midwife works on principle." Cavendish held out his empty cup. "Very well, then, Miss Duncan. Though there will be no drinking of piss, and I must contemplate the purge, I will otherwise accede to your ministrations, but in doing so, I say to you *primum non nocere*."

She took the cup and placed it on her tray. "I've tolt ye afore, I have no French."

"Latin, my dear," Cavendish chided. "The physician's creed—*primum non nocere*—'first, do no harm.' Abide by it, and in turn, no harm will come to you." He flopped onto his back, crossed one leg over the other, and nestled into the pillows, the cap on his head cocked over one eye. "Are we met?"

"Aye," Maggie agreed. "Well met, I'd say."

"I am much fatigued." He waved her away with a flick of his fingers and closed his eyes. "Be about gathering your simples and attend to my cure."

Maggie crossed back to her cabin with her tray. Pleased with the outcome of her meeting with Cavendish, she broke into a grin. "Bloody hell! It would have done me some good to see th' bastard choke down his own piss."

⟨≋⟩

Maggie marched in the lead with a large collecting basket hooked over one arm, lackadaisical Brady Moffat and lumbering Figg in tow. The odd threesome entered the woodlands and followed the well-trod shady path that led to the river. Free of the oppressive stockade wall, Maggie stopped for a moment to breathe deep the air—rich and earthy.

"The dark season," Moffat said, shifting the rifle on his shoulder. "The leaves grown so broad and thick on the trees, they close out every bit of light, even on a bright day like today."

They reached the sun-filled meadow and Figg broke from their triangular formation and gallumped away. By the time Maggie and Moffat caught up to him at river's edge, the giant had shed boots and stockings. He waded with breeches rolled above his knees in ankle-deep water and with childlike pleasure pondered the school of minnows nibbling his toes. As usual, Moffat laid his rifle down and flopped in the shade of a willow. Figg splashed back up onto shore, asking, "D'ye bring our tea, Maggie?" And as usual, Maggie produced Tempie's glazed jug from her basket along with a treat—today, a pan-size piece of buttery shortbread.

"Remember, dinna tell anyone that I'm sharing the viscount's sweeties with yiz," she warned Figg, breaking the sugary biscuit in two and handing him half.

Figg nodded. "'Cause that'd be the end of th' sweeties, aye?"

"And ye dinna want that," Maggie confirmed, "for tomorrow I'm fixin' berry tarts."

"Amen t' berry tarts, sez I." Like some sort of immense squirrel, Figg squatted on his haunches, holding his shortbread in a two-handed fashion, nibbling away at its edge.

"Damn good tea," Brady complimented, swilling freely from the jug.

"Sweet lemon balm," Maggie told him with jerk of her head toward Figg. "Good for those plagued with the farts, if ye ken my meaning."

"Farts?" Brady struck a languorous pose, mimicking the viscount, waving the piece of shortbread she handed him in the air. "Of course—farts! The windy escape backward—the kind more obvious to the nose than to the ears."

"Beg pardon, yer lordship." Maggie giggled and curtsied. "I'm off t' my gatherin' now." She took her basket and disappeared into the tall brush growing along the riverbank.

Moffat handed Figg what was left of the tea and lay back in the grass. "Keep an eye on the midwife, Figgy. I'm going to catch a nap."

Figg nodded, several crumbs from his teatime treat stuck in the snot leaking from his nose. He slurped down the rest of the tea, tossed the empty jug aside, and splashed back into the water.

Maggie roamed along the riverbank to gather the wood sorrel she purported to need. After collecting a goodly amount, she stood upright. She could see Figg stumbling along the waterside, sausage fingers grasping at empty air, trying to capture a yellow butterfly flitting about his immense head.

"*Hoy! Figg!*" Maggie shouted, and caught his eye. "I'm goin' upriver a bit."

The big man acknowledged her with a wave. Maggie carried on in gathering mode, meandering slowly, scanning the flora and fauna at her feet as if on the prowl for something of import. *But a few more days of this deception . . .*

At first, the viscount seemed dedicated to improving his health, abstaining from alcohol for three whole days. Maggie plied him with sweet puddings and trifles, and brewed refreshing tonics and teas—sedating the man with belladonna as often as she dared. But in battling his cravings, Cavendish convinced himself it was only the hard liquors, like rum and brandy, that were responsible for the damage to his liver.

"A fine port," he proposed. "A single goblet served post the evening meal to aid poor digestion and build robust health." Maggie did nothing to disabuse him of the notion, and as she expected—much to her delight—the drunkard could no more stop at a single goblet of wine than a papist monk could stop at buggering a single boy. The viscount's one goblet led to a fearful two-day binge.

While spewing yellow bile into the pisspot Maggie held for him, Cavendish vowed to God with weak fist raised, "I forswear strong drink!" and for two days now, the viscount again suffered the throes of withdrawing from his reliance upon alcohol.

Never had she encountered a human being with mood so foul—his every utterance saturated in vitriol. The man was so exceedingly ill-tempered, nothing could be said or done to please him. Harboring not an ounce of pity for the man, and loath to aid him in any way, Maggie was sorely tempted to feed him a rum toddy and set him again on the road to ruin.

Soon I'll be away from tha' spawn o' th' devil . . .

She had given up on the notion of rescue. Maggie just couldn't fathom how Seth would be able to penetrate the station's defenses. The very moment Cavendish agreed to allow Maggie the freedom of the forest to gather the simples she needed, she began to contrive her escape.

Since she was now responsible for preparing the viscount's meals, she gained access to the stores. Even under Connor's gimlet eye she managed to filch pocketfuls of cornmeal and strips of dry cured beef. A two-point woolen blanket found its way into her basket. A tinderbox, complete with flint and steel that someone had left behind at the cookhearth, crossed the fortyard hidden in the folds of her skirt. While Cavendish snored off his excess in a belladonna stupor, she slid under his bed and retrieved Simon's dagger still lying there. And today, as the sparrows trilled in the dawn, she snicked a hatchet from the woodpile.

Maggie ceased foraging upon reaching a rotten tree stump overgrown with moss and sprouting mushrooms. She checked over her shoulder. Moffat still napped. Waist-deep in water, Figg stalked the river, trying to noodle a trout from the water using naught but his huge ham hands. Maggie crouched down, reached under her skirt, and slipped the knots in the strings securing the recently acquired hatchet to her calf, adding it to the blanket, knife, and tinderbox she'd cached inside the stump.

Almost ready . . . Within the week she would set out on one of their jaunts into the woods with a jug of special tea in her basket. *And after the bastards nod off*—she smiled—*I'm away.* She'd keep to the river. *Like a Red Indian, leavin' no tracks* . . . By the time any alarm was raised, she would be long, long gone.

Maggie cocked her head, noticing a clutch of bell-shaped brownish-yellow flowers growing at the base of a large beechnut, no more than five yards away. She drew closer. Veined petals . . . the leaves hairy and toothed . . . She fell to her knees, not touching the plant. *Henbane!* A potent sedative, perfectly suited for her purpose. She produced the hankie kept tucked between her breasts, and used it to protect her fingers as she plucked the leaves.

"*Psst! Maggie!*"

Startled, she looked up. Tousle-headed Jack Martin peeked out from behind the beechnut. Like one of the brownies from the old tales, the lad's sun-browned face and walnut-dyed clothing blended right into his surroundings.

"I canna believe my eyes." Maggie blinked back tears. "*Jackie!* Is it truly you?" She began to rise to her feet.

"*Stay as you are,*" Jack whispered. "*Listen careful like.*"

The lad's impish grin cheered Maggie to no end, but she fought the urge to hug him tight to her breast and kept at her task as if he weren't there.

"*Push your basket closer.*" Jack placed a coil of knotted rope into it. The lad kept his voice low and spoke slowly. "Set your water barrel near the chimney and wait for the dark of the moon tonight . . ."

"*This night?!*" Maggie glanced up, her heart aflutter.

"Mm-hmm. 'Cause the moon's on the wane," Jack explained, then reverted back to reciting the message. "At the dark of the moon, climb up the barrel, onto the roof . . ."

Maggie pictured the pitched roof of her cabin; its clapboards sloped upward from just above the door's lintel piece to meet the stockade wall at a point three-quarters of the way up. She should have no problem scaling the wall from that vantage.

". . . Secure the end and fling the rope over the wall. Tuck up yer skirts afore ye commence t' shimmy over." Jack continued methodically. "Bring naught with ya. Mind the night patrol. Stay out of the clearing and keep to the tree line. A shuttered lantern will await at Mam's grave. Use it only if you have to. Meet up with us at the Berry Hell. Can you do it?"

"Aye." Maggie nodded.

"MAGGIE!" Figg bellowed.

Keeping her head down, she reached out and grabbed Jack's hand. "How does everyone fare?"

"'Ceptin' fer worryin' over you, we're all of us just fine," Jack assured her with blue eyes glimmering excitement. "Best git, afore them fellas come a-lookin' fer ya."

She popped upright to see Figg splashing through the shallows toward her; hands cupped to his mouth, he hollered again, "MAG-GIIEE!" Moffat was also on his feet heading her way, shading his eyes. She cast a glance to Jack, crouched behind the beechnut, white knuckles gripping his ancient musket. Waving madly, she called to Figg, "Dinna fash the water so, Figgy, ye'll frighten all the wee fishies."

A look of horror crossed Figg's features and he stopped stock-still. "Brady's ready t' turn back."

"Aye—" She waved to Moffat and halted his progress. "Tell him I'll be there in a tic." She turned back and whispered, *"To-night!"* sending Jack away with a smile. The boy scooted like a rabbit, from tree to tree, disappearing as suddenly as he had appeared.

Maggie eyed the sturdy rope he'd left in her basket. Henbane forgotten, she snapped off more than a dozen large burdock leaves, arranging them to conceal the rope before hurrying back to the meadow.

"I don't like you wanderin' that far," Moffat chastised. "Have you what you need?"

"Aye that." Maggie turned on her heel and skipped to the path. Moffat whistled Figg in, shouldered his rifle, and followed after her.

The weight of the hemp rope in her basket pleased her so, Maggie had to restrain from bursting into song as they hiked back to the station. Seth's message was heaven-sent, and the prospect of joining up with them filled her heart so's to over-flow the brim of it with joy. Rushing through the station gates, she didn't stop at the cookhearth to speak to Tempie—hard at work preparing the evening fare—but made straight for the cabin.

Aurelia sat on a bench outside the cabin door with a tin washtub between her legs, busy scrubbing wine stains from linen with a stiff bristle brush.

"Come in, Aurelia," Maggie said, crossing the threshold. "I've somethin' t' show ye."

Wet linen was shoved under soapy water. Aurelia dried her hands on her apron and stretched the muscles in her aching back.

"With speed!" Both hands clenched tight on the basket handle, Maggie waited in the center of the room, barely able to contain her glee when Aurelia entered the cabin. "I'm leavin' *tonight*! D'ye ken what I'm sayin'?"

"Shhh!" Aurelia cast a worried glance over her shoulder and dropped her voice. "You oughtn't be telling me this . . ."

"Look here." Maggie lifted the layer of burdock leaves and revealed the rope. "From Seth . . . I'm goin' over the wall at the dark of the moon tonight."

Aurelia quickly pushed the leaves back to cover the rope. "Are you crazy?" she hissed.

"I'm leaving this wretched place! Och, lass, I wish yid come with me . . ."

"Maggie?" A thick voice questioned, startling the two young women so intent on their conversation, neither of them noticed Figg's massive frame darken the doorway. He didn't enter, but was crouched down, peering inside. He held out Tempie's jug, saying, "Ye left this behind."

Maggie pressed the basket into Aurelia's hands and stepped forward to accept the jug from the giant's hand. "Thanks, Figgy," she said, forcing a giggle. "I swan, I might forget mine own head if it weren't attached." Figg shuffled backward and she stepped out the door.

"Maggie'll be needin' this jug, sed I." He snuffled and snorted.

"'Tis true . . . for our tea on the morrow." Taking him by the elbow, Maggie aimed him toward the cookhearth. "Remember, berry tarts, aye?"

"Amen t' that. Amen t' berry tarts, sez I."

Maggie sent Figg off with a little shove and a gay wave. "Till tomorrow." Arms crossed over her chest, Aurelia came to stand beside her. Maggie hugged the jug. They watched Figg as he ambled off in his odd way with arms swinging to and fro, to join Connor under the tarp.

"D' you think he heard?"

Maggie shrugged. "He's a dunderhead." She tapped a finger to her temple. "A clouty dumplin' for a brain. His only concern is for his tea."

Connor glared daggers from across the yard. Aurelia flustered. "I'd best get back to my chores. I don't want him comin' over here, nosin' around."

"And I promised his lordship a tonic." Maggie turned in to the cabin, feeling Connor's nasty bug eyes drilling a hole in the back of her head. She shut the door, found her basket, and set it on the small table where Tempie prepared her simples. As Maggie dug down to the bottom, salvaging the sorrel leaves squashed under the rope, she went over Seth's instructions again. *Set the water barrel near the chimney . . . wait for the dark of the—*

A muffled commotion erupted outside. The door flew open and Brady Moffat stormed into the cabin. His eyes swept the room and settled on the basket. Maggie lunged for it. He caught her by the arm and scattered the leaves in the basket to reveal the rope.

"You little fool." Grabbing the basket, Moffat dragged her out into the fortyard.

Maggie stumbled over tree roots and stones, struggling to keep up with Moffat's long stride as he jerked her along. Their tussle caught the attention of henchmen and slaves, who began to wander toward the blockhouse like strings of ants drawn to spilled honey.

Moffat pushed Maggie to sit on a tree stump next to Aurelia and went inside the blockhouse with the basket. The laundress sat with head bowed, the palms of her hands pressed together and trapped between her knees. Tearful eyes met Maggie's. "Figg told 'em," she hiccuped. "And then I had t' tell 'em . . . tell 'em *everything*."

Maggie put her arm around Aurelia's slim shoulders. "Dinna fash. Ye had no choice."

Figg came through the door, oblivious to their presence. He leaned against the frame, happily munching on a large piece of shortbread.

Maggie laid into him. "Ye huge telltale! Ran straight to Connor, did ye?"

The giant shook his shaggy head; shifting his weight from one foot to the other, he stuttered, "O-over th' wall, ye sed . . ." His squinty eyes were glued to the bulbous toes of his hobnail boots. "There go my berry tarts, sez I . . ."

"Fuckin' eidgit!" Maggie bent, grabbed a stone, and flung it at him. "Great bag o' guts! More guts than brains if ye think I'm goin' t' fix any tarts for ye now." She pitched another stone at him, hitting him square on the forehead.

Figg cowered against the wall, whimpering, "Th' end of the sweeties, I s'pose . . ."

"Amen t' that." Maggie snatched up another stone. Aurelia grabbed her by the wrist.

"Leave him be. He's a simple fella—concerned for his tea, just like you said."

Maggie heaved a sigh. The stone tumbled from her unclenched fist. "I am a fool undone by a fool."

A crowd gathered—more than a dozen backwoodsmen leaning on their rifles, some puffing on queer long pipes. Slaves called in from the field formed a second, larger group, hovering loosely nearby. Maggie could see Justice and Achilles had come around to stand vigil in front of the forge. Sweat-drenched, the smith stood with muscular arms folded over his bare chest, shining in the setting sun like a piece of polished ebony.

The blockhouse door creaked open—wraithlike Connor the first to slink out followed by grim-faced Moffat. Figg pulled upright, snuffling and swiping his snot onto his sleeve. Castor and Pollux scurried out to take up positions at either side of the doorway. Aurelia grabbed hold of Maggie's hand. The muttering crowd quieted and inched forward when Cavendish emerged.

No longer dressed in an invalid's nightshirt and robe, he had donned a crisp shirt with lace cravat. A sober black waistcoat topped buff breeches—fit to his leg without a wrinkle—and gleaming oiled boots. He stood with his back to the two women, riding crop in hand, and addressed the crowd.

"Escape," Cavendish announced, officious and clipped. "A most serious offense." He tapped the crop to his boot. *Tot. Tot. Tot.*

"It is compulsory for all to witness the miscreants peeled and scourged at the post. Mr. Moffat shall lay thirty lashes on the bondwoman for intent to escape and incite insurrection." The crowd began to buzz. Cavendish raised his voice. "And fifteen lashes on the mulatto laundress for her complicity."

Maggie shot to her feet, aghast. "Aurelia's innocent! 'Twas my doing. *Mine alone!*"

The viscount turned on his heel and marched inside. The twins hurried after, closing the door behind. Moffat stepped up with a length of leather cord and bound Aurelia's wrists, handing the dangling lead to Figg.

"Brady, please!" Maggie beseeched as he bound her wrists in like fashion. "Ye canna mean to whip Aurelia . . ."

He wouldn't answer—would not even meet her eye.

Figg and Moffat pulled Aurelia and Maggie by their leads like a pair of sheep being led to the shearing. Rifles shouldered, the crowd shifted to shuffle along. Maggie cast around in desperation; searching faces in the crowd, she spotted Simon Peavey orbiting the periphery and called out to him, *"Simon!"* Their eyes met for a moment—and in that brief moment, despair doused the tiniest hope flickering in her breast as Peavey shook his head, turned, and disappeared from her field of vision.

Thirty lashes . . . fifteen for poor Aurelia . . . The sentence the viscount levied rang in her head like a cacophony of church bells clanging on Christmas morning. *Thirty lashes . . .*

One of the seamen aboard the *Good Intent* had taken twenty lashes for stealing rum and Maggie had treated his wounds. A big, burly lad, and he couldn't walk for days after. *Thirty lashes . . .*

Brady tugged on her lead, pulled her to the center of the fort-yard where the whipping post loomed. A single iron ring pro-truded from the top of the stout oaken beam—raw wood, a foot and a half square by seven foot tall—planted upright in the dirt. Aurelia looked over her shoulder, eyes wide, her lower lip caught on her teeth. The crowd fell into a half circle facing the post.

"We'll start with the nigger lass," Connor announced. Figg led Aurelia to stand to the right of the post. Aurelia raised her face to the crowd and changed before their eyes. Like bright liq-uid lead hardening to dull gray, her features lost their life light. She stood stoic and stiff, emotionless and blank.

Aye . . . Maggie thought. *Aurelia kens well what happens here . . .*

Connor stepped forward, drawing a large knife from the sheath on his belt. Maggie gasped, but Aurelia did not even suf-fer a flinch—did not struggle or protest when the Irishman sliced through the laces on her bodice. She stood still as a stone statue while Connor ripped and tugged her clothing, rendering her na-ked from neck to waist.

Maggie's stomach lurched. She craned her neck to look be-yond the forest of rifle barrels and the wall of white men surging forward. The black slaves who had gathered to hear the judg-ment floated along the fringe with fearful eyes. She could see Tempie, sitting with her hands clenched in her lap on the bench outside their cabin door. Justice, Achilles, and Simon stood in a row before the forge. *What could they do? Nothing.*

With hands bound, Maggie turned and clutched Brady's sleeve in both fists. "'Twas my doing . . . lay Aurelia's lashes on my back . . . let me stand in her stead . . ."

"You're mad." Brady pried off her grasping fingers. "Your own thirty will be hard to take. Forty-five would kill you certain."

"Ye would do me a service, Brady, for I'd be dead and happy for it."

Figg tied Aurelia's lead to the ring at the top of the post, stretching her arms over her head, pulling the skin on her back tight to receive the bite of the lash.

Aurelia drilled the balls of her bare feet into the loose soil, planting them firmly. She leaned in and pressed her forehead into the post.

Connor took control of Maggie's lead and handed Brady a coiled whip. The crowd stilled. Moffat stepped to stand beside Aurelia. He loosed the coil of braided cowhide to unwind and slither at his feet.

"Brady, *please believe me!*" Maggie threw herself forward, falling to her knees with supplicant bound hands. "Aurelia did naught to earn a single lash from yer whip . . ."

Connor grabbed Maggie by the arm and dragged her back.

"Please . . . Brady . . ."

"It's not for me to say." The words burst angry from Moffat. "I but follow the orders of the man who puts silver in my pocket— in all our pockets," he added, drawing assenting grunts from the crowd.

"And what sort of man does that make you, Brady Moffat?" she spat back at him.

Connor gave her a shove that sent her sprawling. "Shut yer gob!"

"What does that make any of ye?" she snarled at the crowd, rising to her feet. "All of ye—supposed freemen doin' the bidding—th' dirty work—for the likes of that tyrant. *Arse-lickers! Th' lot of ye!*"

Connor grabbed Maggie up by the shoulders and shook her like a rag doll. "I said shut yer gob or be gagged!"

Palpable unease wafted through the restless crowd. Men shuffled their feet. Eyes cast downward, Maggie tore away from Connor.

"I hoped it would be different," Maggie declared. "Hoped th' New World proved better than th' old I left behind . . ." Connor chased after her as she skirted along, appealing to the turbulent crowd. "Are we doomed t' bow and scrape t' them what are called our betters? Doomed to accept injustice piled atop injustice?"

"No!" Gruff voices joined in her dissent.

Connor slapped Maggie across the face and seized her by the arm.

"We are all his slaves when we do naught to stanch the tyrant's hand," Maggie screamed as Connor tugged her away. "Th' whole lot of us! Black *and* white . . . *SLAVES!*"

Connor shouted at Moffat. "DO IT!"

Moffat threw his arm. The whipcord whistled and hissed, landing with a hard crack across Aurelia's golden shoulders. Followed by another . . . and another. Her toes dug into the ground; spine twisting, she flinched in anticipation of every blow, taking her punishment without uttering a whimper.

The crowd fell quiet, spellbound by the spectacle. Maggie fought the urge to look away, wincing at the purple welts raised with every stroke.

"Apply the whip with force, Moffat," Connor warned.

Brady grit his teeth and glared at the scrawny Irishman. The next stroke buckled Aurelia's knees and plowed a bloody furrow into her flesh. Aurelia began to tremble. The remnants of her blouse and shift bunched red about her waist, soaked with blood flowing down the channel of her spine. Her glorious curls tinged as if dipped in crimson paint. Writhing in absolute agony, Aurelia loosed a scream at the tenth stroke.

Maggie turned away to see Simon and Achilles struggling to

hold Justice at bay. She closed her eyes, but could not close her ears to the whip's malevolent hiss, or to Aurelia's pitiful screams.

Crack.

Crack.

Moffat delivered the final two strokes and cut the thong binding Aurelia to the post. She slumped into a bloody pile at its base. Maggie made to go to her, but Connor held her back.

Tempie pushed through the crowd. She draped a sheet over Aurelia. Scarlet blossoms bloomed where the linen clung wet to the wounds. The root doctor whispered into Aurelia's ear and got her to stand on her feet. Justice broke through, and as Aurelia struggled to take her first faltering step, he scooped her into his arms and carried her away. Tempie followed close behind.

Connor pulled Maggie to the post.

Maggie tried hard to be as brave as Aurelia, tried to move her mind away from the chaos of leering faces. Moffat wiped the whipcord clean with a scrap of leather—drops of blood and bits of flesh plopped into the dust. Maggie doubled over and emptied her stomach to splash on Connor's boots. The somber crowd burst into laughter.

"Fuckin' bitch!" Connor swore, shoving Maggie aside. He plucked the never-used kerchief from Figg's pocket, wiped his boots clean of puke, and handed it back. Figg stuffed the stinking thing back into his pocket, then threaded Maggie's lead through the ring at the top of the post.

Like the sound of a bagpiper gone mad, a screeching hum droned in her ears as her arms were pulled taut above her head. Panic choked her vomit-stung throat upon hearing the fiendish zing of Connor's blade drawn from its sheath.

Moffat stayed the Irishman's hand. "White women are flogged clothed."

"Himself said 'peeled and scourged.'" Connor jerked away. "White or no, the lass will be stripped." His pinched face screwed into an angry twist. With eyes bulging and Adam's apple bobbing, he cut and ripped Maggie's clothing to ribbons, exposing every inch above her waist to the whip.

Hot with humiliation, she shivered, the evening breeze carrying a chill to her sweaty, bare skin. In a struggle to maintain composure, she focused on the moist, dark circle staining the beam—the spot where Aurelia had leaned her forehead.

Maggie squeezed her eyes tight and pressed the length of her body into the whipping post—trying to become one with it— stout, strong, and lifeless. The rough wood grain bit into her breasts. Her heart pounded in her ears.

The first crack of the whip, sharp as a pistol shot, snapped Maggie back into the moment. Moffat rained five strokes in quick succession. Searing lines crisscrossed her back from shoulder to shoulder. The smell of fear and blood drifted in and out her nose, the copper taste of it in her mouth where she chewed a hole in her cheek to keep from crying out.

Her knees weakened, but she forced herself to maintain her stance, grateful for the post propping her. The strain on her injured shoulder added to the pain she bore. Blood oozing from the lacerations drizzled down her back and itched like the devil.

A shower of ruby droplets scattered through the air with each resounding thwack of Moffat's whip. By the tenth stroke Maggie no longer cared about courage. Nor did she care who saw her writhing naked—or heard her scream and beg for mercy. Life continued to rush through the chambers of her heart, pumping a steady stream of torment straight to the very marrow of her bones.

After the twentieth stroke her eyes fluttered. She gazed up to the North Star, visible in the darkening sky, and gasped a fervent prayer, "Kill me now."

Stepping back, Moffat tossed the whip to land in a sinister wriggle at Maggie's feet. "That's enough," he said.

Connor sputtered, "Thirty lashes have been ordered . . ."

"I don't care. I'm done. Twenty's more'n plenty."

The crowd joined in. "Aye, Brady's right."

"More than enough . . ."

The viscount's malevolent voice cut through the maelstrom of pain in Maggie's head.

"Take up the whip, Mr. Moffat, and apply the punishment with precision," Cavendish ordered—terse—almost shrill.

The wounds on her back began to cool on the breeze. Maggie turned her head, pressing cheek to post, blinking hard to clear her eyes of tears. The viscount stood waiting on Brady's response, a cut-crystal goblet of claret glistening like a precious gem in his hand.

"Apply them yourself, if you're so eager," Moffat replied, kicking the handle of the whip toward him. One of the bystanders handed Brady his rifle.

Cavendish bristled. "I will not abide blatant insubordination."

Many of the rifles formerly on shoulders now rested in crooks of elbows, faces glaring, Moffat's among them. Connor sidled up to the viscount.

"Think twice, m'lord," the Irishman hissed. "Some of these men are dispossessed by yer hand. They are discontent and armed. Yer better off forgivin' the lass a few tickles o' the lash than risk fomenting mutiny amongst 'em."

Cavendish shrugged Connor off and heaved his goblet at the post. Cut crystal exploded into diamond shards; a stream of fine red wine ran a rivulet down the post and puddled under Maggie's toes.

"I will not bend to the will of this rabble." The viscount snatched up the whip, whirled it over his head, and released it to strike.

Figg flailed out one immense arm and caught the sting of the blow, the leather cord whipping around his thick forearm. In an almost elegant motion, the giant jerked the whip from the viscount's hand and sent the thing sailing over the stockade wall. Moffat stepped up to cut Maggie down.

"LEAVE HER!" Cavendish shouted. He and Moffat locked eyes. "You overstep your bounds, Mr. Moffat. *My* bondwoman stays as she is until I order otherwise. Move along and be about earning the generous wage I pay you."

Brady Moffat hitched the gun on his shoulder and took a step back; mumbling "I-I need a drink," he turned and marched to the cookhearth.

Cavendish faced the griping assembly still suffering the throes of witnessing the whipping gone awry. "Drinks all around!" he announced. "Double ration of grog for all who apply at the cookhearth."

Appeased and diverted by the lure of rum, the sedate mob shuffled and grumbled away. Smiling, Cavendish tipped his hand in mock salute as the crowd disbanded. "Gentlemen! I commend you on the pliability of your conscience!"

He turned to Connor. "Send two bottles of the Canary and Brady Moffat to me."

Connor nodded, but before he could scurry off, the viscount grabbed the Irishman by his stringy arm. "Best have a chat with your brother—Figg forgets his place."

Maggie moaned and closed her eyes.

Footfalls crunching—dwindling—dwindled away.

Time passed with the tick of her blood dripping drop by drop into the dirt. A gravelly caw and ominous wing thumping caused Maggie to roll her head back and glimpse a row of greasy black crows collected to perch along the top of the stockade wall. The hated whipping post now Maggie's only friend, she leaned into its embrace and whispered one last prayer.

"Death—come with speed . . ."

22

Angels and Demons

A whisper.

"Catch her . . ."

Her arms dropped weighty to her sides.

Caught in strong arms and laid onto a sheet, wrapped tight.

My shroud.

Lifted at legs and shoulders and carried away.

Maggie watched the black sky move above her—watched the sliver of the waning moon dip into the grasp of a six-fingered cloud. Her ragged breathing caught the solid night smell—earthworms and fresh-turned soil. The trek to the other side proved endless and she bounced along pondering the shadowy shapes carrying her to her grave.

Angels or demons?

Completely numb, save for her arms crawling with ants, she tried to speak. Her tongue, fat and dry as if coated with cotton lint, kept her questions caked in her throat. The sky, the clouds, and the moon soon disappeared into inky, total darkness.

They came to a place fraught with horse sweat on leather—beasts snorting and stamping in anticipation of a journey. God's low whisper prepared her. "You're going t' ride now."

"T' h-heaven?" Maggie croaked.

No one answered.

Lifted by many hands onto horseback. A dark angel clasped her in warm arms—kept her steady in the saddle. He flicked the reins and all moved forward—creaking saddles and jangling tack—many hooves muffled in thick, damp humus.

Cool fingers pressed her cheek and forehead. "She's burnin' up . . ."

"Gib her de drink," another voice suggested.

Maggie's angel rider held a bottle to her lips, and very thirsty, she drank deeply, then gagged, spitting and sputtering—the hellish water bitter and brack.

"Keep her quiet till we reach the river," God warned.

"I've nae gold . . ." Maggie worried, agitating, trying to free her arms trapped in the winding sheet. "I need coin . . ."

"*Keep her still!*" God's whisper grew harsh.

"I hav' nae coin . . ."

Her angel's rough hand covered her mouth, stifling her moans. His voice cooed in her ear, "Don't worry. I have a whole bagful of gold . . ."

Maggie relaxed in Simon's arms, her head flopped forward. He shifted her weight to rest against his chest, muttering, "Why's she fussin' so fer gold?"

Coming to ride alongside, mounted on a stolen gelding, Justice rasped, "She thinks she's passed on."

In the lead, Achilles turned in his saddle, whispering, "An' she need gold to pay de ferrymon . . . to cross over de riber of death . . . to dat place beyond . . ."

"All of you—*pipe down!*" Moffat admonished from the rear.

Maggie began to thrash again, mumbling about coins and salt.

"Swallow yer medicine," Simon whispered in her ear, and held the bottle to her lips. The astringent smell of the boneset tonic revived her to thrashing. Simon struggled to keep her from pitching out of the saddle and implored, "Aurelia, can y' talk to her?"

"Aurelia's in heaven," Maggie moaned, "an' I'm goin' t' hell . . ."

"We ain't dead yet—" Aurelia's weary voice sounded like a clear bell pealing in the dark. "And we ain't goin' t' hell, crazy girl—we's just runnin' away."

⌖

Tom hit the trail before dawn and kept to it hours after dusk, traversing the many overmountain miles from the hunting camp to the Martin homeplace in a scant seven days. Upon seeing Seth's cornfield open bright at the end of the forested trail, he put a kick in his gallop and ran the last few yards.

Not a breath of smoke rose from the chimney of the familiar cabin perched on its rise. Tom lost the spring in his step passing through the dusty gleaned field, infested with crows cawing and flapping. He wound down to stand in a dooryard void of dogs, children, and chickens, listening to the open door and window shutters creak a lonesome song on the evening breeze.

Too late . . .

Tom wandered the dooryard, got down on his hunkers, and traced fingertips over the hard-packed dirt, trying to make sense of the dim jumble of tracks. Rain had obliterated most of the sign. *They're gone some days now—hard to tell where to.*

He'd thought for sure he'd catch them before they left. Tom leaned in on his long rifle, caught off guard by the depth of his disappointment. Unused to the business of love and still a bit bewildered by the notion of being so tethered to a woman, he stared at the forlorn cabin and a tremor of unease whiffled down his spine. The prospect of sharing the rest of his life with Maggie brought him peace. But the counter—the possibility of spending life without this particular woman—cast a dark shroud over his heart near to suffocating.

Someone at the station's bound t' know something . . . Tom turned on his heel and made for the ridge trail to Roundabout.

Seth had teased him once—he said Maggie had caught him in her snare—and Tom recollected how he had scoffed, offended by the mere notion.

Seth sure had the right of it. Tom had marked Maggie in his sights aboard the *Good Intent,* and the first moment her deep brown eyes met his, like flint to steel, a spark flew between them. He marched along the ridge trail at the quickstep. The sooner he found Maggie, the sooner he could gather her into his arms.

And under that perfect sky, I will bury my face in her hair and beg forgiveness for all my rank foolishness.

Bounding down the final set of switchbacks that led to the valley, Tom stopped cold in his tracks at the base of the trail. A pillow of turned dirt was mounded in the shade of a young chestnut tree, evidence of the sad news Duncan had relayed.

NAOMI MARTIN
1735–1763

Crude block letters incised upon a jagged slab of limestone marked her resting place. A tin lantern and three withered bouquets tied with precious bits of red ribbon were propped around the base of the tombstone.

Heart-wrenched, Tom fell to one knee at the graveside, picturing Winnie and Jack with Battler in hand, gathering only the prettiest flowers for their mam. He wondered at the spent lantern perched there, imagining poor Seth grieving into the dark of night. Tom pressed the flat of his hand to the grave and whispered, "A fine woman—and well loved. The good thee did will live on in the lives of those thee loved."

He turned from Naomi's grave to the fort. The gates were closed. A lone sentry paced the roof of the blockhouse. When Tom'd left, a little more than a month before, the field surrounding the station had been speckled with tree stumps and riddled with stones. Now he found it cleared, plowed, and lined with row upon row of precisely formed hummocks. A dozen Negro slaves worked the rows, preparing tobacco beds.

The clang of iron on iron sounded from beyond the stockade wall, calling in the fieldhands for their evening meal. They shouldered mattock and hoe and fell into ragged file. The gates swung open and slaves trudged forward. Tom jogged to the head of the column and passed through the open gates.

Changes wrought during his absence came immediate to his eye; most blatant—the blood-bespattered whipping post centered on the fortyard.

Bright, fearful eyes shone from the many dark faces tracking his movements. Tom pushed his hat back on his head and hiked his rifle onto his shoulder. The station he and the others had built as a haven for settlers had become a cruel prison for these poor people, condemned to a life of backbreaking labor in order to enrich a rich man's coffers. The sight and smell of slavery never set well within Tom's Quaker soul. Resisting an urge to take his leave, Tom searched beyond the many black faces for one familiar, determined to gather information and be quick on his way.

Weary slaves shuffled step-by-step to the cookhearth, where a tiny Negress wearing a red headscarf dished beans from a huge kettle. The little woman stopped mid-ladle when she spotted Tom. To his surprise, she gave him a bold once-over and beckoned to him with a crook of her finger. At the same time, the sentryman atop the blockhouse called down.

"Be that you, Tom Roberts?"

"Hamish!" Glad for a familiar face at last, Tom went to stand in the shadow of the blockhouse. "What in all hell you doin' up there, Macauley?"

"Och." The big Scotsman shook his shaggy head in disgust. "I find meself in dire need of ready silver." Hamish shrugged and sat down, deerskin-encased legs dangling over the edge of the rooftop. "Overcharged my rifle—drunken bollocks that I am—blew out the barrel."

"Bad luck."

"Aye, for I was verra partial t' tha' weapon, na? How went yer hunt, Tom?"

"Not much luck either, I'm afraid . . ."

"Well, if'n yer lookin' t' earn, this English bugger is lookin' to hire . . ."

"Not me, brother—thanks all the same." Tom squinted into the red-orange sun ball setting beyond Hamish's broad shoulders. "Tell me, did you hear where Seth headed?"

"Seth? Naw . . ." Hamish scratched inside his shirtfront. "I didna hear a word."

The blockhouse door crashed open and the Englishman, brandishing a crystal goblet of red wine, stepped out in stocking feet.

Cavendish . . . Tom recognized him. The selfsame bastard who had dogged Maggie aboard the *Good Intent*.

Identical-twin black boys dressed in the silliest costumes Tom had ever seen followed after the man. One boy carried a pair of polished black boots. The other, a bottle. The pasty nobleman glanced at Tom, then snapped at Hamish, "What say you, sentry? Allowing access to my demesne to armed strangers?"

Hamish scrambled to stand. "Th' man's no stranger to the station. This here's Tom Roberts—one of the finest hunters and trackers west of the fall line."

The viscount eyed Tom with interest. "The finest, you say?"

"Aye, m'lord."

Tom winced at Hamish's use of the title.

Cavendish swaggered forward, sipping from his cup. "You seek hire, sir?"

"Hire?" Tom snorted. The nobleman was not at all as he recalled seeing him last—all silk and lace, bewigged, powdered, and primping. "M'lord" reeked worse than a dockside whore three days after a ship of the line'd made port—a noisome compound of lavender water, puke, and piss that forced Tom to take a step back. Greasy strands of unkempt hair hung to the man's shoulders. His disheveled shirt, though stitched of finest linen, was thoroughly stained with gravy, wine, and Lord knew what all. Tom would be willing to wager more food and drink had splashed onto the man than into him.

Cavendish snapped his fingers. The bottle boy refilled his glass. "I offer bounties . . ."

"Bounties?"

". . . and as I am anxious to recover stolen properties, these bounties are more than generous."

Tom shook his head. "I'm no slave catcher . . ."

"I require your services. My men have been scouring the countryside these five days to no result." Cavendish sat down on a tree stump and the boot boy fell at his feet. "You'd be seeking slaves and horses among thieves and whores—my sentryman will furnish you with complete descriptions. Twenty pounds offered for each slave or horse recovered. Thirty each for the thieves Moffat and Peavey. Fifty for the bondwoman."

"Bondwoman?" Tom slipped the bedroll from his shoulder to land at his feet. He dropped his shot pouch atop it and gripped his rifle in both hands. "A white woman?"

Cavendish stood and stomped feet firmly into footwear. The viscount hiccuped and wavered a bit. "Indeed. I place a high value upon my precious bit of white quim." He held his glass up to catch a ray of light and admire the claret's glow as he spoke. "Though she proved most unwilling at the moment of amorous congress—bent over my writing table, the midwife nonetheless provided a suitably tight ride—"

The butt end of Tom's rifle smashed across the viscount's face, sending him flying onto his back with legs and arms unfurled. In a blink, Tom was upon him with the barrel end pressed to the man's gulping throat.

Cavendish lay perfectly still. A purple welt inflamed his right cheek. Wide eyes glued to the angry finger on the trigger.

Hamish leaped from the rooftop. Landing in a dusty thump, he called, "Put by yer weapon, Tom!"

With eyes narrowed to mere slits and mouth a grim line in his stubbly face, Tom's lips barely moved when he spoke. "I find the bastard's done some harm to Maggie, Hamish—"

"Ye do yer lass no favors swingin' from the gibbet, Tom. This man has means."

Tom considered a moment, then shouldered his rifle.

Cavendish sighed in relief and began to sit up.

Tom planted a moccasined foot on the man's chest and pinned him down like a june bug in the dirt. His skinning knife zinged from its sheath. As Cavendish thrashed and flailed, Tom bent over with his full weight bearing down upon the man's breastbone. He gripped a topknot of hair in one fist, immobilizing the viscount's head.

"Madman!" Cavendish gasped, pleading, *"Sentry!"*

Tom put the honed edge of his blade to the man's forehead, and there he carved the letter *R*. "I mark you a Ravisher of Women—"

"Tom, tha's enough—*Tom!*" Hamish grabbed Tom by the arm, but he shrugged free and inserted the sharp tip of his blade inside the viscount's left nostril.

"I expect, sir, one day soon, something fatal will befall you—" And with a flick of his wrist, Tom slit the nobleman's nose and stepped back.

"I'm cut!" Cavendish bounced upright. Blood spurtled from the nose wound and drizzled from his forehead, pooling in a cupped palm held beneath his chin. "Sentry—*I'm cut!*"

"Aye," Hamish agreed. "An' yer lucky tha'—ye may well have been shot."

Cavendish reached up and gingerly fingered the torn nostril. Eyelids fluttered. He fell back, unconscious.

"G'won, best git." Hamish pulled Tom away. "Th' bastard's henchmen are due back."

The twins shoved gun and gear into his arms. Hamish pushed Tom past the curious slaves congregated to view the commotion. Tom stopped short and delved into his pouch. He handed Hamish a handful of Spanish dollars.

"For the repair on your rifle . . . take it," he said with a wry smile, "for I fear I've cost thee employment."

Hamish grinned, and pocketed the coins. "But a wee loan, lad. Much appreciated." They shook hands.

As Tom passed through the gates, the tiny Negress rushed up, waving Tom's black felt hat and shouting, "Mister! *Mister!*" Tom reached to take his hat, but she held tight to it. "You Maggie's man?" she asked.

"You know Maggie?"

"Mm-hmm . . . she pines for you—d'you aim to git her back?"

"If I can find her."

"That renegade fella, Simon. He done took 'em." The woman cast a suspicious glance back to Hamish. Her voice dropped to a whisper. "Took 'em to his folk—his Injun folk. You unnerstan' what I'm tellin' you?"

"Yep. I know where t' go—thank you, ma'am." Tom dropped his bedroll at the slave woman's feet. "A hindrance to me—keep it." Flattening his hat, he stuffed it under his belt and arranged the strap of his rifle so the gun lay diagonal across his back. Tom loped out into the field, looked to the setting sun, veered left, and took off, full speed.

❦

The weary group of horsemen trotted through the field toward the station. Well past the dinner bell, Connor leaned toward the man riding alongside him. "I hope Tempie put a bit by for us. I swear t' Christ, I'm so hungry, I could eat a nun's arse through the convent fence." The laughing group slowed to a standstill before the closed gates. The Scotsman whom Connor had engaged to keep sentry was nowhere to be seen.

"Fuckin' Scots," Connor cursed. After spending five days with arse bones grinding the saddle, he longed for a hot meal and a good smoke, followed by a noggin of rum and his head to his pillow. He urged his fire-shy mount to the head of the torch-wielding, ragtag slew of rascals he traveled with, and shouted into the dark, "Macauley! Figg!"

No doubt Figg slept snug in his bed, belly full of grog and beans, snoring off a good drunk. Unmonitored, his large brother tended to idle drunkenness. "Fuckin' Figg. Thick as shite an' half as useful."

When the viscount had ordered him to accompany the trackers, Connor hated leaving Figg behind, but he understood the bounty-hungry Virginians would not tarry on this trek. Hardened to the trail, they moved fast and relentless. Figg would've proved a huge burden, to the horses in particular. Connor had hired Hamish Macauley, admonishing him to mind Figg and the fort.

"Hoy, the station!" Connor shouted. "For Christ's sake, will someone open the fuckin' gates!"

At last the big latch klunked open. The gate wailed on its hinge and scraped a slow half arc in the dirt. Connor was surprised to see the viscount's twin body servants with their shoulders to the gate.

The party clipped-clopped into the fortyard. The few slaves who were still awake ran up to grab reins and see to the horses. Tired and hungry, the trackers headed straight for the cook-hearth. Connor dismounted and questioned the twins. "Where's Figg? Where's the sentry?"

"Figg, he in his bed," Castor offered.

Pollux added, "The sentryman, he took off."

"Took off?"

The twins nodded with vigor.

"Fuckin' worthless Scots," Connor muttered under his breath.

"Marse Cavendish want t' see you." Castor jerked his head to the blockhouse.

Pollux added, "Toot sweet, he say."

Given not a moment's respite from the saddle before having to face his employer's certain displeasure, Connor sighed and ground the heels of his palms into his eye sockets.

Th' Scots bitch must be a devilish good piece. Very keen on recovering his white woman, the viscount had spared no expense in the hunt. The trackers diligently roved the frontier for five days, hoping to claim the bounties offered. But aided by expert huntsmen like Moffat and the renegade Peavey, the horses, slaves, and bondwoman had seemingly vanished into thin air. Connor grumbled, "Fuckin' Scots. Fuckin' niggers. Fuckin' Injuns— *fuckin' Scots!*"

Castor tugged at his sleeve. "Would you ask him, Mr. Connor—ask him if we can cut Aunt Tempie down—"

"Cut her down?"

"She been whipped, and left at the post."

"*Whipped?!*" Connor spun and squinted at the dark. In the light of the waning moon, he could make out a shadow huddled close to the whipping post. "Who whipped her?"

"Marse Cavendish made Figg do it," Pollux said.

Connor groaned.

Castor said, "He had Figg lay ten lashes to her after she stitched his nose."

"Stitched his nose? Whose nose?" Too tired and impatient to wait on the answer, Connor shoved by the boys and marched to the blockhouse. He knocked.

"*Entrez.*"

Connor took a deep breath before pushing open the door. The speaking of French always boded ill.

The viscount was never one to stint on candles, but this night

Connor found Cavendish in the shadows, hunched over his writing table scrawling away, the room lit by a spartan, pierced tin lantern emitting the faintest dappled glow.

Scribbling another foul screed to the duke, Connor guessed. He made a point to review the viscount's outgoing correspondence and never posted the most vicious letters—as a kindness to the duke and duchess.

Waiting to be addressed, the Irishman laced his fingers behind his back, the room still but for the sporadic tick of pen to inkwell, the scratchings of the goose quill, and the shuffle of his boots as he shifted from one foot to the other. Without glancing up, the viscount finally spoke.

"What news, Mr. Connor?"

"I'm afraid none, sir." Connor's Adam's apple bobbed erratic along the stalk of his neck. "The thieves have vanished. The trackers declare the trail cold."

"I disagree. The trail is quite warm." Cavendish pulled himself upright and flipped the tin door on the lantern open, illuminating his face.

"Jaysus!"

Variegated shades of blue, violet, and green colored the right side of the viscount's face, looking much like a bag of bruised plums. The flesh swelled so's a mere crease existed where an eye should be. At least a dozen knotted, coarse black threads laddered the left side of his nose, evenly spaced like hatch marks in a ledger. The stitched wound was pink and raw and just beginning to crust. A strip of linen bandaged his forehead, stained rusty just above the bridge of his injured nose. Cavendish spoke as if nothing were amiss.

"On the morrow, Mr. Connor, assemble enough provender, lead, powder, *et cetera,* for you and me, and four men of your choosing . . ."

"M'lord, surely ye do not intend to travel sore wounded as ye are . . ."

"Bring enough supplies, *Connor*"—the viscount raised his voice, wincing at the effort—"for you and me and four of the best men. A *posse comitatus*, as it were. Ready them for the most expedient departure, for I assure you, I will be fit to travel."

"Aye, m'lord." Connor bowed his head, unconsciously rubbing his sore backside.

"Do not be so put-upon, sir." Cavendish laid down his pen and rose from his chair.

Quick to offer an arm, Connor assisted the viscount to his bed. "M'lord—tell me—who did this horrible thing to ye?"

"We shall find the man by heading due west . . ." Cavendish lowered himself to sit.

"*West?!* Beyond the mountains?"

"Yes, beyond the mountains, you dolt. Indian territory." Cavendish swung his legs up onto the mattress and sank back into the pillows. "The whip's tickle extracted the information I required."

"Tempie?"

The viscount nodded. "Due west into Shawnee territory. Peavey's village along the Scioto River harbors the hell-born Scots witch. Her familiar makes his way there as we speak."

"He who cut you so?"

"A rank blackguard by the name of Tom Roberts. Upon him, I shall rain havoc."

"M'lord, perhaps ye need reconsider this course," Connor reasoned. He took one candle from the candelabra, touched the wick to the flame in the lantern, then lit the others with it. "There is no need for ye t' risk further harm. We've the man's name and destination. I'll gather the lads and offer a handsome bounty—"

"*Blast your eyes!*" Cavendish sat up and tore the bandage from his head. Glistening in the candle glow, droplets of red-tinged matter oozed from the angry *R* sliced into his flesh. Connor took a step back.

"*Do you see, sir?*" the viscount railed. "Do you see what this scoundrel has done to me? My life—my very existence thrown completely out of kelter. I will never, NEVER be able to show this face in true society. London will never be more than a pleasant memory for me now. The bondwoman and her rabid lover have condemned me to float forever, here, among the dross of humanity." The viscount slammed his head back into the pillows, clenching fistfuls of linen.

"Ready the men, for I will not be dissuaded, Mr. Connor." The flicker of candle flame danced in the light of his one good eye. "I *will* appease my bloody thoughts."

23

Long Knife Man

Maggie whispered so as not to wake the children. "So are ye comin' along, or no?"

Aurelia curled up tight within her wool blanket. "No . . . not today . . ."

Simon's older sister, Noolektokie, stood beside the low doorway of the bark-covered hut tying off her glossy black braids with bright blue ribbons. "Mag-kie," she said with a pretty smile. "*Pe-ee-wa* . . ." Grabbing her digging stick and a bushel basket from the stack of many, the Shawnee woman gestured for Maggie to follow.

Maggie stamped her feet to the rush-mat floor—the new moccasins Simon'd made for her had yet to conform to the shape of her feet. She secured a sheathed knife about her waist with a length of buffalo tug, and adjusted the woven garters on her deerskin leggings. Slipping the strap of a leather pouch containing flint, steel, and dry tinder over her head and arm, she snatched up a basket and hurried to catch up with the village healer.

The cluster of perhaps one hundred *wegiwas*—simple pole-and-birchbark huts—was arranged around a large, log-built council house. Deep in Indian territory, the Shawnee village of

Kispoko hugged a soft grassy bend along the Scioto River, and it had taken them four days traveling on horseback and by canoe to reach it. Maggie did not recall much of their journey. She'd been among the Shawnee a full fortnight, and still could not shake the unsettled feeling of having been plucked by the hand of God from the whipping post at Roundabout, and dropped into Noolektokie's lodge.

Simon's sister's name meant "Smooth Water," and true to her name, Noolektokie glided quickly through the village, her long, heavy braids swaying with her stride like lengths of rich silken rope. The healer turned and urged Maggie to make haste with a wave of her hand. *"We-witippie!"*

Like Maggie, Noolektokie was dressed in typical Shawnee garb—a short leather skirt, a knee-length overblouse, and a pair of thigh-high leggings—but unlike Maggie's utilitarian castoffs, the details of the healer's attire bespoke her vaunted status among her people.

Noo's leggings were fashioned of red worsted wool and trimmed along the side seams with a fringe of white rabbit fur. Rainbow strands of trade beads hung in thick coils around her neck. Etched silver bands cuffed both wrists, and a hammered silver disk—as big as a Spanish dollar—dangled from one ear. Her overblouse was made from the prized, supple underbelly of a baby buffalo, its yoke and sleeves adorned with rows of colorful ribbons and affixed with many tin cones that tinked softly as she wound a path between *wegiwas*.

The sun had yet to crest above the tree line, and smoke wafted from few lodge roof holes. By the time Maggie and Noo reached the outskirts of the sleepy village, their moccasins were drenched with dew. Chill morning air showed their breath, raising goose bumps. Maggie's wounds had healed clean to but bits of scab clinging to shiny, pink stripes across her back, and she suffered a twinge as the new skin drew tight to her bones.

Maggie and Aurelia had spent their first days in the village side

by side, flat on their bellies in the healer's *wegiwa*. Noolektokie
bathed and dressed their awful wounds with a soothing balm. She
banished their fevers with herbal teas, and fed them sweet corn
puddings and fortifying stews to strengthen their ravaged constitu-
tions.

Maggie clambered after Noo, up a steep escarpment, to enter
the mist-shrouded woodlands bordering the river. Ancient stands
of hemlock, birch, oak, and sugar maple forested the rugged
foothills rising from the river valley. The woods were teeming
with wildlife come to fatten on fruit-bearing understory trees.

"There's a likely tree!" Maggie shouted, running ahead, keen
on harvesting a basketful of delicious pawpaws. She could not
get enough of the sweet, custard apples since the day Noolektokie had introduced the fruit to her. They dropped their baskets
on the ground and began to pluck the yellow oblongs bunched
like grapes on the low-slung branches.

The shift of season filled the air with the ripe smell of decay
and the rustle of dying leaves on the trees. A flock of geese
honked southward, and plump squirrels skittered from limb to
limb, cheeks stuffed with buckeye and beechnuts. Worry knotted
Maggie's gut and furrowed her brow. *Soon the trees will be
barren . . . rivers frozen over . . .*

When she lay in despair, recovering from her ordeal, Simon
had urged her to get well, and she made him promise to take her
back to Seth and the children before snow and ice made travel
impossible. Now that she was fit and anxious to travel, Simon
avoided her. And for the last three days, Maggie had not seen
hide nor hair of him. Bringing her foot down hard on a windfall
pawpaw, she mashed it to a pulp, and hissed, *"Simon!"*

Noolektokie tossed a pawpaw into the basket and arched a
brow at the mention of her brother. "Penagashea?" she asked.

The ironic appropriateness of Shawnee names never failed to
amuse. Simon was called "Changing Feathers," for his habit of
moving back and forth between the white and Indian worlds.

"Aye—Penagashea." Maggie punctuated Simon's Shawnee name with a disdainful Scottish harrumph. "Penagashea make Mag-kie crazy." She squinched her face, clutched at her hair with both hands, and shook her head back and forth.

Noolektokie understood the sentiment and laughed. "O-ho!"

Though grateful to Simon for bringing her and the others out from bondage, Maggie had been honest with him from the start. She told him point-blank that he must take her back over the mountains, and he promised he would. The prospect of living out the rest of her life among Red Indians was almost as unbearable as fulfilling the terms of her indenture for Cavendish.

Maggie's morning outings with Noolektokie were the highlight of an otherwise fear-fraught day. She spent most of her time hiding inside the *wegiwa* to avoid the angry glares and bitter sentiments of Kispoko's inhabitants. Whenever she ventured out on her own, she was spat upon. Children shouted names and pelted her with clods of dirt. And once, when she was fetching water, an angry old woman followed after her, rapping her on the head with a wooden spoon while dishing out a vile harangue.

Throughout the village, blond, chestnut, and carrot-red scalps were proudly displayed on lodge poles—a frightening reminder that after seven long years of war allied to the French, the Shawnee harbored no great fondness for the British.

I canna change my feathers. Maggie picked pawpaws, bemused, for on the other hand, the sharing of a common enemy—the white man—caused runaway slaves like Aurelia, Justice, and Achilles to be warmly welcomed into the tribal fold.

Affable Justice exhibited his value at once, setting up a primitive forge and repairing a host of broken guns, leaky pots, and kettles. Aurelia's skill with the needle helped her to bond with the native women, and her nimble mind easily picked up the complex language Maggie struggled so to comprehend. Young Achilles fell right into the Indian pattern of life, so similar to the life he'd been torn from in Africa. He traded his slave clothes for breechclout and fringed leggings. Armed with a bow of his own devising, he endeared himself within the first days of his arrival, chasing down and killing a fat she-bear, earning himself the name Mkateelenalui—Black Arrow.

Noolektokie picked up her basket and moved on to a stand of tall flowers. "Mag-kie!" she called out. Dropping to her knees, she began to dig.

"Faerie candles!" Maggie said aloud the name she made up for this particular American flower. She'd always been partial to the droopy white plumes with their odd, haylike aroma. She crouched beside the healer in excitement. "Ye ken—them being so bonnie, I always figured they must be good for somethin'."

Noolektokie prized free a stout section of root, dark and gnarly on the outside, creamy white on the inside. "*Mkatee co-hosh,*" she said. Brushing off clumps of dirt, she handed the root to Maggie.

"Aye . . . *mmm-ka-tee co-hosh,*" Maggie repeated, with brow furrowed. *Now for the difficult bit . . .* "But what d'ye use it for? Eh . . . *cohosh* . . ." She searched through her scant Shawnee vocabulary. ". . . *wee-thenie*? To eat?" She pretended to bite into the root.

"No, Mag-kie . . . *chobeka.*" Noolektokie rose up on her knees. With graceful movements, she indicated a large belly, then mimicked rocking a baby, then again indicated a large belly. "*Chobeka ho-tohcoo kweewa . . .*"

"*Kweewa*? Woman? Pregnant woman?" Maggie indicated a large belly, then mimicked pushing and straining like a woman in labor. "*Chobeka*—medicine—for *kweewa* in labor?"

"Aye!" Noolektokie used one of her few English words, nodding and smiling wide.

Maggie babbled on as they harvested the black cohosh root. "I'll take yer heathen word for it, lass, for though ye may lack English, ye surely ken yer remedies—aye?"

"Aye!" Noo agreed.

Shots rang out—coming from the river—followed by the Shawnee halloo—"*Chi-chi-lo-a! Chi-chi-lo-a!*"—and more shots.

Noolektokie's hand flew to her mouth. "Waythea!" She gasped her husband's name, jumped to her feet, and pulled Maggie to stand. The two gathered their baskets.

In an effort to maintain control over their shrinking homelands, the Shawnee had joined forces with the Ottawa chief Pontiac and many other tribes laying siege to forts and terrorizing settlers up and down the frontier. Kispoko's war party had returned, hopefully with Noolektokie's husband unscathed among them.

They ran to the ridge and could see four large canoes filled with bare-chested warriors paddling toward the village. Noo hugged her basket to her chest; eyes twinkling with tears, she bounced on the balls of her feet and pointed to the last canoe. Exclaiming "Waythea!" she took off, scrambling down the escarpment, dribbling a trail of pawpaws behind her.

Maggie lost sight of Noo in the stream of villagers spilling forth from *wegiwas* and swarming toward the returned warriors like bees toppled from their hive. Maggie hurried down the established path leading back to the village.

Wives, mothers, and children embraced husbands, sons, and fathers. Young men who had remained behind—Simon and Achilles among them—splashed into the water to help beach the canoes. Old men emerged in regalia, and gathered in a dignified group at the doorway of the council house to officially welcome the victorious men home.

Waythea is back—Maggie wandered through the bustling throng hiding behind her basket, her bottom lip caught on her teeth. *We'll need new lodgings, Aurelia and me . . .*

The returned warriors began to disengage from their families and head toward the council house, many with freshly shorn scalps swinging from their belts—hanks of bloody hair attached to tattered skin with globs of fat and bits of blood vessels still clinging to the unscraped flesh.

Maggie hugged her basket and scooted into the shade of the closest *wegiwa*. Leaning a shoulder to a stout lodge pole, she spotted Noolektokie and her husband strolling arm in arm. Two scalps dangled from Waythea's belt, one curly brown, the other, golden blond.

Pawpaws tumbled onto the soft loam as Maggie retched sour bile. Bent over the puddle of yellow spittle, blinking teary-eyed, she glanced around hoping no one had noticed her weakness. A group of five warriors came her way. She toed sandy soil over the sick and plastered her back to the rough bark of the *wegiwa*, giving over a wide path as they passed.

The warriors' dusky muscled bodies exuded confidence and pride in victory, but the scarlet circles and lines painted around their eyes lent them a devilish countenance. It would be daunting to face these men in battle.

Maggie knelt to gather the spilled fruit and noticed the villagers at the shoreline forming into four files, one leading from each canoe. Hand to hand, they passed the spoils plundered from settlements along the frontier. A group of white captives were herded to stand near the growing pile of pots, clothing, weapons, and sacks of meal. Maggie abandoned the pawpaws and edged forward.

Two small white boys, a young girl, and a British infantryman clustered together near the prow of the lead canoe. The boys were very young—brothers by the look of them. Maggie gauged the bigger lad to be about five years old, and the smaller, no older than three. The girl was taller than Winnie, with dark brown hair pulled back and plaited in a single, thick braid. She held each boy by the hand and her heavy brows drew into a fierce V whenever any Shawnee ventured too near.

Th' lass's fearless. Tha's how she's survived . . . The Shawnee admired such bravery.

The big, burly soldier stood with wrists bound before him, sweat stains patching his red waist jacket. Her countryman wore the bedraggled remnants of his uniform proudly. Maggie recognized the distinctive dark tartan of his regimental kilt as that of the Royal Highlanders—the Black Watch.

He looked like a wild man—handsome face covered with golden-red stubble and mottled bruises—long auburn hair all a-tangle. His boots must have been stolen from him—his feet and muscular calves encased in naught but red-checked hose. He stood tall and defiant nonetheless.

Maggie skirted around the jabbering audience formed in a solid phalanx around the captives and the pile of booty. The old woman, the very one who had rapped Maggie on the head with a spoon, ordered the captives to sit on the ground, poking and prodding them with a staff tied with a fluff of red feathers. The crone harkened to the crowd; waving her feathered stick, she shouted, *"Choyoch-ki, pethe-ta-waloo!"*

The crowd quieted instantly. Pleased, the woman smiled a toothless grin, set staff aside, and pulled forth from the pile a military-issue musket. The harpy held it in her spindly claws, speaking at length until a grinning young man stepped forward. The crowd murmured approval when she placed the gun into his hands. So it went with each item—every kettle, ax, and blanket.

Maggie waved to Simon at the opposite end of the crowd. He caught her eye at the same moment, smiled, and wound around to join her.

In Kispoko, Simon cast aside all reference to his white heritage. He dressed in breechclout and leggings. Drawn over one shoulder and belted at his waist, he wore a red-and-black-striped blanket. He'd plucked his lovely chestnut hair, leaving one thick lock, stiffened with bear grease to stand upright, like a bristly brush mounted to the crown of his head. His scalp lock was dressed with red, yellow, and green feathers, and matching feathers attached to a leather strap were tied around the biceps of his right arm. Silver hoops decorated his ears and a silver bead ornament dangled from a piercing on his nose. Simon took her hand. "You look beautiful, Mag-kie. *Wil-li-thie.* Beautiful."

Maggie jerked her hand away. "When are ye goin' t' take me back like ye promised?"

Simon ignored her question. "There's going to be a big feast tonight."

"And what's to become o' them?" Maggie pointed to the huddled captives.

Simon nodded at the old woman. "Payakootha—she's the Peace Chief. She decides. The little ones and the girl will most likely be adopted. The soldier . . ." He shrugged.

Payakootha prodded the girl to stand front and center. The boys leaped up as well, ferociously clinging to her skirts. The Peace Chief rasped out an order and two men came up to pry the boys away.

The girl drew her shoulders square, held her head erect, and clasped hands beneath budding breasts. She kept her eyes straight. Her chin began to tremble as Payakootha rambled on and on. Heads nodded in approval when a middle-aged couple stepped forward and took the girl away with them.

Simon leaned in and said, "Their only child—a daughter—died from a bad fever."

The crowd also agreed with the appropriateness of the Peace Chief's decision when the brothers were given to a childless couple.

Two warriors grabbed the Scots soldier and pushed him to stand. The Shawnee fell silent and everyone inched forward. Payakootha bent down to pick up a small wooden bowl. She hobbled over to the soldier, dipped her hand into the bowl, and smeared black paste all over his face.

The villagers burst forth in a raucous cheer that sent a chill down Maggie's spine. Women held open palms to the sky, ululating high-pitched screams. Children yipped, yawped, and danced. Men threw their heads back, howling in triumph, and fired shots into the air.

"What's going on?" She clung to Simon in the midst of the tumult, tugging on his arm. "Why'd she black his face?"

Simon met her gaze, his green eyes brilliant with excitement. "The soldier's to be burned!"

A fire crackled in the circular fire pit centered in Justice's *wegiwa*. The blacksmith sat with massive shoulders hunched and he poked at the fire. Aurelia spooned stiff cornmeal mush onto a hot stone. Maggie sat between the two of them, crouched in a brown blanket, staring blankly at a steaming kettle nestled in a mound of glowing embers.

Justice's deep rumble broke their silence. "The Injuns seem t' have calmed considerable since th' dawn light." He leaned back, grabbed a stick of wood, and tossed it onto the blaze. A swirl of sparks and smoke billowed to fly up and out the roof hole. "But I swan, I will hear that poor man's pitiful moaning ringing in my ears fo' many a day t' come."

"That had t' be the most terriblest thing I ever heard . . ." Aurelia shuddered and swiped back the tears sprung to her eyes. She took up a flat of birchbark and used it to flip the johnnycakes one by one.

"I hope he's dead. He must be dead." Maggie clinched her blanket beneath her chin and stared into the flames. She dared not shut her eyes for more than an instant, for when she lingered in the darkness, she saw it all again.

They'd stripped him naked and painted him all over with a gritty black stain made from charcoal mashed in water. The villagers armed themselves and formed two parallel lines from the shoreline to the council house. The soldier was made to run this gauntlet, all the while fiercely beaten with sticks and pelted with stones. Simon broke away from Maggie and joined in, baying like a wolf when he dealt a fearsome blow to the man's head with the pipe end of his tomahawk.

The Shawnee gathered in the clear area in front of the council house, where a tall stake had been pounded into the ground.

Firewood was piled off to the side. The soldier's wrists were bound and his neck was secured with a long cord and tied to the stake, leaving him enough slack to wander around it like a tethered dog.

To the man's credit, he bore every bit of this treatment with great patience and stoic dignity. Seven or eight yards off to the side, a handful of women kindled a large fire. As the flames rose, Payakootha and the other elders laid the ends of their staffs into the flames.

As if on signal, two warriors leaped forward with hideous cries. One held the struggling Scotsman firm by the shoulders; the other sliced off both of the soldier's ears.

They tossed the bloody ears into the dirt. The crowd celebrated, whooping and leaping about. A gang of young boys made a game of kicking the severed appendages back and forth.

Blood pulsed from the gaping wounds and ran down the soldier's neck, but throughout the awful ordeal, he did not cry out, not once. To the crowd's delight, he stomped around the post, glaring, pounding his chest with bound fists, shouting, "'S mise Lachlan Maclean's ann á Ardnacross á tha mi! D'ye hear tha'? I'm Lachlan Maclean of Ardnacross on the Isle of Mull, and I fear only God!"

Maclean's brave declarations boldly delivered in Maggie's native tongue tore at her heart. She could no longer bear witness to his torture. She pushed through the crowd to where Simon stood at the forefront and latched onto his arm. "Put an end to this madness!"

Six warriors marched forward, each taking hold of one of the long staffs burning in the fire. Armed with the flaming brands, they circled the stake, and no matter which way Maclean turned, he could find no respite from the heated tips pressing into his naked flesh. Women ran to scoop up bucketsful of coals and spill them around the stake so's the Scotsman's limited path was strewn with hot embers. Maclean stumbled and fell onto the smoldering coals. The smell of burned hair and scorched, bubbling flesh seared Maggie's nostrils.

An old man ran in shouting. He pressed his foot to the prone man's neck and lopped off a chunk of scalp, holding the bloody thing over his head for all to see.

Almost every square inch of Maclean's flesh was either burned, blistered, or bleeding, but the Scotsman pushed himself to stand on wobbly legs and continued to rant. "Th' Macleans, ye fuckin' heathens! We were there at Stirling . . . at Sherrifmuir . . . at Culloden . . ." Inured to pain, he shambled back and forth, around and around the stake. "An' as sure as there's a hole in yer arse, ye willna hear me beg mercy . . . *never! NEVER!*"

Payakootha took a brand from the fire and scraped the glowing end to the raw bone on Maclean's head, generating a spray of sparks that had her cackling with glee.

Maggie tugged on Simon's arm; with tears streaming down her face, she pleaded, "Make them stop!"

"Are you mad?" Simon jerked away and waved his arm to the crowd shrieking with bloodlust. "Even if I wanted to, I wouldn't be able to stop them now."

"I'm Lachlan Maclean, grenadier with the Royal Highlanders Forty-second Regiment of Foote!" the Scotsman cried out as he shuffled like a drunk through hot ashes. "And I curse yiz all, ye red-devil whoresons!"

Two big warriors grabbed Maclean by the arms. A third stepped up with knife upraised. Maggie thought for sure this would be the merciful end.

So did Maclean. He threw out his chest, closed his eyes, and raised his face to heaven.

The warrior with the knife jammed his thumb into the Scotsman's mouth, and pried it open. When he turned back to face the audience, he displayed Maclean's severed tongue skewered on the tip of his knife. He flicked the bloody thing to sizzle on the coals.

Maclean dropped to his knees, gagging, spitting blood.

Maggie could bear no more. "Kill him, Simon—shoot him."

"Shoot him?"

"I beg ye," she sobbed, clinging. "Shoot the poor man."

"No!" Simon pulled away. "We need this vengeance—vengeance for all that is lost to us."

Maggie tore at the rifle slung over his shoulder, shrieking, "Give me yer gun, then, ye fuckin' heathen. Give it to me an' I'll do it. I'll shoot him, ye coward . . ."

It was then Simon slapped her. Slapped her across the face hard enough to knock her down. He hauled her away—dragged her kicking and screaming into Justice's *wegiwa*.

"Keep her in here," he said, "for she's apt t' get herself killed."

Maggie stayed the awful night with Justice and Aurelia. The three of them trying with all their might to close their ears to the suffering wails and insane shrieking . . .

Aurelia broke Maggie's reverie, setting a johnnycake and a tin cup of hot tea beside her. "You should try an' put somethin' in your belly."

Maggie shook her head no.

"Then you should lie down and rest . . . ain't none of us got a wink o' sleep last night."

"That's a good idea," Justice agreed. "It's quiet now." He lay flat back with his arms folded under his head. A shrill yipping pierced the silence. Justice bolted upright.

"*She-mano-se! She-mano-se!*" More shouts. Hurried footfalls beat a path around their *wegiwa*.

"Y'all wait here," Justice ordered, taking up a stout club of firewood, his eyes very wide and white in his face. "I'm goin' t' see what's goin' on."

Maggie and Aurelia followed him out the door. Morning fog and smoke clung to the bark-covered domes. They stayed near the doorway wondering at the commotion—dogs barking, Indians tumbling barefoot and bare-chested from their snug lodges, scurrying toward the village center. Justice sprinted back, dodging through the moving tide like a salmon swimming upstream.

"White man—come out of the trees—" he gasped.

Maggie grabbed his arm. "Soldiers?"

Justice wagged his head back and forth. "No. One of them they call *She-mano-se*—a long knife man."

"A slave catcher?" Aurelia half slunk back into the doorway.

"Might be . . . best lay low." Justice took a deep breath. "He must be crazy for sure—white man comin' in here by his lonesome."

Maggie went back into the lodge and snatched up her blanket.

"You best stay put, woman," Justice warned.

Maggie threw the blanket around her shoulders. Aurelia grabbed her by the wrist. "That man may well be a slave catcher. Remember, they's huntin' you, too."

"He might be a French trader, and may well be my only chance to get away from here." Maggie pulled free and draped the blanket over her head. "I'll be careful." She ran to join the Indians gathering at the council house, where the bones of Lachlan Maclean lay smoldering on the coals.

The shouting died down—replaced by an uneasy mutter and shifting of shoulders. Maggie pulled at the blanket edges; ensuring that her face was well shadowed within, she wended her way to the front of the crowd.

It was as if someone pounded the wind from her lungs. Her knees buckled. The blanket slipped to her shoulders and she clutched both hands to her heart, unable to believe her eyes.

Tom Roberts faced the Shawnee unarmed, dressed in naught but breechclout and the beaded strap of his shot pouch diagonal across his bare chest.

He looked like a ghost—a phantom risen from the swirling eddies of mist and smoke. His long, loose hair lifted on the breeze, crow's-feet gathered at the corners of his shining blue eyes, and he smiled serene. In his arms he cradled a pure white fawn.

24

The White Fawn

Tom knew for certain he was a man in love in that moment. When he saw Maggie, his heart overflowed with joy, and try as he might, he could not help but smile.

In the blink of an eye, he watched Maggie's shock mingle with relief and happiness. She made as if to run to him and Tom had to warn her off with a brusque shake of his head. Her shoulders stiffened and her smile coalesced into a wary pucker, as suddenly she was aware of their precarious situation.

Indian clothes become her ... But she looked much thinner than when he'd seen her last. Deep shadows rimmed her eyes and a fading bruise colored the left side of her gaunt face.

Cavendish ... Tom breathed deep to quell the lurch in his chest. *I should have killed the bastard* ... He gave his head a shake to dispel his vengeful thoughts. *Not now ... keep your wits about you ...*

Tom waited with his back to the council-house door. To his left, an ominous, blackened stake stood sentinel with him—the charred bones of some poor devil scattered in the smoking ashes. He eyed the crowd assembling. Several hundred Shawnee gathered around the clearing, a score or more of able-bodied warriors among them. No one made a move to rebuke him or question his presence.

"You've confounded them," Tom whispered into the fawn's twitching, oversize ears. He hugged the baby deer tight and its sharp, puny bones and bristly hairs bit into his bare chest. The fawn trembled; pink nose quivering, it studied the scene with eerie pink eyes.

Tom could not believe his good fortune when he'd found the oddling curled in the dew-soaked shade of a laurel tree the day before. He had once seen the hide of a white beaver—and once thought he saw a white squirrel darting among the trees, but he had never ever seen a white deer. Pure-white animals, especially larger species like deer and buffalo, were so extraordinarily rare, Indians considered them magical beings come direct from the spirit world.

At last, the elders came forward in slow procession, their stooped frames swathed in striped wool blankets. A grizzled old woman bearing a red-feathered staff led five old men to stand in a row, shoulder to shoulder, before Tom.

Tom squeezed the fawn, threw shoulders back, and addressed his audience in Ojibwe, the trade language common to all Algonquian tribes. "Grandfathers! Grandmothers! Brothers and sisters! I greet you in peace on this fine morning! I am Ghizhibatoo, son of the Deer Clan of the Anishnaabe."

"O-ho! Anishnaabe!" The crowd buzzed, very surprised that an English white man—a Long Knife at that—could claim kinship to the original people, the Ojibwe from the north. Maggie's lips parted in amusement. She gave her head a little shake.

Tom took a step forward and offered the white fawn with outstretched arms. "I, Ghizhibatoo of the Deer Clan, give this deer to the Shawano—a token of good wishes from my totem." He counted on his Ojibwe name, "Swift-footed," and his ties to the Deer Clan to enhance his gift's significance and value.

The old man standing directly opposite stepped up and, with great reverence, took the baby deer into his withered arms. The chief communed with the fawn for a moment, staring into its blinking pink eyes, stroking the soft white velvet between them with a gnarled finger.

A pretty woman—a medicine woman, by the otter skin bag she carried on her hip—came forward and pulled a length of cordage from her pouch. She fashioned a lead and slipped it over the animal's head. The old man set the fawn on its feet. The medicine woman took the lead and walked with it, skirting the edge of the crowd, displaying the gift for all to see.

The sight of the delicate being capering on spindly legs, with tiny pink hooves dancing on the hard-packed dirt, acted like a stone tossed into still water, sending a ripple of happy wonderment radiating through the crowd. Such a beautiful thing could only bring good luck. The villagers jostled for position and a crop of hands darted out to touch and stroke the fawn's ethereal whiteness as the medicine woman passed by.

Shrouded in their blankets like bats wrapped in their wings, the elders kept aloof from this hubbub. Tom dug into his pouch for the tobacco Duncan had given him back at the camp.

"Wise ones!" The cured tobacco looked like a black snake curled in a figure eight, resting on his open palms. "Share this tobacco when you consider great things and smoke from the same pipe."

The old woman snatched the leathery twist and put it to her nose. She gummed a grin, and the tobacco disappeared inside the folds of her blanket. The elders drew together, nodding and whispering. Tom looked over at Maggie and winked. His gifts had been well received. Everything was going well.

The chief who had accepted the fawn stepped front and center to speak. Tom found it difficult to gauge his age. The elder's silver hair was undressed and flowed in wisps to shoulders hunched with rheumatism. His brown face, like the shell of a walnut, was fissured with deep wrinkles, but his voice carried strong and his eyes shone bright with intelligence.

"I am called Skootekitehi," he announced with much pride. By his name, "Fire Heart," Tom figured the old man must once have been a fierce and determined warrior. "We welcome you, Ghizhi-batoo. You honor our village with fine gifts. We are grateful, but we wonder—what can the Shawano offer the son of the Deer Clan?"

This was his moment. Tom drew a deep breath and threw his arms wide. "Grandfathers and grandmothers! Brothers and sisters!" His voice boomed. "You see before you a man chasing a dream."

"A dream, o-ho!" The open space of the clearing shrank as the throng closed in to hear his words. Heads wagged. Maggie shifted forward with the jabbering crowd. The reaction pleased Tom. He'd hoped the Shawnee would be sympathetic to the notion of a dream quest. Considered to be messages from the Great Spirit, dreams were never taken lightly among the Ojibwe, and extraordinary efforts were regularly expended to make sense of one's dream visions.

"In the awake world," Tom began, his eyes locked with Maggie's, "I knew a woman. She was a very good woman, but I treated her badly." And though he knew she could not fathom a word he said, Maggie seemed to understand nonetheless. She drew a shuddered breath and her bottom lip caught on her teeth. "The hunt called to me, and I left this good woman behind with angry words."

"The hunt . . ." Men nodded in understanding. "Left her behind . . ." Women shook their heads in disgust.

Skootekitehi shot a glance over his shoulder at the old woman who had taken the tobacco and suggested, "Life with a woman can be trying."

"Yes, Grandfather, but equally, life without a woman can be more so. The woman I ill-used now haunts my dreams. Plagued by these visions, I find no rest. I have no appetite for good meat and sugar. No desire for the hunt . . ."

"*Coo-wigh!*" A sharp scream interrupted Tom's speech. Grunted complaints resounded through the crowd as Simon muscled his way to the front lines, pushing and shoving to take a stance at Maggie's side. Tom duly noted the war club gripped in Simon's ready fist.

"*Coo-wigh-wigh-wigh!*" Simon screamed again, his sinister face painted red across the eyes like the mask on a raccoon. Maggie drew her blanket tight, shuffled sideways, and linked arms with the medicine woman holding the fawn on its lead.

Clearly annoyed by Simon's rude interruption, Skootekitehi flicked his fingers. "Go on, Ghizhibatoo . . ."

Tom continued: "I woke with the moon high in the sky and spied the white fawn shining beneath a laurel tree. I rubbed my eyes, thinking myself still in the dreamworld. But I was awake, and when the white fawn ran away, I was compelled to follow its tracks."

A murmur of agreement whiffled around the clearing.

"Of course."

"Anyone would do the same."

"Grandfathers and grandmothers! Brothers and sisters!" Tom threw out his arms. "The white fawn led me here—to your village."

"O-ho!"

"The Long Knife lies!" Simon stepped forward, brandishing his club. "His white-man tongue spreads lies like wind spreads fire."

Tom did not waver. He stood his ground and held his hands out, palms up. "You can see I have come in peace, brother, unarmed—"

"Brother! *Pah!*" Simon spat into the dirt.

"Control yourself, Penagashea," Skootekitehi warned. "Ghizhibatoo has the protection of the elders, and we would hear him speak . . ."

Simon sputtered, "But he lies, Grandfather . . ."

The medicine woman grasped Simon by the arm, scolding, "Show respect, little brother."

"Leave me be, Noolektokie." Simon shrugged free of her grip. "I say he lies!"

Tom played to the audience, his arms outstretched. "The white fawn did not lie to me, for I see my dream-vision woman standing among the Shawano—there!" He pointed to Maggie, whose eyes grew wide in their dark circles.

"No!" Simon snarled. "Ghizhibatoo lies!"

"The white fawn does not lie," someone shouted from the crowd.

Simon protested. "No! Mag-kie is my woman. I saved her!"

"Penagashea . . ." Noolektokie tried to reason with her brother. "The white fawn showed him the way . . ."

"Listen to what the fawn tells us!" a woman called out.

"Wise ones!" Tom shouted above the uproar. "Let me have my dream-vision woman!"

"*No!* Mag-kie belongs to *me!*" Simon grabbed Maggie by the arm.

Maggie jerked away, stumbling backward.

With one hand, Noolektokie hung tight to the skittish fawn's lead; she laid the other on Simon's shoulder. "Little brother, Ghizhibatoo was brought here by the white fawn."

With a growl, Simon tossed his war club away and shoved his sister aside. Maggie moved back, pressing into the burgeoning crowd. Tom rushed forward.

Catching the sun for an instant, bright steel flashed from Simon's sheath—and in the same instant, Simon drew his sharp blade across the fawn's white, white throat.

In the silence of stunned dismay, Tom grappled with Simon, wrested the knife from his fist, and flung it aside. Others stepped up to separate the pair. Struggling, Simon was restrained in a grip between two big warriors.

The fawn staggered a few steps, then collapsed into a broken pile. Noolektokie dropped to her knees beside it, tears streaming down her face as she stroked the baby's brow. Blood pulsed from the gaping wound, pooling into a scarlet mirror around its head. Pink eyes fluttered to close.

Many amid the uneasy crowd clutched amulets for protection against the bad medicine of seeing such a thing. The elders gathered to stand over the dead fawn. Skootekitehi shook his head. He turned his back on Simon and faced Tom.

"Ghizhibatoo of the Anishnaabe—you have honored us and behaved as a true human being. Take your dream-woman, and may the Great Spirit direct your way."

Simon heaved himself forward like a spitting snake. His guards held firm. He calmed, and a malevolent smile crossed his face. In English he shouted, "The day will come soon when I find you in my sights, Tom Roberts!"

Tom turned and, in English, calmly replied, "And I'll be waiting for you. Grease it, paint it—no matter—that white skin of yours makes a good mark to shoot at."

"Let's go"—Maggie's fingers wrapped his wrist—"afore the heathens change their minds."

Tom caught Skootekitehi's eye and called out, "Thank you, Grandfather!"

The old chief drew himself tall and swept one arm up to the sky, shooing them on their way. The crowd parted like prairie grass in a high wind. Tom clasped Maggie's hand in his, and together, they ran for the woods.

25

The Warrior's Path

Tom held tight to Maggie's hand as they ran into the forest. They flew past the pawpaw trees, past the stand of black cohosh flowers, darting between elm, oak, and maple, running deep into the dense woods until even the faint deer track they followed disappeared. And just when Maggie's legs began to falter and she thought her burning lungs would burst, Tom careened to a halt at the base of a huge, ancient chestnut.

Panting, he fell to his knees at the north side of a tree so large it would take four men with arms outstretched to circle its girth. He pawed through the pile of chestnut leaves and revealed a makeshift stone wall blocking the vertical hollow formed where a thick root curved up to meet the trunk. Tom tossed the rocks aside, reached inside, and pulled out his cached gear—a worn pair of moccasins, a bundle of clothes, rifle, knife, tomahawk, and a rectangular rawhide parfleche.

Maggie leaned forward, gulping air, her hands on her knees, black braids swinging like twin pendulums. "Och, Tommy . . ." she gasped, "but aren't ye a sight for sore eyes!" She laughed in relief. "A madman ye are—steppin' willing into that nest o' vipers—a madman!"

"I do have a knowance of Indian ways." Tom chuckled; hopping on one foot, then the other, he tugged on his doeskin leggings. "Worded in the proper fashion, accompanied by the proper gifts . . . 'twere no great peril." He led the legging strings along his hip and tied them to the belt of his breechclout.

"No, Tom. There *is* peril in that village," Maggie insisted, her voice suddenly tense, her shoulders stiff. "They killed a man last night. Tortured him." She sank back to lean against the tree with her hands to her ears. "And then, when I saw ye standin' there beside his scorched bones . . ." She shuddered. "I've no th' words to thank ye for comin' for me."

Tom rolled onto his seat and tugged on his moccasins. Springing up, he unfurled his faded blue hunting shirt with a snap, pushed his arms into the sleeves. He checked the back trail over his shoulder. "It doesn't seem like anyone's after us, but we ought to get a move on nonetheless."

Maggie nodded, sponging sweat from her face with the hem of her loose calico blouse. "Keep movin', aye—that Simon—he'll be after us for certain, na?"

"I looked the man square in the eye, Maggie, and there's somethin' dead up that stream." Tom dove inside his shirt and popped his head through the neck hole. "I plan to lay many a mile betwixt him and us . . ." He buckled a wide leather belt over his shirt and shoved the handle of his tomahawk into it, seating it firm. "I'm tellin' true when I say I don't intend to lose you again."

"Lose me!" Maggie drew a stuttered breath, pressed back against the chestnut, bitter wariness furrowing her brow. "I was never lost to you, Tom."

Tom abruptly ceased his practical scrambling and pure remorse filled his blue eyes. "I was a fool to have left you behind." He stepped forward and took Maggie by the hand. "Believe me, I've been plain miserable—wanderin' lost since the day we parted." He pulled her close and buried his face in the slope where her shoulder met her neck, whispering rough into her ear, "But now, Maggie—now with thee in my arms—I am found."

Maggie twined her arms tight about his waist and breathed deep. The smell of him—a fusion of sweat, gunpowder, leather, and crushed leaves—soothed the raw patches scraped onto her soul. She pressed palms to Tom's broad shoulders, calmed by the subtle motion of muscles moving over his bones. "Aye . . . so we're both found."

In an awkward, halting movement, they met in a soft kiss. Maggie dipped her head, placed an ear to his chest, and smiled at the sound of his heart thrum-thrumming in unison with her own.

The treetops churned on a breeze and a scatter of yellow leaves trickled down around them. Ripe chestnut burs loosened and bounced rattling through the branches, thudding into the soft forest floor. One thunked off the top of Tom's head.

"Ouch!" Tom pulled away, rubbing his noggin. He picked up the bristly bur and laughed. "I guess Grandfather Chestnut's urgin' us t' get a move on." Tom scrambled to shoulder his shot pouch and powder horn. He pulled the plug on his horn to check the condition of his powder. "Ah-yep, as dry as a nun's—" Tom caught Maggie's eye and grinned without finishing the sentiment. "C'mon, then . . . you carry this." He handed the parfleche to Maggie.

She flipped open the flap on the stiff leather case. About two dozen strips of venison jerky kept company with a handful of dried apple slices and a small sack of parched corn. Maggie slipped the braided jute strap over her head to lie diagonal across her chest, positioning the parfleche to rest on her hip. "So where're we headin'?"

"I've a raft in the weeds a few miles downriver. We'll pole down the Scioto and cross the Ohio. We're afoot from then on—following the Warrior's Path to the Gap." Tom dug through his pouch and found his red garters. "I'm not goin' t' scrub around it, Maggie. I am no faint heart, but I do not relish travel-in' with my back to Peavey's rifle. So it's goin' to be a hard go from before daybreak to past nightfall." Tom pointed to her feet. "Best tighten the wangs on your footwear."

Maggie nodded and dropped down to secure the laces of her moccasins with a double knot. Tom knelt on one knee beside her, tying finger-woven garters below each of his knees. He stood and slipped the blade end of his hunting knife into the garter on his right leg.

"If we're clever and careful, Simon won't be able to find us. Once we cross the mountains, he won't know where t' find us." Tom took up his rifle. He flipped open the frizzen and blew the prime from the pan. "We'll be cold-campin'—no fire, no hunting." He tapped fresh black powder granules into the pan, flipped it shut, and nodded to the parfleche she carried. "What you carry there and what we can forage along the way is all the provision we have." He slipped the strap of his rifle over his shoulder and set his wide-brimmed hat on his head.

"I'll take a few o' these chestnuts." Maggie gathered up the half-dozen burs lying in the leaves around her, stuffing them into her pockets. "They're best roasted, but not so bad raw. Pawpaws are ripe as well. We'll do all right."

Tom offered his hand and pulled her to stand. He peeled away a sweaty curl pasted to her cheek and tucked it behind her ear. "Thee must know this—I mean to share a large portion of thy life, Maggie Duncan."

"Aye, lad." Maggie smiled at his slip into the Quaker-speak. "Yer my man, an' I'm yer woman." She reached up on tiptoes and kissed him quick on the lips.

"Good." Tom squeezed her hand. "Then let's away."

Noolektokie decided to cure the hide with the hair on and tiny tail intact—to remind the Shawano of the fawn's pure-white beauty, and to prove to future generations that they had indeed been blessed by the presence of such a magical being.

She spread the flayed fawn skin on the ground and cut a measured series of small slits around its perimeter. Using buckskin thong, she laced the skin through the slits and around a sturdy pole frame, stretching the hide taut and even, the line of the spine true to center. Noolektokie leaned the prepared frame against a large oak. Normally when working hides, she would sit with other women and they would chitter like gray squirrels about children, husbands, and recipes. Today, none of the other women joined her.

She sank down to sit cross-legged before the frame and pulled her medicine bag onto her lap. The elders had enjoined her to this task and the responsibility weighed heavy upon her shoulders. In preserving the white fawn skin, she hoped to undo some of the damage her brother had wrought.

Her tools were arranged in a row on her right—a toothed bone scraper for fleshing the hide, the fawn's severed head with its cranial cap removed and oily brains exposed, a smooth bevel-ended hickory stick for working the brain solution into the skin, a palm-size pumice stone for a final scouring after the skin'd dried, and embers she'd culled from her fire, glowing in a small clay pot.

She placed the clay pot before the framed skin. From her medicine bag she produced a small leather envelope filled with a handful of tobacco crumblings. She sprinkled a generous pinch onto the embers and fanned the acrid smoke to billow up. Noolektokie pushed the smoke with cupped palms, up to the evening sky.

"Spirit of the White Fawn—I call upon thee. Grant me the skill to honor thy beauty."

Laying her scraper at center, she leaned in and scraped a curl of fat and flesh from the skin. Intent on her task, she did not hear old Skootekitehi come upon her, and she startled when he spoke.

"Payakootha has approved. Your brother will join with your man, Waythea, in a war party heading over the mountains to raid on the Long Knives. They will travel the Warrior's Path."

"My brother seeks to possess what cannot be possessed." Noolektokie shrugged and shook her head. "Whatever happens—even if he kills Ghizhibatoo and makes Mag-kie his woman—Panagashea will not succeed."

The old man nodded. "Waythea makes ready to leave. He asked for you."

"Please tell Waythea I will be along, Grandfather."

Noolektokie drizzled a gourd of water over the skin to keep it moist. Before leaving to bid farewell to her husband, she tossed what was left of the tobacco onto the embers and closed her eyes. The smoke floated up toward the heavens and she whispered one more prayer.

Connor added a stick of deadfall to the growing pile in Figg's outstretched arms. He jerked his thumb and said, "Would ye take a look at that preening peacock . . ."

Some twenty yards off, the viscount stood alongside the creek in the small clearing where they'd set up camp for the night. He wore a faux-military coat—a bright red wool affair trimmed with official-looking gold braid and regimental lace. Two silver-bound pistols jutted from the blue satin sash belted at his waist. Since the day they'd left Roundabout, he had taken to wearing an elaborate small sword, a light but deadly thrusting weapon. With one booted foot propped on a rock, he angled a mahogany-framed mirror to the light of the setting sun, contemplating his reflection.

Connor snickered and piled more wood onto Figg's burden. "All th' glass-gazin' in the world'll never change the fact that he's a fuckin' ugly bastard, fancy red coat or no."

The viscount's wounds had healed rudely. The *R* carved onto his forehead festered angry red and oozed putrid matter around the edges of the scab. Frayed stitches holding the raw edges of his nostril together seemed to strain with swelling that would not abate. Overall, he exhibited an unhealthy pallor, his eyes gone so yellow with jaundice as to look like a pair of piss holes in the snow.

"Glass-gazin'," Connor snorted. "Him with a face like a plateful of mortal sin . . ."

Figg chortled, "Like it caught fire, and been put out with a spade."

Connor slapped his knee. "Good one, Figgy."

The viscount set the mirror aside and called out, "Will you two lackwits hurry along? There's a plaguey chill in the air . . ."

"Aye, m'lord." The little Irishman smiled, waved, and wandered farther away. He found a nice long branch, braced a foot to it, and cracked the length into sections small enough to carry. "Hurry, the bastard says. D'ye think he might deign t' lift a finger and help us see to the camp?"

Figg shagged his massive head negative as his brother continued to rant.

"Not him. If work were a bed, yer lordship there would sleep on the floor." Connor struck a foppish pose with wrist limp, and mimicked, "'Gather four of the best men'—what a load o' shite! As if anyone's fool enough to follow that utter arsehead into Indian territory."

After a moment's reflection, Figg noted, "We followed him—you an' me . . . an' Crab . . . an' there was them two slaves afore they run off . . ."

"Brilliant, those two. They knew well enough to flee a sinking ship."

After only two nights in the wild, the Negroes they'd brought along as porters disappeared with most of the meal, parched corn, and dried meat. Worst of all, with the slaves gone, all the hard work fell square upon Connor and Figg.

"Crab's still aboard the sinkin' ship wi' us . . ." Figg offered with some optimism.

"Crab's a drunken sot. You and me—we're fools." Connor shrugged his bony shoulders. "C'mon, let's get a fire goin' and hope Crab brings in some meat for our supper."

"Amen t' meat, sez I."

Cavendish's vengeful expedition had been cursed from the onset. He had a hard time convincing any frontiersmen to venture into hostile territory in pursuit of Tom Roberts, who seemed to be held in high esteem among the rough fellows. In the end, offering a goodly amount of silver, Cavendish was able to coerce a single drunken scoundrel to act as their scout.

"Awright . . ." Obediah Crabtree agreed, sealing the bargain by hawking up a glob of tobacco-tinged mucus to splat in the dirt. "I can take yiz as far as Peavey's village on the Scioto, but there's where we part company. I hold no quarrel with Tom Roberts, and I've lived this long avoidin' Injuns wherever possible."

True to his word, Crabtree led them through the wild woodlands cloaking the Blue Ridge, through the mountain pass into the country called *Kenta-ke*. They traveled up toward the Scioto River by way of an ancient trail known as the Warrior's Path.

The viscount did not travel light. Two packhorses were required to haul his luxurious accoutrements. As his lordship could not be expected to sleep without shelter, or on the ground, Connor and Figg set up a canvas tent and a camp bed complete with feather mattress and pillow every night. Conspicuous among the furnishings and extensive wardrobe the viscount insisted on traveling with were no fewer than two ten-gallon casks of French brandy.

Figg dumped the wood next to the circle of stones they'd prepared as a hearth for their fire. Cavendish shed his weapons and jacket, unfolded his canvas camp chair, and planted it next to the fire ring. He authorized Figg to decant two bottles of brandy—one for himself, and one for the men to share. Connor found his tinderbox and set to kindling a fire.

"Ho! The camp!" Obediah Crabtree shouted. Their guide slipped out from a tangle of mountain laurel with a tom turkey slung over his shoulder. Connor grinned. He had to concede—Crab had yet to fail in providing for their supper.

A narrow, loose-knit man, Crab shambled toward them dressed in dirty, droopy buckskin from head to toe—shirt, clout, and fringed leggings. His gaunt cheeks were covered with a patchy dark stubble. A wild ridge of bushy brows shadowed deep-set eyes. Hatless, he had taken to wearing a sweat- and salt-stained scrap of linsey tied gypsy style around his balding pate.

"Well done, Crabby!" Figg licked his lips. "Amen t' turkey bird, sez I."

"Picked a bunch of custard apples." Crab's possibles pouch bulged with yellow fruit.

"Make haste with supper, sir," Cavendish ordered. "The stomach worm gnaws."

"Aye aye, Cap'n." Crab rolled his eyes at Connor, and the two of them exchanged an amused glance. The hunter set to work, briskly plucking feathers. Connor kindled a good-size blaze. Crab had the bird eviscerated and roasting on a spit just as the stars began to pop onto the sky.

Connor, Crab, and Figg sat on the ground in a semicircle on one side of the fire, taking turns tending the meat, the fire, and their brandy. On the other side, perched in his chair, Cavendish sat in sullen silence, sipping Armagnac straight from the bottle, glaring at the flames.

"Ye keep a fine supply, Cap'n, an' that's of some import." Crab saluted the viscount and took a swig of brandy. "I'll tell ye boys, once, when I was out hunting buffeler with Ned Hatch, we'd badly misjudged our supply and run through all our rum premature like."

"Misjudged!" Connor derided, snatching the bottle away from him. "Drunken sot."

"Hard work—butcherin' wild beef." Crab dug a finger under the kerchief on his head for a scratch. "Yep, we were desperate for drink, so we did like the Injuns do, and took t' sucking the water and sludge from the butchered buffeler guts."

"If that isn' the most disgustin' . . ." Connor shuddered.

"'S truth. 'Tweren't anywhere near as fine as this Frenchy swill. Fermented grass mostly." Crab plucked something from behind his ear, examined it for a moment before flicking it into the fire. "It tasted kinda like ale what'd turned—but it served to make us drunk, and that was all we cared for." The skin on the bird crisped golden, and when Crab pierced it with his knife, the juices ran clear.

"Ho! The camp!" A shout resounded from the murky tangle to the north.

Crab was the first to his feet. Gun in hand, he squinted, then waved. "Ho! Macauley!"

Smiling, Hamish Macauley entered the circle of light cast by the campfire. "Followed the smell of meat a-roastin' and happily spied th' yellow of yer fire."

The Scotsman and Crab exchanged slaps on the back. The viscount bounded to his feet, brandishing his bottle. "Recreant! *Judas!* How dare you exhibit your face in my presence . . ."

"Now, tha's a fine way t' greet the man what saved yer life oncet." Hamish slipped his gear from his shoulders.

The viscount blustered. *"Saved my life?!* 'Twas *you* who admitted that madman into my demesne—*you* who allowed the blackguard to escape, and *you* who ran off, leaving me sore wounded and in desperate straits."

"Och, quit yer bellyachin'." The big Scotsman plunked himself down and settled comfortable betwixt Crab and Figg. "Considerin' the way ye blethered on t' Tom aboot how ye bent his woman o'er yer writin' table t' ravish, yer lucky t' have gotten by with those paltry cuts an' bruises." Hamish snapped a turkey leg from the carcass. "Ye might recollect, Tom meant t' kill ye. Had his barrel t' yer throat he did. Saved yer royal hide, I did, calming his head and hand."

Cavendish sighed, fell back into his chair, and took a deep swallow from his bottle.

"The midwife is *Roberts's wòman*?" Connor sputtered. "This . . ." He fluttered his hands through the air. "This is all on account of that Scots whore?"

"Yer lordship's manly boasts put Tom over the edge." Hamish

tore a bite from the drumstick. Bits of meat and spittle flew from his mouth as he spoke. "Tom's mad for the lass, ye ken? Why, he paid thirty silver dollars for her lunch basket at the gather-all."

"Thirty dollars!" Crab whistled. "Tom must love th' gal."

"Tom Roberts shall pay dearly for the damage he has wrought unto me." Cavendish drew his knife, leaned in, and sliced a chunk of meat from the bone.

Hamish swiped grease from his chin on his sleeve. "So yer after him now, eh?" The big Scotsman waved the half-eaten drumstick at Cavendish's face. "Revenge on him for carvin' on yer pretty face, na?"

Cavendish smiled and toasted with his bottle. "To quote the Bard, 'Cry havoc and let slip the dogs of war.'"

Connor shook his head in disbelief. Crab tossed a custard apple into his lap. Figg tore off the remaining turkey leg and bit into it.

Hamish gnawed on the knob end of the turkey bone. "Did yiz happen hear how Bouquet routed the Indians at Fort Pitt? The heathens took an awful drubbing at the hands of the Black Watch."

"Huzzah the Crown!" Cavendish toasted with mock enthusiasm.

"Aye, well, Bouquet's victory has served t' stir the hornet's nest," Hamish continued. "War parties—Seneca, Mingo, Shawnee, and more—are raidin' up and down this frontier."

"War parties!" Connor yelped.

"Aye. Best turn tail and head back t' Roundabout. Fort up. Yiz dinna want t' risk being captured." Hamish bit into a custard apple.

"Being captured by them devils is the worst," Crab joined in. "You know, boys, the Catawba had me once, but I escaped afore they had a chance to black my face."

"Black yer face!" Connor squeaked.

Hamish shook his head. "Och, yer no long for this world once th' buggers paint ye black . . ."

"They torture them what's painted black in the most heinous fashion," Crab said. "Remember Joe Sweeney?"

"Poor Joe!" Hamish tsked.

"What happened to him?" Connor asked.

"He was captured by the Shawnee . . ."

"Na, 'twere Cherokee," Hamish argued. "After stripping him naked, they cut th' lad—just a wee slit in his side—fished out one end of his small gut and nailed it to a tree." Hamish shifted position, the flames shining in his blue eyes. "Then the squaws took over . . ."

"Them she-devils are worse than the men. Vicious."

"Aye. They pecked away at poor Joe's bits with sharp sticks—poked and prodding him with burning brands to walk 'round and 'round that tree for hours, winding and unwinding his entrails until at last they tired of it all, and set him aflame."

"M-m'lord, did ye hear?" Connor stuttered. "I-I think we ought turn back—"

"Pay no heed to the Scotsman, Mr. Connor." Cavendish leaned back and crossed one booted leg to dangle over the other. "Clearly, Macauley is in league with Roberts, and has sought us out to dissuade us from our mission. Clever ploy."

Hamish raised his hand open-palmed. "I swear—my every word's the truth."

Connor pleaded, "But if he *is* tellin' the truth, then—"

Cavendish interrupted. "I had thought better of you, Mr. Connor. Indians on the warpath indeed." He sneered. "Consider the Scotsman's tale naught but a ghost story for the campfire."

"Them Injuns ain't no ghost story," Crab added. "Ye have Mac's word on it."

"Pish-posh," Cavendish scoffed with a dismissive wave of his hand.

"Well, no one can say I didna try t' warn yiz." Hamish sucked the last bits of gristle from the leg bone, flipped it into the flames, and rose to his feet. "'Tis no skin off'n my arse one way or t' other. I thank ye fer sharin' fire, supper, and spirits wi' me."

"Where ye headin', Mac?" Crab rose to his feet.

Hamish shouldered his bedroll, pouch, and weapon. "South— as quick as m' legs can get me there." The two frontiersmen shook hands. "Keep a weather eye open, Obediah, and fare well."

Connor woke at the peep of day. He sat upright, stretched limbs stiff with the morning damp, and clutched the warm woolen blanket around his shoulders. To his right, Figg hunkered over the fire ring with a stick, stirring the smoky ashes in search of live coals. To his left, the spot where Crab had curled up for the night lay empty.

"Crab gone hunting?"

Figg shook his head. "Crab's gone."

"Hunting?"

"Just gone."

Connor blinked, then scrambled to his feet. "Don't tell me th' bugger's took off—"

"Aye . . ." Figg carefully tented the handful of live coals he'd raked up with an arrangement of small twigs and cattail fuzz. "Too fond of his hair, sez he, t' have it swing from some Injun lodge pole."

Connor groaned, and fell to his knees.

Figg puckered thick lips and blew the coals to flame.

26

A Melodious Duel

Ee-o-lay!

Tom jerked awake and sat up. He pawed the dim shadows to his right until he laid his hand upon his tomahawk, the blade half buried and haft jutting up at an angle within easy reach.

Ee-o-lay! Ee-o-lay-o!

A wood thrush—its liquid call trilled from the treetops. Tom heaved a sigh and dropped the tomahawk. He turned and traced his fingertips over the dark mound to his left. Maggie lay warm beside him, curled like a fiddlehead fern, with knees hunched to her chest. He rolled onto his side and slid an arm around her. Shifting hip and shoulder, Tom drew his woman close and they sank deep into the pile of duff they slept upon—a bed of soft loam and decaying debris scraped up from the forest floor.

"Wake up, darling girl," he whispered, wrapping tight to her form, the curve of her spine pressing against his stomach and chest.

"Mmm—yer warm . . ." Maggie sighed, and pressed back.

Tom grunted and shoved at the hard edge poking painful under his shoulder blade—the rifle he'd tucked up against his back the night before. Not the most comfortable way to spend the night, but body heat helped to keep the powder charge dry. He rested his hand in the dip at Maggie's waist and gave her a little shake. "Time t' wake, laze-a-bed." Frizzy hairs escaping her sleep-tousled braids tickled his lips.

"Mm-hmm . . ." Maggie agreed, but she didn't budge.

He twirled a finger around her ear.

She swatted at his hand. "I'm so tired . . ."

Tom believed she was tired. While poling their raft down the gentle Scioto the day before, Maggie had recounted all that'd happened since that day he'd left—Naomi's illness and death, Seth's deal with the viscount, rape, bone setting—ending her horrific narrative by lifting the hem of her blouse to show him the scabby raw stripes crisscrossing her back.

They had traversed over fifty river miles on the Scioto, and reached the confluence at the Ohio by noon. Tom dismantled the raft and sent the bits and pieces down the river. They hiked due south till well past dusk. Maggie endured without complaint, but she was much weakened by her latest bout with fever. Tom slowed the pace, stopping often to let her rest, and they did not advance with the speed he'd expected.

Once the moon had reached its zenith, he led Maggie a hard turn off the Warrior's Path. They climbed up to a ridge running parallel to the trail and Tom found a cozy level spot between a large boulder and a stout log. Maggie raked up their bedding and Tom spanned the narrow space with pine boughs to form a small cave of sorts. They crawled in cold and exhausted, falling asleep nestled like two squirrels in a tree hole.

Ee-o-lay! Ee-o-lay-o!

The wood thrush continued to urge them to rise. Tom cupped Maggie's shoulder, and could feel the whip scars through the thin calico of her blouse. His head suddenly buzzed with a combination of severe guilt and pure hatred for Julian Cavendish.

Tom had promised Maggie he would let no harm come to her, and then he turned his back on that promise. If he had heeded

Maggie's wish, and purchased her indenture from Seth, she would never have suffered under the viscount's lash. He dipped his nose to Maggie's hair, breathing deep to allay the conflagration ignited in his chest. Maggie may have forgiven him, but Tom would never forgive himself.

"C'mon, Maggie." He gave her a gentle nudge. "We've got to get goin'."

"Just a few winks more . . ." Maggie begged, drawing his hand back around her waist.

"No. We have t' get up *now*." Peeling away, he severed the bond of shared body heat and crawled out, dragging his gun with him. Maggie whimpered like a puppy and rolled into the warm depression he'd abandoned.

Tom stretched his limbs, rolled his neck, and scrubbed the sleep from his eyes. The waxing moon hung low in the west and the faintest blush of rising sun colored the east. The treetops presented a mottled silhouette against a sky saturated in teal blue. A second thrush joined the first and the pair of songbirds rustled through hemlock leaves, leaping from branch to branch, engaged in a pleasant, melodious duel.

Fog swirled between the trees, leaving the woodland coated in a twinkling of dew. Tom leaned his rifle against the boulder, marched a dozen steps, and loosened the front flap on his breechclout. He took a wide stance at the ridge edge, pushed the fabric aside, took aim, and arched his stream out over the cliff. A thinning mist clung in patches to the treetops, hugging the valley below, but the sky was clear and it looked to be a fair-weather day. He bounced on the balls of his feet, shaking off the last few drops before tucking back and readjusting his clout.

On hands and knees at the opening of their bower, Tom retrieved his gear. "C'mon, Maggie." He pinched the toe of her moccasined foot. "You have t' wake up."

Maggie sat up, yawning. "Seems as if I only just shut my eyes . . ."

Tom sat on the ground. He shoved his tomahawk into his belt and secured his knife to his calf. Maggie scooted out on her rear end from under the pine boughs to sit next to him. She dug into the parfleche. "Hungry?"

Tom shook his head and pulled his rifle onto his lap. "I'll eat on the trail. We need to get a good piece under us today. No tellin' how long afore Simon's trackin' our steps." He untied the soft leather cuff protecting the lock and trigger mechanism, flipped open the frizzen, and wiped the prime out of the pan.

Maggie nibbled on an apple ring. "Yer aye fiddlin' with yer gun."

"Damp can creep in and cause plenty of trouble." Tom dug into his pouch for a tin of tallow. He coated the pan with a thin layer of grease, laying in a thick bead of fat along the edge. He tapped the correct ration of black powder into the pan and snapped it shut. "And we're campin' without fire to boot—I don't want to chance my powder being wet."

"It's truly a hardship—no fire." Maggie shivered and moved closer. "Right now I'd trade my soul to Ol' Scratch for a cup of hot tea and one of Ada's raisin scones." She pulled her legs under her skirt and nuzzled up against his back. "So nice an' warm ye are—cast off heat like a Dutch stove, ye do."

Tom examined the flint caught tight in the jaws. A dull flint would not strike a reliable spark. He ran his thumbnail across its edge, shaving off a curl of fingernail in the process, satisfied with the sharpness.

Maggie pointed to a little red feather jutting out from the side of the lock. "What's that pretty there? A good-luck charm?"

"Naw—that's my plug for the touchhole to keep the damp from seepin' into the barrel." He removed the feather and slipped it inside his moccasin.

"This damp surely seeps into th' bones, na?" Maggie rose to her feet with arms crossed over her chest and rubbed her arms briskly, shifting from one foot to the other. "I'm goin' t' find a bush. I'll be back in a tic, aye?"

"Tend to your business and then we're off."

Tom found a rag inside his pouch and wiped the barrel and stock. Paying special attention to the intricacies of the lock, he checked for rust. His biggest concern was for that which he could not see—the condition of the powder charge packed down the barrel. He'd gone two days without firing his weapon, and with every passing day, the chances of misfire increased tenfold. Tom looked up at the brightening sky.

Later today, after we get a few miles under us . . . With better light, he would take the time to dismount the barrel from the breech, push out the charge, and reload with fresh powder.

Maggie scurried back. "Tom!" she whispered loud. "Hoy, Tommy . . ." she called to him with a frantic wave. "Here. Come here. *Quick.*"

He followed after her, past a copse of scrub pine to a rocky promontory sporting a fine view of the valley below. Maggie pointed down to an opening in the trees, a canebrake, maybe five miles distant. "Look there," she said. "D'ye see 'em?"

Tom did—a double file of Indian warriors moving along the trail at the quickstep. "That close," he muttered.

"D'ye think it's Simon?"

"C'mon." He grabbed Maggie by the arm and pushed her along, stopping only to gather pouch, powder, and parfleche. They scrambled down the steep hillside, sending a scatter of scree and debris skittering along with them. Tom glanced back with regret at the clear sign they left for anyone bothering to course their trail.

Maggie saw it, too. "They're bound to catch us."

"To the creek." Tom pulled her along. "We'll travel the creek—confuse the sign . . ."

"Aye? Ye think we can outrun them?"

"We will outfox 'em." Tom stopped cold and sniffed the air. "D'you smell that?"

Maggie turned upwind and drew a breath. "Smoke?"

He nodded; both hands on his rifle, he pulled the hammer back to full cock, crouched a bit, and moved a few steps forward. He stopped and smelled the air again.

Maggie tugged at his shirttail. "Indians?"

Tom walked slow, sniffing again. "Horses and . . . bones . . . burned bones . . ."

In the distance a gunshot boomed, sending a racket of birds flapping into the sky.

"Megstie me!" Maggie yanked on Tom's shirt so hard it choked him around the neck.

Tom shook Maggie off and watched the birds fly away. Deep furrows lined his brow. He moved in the direction of the blast, muttering, "Pistol fire?"

Clinging to his shirttail like a bur on a long-haired dog, Maggie followed close behind. "What is it, Tommy?"

"Shhh!" He cocked his head.

Clear as a bell, the high-pitched whinny of skittish horses reached their ears. Tom turned and met her with hard blue eyes, both hands on his rifle in a white-knuckled grip. "Promise thee will do exactly as I say. Promise?"

"Let's just go." Maggie pulled on his shirttail. "Away t' th' creek . . . like ye said . . ."

"Promise me—exactly as I say."

"Aye." Maggie nodded. "I promise."

He motioned with a jerk of his head and she followed him. They left the trail and wove a path through a thick tangle of mountain laurel, crouching and dodging to avoid hitting their heads on limbs and branches. Soon they could hear voices. Tom fell to his belly in the dirt and motioned for Maggie to do likewise. They shimmied forward like snakes and peered through dense foliage into a clearing in the wood.

A sharp breeze cut a windblown path through the foot-long grass carpeting the clearing. About thirty yards off, a thin stream of smoke twisted up from a ring of stones, painting a dark gray line on the sky. Staked near the creek, a white canvas tent fluttered on the morning breeze, and an agitated pair of brown horses snorted and stamped next to a large pile of goods. A small, babbling man together with a bearlike, silent man stood with hands raised over their heads.

And near them, with lank hair unbound, disheveled in a red frock coat and stocking feet, stood Cavendish, arm extended, his pistol trained on the odd men. The viscount and the small man exchanged heated words, but Tom could not make out exactly what was being said. "Those two . . ." he asked Maggie. "Are they armed?"

"Th' wee one—Connor he's called. He always carries a brace o' pistols."

"And the big fella?"

"Figg?" She shook her head. "I've never seen him with a gun. He's simple—does as he's told—beat Joe Mulberry t' a pulp when ordered."

"Right." Tom began to rise to his feet.

Maggie grabbed him by the shirtsleeve, her dark brows tilted with anxiety. "Dinna bother with tha' lot. Let's away while we've th' chance!"

Tom shook his head. "We need those horses."

"But the Shawnee . . ." She dug her fingers under the muscles of his arm. "Simon—he must've heard the shot . . ."

"And sees the smoke as well. We *really* need those horses." Tom pried her hand away. "I know what I'm about, Maggie. Stay right here. Understand? Don't budge."

A small squeak sounded from the back of her throat. She blinked tearful eyes and nodded. Tom scrambled to his feet and entered the clearing. So fully occupied by their own drama, the threesome at the end of the field took no notice of him. Tom braced his rifle to his shoulder and called, "CAVENDISH!"

The viscount turned. His quizzical squint widened to round

eyes and raised brows, serving to squash the sanguine *R* carved on his forehead illegible.

Tom's finger crooked over the trigger. "I'll have those horses or your head blown off!"

A smile crept across the viscount's face. He leveled his pistol at Tom and shouted, "I have a grievance with you, sir!"

"And I have you in my sights. Throw down. Have your man Connor there bring those horses to me now."

Cavendish answered by steadying his aim with a hand supporting his wrist and both men triggered their weapons in the exact same instant.

Tom's rifle ignited with a puff and a bright flash in the pan, but the charge did not fire.

Cavendish's pistol boomed. A cloud of sulfurous smoke bellowed up and a lead ball whizzed across the field to thud into Tom's flesh.

It was as if a huge invisible mallet had swung down from the heavens and slammed hard into his left shoulder. Tom spun back. His rifle jerked from his hands. The blow staggered him back several paces. He struggled to maintain a stance and capture a breath.

The horses screamed and bolted.

Maggie cried out, *"Tom!"*

Cavendish glared across the field; his chest rose and fell in a great huff of exasperation. He turned in to his tent, the spent pistol in his hand trailing a white plume.

Connor tore off hollering, "C'mon Figg, c'mon!" as he chased after the spooked horses.

Figg stood rooted with arms still up in the air, his big head roving from side to side, following the crazed horses and Connor zigzagging across the field.

Tom took a deep breath and formed a fist, clenching his left hand so tight, jagged fingernails bit into his palm. He bent his elbow, tugged open the rent in his shirtsleeve, and picked at scarlet-imbued shreds of linsey embedded into the raw wound. Blood bubbled from a neat round hole in his biceps and trickled rivulets to his elbow. Reaching around, he fingered ragged skin and sticky ooze on the back side of his arm. An exit wound. The ball had passed through the flesh, only grazing the bone.

Cavendish emerged from his tent with a powder flask, eyes hooded in concentration as he tapped the requisite grains into the priming pan.

In a heartbeat, Tom gauged the span between them and judged the speed of his foe's reloading. He broke into a trot.

Cavendish sifted a measure of powder down the barrel. He looked up, squinting. Surprise combined with annoyance to distort the ruddy *R* anew. He hurried to thumb ball and greased patch into the muzzle.

Tom picked up speed as he moved upfield. He slipped the tomahawk from his belt, the weight of the iron ax in his right hand, a comforting counterbalance to the throbbing heaviness settling in his left. Throwing a kick in his gallop, he broke into a full-on, stretch-legged sprint.

The viscount struggled to pry the ramrod from its place beneath the barrel, eyes ricocheting from his task—to Tom closing the gap—back to his pistol—then back to Tom charging across the field.

Fingers fumbled. The ramrod tumbled free—lost in the tall grass. Cavendish fell to his knees, slapping the ground with a hysteric flat hand. Locating the ramrod, he leaped to his feet, seating the ball firm to the powder with one stroke. He raised his weapon, taking aim at the man barreling toward him, and pulled back on the hammer.

Bearing down at full speed, Tom slammed head and shoulder into the viscount and sent him sprawling. The pistol flew into the air, spinning end over end, disappearing with a thump in the grass. The momentum of the charge carried Tom paces beyond Cavendish.

The viscount scrambled to stand, and with Tom right on his heels, he hastened to the fire ring to snatch up the scabbard strung over the camp chair. His sword zinged out. Tom's tomahawk swung a wide arc. Cavendish parried the blow.

Edged weapons met in a clack and tangle of tempered steel and hickory wood. Locked in struggle, each man pressed forth straining, faces mere inches apart. Tom's eyes met with a pair yellowed and dull. Stitches gummy with pus held the viscount's festering nose in one piece, and the scabrous *R* on his forehead cracked and seeped matter. Cavendish was fueled by a deep-seated thirst for vengeance, and Tom could feel his own strength waning, draining from the hole in his arm.

Cavendish hissed through clenched teeth, "Sing a psalm, good sir, for after I dispatch you in handsome style, I mean to fuck your whore atop your rotting corpse."

Twisting and working the curved head of the tomahawk down the sword, Tom hooked on to the ornate hilt. With one hard jerk, he flung the viscount's weapon aside.

Mouth agape, Cavendish stared at his empty hand, fingers twitching.

Tom flipped the tomahawk into his left fist and unsheathed his hunting knife with his right hand. He dipped and spun behind his foe. With a sweeping motion, he sliced through white stocking and taut tendon, meeting gritty resistance as the honed edge bit into the bone just above the viscount's left heel. Like a marionette with a severed string, Cavendish crumpled in a heap.

Maggie came dashing across the field.

Tom leaned in on his knees and gulped for air. His arm buzzed with a sensation akin to being stung repeatedly by a hundred bees.

Shouting "CONNOR!" Cavendish crawled toward the camp chair, dragging his crippled leg, leaving a trail of bright blood on the green grass.

Connor ignored his wounded master. Having succeeded in

maneuvering one of the geldings to a standstill, he grabbed fist-fuls of coarse mane and pulled his spare frame onto the horse's back. With a wave of his hand he shouted, "C'mon, Figgy! We're off!" Wheeling his mount, he splashed across the stream, gallop-ing into the woods beyond.

Figg lowered his massive arms. With brow beetled in confu-sion, his gaze shifted from retreating Connor, to Maggie running toward Tom, to Cavendish struggling to pull himself up onto the camp chair, and back to his brother galloping from sight.

Cavendish plopped into the chair and leveled an order. "*Figg!* Do as I say—thump that man soundly. Thrash him! DO IT NOW!"

Tom had never seen a man grown as large and thick-built as the Goliath lumbering toward him. The girth of the man's chest rivaled that of a fifty-gallon barrel. Each of his upper arms equaled the size of a smoked ham, and his clenched fists were like iron anvils. Tom stood upright. He sheathed his knife, trans-ferred the tomahawk to his good hand, and balanced on the balls of his feet, ready to do battle with a giant.

Maggie ran up and planted herself between the two men, shouting, "No, Figg! *No!*"

Figg lurched to a halt. With a playful wriggling wave of his sau-sage fingers, he grinned gap-toothed and said, "Hoy, Maggie!"

Cavendish groaned. "You great, hulking, leather-headed idiot. Take the man down, Figg! *Take him DOWN!*"

"If any harm comes to this man, Figgy," Maggie warned with an admonishing finger, "I will never again share my teatime sweeties wi' ye—d'ye hear me? *Never!*"

"Awright, Maggie." Figg wagging his ginger head. "I hear ye." As a sheepish aside to Tom, he added, "Maggie makes th' best sweeties, um-hmm . . . amen to teatime, sez I."

Tom heaved a sigh and slipped his tomahawk into his belt. "You best come along with us, big fella. There's a war party coursing this trail." Figg nodded and followed Maggie and Tom to the campfire. Tom picked up Cavendish's spent pistol lying near the tent and stuffed it into his belt. He winced, supporting his left arm as he scoured the grass. "Help me find this pistol's mate."

Maggie fussed at Tom's bloody shirtsleeve. "Och, this wound needs cleanin' and dressin' . . ."

Tom shrugged her off. "No time now—find that gun."

"Here 'tis, mister." Figg came up with the loaded pistol pinched between thumb and forefinger. He held the gun at arm's length, as if it were a spitting snake. Tom added the pistol to his belt and marched to stand before the viscount. Figg and Maggie scurried to follow.

Cavendish sat gasping in his chair. "Think twice on how you mean to handle this situation," he threatened as the threesome approached. "Do not forget, I am a peer of the realm."

"Yer the devil's get," Maggie snapped, "and if ye had a pair, I'd saw yer bollocks off with a dull blade and leave ye t' drip dead."

The viscount looked beyond Maggie and pulled a perfumed kerchief from his sleeve, pressing it to his nose. "Harness your hedge-whore, Roberts, for she fouls the very air I breathe."

In the blink of an eye, Maggie plucked the knife from Tom's calf. "And that'll be th' last breath ye ever take, ye shit-sack . . ."

Tom lunged and caught Maggie around the waist.

Cavendish shrank back. "A peer of the realm, sir! It will not go well for any of you if I am killed . . ."

"Ah, lordship, it's plain you don't quite understand." Smiling, Tom grasped Maggie's fist still clutching the knife and peeled it open, finger by finger. "It's not a matter of 'if'—it's but a matter of *how*."

Maggie released the knife with a sigh.

A musket shot resounded in the distance, casting up a flurry of squawking birds.

Tom slipped his knife into its sheath. He gave Maggie a nudge, signaled Figg with a wave, and the three of them took off jogging toward the trees.

Cavendish sputtered, "Come back here! You cannot mean to leave me behind!"

Maggie tugged Tom by the shirttail. "Yer just goin' t' leave him?"

"He gives off an ill-savour—a coward in a red coat—the Shawnee will not be able to resist such a prize." Tom urged her along with a shove to her shoulder. "Get goin'—*go!* Into the trees." Tom and Maggie spurted ahead. Figg gallumped behind.

"Roberts, please!" the viscount screamed. "I will pay you! Dutch silver . . ." Shrill war cries sounded from the opposite end of the field. Shoulders heaving, Cavendish sobbed, "You cannot leave me here! Figg! *Maggiiee!*"

At the sound of her name, Maggie slowed and glanced over her shoulder.

Cavendish gripped the arms of the chair. *"Mercy! I beg, MERCY!"*

Tom jerked Maggie by the arm and pushed her forward.

"Come on. The longer they tarry with him, the better for us. Now run—*RUN!*"

⚬✦⚬

The Shawnee war party burst into the clearing. Encountering no resistance, they raced across the field, yipping, screaming, and discharging weapons.

Several warriors tore past Cavendish in his chair to dive into the canvas tent, tossing its contents. Others rifled through the camp boxes, finding tobacco, lead, gunpowder, and other valuable accoutrements. They exulted over the portmanteau packed full of clothing. A pair of swift-footed braves chased after the loose horse. Several Indians sounded a celebratory halloo and hoisted two brandy kegs into the air for all to see.

While his boisterous fellows plundered the campsite, Simon Peavey hung back, reconnoitering the field. Following the trampled buffalo grass leading to the campsite, he halted and hunkered to examine a spray of crimson droplets dotting the dew-soaked ground. Three paces beyond, half-hidden in tall grass, he found a spent rifle. Simon rubbed a thumb over the distinctive silver heart inlaid in the polished stock. He pressed the tip of his nose to the lock.

Warm.

He rushed to join Waythea.

The war party leader hovered over the cringing captive, who sat clutching the arms of the same kind of chair the British generals carried with them when they went to war. Waythea issued an order and two braves none too gently hoisted the wailing Englishman to his feet. Simon raised a brow—the man was none other than the Viscount Julian Cavendish, dressed, for some reason like a military officer.

Waythea closed in to inspect the squirming viscount's red coat, fingering the adorning gold braid. He eyed the slit nostril and traced a disdainful finger over the odd scabby mark on the white man's forehead.

"I'm a peer of the realm, sir." Cavendish recoiled with a grimace, crinkling his nose. "My father, the *duke*, will pay a goodly sum for my safe return."

"*Anglais.*" Waythea spat out the word.

Cavendish brightened. "*Mais oui! Je suis Anglais. Mon père—*"

Waythea slapped him hard across the face.

Simon stepped forward to show Waythea the rifle. "Look, brother—Ghizhibatoo's weapon—still warm. He was just here—him and Mag-kie."

Cavendish squinted, whimpering, "*Mr. Peavey?* Is that you, Peavey?"

Waythea laughed and hefted the rifle. "*O-ho!* You have found a very fine rifle." He gazed down the sights. "A hunter with a gun such as this would seldom come home empty-handed." He handed it back.

"You were hoping for a new gun, brother." Simon offered the

rifle with both arms extended. "Take this one and relay the order to move onward. Let us go, Waythea, while Ghizhibatoo's track is still warm."

"It *is* you, Mr. Peavey!" Cavendish heaved a great sigh of relief. "How fortuitous! I almost did not recognize you so outlandishly native, babbling the heathen tongue with such dexterity." He jerked a chin to Waythea. "Inform this rather pungent savage—tell him—as a token of my enduring friendship, *et cetera, et cetera*, he is to take freely of anything he desires. Quickly now—tell him."

Both Simon and Waythea ignored the interruption. Waythea smiled and slipped the rifle strap over his shoulder. "I do need a new gun and I thank you, Penagashea, but the only order I will issue is one to head homeward. There is more than plenty here. I see no need to range any further." He belted the viscount's scabbard around his waist. Grinning, he displayed the sword before slipping it into its sheath. "Fine goods, brandy, *and* an English soldier. What luck! One day out and we return to the village in good stead—not one of us injured or killed—and all of us with ample time to ready for winter."

"But, brother—Ghizhibatoo's trail grows cold."

Waythea shrugged. "Your fight with Ghizhibatoo is your fight. We are finished here, Penagashea. You are free to do as you wish, but the rest of us go home to sleep with our wives."

The war party leader bent to examine Cavendish's wounded leg. "This one will not run," he said to the two braves who held the viscount upright. Waythea marched on to organize the transport of booty for the trip home. The braves dropped Cavendish into the chair and followed after.

Wincing and gasping, Cavendish looked to Simon and sputtered, "Did you let it be known I am a man of means? What is it these heathens desire? Guns? Brandy? It is to our advantage you speak this peculiar gibberish. Make whatever promises necessary and then get me back to Roundabout."

Simon lashed out and cracked the viscount across the face with the back of his hand. "Which way?" he demanded.

Stunned and confused, Cavendish rubbed his cheek, bloodied spittle dribbling down his chin. "W-way? T-to Roundabout? Y-you know these paths better than I . . . it will be well worth your while to represent my cause . . . well worth your while. I hold letters of credit in Richmond. I can offer you—"

Simon silenced the incessant blather by slipping the tip of his knife into the viscount's nose. "You're wasting time—which way did they head? Roberts and Mag-kie?"

Cavendish's neck stiffened and his eyes crossed to sight the bright blade penetrating his intact nostril. Gasping staccato gulps, he raised a quaking hand and pointed south.

With a jerk of his wrist, Simon slit the viscount's nose.

27

Changing Feathers

Tom's heart thumped a rapid tattoo in his chest. With every jarring footfall, agonizing hot spikes darted from his left shoulder down to his fingertips. The pain sapped his strength, turning his legs into leaden weights. He struggled to keep the pace, but Figg and Maggie quickly outdistanced him. They ran hard and fast, dodging through the dense woodland as Shawnee yips, yells, and musket fire faded beneath the pounding of their feet on the forest floor.

Maggie cast a worried glance over her shoulder. She snatched Figg by the shirttail. The big man skittered to a stop and they waited for Tom to catch up.

Tom lurched forward, urging them on. "Run. *Run!*"

Maggie shook her head. "Look at him—bloodier than a butcher boy . . ."

"Pale as the tinker's arse, he is," Figg huffed in agreement.

Maggie ripped and tore a six-inch band of calico from the hem of her blouse. "I'm goin' t' bind that wound."

"No time for that." Tom waved her off. "Not with Peavey on our trail."

"Ye'll bleed t' death afore he finds ye. Stop—catch yer wind and I'll bandage yer arm."

"Awright." Tom pulled up gasping, falling back against a huge buckeye tree. "Be quick about it."

Maggie wrapped his upper arm tight, tying the calico off in a neat square knot directly over the wound. "There, I wager yer arm feels better already, na?"

A sharp crack, like close-by lightning, echoed through the trees. Tom shouted, *"Take cover!"*

The three of them ducked to hunker in a huddle at the base of the buckeye just as a lead ball whirred past and thunked into an elm behind them, scattering a spray of woodchips. Tom pulled the pistols free from his belt and tossed them onto the ground at his feet. He dumped the content of his pouch and jerked his chin toward the elm. "Rifle shot—it's got to be Peavey." He set the one loaded pistol aside. Holding the spent pistol in a trembling left hand, fingers stiff with pain, he unstoppered his horn and managed to pour a sloppy measure of gunpowder down the barrel.

Maggie tugged at Tom's shirtsleeve. "Oughtn't we run?"

"Can't seem t' lay a hand to my shot bag . . ." Tom raked through the scattered pile. "Never mind." He snatched up a small drawstring sack. "Here 'tis. Find my patch box."

Maggie rooted through the odds and ends and handed him a small wooden box. "Let's head to the creek—confuse the sign like ye said afore."

Tom peeled off a greased patch. "Too late for that. He has me in his sights and will dog my tracks to kingdom come. I have to make a stand here and now—and, Maggie . . ." Tom paused, looking her deep in the eye. "Thee must do exactly as I say. Promise?"

"I promise." Maggie nodded. "D'ye hear tha', Figg? Ye must promise t' do exactly as Tom says."

Figg huddled closer, wagging his giant head. "Aye, Maggie. I promise."

Tom wrapped a patch around a lead ball and thumbed it into the muzzle. "Blast!" He dumped the load from the barrel. "My rifle shot's too small for this pistol." He dropped the pistol, pulled his knife from its sheath, and cut a small square from Maggie's buckskin skirt.

"Listen close, Maggie. I want you and Figg to take off—keep to the trees and head south—I'll catch up when I finish here."

"Are ye mad?" Dumbfounded, she gestured to his left arm, soaked in blood.

"There's short range to these pistols. I have to draw him in close and I can't be bothered with the two of you about." Tom rammed a new load down the barrel, the thicker buckskin patch taking up the difference in caliber. He glanced up and forced a smile. "I'll catch up, Maggie. You'll see. Now get going. G'won. I'll catch up."

"I willna. Ye must be daft t' think I would."

Another shot cracked and whirred through the trees. The three of them flinched into a tighter crouch. This time the ball plowed through a limb directly overhead, raining bits of debris onto their heads.

"He's close." Tom stood and stuffed the pistols into his belt. "Maggie, you and Figg must leave now, while Peavey reloads."

Maggie leaped to her feet and clutched at his arm. "I willna leave ye, lad."

Tom shoved her away. "Go! I don't want you here. *GO!*"

She stumbled back, knuckled the tears from her eyes, folded her arms across her chest, and hissed through clenched teeth, "I'm stayin' put."

"By God! Thee will do as I say!"

Figg stepped between the fractious pair. He grabbed Maggie around the waist and tossed her up and over his shoulder like a sack of meal, clamping one massive arm over her thighs.

"Set me down!" Maggie twisted and squirmed, pounding big beefy shoulders with useless fists. "Set me down, Figg!"

"Ye promised Tom, Maggie."

"Good man." Tom pressed his hunting knife into Figg's great palm. "I'm counting on you to keep her safe. Off with you now." He sent Figg on his way with a slap on the back. "Keep to the trees—"

Maggie lifted her tear-streaked face and cried out, "Yer an angersome man, Tom Roberts, but I love none but you. D'ye hear? None but you!"

Tom watched Figg lope away with Maggie bouncing on his shoulder, her arms outstretched.

"If I could but live through this," he muttered, "I will gratefully spend the rest of my life in those arms."

A third rifle shot sounded and Tom pressed back against the buckeye. The lead ball buzzed past, tearing a furrow through the bark at eye level. Knowing Peavey would reload before showing himself, Tom pulled one pistol from his belt and waited before peering around the tree trunk.

Twenty yards away, Simon crept out from a thick tangle of mountain laurel, rifle stock firm at his shoulder. A heavy oaken war club, curved like a cutlass with a smooth, round ball carved at the striking end, dangled from his waist. He had stripped down to breechclout and leggings, and the morning sunlight dappled his tanned skin, blending his body into the surroundings. Simon slipped through the trees, stalking his prey without registering a sound.

Tom drew a deep breath and stepped out from behind the buckeye. Shouting "PEAVEY!" he feinted to the left, then dove to the right.

Simon swiveled, fired, and missed.

Tom landed in a somersault, bounded to his feet, and discharged his pistol. The shot grazed a bloody stripe along Peavey's thigh muscle.

Not even bothering to glance at his leg, Peavey tossed his smoking rifle, loosed his war club, and charged forward, full speed, screaming. *"Coo-wigh! Coo-wigh-wigh!"*

Tom yanked the other pistol from his belt. He brooked a firm stance, cocked back the hammer, and braced his right wrist with his weak left hand. Peavey sped toward him, a blur in the lingering smoke and haze. Tom squeezed the trigger. The shot spun off target. Simon swung the club in a wide arc and struck Tom a blow square on his bloodied arm.

Sharp arrows of pain coursed through the very marrow of his bones to burst into his brain. Tom's legs buckled and he dropped to his knees. Peavey toppled him with a pair of vicious blows to the ribs. Choking and coughing up gobs of bloody spittle, Tom rolled onto his back, striving to free the tomahawk from his belt. Simon bent close and easily twisted the tomahawk from Tom's feeble grip. He flung it aside. Planting a moccasined foot on Tom's chest, he pinned him helplessly to the earth.

Tom rasped between ragged breaths, "Do what you will with me, Peavey, but let Maggie go in peace."

"Always such a hero." Simon sneered. "You were the one that left her behind—left her to that English pig!" With his full weight pressing down on Tom's chest, he snarled, "I saved her. She's mine now—MY dream-woman—MINE!" Peavey stepped back and raised the war club over his head to strike.

"SIMON!"

He froze at the sound of his name, glanced up, and saw Maggie running with Figg gallumping along at her heels. In that spare moment, jealous rage coalesced into sweet longing. Simon's eyes grew as soft as springtime, revealing a young man desperate in love. His arm dropped.

"I'll go with ye, lad," Maggie cried out. "I'll do whatever ye say—I'll go with ye willing! Just dinna kill Tom. I canna bear for him t' die! I canna bear it."

Simon's shoulders rose and fell in a sigh of true understanding.

Looking down at Tom, his green eyes narrowed and turned hard as glass. He swung the club up to deal the deathblow.

"NO!" Figg whipped his arm, hurling the knife in his hand to fly end over end, sinking the blade deep into Peavey's chest.

The heavy club thumped to the ground and Simon sank to his knees, clutching the knife embedded in his heart. Tom pushed up on his elbows and caught Simon as he fell. Maggie ran up and helped lower him to lie with his head cradled in her lap.

Simon gazed up with eyes once again the verdant green of new leaves in the springtime. *"Mag-kie . . ."* He breathed her Shawnee name.

"Sha, laddie . . ." Crooning softly, Maggie stroked his cheek. She pressed a palm to his chest and the diminishing beat of his damaged heart.

Simon fought to garner a breath and grasped at the air for her hand. "Mag-kie? *Mag-kie!*"

She took his frantic hand and held it to her breast. "I'm right here, lad . . . right here."

He flashed a boyish smile. His eyes fluttered shut, and as life left him he whispered, "I loved you—I did."

A shuddered sob choked in Maggie's throat. She laid Simon's head gently on the ground and leaned into Tom.

"As slippery as a river trout, she is," Figg mumbled as he shuffled to stand over them. "Tried t' keep her safe—tried—but she squirmed away." Stunned and confused, he stared down at Simon's dead body. "I din't mean t' kill him, but he meant Tom harm, an' no harm must come t' Tom—Maggie sed, no harm . . ." Huge shoulders heaved and he began to cry.

"Aww, Figg . . ." Tom strained his neck looking up at the tearful Goliath. "You're a good man—brave and true. You saved our very lives."

Figg blubbered on, "But Simon's dead and Maggie's vexed with me . . ."

"Och, Figgy, ye silly great gowk. I'm not vexed, just a bit sad is all." Maggie tugged the big man by the thumb, drawing him down to sit beside her. She threw her arms around his tree-stump neck and kissed his tearstained cheek. "Dinna fash so. When we get back home, I will bake ye a double batch o' shortbread."

Figg swiped his snotty nose on the back of his hand. "D'ye hear, Tom? A double batch."

"Set aside your dreams of shortbread." Tom braced against Figg and struggled to his feet. "Looks like we've got company."

Following Simon's trail, the Shawnee war party broke through the brush in solemn, single file. Figg and Maggie rose to stand at either side of Tom and she whispered, "What do we do now?"

Tom chuckled then winced. "Not much."

"Ye see the fella wearin' the blue blanket? The one comin' straight for us?"

"The one carrying my rifle?"

"Aye. He's called Waythea. He's known as a reasonable man. Talk t' him."

Standing unarmed, with his knife buried to the hilt in a Shawnee warrior dead at his feet, Tom was not as confident in his negotiating capabilities. He waited what seemed an eternity as the armed band marched to stand in a close circle around them.

The war party presented an odd sight. A number of the Indians had donned goods they'd plundered. A few of the tawny warriors were garbed in ruffled lace shirts, and one very serious brave was proudly decked out in the viscount's velvet nightcap and silk dressing robe.

Cavendish was dragged forth last, his arms slung over the shoulders of two young braves, face bloodied, anguished eyes catatonic in terror.

Waythea stood over Simon's dead body, shaking his head. "My wife will tear her hair when she learns of her little brother's death."

Tom's lungs ached with every breath and he fought back a

wave of nausea. With his head spinning, he struggled to find the correct Algonquian words.

"Please know . . . know that I never meant for things to come to this pass." Tom wavered and Figg caught him up, saving him the humiliation of dropping bung end in the dirt.

Waythea held up a hand. "We will take our brother home to be buried. Perhaps in the next world, Penagashea will not be as lost as he was in this one." Whisking his blanket from his shoulders, he spread it on the ground and rolled Simon's body onto the makeshift bier. Six warriors came forward to stand three on either side. They hoisted the blanket and marched away.

Figg lowered Tom to rest on a fallen log.

Waythea turned to leave. He paused and turned back.

"It is a sad day, Ghizhibatoo," Waythea said, "but not unexpected. After all, Penagashea did kill the white fawn." He slipped Tom's rifle from his shoulder and set it on the ground at Tom's feet. "Go in peace, brother." The war leader strode away, waving his fellows to follow.

Wincing, Tom reached down and tugged his rifle onto his lap. Maggie and Figg sat down beside him and they watched the Indians maneuver in orderly retreat.

Cavendish stirred, roused by the movement and the deference shown to Tom. "Roberts!" he cried. "Parlay with the heathens on my behalf. Anything I have is yours—Spanish dollars—the Scotswoman—name your heart's desire!"

Tom shut his eyes, drew a deep breath, and ran his hand down the smooth iron barrel. He traced a fingertip over the silver heart embedded in the rifle stock.

"Ye ken, Tom," Maggie said. "A bullet in his brain would be a kindness."

Shaking his head, Tom shrugged. "Wet powder . . ."

Writhing and screaming, Cavendish cried, "Roberts! Help me! I beg you!" The viscount's captors silenced his pitiful pleas with a musket butt to the head. Dragging his slouched body, they disappeared, lost in the tangle of mountain laurel.

Tom struggled to stand. "Lend me a hand there, Figg."

"Och, Tom!" Maggie scolded. "Bide a wee! Ye need t' rest."

"Ah, Maggie . . . it's been so long since I last et, my belly is cursing my teeth." Tom handed her his rifle and draped an arm over Figg's broad shoulder. "What we truly need is a warm fire and something to eat. What d'ye say, Figgy?"

Figg grinned wide. "Amen t' that, sez I."

Epilogue

The Blue Ridge

"There they are, Susannah!" Maggie pointed. "D'ye see 'em? Up there, at the top of the ridge."

Leaning on their long rifles, Tom and Seth stood on a broad promontory jutting out over the valley—tall man, small man—sentinels silhouetted against a golden sky.

"Hoy, lads!" Maggie called with a wave. "Lend a lass a helping hand, aye?"

Tom and Seth turned as one. Surprised smiles graced their faces. The men set weapons down and hastened to assist the women up the steep rickle of stones.

Susannah seated baby Alexander firm on her hip and clasped Seth's hand. "The camp's settled, an' we've a fine rabbit stew on the boil."

"So we decided t' come an' see the lay of the land," Maggie added.

Tom pulled Maggie up and led her to the edge. He swept his hand across the view—a vast expanse of dark pines and bright broadleaves cloaking rolling hills. "There it is. Our claim—from that tight bend in the river straight north to that limestone cliff."

Seth and Susannah came to stand beside Tom and Maggie.

"My place is just west of Tom's. Can ye believe it, Susannah?" Seth rested a hand on her sturdy shoulder. "Surveyed, lined out on paper, and recorded—legal and proper!"

Maggie smiled and noted how Seth's hand lingered on Susannah's shoulder, and how Susannah didn't seem to mind.

Friday, Patch, and Little Black came scrambling up, followed by Jack, Winnie, and Mary. Bonnet strings flying, Mary ran up and gave her mother a hug. Jack raised a ruckus, leaping about with arms over his head, proclaiming, "I'm king of the hill! King of the hill!"

Winnie shouted, "Down with tyrants!" and pulled Jack into a headlock for a good knuckle scrubbing.

Susannah's brow furrowed. "Where's Battler?"

Mary pointed down trail. "Here he comes."

"Whoa, Figgy, whoa!" Astraddle tall, broad shoulders, Battler held tight to Figg's ears. Figg swung Battler off and sent the boy to sclim up and join the others.

"C'mon up, Figg," Tom urged.

"Naw, Tommy." Figg shook his great head. "Not one fer heights, am I."

Battler marched over and tugged Susannah's skirt. "I'm hungry!"

Seth snatched Battler into his arms and tickled his pudgy belly. "Leave Susannah be, ye wee hellion."

Breathless between giggles, Battler insisted, "But I'm hungry, Da. I'm hungry."

"It is almost supper time," Susannah reminded Seth.

"All right—too crowded up here anyway." Seth herded children and dogs down off the ridge. "Come along, my rascals, come along! Let's go—back t' camp with every fetchin' one of ye."

"I'll quick fry up some johnnycakes," Susannah said, passing the baby down to Seth. "That ought to tide 'em over."

"Amen t' johnnycakes!" Battler cheered. Figg hoisted Battler onto his shoulder and fell in with the crowd heading down the hill.

Maggie bunched her skirts in her fist. "I ought to go help Susannah . . ."

"Stay—" Tom caught Maggie by the arm. "Let it be just the two of us for a bit." He cupped the round curve of her belly. "After all, it won't be too long before we'll be three."

"Och, we've a few months left t' us yet, lad." Maggie cozied into Tom's embrace. Wrapping her arms about his waist, she leaned her cheek to his chest. Tom sighed and nuzzled her hair. The din of dogs and the Martin family faded on the April breeze, and together, Tom and Maggie watched the sun inch into their horizon.

Midwife of the Blue Ridge

by Christine Blevins

READERS GUIDE

1. "The lass became Hannah's shadow, attending the births, nursing the sick, tending the injured, and laying out the dead." Maggie Duncan was trained in midwifery from a very young age. How do you think her occupation as a midwife adds to the development of her character and to the telling of the story?

2. What are some of the political and social forces that draw Maggie Duncan and Tom Roberts together? What drives them apart?

3. Themes of independence and slavery fuel the novel's plot. What are the virtues and inequities inherent in the system of indentured servitude as portrayed in this story? How do you think the system affects Maggie's life? In what ways does her servitude differ from slavery?

4. The Jacobite Rebellion of 1746, the French and Indian War, and Pontiac's Uprising are three of the wars mentioned during the course of this novel. How does war affect the individual childhood experiences of Seth Martin, Maggie Duncan, Simon Peavey, and Mary Bledsoe? How do you think war functions as a catalyst for change?

5. *Midwife of the Blue Ridge* is set during a time when the colonies were expanding into Native American territory. How does the resultant culture clash manifest itself? How are the differences in attitude toward Native Americans—as displayed by Tom Roberts, Simon Peavey, and Maggie Duncan—a result of their direct exposure to Native American culture?

6. The women in this story deal with many hardships and much uncertainty. What are some of the different ways in which the female characters cope and persevere in the face of adversity?

7. In the eighteenth century, death was often sudden, childbirth was dangerous, and infant mortality was high. Illness or violence could, and frequently did, decimate entire communities. Discuss the effects these eighteenth-century realities had on the lives of the settlers, and compare their experiences to your own in the twenty-first century.

8. At one point in the story, referring to his rifle, Seth tells Cavendish, ". . . a lout like me can sink a ball in yer brain from one hundred yards with one of these." Discuss the role of the gun in the novel and the impact of gun ownership on eighteenth-century Colonial America.

9. Figg transforms from mindless brute to unlikely hero over the course of this story. How do Tom's heroic deeds compare with those of Figg? Do you think any of the female characters can be considered heroic?

10. Which elements of eighteenth-century frontier living were the most surprising or interesting to you? Do you think you would have been able to survive a life on the frontier in Colonial America?

11. Given what you know about the characters, how do you envision they carry on with the rest of their lives?